EAST RENFREWSHIRE

970

D1344594

Ruth's Journey

ALSO BY DONALD McCAIG

Ruth's Journey

DONALD McCAIG

**SIMON &
SCHUSTER**

London · New York · Sydney · Toronto · New Delhi

A CBS COMPANY

First published in the US by Simon & Schuster, Inc., 2014
First published in Great Britain by Simon & Schuster UK Ltd, 2014
A CBS COMPANY

This paperback edition, 2015

Copyright © 2014 by Stephen Mitchell Trusts

This book is copyright under the Berne Convention.
No reproduction without permission.
® and © 1997 Simon & Schuster Inc. All rights reserved.

The right of Donald McCaig to be identified as author of this
work has been asserted in accordance with sections 77 and
78 of the Copyright, Designs and Patents Act, 1988.

1 3 5 7 9 10 8 6 4 2

Simon & Schuster UK Ltd
1st Floor
222 Gray's Inn Road
London WC1X 8HB

www.simonandschuster.co.uk

Simon & Schuster Australia, Sydney
Simon & Schuster India, New Delhi

A CIP catalogue record for this book
is available from the British Library

Paperback ISBN: 978-1-47113-921-5
eBook ISBN: 978-1-47113-922-2

This book is a work of fiction. Names, characters, places and
incidents are either a product of the author's imagination or are
used fictitiously. Any resemblance to actual people living or
dead, events or locales is entirely coincidental.

Printed and bound by CPI Group (UK) Ltd, Croydon, CR0 4YY

MIX
Paper from
responsible sources
FSC® C020471

Simon & Schuster UK Ltd are committed to sourcing paper
that is made from wood grown in sustainable forests and supports the Forest
Stewardship Council, the leading international forest certification organisation.
Our books displaying the FSC logo are printed on FSC certified paper.

For Hattie McDaniel

"My own life even surprises me."

A huge old woman with the small, shrewd eyes of an elephant. She was shining black, pure African, devoted to her last drop of blood to the O'Haras, Ellen's mainstay, the despair of her three daughters, the terror of the other house servants.

—MARGARET MITCHELL, *GONE WITH THE WIND*

Whither thou goest, I will go; and where thou lodgest, I will lodge: thy people *shall be* my people, and thy God my God: where thou diest, will I die, and there will I be buried.

—BOOK OF RUTH

PART ONE

Saint-Domingue

HER STORY BEGAN with a miracle. It was not a remarkable miracle; the Red Sea did not part and Lazarus didn't rise up. Hers was one of those everyday miracles that part the quick from the dead.

The miracle happened on a small island which had been a very rich small island. The island's planters called it the Pearl of the Antilles. Three weeks after *The Marriage of Figaro* opened in Paris, it played Cap-Français, the small island's capital city. The island's planters, overseers, and second sons ruled sugar and coffee plantations that made rich Frenchmen richer and propelled unimportant shipping merchants into the bourgeoisie. Every year the island produced more revenue than all Britain's North American colonies combined.

But that was olden times. These days fertile cane fields lay fallow under thick black ash, and the broken cornerstones of once grand mansions peeked beneath rude thornbushes.

If they were prudent and kept to the roads, Napoleon's soldiers could still patrol the Plaine-du-Nord at least as far as Villeneauve. Their ring forts were safe enough.

But when night fell they bivouacked inside those forts or returned to Cap-Français. Day or night, the mountains belonged to feral hogs, goats, insurgents, and Maroons.

———

The afternoon of the miracle, the woman who would become the child's owner and almost mother sat beside her window looking east over the broken rooftops of the capital and the mastheads of the blockaded French fleet to the gentle azure bay because every other vista rejected hope. And Solange Escarlette Fornier turned to hope as the fleur-de-lis inclines persistently to the sun.

Though Solange was young she wasn't beautiful. Two years ago on her wedding day, in her grandmother's Flemish lace gown and jewels, Solange had been plain. But those who spared Solange a second glance often found time for a third, lingering on her high cheekbones, her cold gray-green eyes, her arrogant Gallic nose, and her mouth, which promised much it withheld.

That second glance revealed how this young woman's loneliness made her invulnerable.

Solange Escarlette Fornier had been reared in Saint-Malo, the thriving port on the Breton coast. She understood her home, and when she spoke her hands employed the subtle gestures of the native. Solange knew how Saint-Malo skeins had been wound by what hands and of what wool.

Here, on this small island, Solange Escarlette Fornier was a cipher—a provincial bride without influential Paris kinsmen, married to an undistinguished captain in a dying army. Solange couldn't understand why these terrible things were happening, and though she blamed her husband, Augustin, she reserved more blame for herself: how could she have been so stupid?

Among Saint-Malo's bourgeoisie, the Forniers were "considerable" and the Escarlettes "redoubtable." Henri-Paul Fornier and Solange's father, Charles, hoped to join their houses with marriage.

Henri-Paul's schooners would carry Escarlette manufactures, while Escarlette influence could tame greedy port officials. Every ship needs two anchors.

Courteously and candidly, the fathers evaluated the prospective bride and groom for, as another Breton saying has it, "love and poverty make an untidy household."

Love? In the presence of Charles Escarlette's eldest daughter, young Augustin Fornier was blushing and speechless, and if Solange was indifferent to her suitor, no matter. Doubtless, like countless girls before, Solange would come around.

Poverty? During the fathers' dotal discussions, the son's prospects were carefully balanced against the daughter's substantial dowry.

To the marriage, Augustin would bring ninety percent (Henri-Paul reserved an interest) of a distant plantation: the Sucarie du Jardin of 150 hectares, improved by a great house ("a Versailles!"), and a modern sugar mill ("the whiter the sugar, the better the price, is it not so?"), and forty-three ("docile, loyal") field hands no younger than fifteen or older than thirty years, not to mention twelve female slaves of childbearing age and numerous children, some of whom would survive to enter the workforce.

Henri-Paul produced records of quarterly receipts deposited in the Banque de France.

"One hundred twenty ecus," Charles said. "Commendable." He hummed as he riffled the papers and paused to jot a note. "Very handsome. Have you more recent accounts? From the last three years, perhaps?"

Henri-Paul took his pipe from his pocket, considered but put it away. "Events."

"Just so. Events . . ."

Charles Escarlette knew there could be no recent accounts, but he'd indulged himself, just a little.

Twenty years earlier, when Henri-Paul mortgaged two small coastal schooners to buy a sugar plantation on a Caribbean island few Saint-Malouins had heard of, Charles Escarlette hadn't been among the loudest scoffers, but he had raised an eyebrow.

Henri-Paul's "improvidence" became "sagacity" when European demand for sugar doubled, tripled, and quadrupled. Even the poorest household must have its jams and cakes. No soil was better suited for sugarcane than the small island's, and no plantation refined whiter sugar than the Sucarie du Jardin. The first year Henri-Paul owned the plantation, his overseer delivered profits which reimbursed the purchase. Subsequently, Henri-Paul had used profits from this venture to expand his fleet to eight coastal vessels (which became his elder son, Leo's patrimony), and the Forniers were invited to join la Société des Expéditeurs et des Marchand, at whose annual ball Henri-Paul (who'd had one glass too many) clapped Charles Escarlette on the shoulder and addressed him with the familiar "tu."

That unfortunate "tu" is why Charles asked for accounts which could not possibly be forthcoming.

For ungrateful slaves on that rich small island had revolted against their legitimate owners. As the slave revolt spread, metropolitan Frenchmen independently started a revolution of their own and executed their king. The revolutionary government, those unbusinesslike Jacobins (who lived in Paris and probably didn't own one cubit of one sucarie!), in an excess of "Liberté! Égalité! Fraternité!" had freed every French slave!

Some years later, with Napoleon Bonaparte controlling the French government, conditions on the small island remained disordered, dangerous, and distinctly unprofitable. A self-appointed Negro governor-general sought to retain ties with France (while distributing its finest plantations to his supporters), and other rebels contested his rule and stole plantations for themselves.

Charles Escarlette understood that Henri-Paul wouldn't have assigned ninety percent of the Sucarie du Jardin to his son Augustin if profits had been guaranteed, but he smiled in a most agreeable manner and opened a bottle of Armagnac sealed the same year the late lamented Louis ascended the throne. Henri-Paul was appreciative.

On his second glass Henri-Paul noted that Solange's hips and breasts could produce and nourish strong grandsons but added, "My Augustin won't wear the pants in that family."

Charles swirled his Armagnac to savor its bloom. "Augustin will always need guidance."

Gloomily, "He would have made a good priest."

Snort. "He doesn't eye my daughter like a priest!"

"As some priests do, perhaps."

Instant bonhomie. The two, who'd been anticlerics in their youth, chuckled. Charles Escarlette tumped the cork back in the bottle and offered his hand. "Tomorrow, again?"

"At your convenience."

―――――

Augustin Fornier was not entirely unsuitable as a prospective son-in-law, but he wouldn't have been chosen except for that faraway sucarie and the intervention of Napoleon himself.

As Charles and Henri-Paul wanted the Sucarie du Jardin restored to French ownership, Napoleon wanted the small island's wealth delivered to France instead of enriching quarreling Negroes who had been French property until a stupid Jacobin mistake was made. Moreover, pushy Americans had been sniffing around New Orleans, hub of the enormous Louisiana Territory, and a strong French force on the small island would check American ambitions. The French and British were presently at peace, the seas were open, and Napoleon's splendid army had very little to do. The First Consul entrusted command of a large expeditionary force to his own brother-in-law, General Charles-Victor-Emmanuel Leclerc.

After his discussion with Fornier, Charles Escarlette interviewed Ricard d'Ageau, who'd lost an arm at Austerlitz, becoming thereby Saint-Malo's authority on military matters. Ricard gratefully accepted Escarlette's second best cognac before laying a judicious finger aside his nose and announcing that after Leclerc's expedition landed and reassembled, there'd be three, perhaps four skirmishes, Leclerc would edify the populace with hangings, and affairs would return to normal within weeks, not months. Faced by French guns manned by Napoleon's veterans, "Les Nègres will run like Toulouse geese."

"And then."

"Ha, ha. To the victor goes the spoils!"

This last prognostication fit all too perfectly with Charles Escarlette's suspicions, and he spent a restless night and was grumpy at the breakfast table. When Solange asked her "dear Papa" if something was wrong, he replied so sharply, she stared at him as if he were a lunatic encountered on the street.

But not long after, his mind and duty became clear. It only remained to get Henri-Paul ("tu" indeed!) to understand the reality and opportunities of the situation.

Augustin Fornier had spent two chaparoned afternoons with his young potential bride. Though innocent of the fairer sex and life beyond the walled courtyard of the Fornier establishment at 24, rue des Pêcheurs, even Augustin—when his love delirium subsided— even Augustin knew his beloved Solange Escarlette was provincial, haughty, indifferent, and self-absorbed. What of it? Love is no bookkeeper.

He ached for her. The mole beside her left eyebrow was located exactly where the perfect mole should be, Le Bon Dieu had designed her breasts to repose in Augustin's hands, her plump buttocks were shaped so he could clasp her to him. Imagining that triumphant moment when he'd possess Solange ruined Augustin's sleep and twisted his sweaty sheets into ropes. Can one build a marriage on desire? Augustin didn't know and didn't care.

Solange thought marriage would mean a week of lording it over her unmarried sisters and the tedious duties of the marriage bed with a man she thought nice enough. Duty was duty, not so? Her father had arranged her christening, her schooling to twelve years, and now her marriage. That was how things were done in Saint-Malo.

The deal was struck and the pair wed. With a loan two points above the prime rate, secured by the sucarie, Charles Escarlette purchased a sublieutenant's commission in the Fifth Légère for his son-in-law.

As a boy, Augustin had been pacific. When other boys flourished wooden sabers, Augustin worried someone might poke his eye out. When those boys became men and their stick swords sabers, the glistening steel made Augustin shudder. But his father-in-law explained: "The Sucarie du Jardin is your entire competence; not so? After General Leclerc breaks this revolt and our Negroes return to work, will the Sucarie du Jardin return to its rightful owners or to one of Leclerc's favorite officers?"

Charles clapped Augustin on the back. "Don't worry, my boy. It'll be over before you know it and"—he coughed—"I'm told Negro women are . . . primitive."

Augustin, whose possession of his bride had been rather less thrilling than he'd hoped, thought "primitive" might not be the worst thing in the world.

Henri-Paul blamed his son's "indiscreet ardor" for the "régime de in fiparatum de bient" he'd been forced to accept. Solange Escarlette Fornier's substantial dowry had been deposited in the Banque de France—in Solange's name.

"My dear friend," Charles encouraged his new relation, "they will need that money to restore the sucarie. Before the year is out your ten percent will be earning again."

Solange thought she might rather enjoy being mistress of a Grand Plantation, and her sisters were quite annoyed at her presumptions. She'd be gracious, kind, and, if not beautiful (Solange was a realist) very, very well dressed.

Sundays after Mass she'd entertain other planters' wives, serving tea with her grandmother's cobalt blue and gold Sevres tea set. She'd be wearing her grandmother's necklace, and a servant would stand behind each chair, fanning her friends.

The new-minted couple embarked in Brest and sailed west through choppy winter seas for forty-two days. Augustin's sublieutenant rank commanded a bunk in a minuscule cabin the newlyweds shared with two unmarried officers no more important than they. Pretending they didn't see or hear what inevitably they must was delicacy's refuge. Since there wasn't enough room to quarrel, Solange made do with her eyes.

For one splendid moment the morning of January 29, it all seemed possible. On the crowded deck as the small island grew larger, Solange slipped her little hand into her husband's. Perhaps her sweet dependency brought the tears to Sublieutenant Fornier's eyes, but perhaps it was the island breeze, spiced with gentle languorous perfumes. It was true! The officer-planter and his bride inhaled the promise of the Pearl of the Antilles.

Since insurrectionists had removed channel markers in Cap-Français's harbor, General Leclerc's expedition, including the Fifth Brigade and its novice sublieutenant, sailed down the coast to make their landing and Solange had the minuscule cabin to herself.

While the French fleet waited for Leclerc to strike, insurgents set fire to the capital city and a bitter stench masked the aromatic breezes. To hell with the navigation markers! The admiral sailed in and moored at the quay. The French landing party was sailors, marines, and civilians like Solange, brandishing an unladylike dagger and greeted by several hundred black children calling "Papa Blan, Papa Blan" (White Father). As the landing party looted, Solange commandeered children to carry Fornier baggage to a neighborhood which had been spared the flames.

Solange perched on the stone stoop of a small two-story stone house with her dagger across her knees until that evening, when General Leclerc's forces arrived to join the looting. Two days later, an officer with proud grenadier's mustachios informed Solange that not enough houses had survived the fire and hers was required for superior officers.

"Non."

"Madame?"

"Non. This house is small and dirty and everything is broken, but it must suffice."

"Madame!"

"Will you remove a French planter's wife by force?"

Later, Augustin made himself scarce when other officers made futile attempts to dislodge his wife.

———

For a time Napoleon's plan succeeded. Many islanders welcomed French help to end the revolt, and many of the governor-general's black regiments joined the French. Houses were repaired and re-roofed, and Cap-Français rose from its ashes. Leclerc sent most of the French fleet home. Many rebel commanders renewed fealty to France and its First Consul. The self-appointed governor-general was enticed to a peace conference, where he was arrested.

The Forniers drove out to inspect their sucarie. It was a cool misty morning on the Plaine-du-Nord, and Solange wore a wool wrap. The plain was dominated by hulking Morne Jean, which gave birth to big and little streams interrupting their passage.

In tiny villages, silent, emaciated children peeked at them and feral dogs slunk away. Some cane fields had been abandoned to brush, some subdivided into the small garden tracts and rude dwellings of the new freedmen; a few were solid with unharvested cane. They forded gurgling creeks and were ferried across the murky Grande-Rivière-du-Nord, whose banks were littered with broken limbs and tree trunks deposited by winter floods.

South of the Segur crossroads, they turned in to their fount of future happiness: the Sucarie du Jardin.

They had read the overseer's reports, deeds and plats of a remote, mysterious Caribbean plantation; today they left real wheel marks in a disused lane in cool shadow between walls of sugarcane waving above their heads. "Vanilla," Solange whispered. "It smells like vanilla."

Cane rustled. Anything might be concealed in that cane, and they were relieved emerging into sunlight on the cobbled drive fronting a two-story plantation house which hadn't been as grand as their imaginings even before it was burned. Blue-gray sky, punctuated with blackened roof beams, filled upper-story windows. Rubble spewed out of what had been its front door.

"Oh," Solange said.

The faint WHOOSH would be the sucarie's Negroes fleeing through the uncut cane. "We will build anew," Augustin said.

Solange asked, "Do you think we can?" and rested her hand on his knee.

Theirs. The shattered house, the burned sugar mill with its bent and broken axles, shafts, and gears—*theirs.* Plans excited their minds. They explored the undamaged Negro hamlet—*theirs.* Each worker's reszide was protected by a bright green wall of interwoven ropy cacti—when Augustin put out a curious hand, he retracted it and sucked his finger while Solange giggled. Each reszide's yard had been pounded hard as cement and swept. Augustin ducked to step into a dim interior. Solange coughed. Her husband's head almost touched the smoke hole, which amused her. Tattered mats were rolled beside a large basket for collecting manioc. The kettle on the hearth had whitish foodstuff caked in the bottom. Augustin imagined himself instructing Negro children in the glories of French civilization. He anticipated their gratitude and joy. Solange picked up a well-turned porcelain bowl, but the edge was chipped so she tossed it away.

Planter accounts had warned about gardens like the well-tended one behind this hut. Field hands *would* expend their energy on their gardens rather than their master's work. Augustin announced a proprietor's decision. "*Our* Negroes *will* complete their sugar work *before* this . . . frivolity!"

Solange vaguely wondered if they'd also have a house in town.

The sun smiled down on their life from today to forever. They— just the two of them—they could make something here. *Theirs.* Augustin swelled with pride. He would capture and return errant workers to the Sucarie du Jardin. Wasn't it their home too? Wasn't it as much their life as his? When a breeze ruffled the cane, the cane rattled. What a lovely sound!

"The house . . ." he said. "I am glad the house is burned. It was too small. Unsatisfactory."

She said, "We will build a better one."

In the mansion's neglected flower garden, Augustin spread his cape beside a rosebush whose husks whispered of possibilities. They would be rich. They would be good. They would be loved. They would do as they pleased. Solange opened herself to Augustin in the fine delirium of love.

Alas, after the Negro governor-general was deported to France, fighting intensified, the countryside became unsafe, and the Forniers never again visited the sugar plantation which had embodied so many hopes. Solange's husband no longer spoke of what he did when he was soldiering. He was promoted. He was promoted again but took no pride in it. Augustin no longer enjoyed balls or theater, and the most amiable witty conversation bored him. Captain Fornier stopped going out into society.

With summer came the yellow fever.

An odd theory was popular with credulous French officers: they were losing to *unnatural* forces. Many years ago, even before the Jacobins freed the slaves and long before Napoleon sent Leclerc to reenslave them, a voudou priest was burned in Cap-Français's public square. Superstitious Negroes believed this particular priest could transform himself into an animal or insect and thus could not be killed. But ha, ha, monsieur: his fat bubbles like the other's! Although the voudou priest's ashes were scrubbed from the cobblestones, that summer saw an unusual infestation of mosquitoes and the first yellow fever epidemic.

The fever burned. The sufferer gasped for water. Then his brain was squeezed as a strong man juices fruit. The condemned man remained clear-minded, so his dearest illusions were exposed as the lies they'd always been.

Then surcease. Quiet. Ease. The fever departed and the head stopped throbbing. One drank cool water and lay back. A kindhearted soul washed the filthy sweat from one's body. Many victims dared to hope.

Some of the most devout lost their faith when the fever returned and black blood streamed from the nose and mouth and the black vomiting and the stream of filth.

For Le Bon Dieu's doubtless good reasons, He spared Augustin and Solange, but most of Napoleon's expedition died faster than they could be buried. Though interred with more pomp and dignity than tens of thousands of his fellow soldiers, General Charles-Victor-Emmanuel Leclerc was just as dead.

The general's wife departed on one of the last French ships to leave the small island, because one year after the French-British peace treaty was signed, it came unsigned and a British squadron blockaded the island.

With the British came news that Napoleon had sold the Louisiana Territory to the Americans. French survivors on the small island knew Napoleon had sold them too.

After General Rochambeau took command of the besieged French forces, a febrile gaiety descended on the capital. Abandoned by their nation and their Emperor, officers, planters, wives, and Creole mistresses frolicked at nightly balls. Though *The Marriage of Figaro* was just a memory, popular entertainments filled a theater whose broken roof was open to the night sky. Bats swooping through the roof beams alarmed women in the audience.

Solange wasn't naturally sociable, but she understood that in these circumstances to be disconnected was to die. Although she'd rather be walking the beach alone, she ignored her inclination and attended nightly balls or the theater. When Augustin no longer accompanied her, her faithful escort was Major Alexandre Brissot, an unusually handsome officer a year or so older than she. Since he was General Rochambeau's nephew, Major Brissot offered protection above his rank, and though Solange might have permitted certain liberties, he never asked for them.

Solange was a realist. Whatever Brissot might be, she was grateful for his protection. Back home, Solange's expectations had been what was due every Escarlette: a modestly successful, mostly faithful husband with an adequate competence and respectable position. Nothing in Saint-Malo had prepared her for unburied fever victims changing shape on the street or the greasy tang that rose up in her throat. Her imaginings hadn't included choking smoke snaking through the streets of a besieged city or a plantation they owned but daren't visit ever. Her husband's eyes were so strange! Her husband, the man she lay down beside!

After twenty-eight months, six days, and twelve hours in Hell, Captain Augustin Fornier had seen and done worse than his nightmares. Augustin had spurned too many mercies and shut his ears to too many piteous pleas. His ordinary French forefinger had pulled the trigger, and his own awkward hands had adjusted the nooses.

His own wife said, "When we defeat these rebels, they must put everything back as it was. Exactly as it was!"

He agreed knowing nothing could be put back, nothing was as it had been.

As his father suggested, Augustin would have made a good priest. These days, he didn't know which of his mortal sins would damn him.

Today's patrol was a fool's mission: pursuing an escaped slave, one Joli, body servant to General Rochambeau's nephew Alexandre Brissot. This pursuit made no sense. Slaves ran away every day, dozens, hundreds, thousands of them.

Perhaps it was the horse Joli stole. Perhaps the horse was valuable. Augustin obeyed orders. What was proper to a soldier and proper to an executioner was no longer a meaningful distinction.

For some reason the general wanted Joli's head. Despite the slenderness of human necks, removing the head is no easy matter. Unless the saber strikes just so, where two vertebrae meet, the blade hangs up in bone while severed arteries spout blood over one's white pantaloons.

Joli's hoofprints switchbacked through abandoned coffee plantations along the mountain above the Plaine-du-Nord.

Augustin and his sergeant rode mules. Ordinary soldiers caught their breath when they could. In far-off Saint-Malo it would be fall. Cool, agreeable fall.

Terraces opened between rows of coffee trees far above that

gentle promise, the amiable blue sea. The British squadron didn't try to conceal themselves: three frigates (one would have sufficed) sailed lazily to and fro. A child's toys. What did they know, those bored English officers with glasses trained on ruined Cap-Français and Morne Jean looming over the city? How Augustin envied those officers.

The incline became too steep for coffee growing, and the cart lane narrowed to a footpath and finally a track for the island's huge rodents and wild boars. Augustin dismounted and led his mule. Sweat poured into his eyes. Pulling, climbing, hacking, lunging through brush that clung to them like rejected lovers, some soldiers cursed, others murmured prayers they'd learned as children. The most optimistic French soldier did not believe he'd ever see France again. Every man knew he was *mort, décédé, défunt.* Sometimes they sang a cheerful song about Monsieur Mort, what a good fellow he was.

Mort oui, but not just now! Not this morning, not as long as dew clung to these un-French leaves and odd insects celebrated their insignificant lives and an ungrateful sun blistered their foreheads. Tomorrow, Monsieur Mort, we shall rendezvous. As you wish. But not today!

———

Augustin Fornier's life might have been different. If only Fortune had smiled—just a modest smile, Fortune's knowing wink . . . Ah, bien.

And in Saint-Malo he had thought himself unhappy! What a child! What a spoiled foolish child! Yes, Augustin's father was demanding, but had he asked more of his sons than other self-made men? True, Augustin's prospects had been inferior—his older brother, Leo, would inherit Agence Maritime du Fornier—but at least Augustin had *had* prospects!

How happy he had been!

Brush snatched Augustin's coat and sword belt and plucked his tricorner hat off his head so regularly he carried it in his hand.

A red cap clung to the spikes of a thorn tree; a bonnet rouge, one of those "liberty caps" Jacobins had favored and Napoleon detested. The silk twill seemed too fine for a runaway body servant. Perhaps Solange could make something of it.

Augustin clambered onto a clearing on a narrow terrace. A tethered brown and black goat bawled as soon as the patrol appeared.

The door flap of the small reszide had been a carpet which might have come from a grand house. The fronds of the hut's roof were tied with strips from the same carpet.

His sergeant cocked his musket, and the others followed suit.

It was cool here, so high above the plain. A waterfall trickled down a mossy cliff face and splashed into a washtub-size pool.

The goat complained, a green parrot chattered like a wooden mallet tapping a log. A breeze tickled Augustin's neck hair. It must have been pleasant high above the bloody conflict. It must have seemed safe.

The dead girl beside the door hadn't been dead long enough for her blood to blacken. Augustin didn't look at her face. He had too many faces to forget.

Augustin drew his pistol. When he jerked the carpet door aside, death air washed him dirty. Before his nerve failed, Captain Fornier stepped inside.

The old woman had been partially beheaded, and the baby's brains were splashed like red-gray smut across the hearth. The baby's tiny clenched hands might have been a small marsupial's. "We humans are not human," Augustin mused. Vaguely he wondered who'd done it. Maroons? Insurrectionists? Another patrol?

The murderers had overturned, emptied, and scattered, seeking the family's poor valuables.

Augustin hoped the blood he was standing in hadn't got into his boot uppers. Once blood stained the stitching, it couldn't be got out.

The upside-down manioc basket hadn't been disturbed. The marauders had searched, strewn, and tossed away, but they had not overturned the manioc basket, though that basket might have concealed everything they were looking for. The basket was untouched: a smug household god.

When Augustin kicked it, it rolled into a corner.

Revealing an erect, smiling, naked, very black girl four or five years old. The child's feet were blood dipped, as were her knees where she'd knelt beside her slaughtered family. At his stare, she hid her gory hands behind her back and curtsied. *"Ki kote pitit-la?"* she said in Creole. In French she added, "Welcome to our home, sirs. Our goat Héloïse has good milk. Can you hear Héloïse bawling? I would be happy to milk her for you."

Captain Augustin Fornier, who had seen it all, gaped.

The child repeated, "You must be hungry. I would milk her for you."

Augustin crossed himself.

Her smile was illuminated with a child's buoyant charm. "Will you take me with you?"

He did.

PART TWO

The Low Country

Refugees

WHEN AUGUSTIN PRESENTED the solemn, beautiful child to his wife, the angels held their breath until Solange smiled.

Such a smile! Augustin would have given his life for that smile.

"You are perfect," Solange said. "Aren't you."

The child nodded gravely.

After due consideration Solange said, "We shall name you Ruth."

———

Solange had never wanted a baby. She accepted her duty to bear children (as it was Augustin's failed duty to initiate them), and with enough wet nurses and servants to cope with infant disagreeableness, Solange would rear the heirs the Forniers and Escarlettes expected.

But as a child, while her sisters happily advised, reproved, and dressed blank-eyed porcelain dolls, Solange dressed and advised only herself. She thought her sisters too willingly accepted Eve's portion of that primordial curse.

Ruth was perfect: old enough to care for herself and appreciate her betters without asking too much of them. Malleable and willing, Ruth brightened Solange's days. She wasn't the precious, awful burden an Escarlette baby would be. If Ruth disappointed, there were buyers.

Solange dressed Ruth as her sisters had dressed their dolls. Although lace was scarce, Ruth's hems were fringed with Antwerp's finest. Ruth's pretty silk cap was as lustrous brown as the child's eyes.

Since Ruth spoke French, Solange supposed her family had included house servants. Solange never asked: *her* Ruth was born, as if in her own bed, the day Solange named her.

One quiet evening, before Solange closed the shutters against the night air, a pensive Ruth sat at the window overlooking the city. In that dim, forgiving light, she was a small black African as mysterious as that savage continent and just as assured as one of its queens.

"Ruth, chérie!"

"Oui, madame!"

Instantly so agreeable, so grateful to be Solange's companion. Ruth admired those characteristics Solange most admired in herself. Ruth accompanied her mistress to the balls and theater, curling up somewhere until Solange was ready to go home.

Assuaging Solange's grave loneliness, Ruth sat silently on the floor pressed against her mistress's legs. Sometimes Solange thought the child could see through her heart to the Saint-Malo seashore she loved: the rocky beaches and impregnable seawall protecting its citizens from winter storms.

With Ruth, Solange could drop her guard. She could be afraid. She could weep. She could even indulge the weak woman's prayer that somehow, no matter what, everything would turn out all right.

She read fashionable novels. Like the sensitive young novelists, Solange understood what had been lost in this modern 19th century was more precious than what remained, that human civilization had passed its high point, that today was no different from yesterday, that her soul was scuffed and diminished by banal people, banal conversation, and the myriad offenses of life. The daily privations of a besieged city were no less banal for being fatal.

Captain Fornier was stationed at Fort Vilier, the largest of the forts ringing the city. The insurgents often tried and as often, with terrible losses, failed to penetrate the French forts' interlocking cannon fire. Sometimes Captain Fornier stayed at the fort, sometimes at home. The flavor of his bitterness lingered after he departed. Solange would have comforted Augustin if she could without surrendering anything important.

Nothing in Saint-Domingue was solid. Everything teetered on its last legs or was already half swallowed by the island's dusty vines.

There'd be no French fleet fighting their way through the British squadron. No reinforcements, no more cannon or muskets or rations or powder or ball. Without a murmur the Pearl of the Antilles faded into myth. Patriotic dodderers urged uncompromising warfare while Napoleon's soldiers deserted to the rebels or tried to survive another day.

As their dominion shrank, the French declared carnival: a spate of balls, theatrical performances, concerts, and assignations defied the rebels at the gate. Military bands serenaded General Rochambeau's Creole mistresses, and a popular ballad celebrated his ability to drink lesser men under the table.

American ships that slipped through the blockade sold cargoes of cigars and champagne and departed with desperate military dispatches and Rochambeau's booty. Smoke rolled in from the countryside to choke the city until dusk, when it was dispersed by the sea breeze and the hum of clouds of mosquitoes. It rained. Great crashing rains overflowed gutters and drove humans and dogs to shelter.

Solange forbade Ruth to speak Creole. "We must cling to what civilization we can, yes?" When their cook ran off and Augustin could not secure another, Ruth made fish soups and fried plantain, while Solange perched on a tall stool, reading to her.

High officers sent officers on desperate missions in order to comfort their widows.

In Saint-Louis Square, General Rochambeau burned three Negroes alive. In an ironical moment he crucified others on the beach at Monticristi Bay.

Every morning, Solange and Ruth strolled the oceanfront. One morning, the quay was packed with chained Negroes. "Madame, we are loyal French colonial troops," one black man shouted. Why tell her?

Ruth wanted to speak, so Solange hurried her along.

Two frigates sailed out into a beautiful day on the bay, and at low tide, three mornings later, the wide white beach was littered with drowned Negroes. The flat, metallic smell of death set Solange to gasping. When Solange complained to Captain Fornier, his weary, tolerant smile was a stranger's. "What else would you have us do with them, madame?"

For the first time, Solange was afraid of her husband.

———

The morning everything changed, Solange awoke to Ruth humming and the piquant odor of coffee.

Solange pushed the shutters open on a dejected straggle of soldiers below. What day was it? Would Augustin come home today? Would the rebels mount their final attack?

Ruth said, "What does Madame wish?"

What indeed? How could she be so discontented without intending anything?

Solange touched the gold rim of her cobalt blue cup. These walls, the walls of her home, were brute unplastered stone. Shutters of some native wood were unpainted. Ruth's eyes, like the delicate cup, were rich, complex, and beautiful. Solange said, "I have done nothing."

Ruth might have said, "What ought you have done?" but she didn't.

"Like a silly amateur sailor I have drifted into very deep water."

Ruth might have corrected this self-appraisal but didn't.

"We are in grave danger."

Ruth smiled. The morning sun haloed her head. Ruth said, "Madame will attend General Rochambeau's ball?"

Solange Fornier was Charles Escarlette's daughter, redoubtable and shrewd. Why was she reading sentimental novels?

Ruth said, "The general's ball will be held on a ship."

"Does he mean to drown his guests?"

Ruth's face went blank. Had she known one of those doomed prisoners? Solange sipped her coffee. At her impatient gesture, Ruth added sugar.

A cobalt blue teacup on a rude plank table. Sugar. Coffee. La Sucarie du Jardin. The Pearl of the Antilles. The air was clear and cool. Had the insurgents burned everything flammable? Solange could smell the faintest hint of the island's beguiling florescence. How beautiful it all might have been!

"Yes," Solange said. "What will I wear?"

"Perhaps the green voile?"

Solange put her finger to her chin. "Ruth, will you accompany me?"

She curtsied. "As you wish."

Solange frowned. "But what do *you* wish?"

"I wish whatever Madame wishes."

"Then tonight, you shall be my shield."

"Madame?"

"Yes, chérie. The green voile would be best."

When Augustin came home that afternoon, she surprised him

with a kiss. He unbuckled his sword belt and sat heavily on the bed stretching his legs so Ruth could pull his boots off. "Poor dear Augustin . . ."

His puzzled frown.

"You aren't cut out to be a soldier. I should have known . . ."

"I am a soldier, an officer . . ."

"Yes, Augustin, I know. Your frock coat. It is in our sea trunk?"

He shrugged. "I suppose. I haven't seen it in months."

"Make it presentable."

"Are we going somewhere? The theater? Some ball or another? You know I detest these amusements."

She touched his lips. "We are leaving Saint-Domingue, dear husband."

"I am a captain," he repeated stupidly.

"Yes, my captain. Your honor is safe with me."

Perhaps Augustin should have asked what and when and why, but he was exhausted and this was too complicated. He pulled off his uniform jacket. In socks and pantaloons he flopped back, grunted, and began snoring.

He has aged, Solange thought—surprised by her husband's lined, weary countenance. She fled this too tender mood with self-reproach: why have I abdicated my responsibility? Why should a Fornier determine the future of an Escarlette? "Rest, my brave captain. Soon, our troubles will be over."

No, Solange didn't know what she would do She had no words for the bright life flooding through her, that *something* that set her eyes and feet and fingertips tingling. She was certain of only one thing: they must escape the small island. They had nothing here, neither plantation nor rank, nor the false assurance that today would be the same as yesterday. If they stayed they would be killed.

Solange would know *what* to do *after* she'd done it.

It was pure Gallic genius to transform the poor old barnacle-encrusted, blockaded *Herminie* from a cannon-puffing, shot-hurling French flagship into an Arabian seraglio, with red and blue and green and gold scrims fluttering from yards and braces, potted palms stationed on the gun deck, and lamps and candles positioned to imperfectly illuminate nooks as lovers' havens. A military band tooted gallantly, and officers in plumed silver helmets toasted Creole mistresses while Negroes in red and blue turbans slipped among them recharging glasses. In a palm grove on the quarter-deck, Major General Donatien-Marie-Joseph de Vimeur, Vicomte de Rochambeau, greeted his guests. General Rochambeau was explaining the American Revolution (where he'd been his father's aide-de-camp) to an American merchant captain. "Captain Caldwell, do you really believe that General Cornwallis surrendered to General Washington at Yorktown, ending the war and ensuring American independence? You do? Ah, Mrs. Fornier. You have neglected us of late. When was the last time we had the pleasure . . . the theater was it? That miscast Molière?"

The patch on the general's powdered cheek may have covered a chancre, and when he pressed his lips to her hand, Solange repressed an urge to wipe it. "My dear general. In your company I had begun to fear for my virtue."

Rochambeau chuckled. "Dear Mrs. Fornier, how you flatter me. Allow me to introduce Captain Caldwell. Captain Caldwell is Bostonian. The captain may be the only incorruptible man in Cap-Français. Certainly his is the only neutral ship."

The general's smile, like the man himself, was fleshy. "I don't ask how many of my bravest officers have offered Captain Caldwell bribes—'just a small cabin, monsieur' . . . 'a place in the sail locker' . . . 'deck passage' . . . Captain, no names, please. I need my illusions intact."

The American shrugged. "Money's no good if you aren't alive to spend it."

Rochambeau had taken Captain Caldwell to Monticristi Bay, where skeletal remains testified as only they could. Rochambeau beamed. "How true. How very true." He patted Ruth on the head. "Charming child . . . charming . . ."

As Solange withdrew, the general resumed his history lesson. "Lord Cornwallis was so chagrined at his defeat he wouldn't attend the surrender ceremony, so, at the appropriate moment Cornwallis's aide offered his sword to my father, the Comte de Rochambeau. The British surrendered to us French . . ."

The American guffawed. "That makes your father our first president. Anybody tell George Washington 'bout that?"

Solange whispered, "Discover. Learn everything you can," and Ruth vanished like smoke.

The island's passionate, primitive girls had rather disappointed Napoleon's officers. Sad experience had proven that every alluring Creole girl had a brother in jail or a sister with a sick baby or an aged parent who couldn't pay his rent. These dark-skinned succubi brought as many complications as satisfactions into their beds.

Solange's usual escort, Major Brissot, was drunk, sprawled against the mainmast and barely able to raise his polished cuirassier's helmet. She flirted dutifully with admirers, but what these gallants took for vivacity (some thought desire) was impatience. She knew *what* she wanted but not *how*.

Blackmail? On Saint-Domingue, who *wasn't* corrupt? Who cared how many Negroes Colonel X had tortured and killed? General Y's betrayal of French plans to the insurgents? Pish! Major D's sale of French cannon to the enemy marked a new low, but, given the opportunity, what practical man wouldn't have done the same?

In the end, Solange's suitors sought easier conquests, and, beside her untouched champagne glass, she perched on the capstan waiting for Ruth and the child's espionage. The moon marched across the sky, the military band grew discordant and put their instruments down. Laughter, glassware clinking, a curse, a shriek, more laughter. The American captain had gone off with a Creole girl. General Rochambeau had disappeared into the admiral's cabin.

Chewing a heel of bread, Ruth perched on the capstan beside her mistress. She belched, covered her mouth, and apologized.

"Well?"

Whenever the wind changed and blew the British blockaders off station, Captain Caldwell would sail with many heavy chests (thought to contain treasure) consigned by General Rochambeau and an official pouch with military reports and favored officers' requests for transfer carried by the general's personal courier, Major Alexandre Brissot, Rochambeau's sister's son.

Alexandre had been shipped to the colony for conduct which, while not absolutely unknown was best practiced in a small—a very small—circle of peers. Alexandre had been indiscreet. Here, on the small island where murder, torture, and rape were commonplace, he'd been indiscreet again.

"He is a pede." Ruth finished her bread and licked her fingers.

"Of course he is. Major Brissot is the only French officer who always treats ladies courteously."

"Alexandre disgrace General Rochambeau."

Solange blinked. "How could anything disgrace . . ."

"Alexandre and that boy, Joli. He loves him. Give him so many gifts other officers laughin'. When Alexandre uncle find out, he want kill Joli, so Joli run off. Joli ain't come back neither. Best not."

"Joli . . ."

"Alexandre warn Joli to run. General want hang Alexandre but can't 'count he sister son."

Many of the general's guests had attained that plateau where they stayed erect by leaning against something and conversing with simple repetitions they needn't recall in the morning. Servants had appropriated the wine, and the party was well beyond that point that cues the prudent lady's departure. Sober soldiers guarded the admiral's cabin. "Two," Ruth informed Solange. "The general layin' with two tonight." Ruth grimaced. "Womens," she specified.

Hope surged through Solange—not an *idea* nor yet a *plan* . . . "Ruth, back to the house. In my trunk with my other fabrics, you'll find a red silk liberty cap. Bring it to me. Hurry."

A discordant trio of junior officers bellowed a bawdy song: "Il eut au moins dix véroles . . ." A disheveled colonel and his Creole girl exited their candlelit privacy, clinging to each other. When one of Rochambeau's guards winked, Solange pretended she didn't see.

Hope waned, and Solange had almost abandoned her mad scheme when Ruth reappeared and draped the soft silk fabric over her hand. "Madame?"

Ruth's presence firmed Solange. "Over there. That officer with his helmet in his lap. Wake him. Give the bonnet to Major Brissot and say 'Joli.' Solange carefully—oh so carefully!—told the child everything she had to say and do. "Ah, Ruth," Solange said. "I trust you with our lives."

With a downturned hand, the child dismissed her fears. "Little by little, the bird makes his nest."

Solange set her trap in a cabin on the port side, where one small tin lantern illuminated empty champagne glasses and a rumpled coverlet on the narrow bed. She turned the coverlet over and fluffed it. For no particular reason, she stuffed the champagne glasses into a drawer.

When she extinguished the candles, beeswax sweetened the smell of recent sex. Solange removed all of her clothing, closed the lantern, and waited. Once her eyes adjusted, enough moonlight came through the porthole to illumine her trembling, very naked arms.

She heard a stumble outside the door. A clunk. A breathless male whisper. "Joli . . ."

The latch turned, and, naked, she enfolded her prey.

————

Seconds or several lifetimes later, the general burst in behind his nephew, bellowing, "Mon Dieu, Alexandre! You and Joli will shake hands with the hangman!"

Flaring lanterns. Other officers pressed into the cabin behind their general. Solange gasped and covered her nakedness like Eve in the garden. "Alexandre!" the general gasped. "You? This woman?"

The general's round face leered over his nephew's shoulder. "Dear boy! Dear boy! I didn't . . . Don't let me ruin your, your tête-à-tête."

The general's entourage matched his leer.

Solange scooped her gown, clutching it against her nakedness. "Alexandre is my . . . my escort. Please, sir. My husband must not know."

He put a finger to his grinning lips. "Silent as the grave. He shan't hear a word from us, yes, gentlemen?"

Murmurs and muted guffaws.

The general closed the door firmly behind him.

Solange took a deep breath and opened the tin lantern. Humming, and in no particular hurry, she dressed.

Alexandre slumped on the bed, his hands clamping his skull. He vomited between his knees and stared at the mess. Solange opened the porthole, wishing the general had left the door ajar. She buttoned her collar and fluffed her hair. "Pardon me for remarking, Major. But you are ridiculous."

His eyes were so confused and sad, Solange couldn't meet them. "Joli? I thought you were . . . His cap, I gave him that cap. Joli . . ."

"Doubtless your Joli is safe with the rebels. Perhaps he fights against us French. Monsieur, don't try to understand all this. You will understand everything in the morning. May I suggest that tonight this bed is as good as any?"

"I love him." He sobbed a racking, choking sob.

"Ah, monsieur. You were always kind to me."

Ruth appeared in the doorway, looking her question. Solange said "Oui," and the child smiled.

On deck, the stars had faded and the moon hung over Morne Jean. Here and there officers in elaborate filthy uniforms lay like battle casualties. A whore picking a fat captain's pockets glared at the pair.

As she and Ruth made their way home, dawn lightened the ocean and gentle waves gurgled against the seawall. Solange took Ruth's small hand in hers and squeezed it.

Later that same day, while Augustin and Ruth packed, Solange presented herself at General Rochambeau's headquarters. No, she would not discuss her business. Madame's business was of an urgent and familial nature.

After Solange got past his adjutant and shut the door, General Rochambeau greeted her with the smile crocodiles reserve for well-rotted corpses. "Ah, madame. So good to see you. Less of you perhaps, still . . . Tell me, Mrs. Fornier, my nephew is your *escort*?"

"Very often." Solange blushed prettily. "The theater. He's a marvelous dancer."

"Just so. He . . ."

With some effort, Solange deepened her blush and said, shyly, "It is dear Alexandre I have come about . . ."

"Ah yes. Indeed. Madame, some wine?" He went to his sideboard. "Something stronger?"

"Oh no, my general. Last night . . ." (She touched her temple and winced.) "Ah, a married woman must not mix love with wine."

"Madame Fornier, we neither create nor vanquish our desires. Until last night, if you'll permit me, I thought Alexandre . . . Spirited young men . . . young men will . . . *experiment*. To find their true selves, is it not so?"

She smiled sweetly. "General, I must have your counsel. I am a married woman. But it is another I cannot get out of my head . . . his hair, his tender lips, his sensitive eyes . . ."

Had not his blushes been abolished years ago, perhaps the general would have found one now. Instead, he coughed. "As you say, madame. As you say."

"We are destined to be one." Groping for the appropriate sentiment, Solange cribbed from her sentimental novels. "Our love is meant to be. Alexandre and Solange. Our destiny is writ in the stars!"

Rochambeau poured a glass of something stronger. "No doubt."

"General, my marriage . . . a Fornier is not an Escarlette, much less a Rochambeau!"

His nod acknowledged this self-evident truth.

"I accept Alexandre's offer. But he is so . . . unworldly."

"Alexandre's . . ."

"We'll need passports. After we reach France, Alexandre and I will seek our destiny!"

"Madame, I give passports only to the old and the ugly."

"General, you are *so, so* gallant."

"And Captain Fornier?"

"My husband accepts what he cannot change."

"Very well. As you may have heard, my nephew is escorting dispatches to Paris. Major Brissot will need an aide. Does that satisfy you, madame?"

Solange clapped her hands together so smartly, the general winced. "Madame, if you please." He drained his glass, hacked, and swallowed hard.

"I'm so sorry, General. Alexandre respects you above all men, and he is so hurt by those vicious calumnies. If my public embarrassment has refuted those lies, I am satisfied."

Rochambeau rubbed his temples and turned hot eyes on her. "You have attained your goal, madame. Would you hazard it?"

"General, I do not take your meaning."

"Madame, of course you do." He rubbed his temples. "I had thought you . . . unexceptional. Now, I regret I shan't get to know you better. I shall amuse myself, however, imagining you and Alexandre, as you put it, 'writ in the stars.'"

"General, are you mocking me?"

He bowed deeply. "Dear, dear Mrs. Fornier, I would be afraid to."

Three nights later high winds forced the British squadron into desperate tacks to hold their position. Although Captain Caldwell had assured Solange he'd notify her when he was ready to sail, Solange and her family boarded immediately. Solange feared one of those last-minute *so regrettable* mistakes. When Major Brissot and his improved reputation departed Saint-Domingue, the Forniers would depart too. A single portmanteau held their belongings, softer fabrics cushioning the blue and gold Sevres tea set. Jewelry, a few gold louis, and a charged four-barrel pepperbox pistol were stowed in Solange's reticule. She had sewn her precious dower agreement and letter of credit into Ruth's petticoat.

By morning, the British blockaders were blown out to sea and the horizon was empty of their sails, but Major Brissot didn't appear until ten o'clock. Soldiers carried the general's precious trunks aboard and then had to be mustered and counted and two deserter-stowaways plucked from hidey-holes before they cast off. Captain Caldwell was anxious; though officially neutral, American ships carrying French booty were legitimate prizes.

It was brisk and sunny, and the air was brilliantly clean. Beside Captain Caldwell, Major Brissot winced at two shots from the quay. "There but for the grace of God," he murmured.

The captain urged his quartermaster to crack on more sail before turning to his important passenger. "A fine day, monsieur. Excellent. If the winds hold, we'll make swift passage."

Alexandre smiled sadly. "Good-bye, Saint-Domingue, accursed island. Your voudou men have cursed us. All of us."

The captain sniffed. "I am a Christian, sir."

"Yes. As are they."

As the island sank to the horizon, a thin column of smoke lingered above what might have been a plantation, or a town, or perhaps a crossroads where men were squabbling, fighting, and dying.

Alexandre shuddered. "The Negroes . . . They love us, but they hate us too. I shall never understand . . ."

"You are well out of it."

"I have left too much behind."

Captain Caldwell grinned. "You have left less than you think. Have you inspected your accommodations?"

"Sir?"

When Alexandre stepped into his cabin, he was startled to find a small girl serving breakfast to a fellow he may have met somewhere, sometime, and a woman he remembered too vividly. "Madame!"

"Ah. Look, Augustin, it is my lover, Alexandre. Isn't he handsome?"

The husband so addressed set his fork down to examine his rival equally. "Good day, Major Brissot."

Solange said, "Alexandre, your uncle holds violent opinions about whom one may or may not love. My subterfuge spared you and restored your—and your family's—reputation."

Alexandre stuttered his outrage. Why, why had Madame Fornier involved herself in his affairs?

"Sir"—Solange smiled too triumphantly—"I have repaired your reputation at some cost to my own. Don't I deserve your thanks?"

Apparently not. Despite steady winds and exceptionally fine weather, their voyage was awkward and unpleasant. Alexandre sulked. Augustin was depressed. Solange, who had spent her childhood on small boats, was intensely seasick. Ruth was the sailors' favorite. They spoiled her mercilessly with sweets and taught her "American" English. A burly seaman carried her to the tip-top of the mainmast.

"I swayed out over the water," she told Solange. "I could see all the world."

When they landed in Freeport, a fast schooner was waiting for Alexandre and his uncle's booty. Alexandre made an effort. "Madame, you are a formidable woman."

"No, sir. I am 'redoubtable.' Your Joli is lost. Surely there are other Jolis?"

Alexandre examined Solange until her gaze faltered. "Ignorance is always cruel."

———

Although he was sailing for Boston, Captain Caldwell would call at Savannah, Georgia, a city he assured the Forniers was prosperous, cosmopolitan, and where (nodding at Ruth), unlike Boston, slavery was legal. Solange had made all the decisions she could bear to make and Augustin couldn't help. Savannah would have to do.

And, for just two louis, the Forniers could retain their cabin. A bargain, Caldwell assured them. The Irish immigrants he took aboard would have paid more.

Solange and Ruth took the air on the quarterdeck, ignoring the stares and just audible remarks of less fortunate fellow passengers. Solange did wonder if Augustin had left something very important on the island, but she didn't ask. Her husband rarely left the cabin.

In shallow waters off Florida, the weather deteriorated, and the leadsman chanted night and day. Driving rain flogged the deck and the huddled Irish passengers. Two unfortunate infants died and were consigned to the deep.

As they pelted northeast, the rain relented but the wind was biting.

The captain reduced sail as they approached the delta where the Savannah River emptied into the Atlantic. "Mistress, mistress, come look!" Ruth pulled Solange to the rail and clambered up to see better.

"The New World." A burly Irishman betrayed no enthusiasm.

Solange, fresh from quarreling with Augustin, did not need a new friend. "Oui!"

The man's thick dirty hair was brushed back, and he smelled powerfully of the bay rum he'd applied in lieu of soap and water. "You'd be one of them Frenchies the niggers chased off?"

"My husband was a planter."

"Terrible hard work, all that stoopin' and hoein'."

"Captain Fornier was a planter. Not a field hand."

"Betimes rebellions overturns masters and betimes they overturns field hands. Turnabout bein' fair play and all."

"You, monsieur; are you too the debris of rebellion?"

"We are. Me brother and me, the both of us." He smiled. Some of his teeth had been broken, all were stained. "Do you reckon it matters if the hand that fastens your noose is white or black?"

"Sir, don't distress the child," Solange said. "She knows nothing about such matters."

The Irishman studied Ruth. "Nay, ma'am, I reckon this child knows a muchness."

A pilot boat battered over the bar; a seaman in oilskins climbed the rope ladder and had a word with Captain Caldwell before taking his place beside the helmsman, hands clasped behind his back.

The ship eased up a channel through an estuary pocked with brushy islands and pale sandbars. It looked nothing like Saint-Malo. Ruth took Solange's cold hand in her warmer one.

Reluctantly the tide loosed them to slip inland between a wall of gray-green trees dripping with ghostly moss and a vivid yellow-green salt marsh. Directly, this wilderness gave way to a port where big and little ships docked and anchored, beneath an American city on the bluff above their mastheads.

Augustin came on deck blinking in the sunlight.

Savannah's bluff was faced with five-story warehouses, and staircases wriggled back and forth as if embarrassed by what space they required. The docks were frantic with carts and wagons while spindly cranes delivered cargo from ship to shore and reverse.

The pilot eased them alongside this confusion and scurried down his rope ladder indifferent to the shouted promises of New World hucksters: "I want your silks and by Jehoshaphat I'll pay for them!" "British and French banknotes discounted! I have U.S. and Georgia banknotes in hand."

After the gangplank was lowered, their meager possessions clasped fast, the immigrants hurried into their future. A small man in a white waistcoat and top hat confronted Solange's Irishman. "Work for the willing. Stevedores, draymen, drovers, wherrymen, laborers. Irish and free coloreds treated same as white."

As Solange came up the burly Irishman set his bundle down and inclined his ear. He shook his head no, but the small man clutched his sleeve, whereupon, pursued by his top hat, he was flung into the river. "And a Killarney greeting to you, my man. Selling work is a shabby business."

"Silks, jewelry, gold or silver, gewgaws? Madame? You won't find fairer prices in all Georgia."

Solange brushed by with "Invariably, sir, those most eager to help strangers offer the least."

The little family humped their portmanteau up three landings to Bay Street, a broad boulevard where coloreds unloaded cotton bales and rough-cut lumber into warehouses.

Solange rested on a wooden bench wiping her brow. Among the mercantile bustle, gentlefolk exchanged gay greetings, promenading through Negroes and Irish as if they didn't exist. Solange felt poor.

Some shops facing the boulevard were busy, others silent as rejection. A six-horse lumber wagon rumbled by, off wheel squealing. Some coloreds were respectably dressed, others wore rags that scarcely observed the conventions of decency. River breezes refreshed the promenade. Solange dabbed perspiration from her brow. Augustin was pale, silent, and diminished. Augustin could not be sick. That would be too much! Solange elbowed her husband and was relieved by his querulous protest.

She sent Ruth to inquire for a moneylender. The coloreds would know who offered fair value. She told Augustin to remove his outer coat. Did he wish to poach like an egg?

Her husband's smile begged for tenderness, an emotion Solange had less of. In this hard, uncouth new country, tenderness would impede her progress.

A dray braked as its driver berated another. They concluded their loud confrontation by leaning from their perches for vigorous, mutual backslapping.

Solange was so very alone. "Augustin?"

"Yes, my dear." His too familiar, too flat voice. His damnable despair!

"Nothing. Never mind."

Augustin did try. "Dear Solange. Thanks to your cleverness, we have escaped Hell!" His pale lips and jacked-up eyebrows seemed to believe it too. "Le Bon Dieu . . . ah, He has been so merciful."

Was this the man she'd married? What had the island done to him?

Ruth returned with an elderly Negro in tow. "Mister Minnis, he fine honest Jewish gentleman, ma'am," the Negro informed her. "He bein' glad buy or loan 'gainst your jewels and gold."

"Jewels and gold?"

"Oh, yes, ma'am. You pickaninny, she say how much you bringin'. King's ransom. My, my."

Before Solange could correct his misapprehension, Ruth dragged Augustin to his feet. "Come along, Master Augustin," she cried. "Soon you be joyful again."

At Mister Solomon Minnis's residence on Reynolds Square, the servant left them on the piazza, assuring them that "Mr. Minnis be seein' you straightaway, yes, sir: straightaway."

At ten o'clock on a winter morning, Mr. Minnis was unshaven in nightshirt, slippers, and robe, but he bought their silks—including Solange's green voile ball dress—and loaned against her jewelry and cobalt blue tea set. She could have payment in coin or scrip.

"At what discount?"

"Ah, no, no. No discount, madame. The notes are redeemable today, in this city in silver. A branch of the Bank of the United States is established in Savannah, and there's to be a substantial bank building erected come spring. The cotton trade requires such."

Each of Solange's notes assured that the "President and Directors of the Bank of the United States promise to pay twenty dollars at their offices of Discount and Deposit at Savannah to F. A. Pickens, the President thereof, or to BEARER."

"Satisfactory," the bearer said, stowing her notes with the three silver Spanish reals that completed Mr. Minnis's purchase and pawn.

As his Negro servant discreetly removed Solange's valuables, Mr. Minnis asked about Saint-Domingue: Were the Negro rebels as brutal as reported? Were white women subjected to . . .

Solange said rebel atrocities were too harsh and too numerous to relate, but that was then and this was now and her family required accommodations during their stay in Savannah.

Although refugees and immigrants had strained Savannah's modest housing stock and not a few families camped in the squares, Mr. Minnis knew a widow who might rent the coachman's apartment over her carriage house.

They moved into two bare rooms that afternoon and Solange engaged a cook.

Impoverished immigrants competed for laboring jobs with colored servants, like Solange's cook, who'd been rented out "on the town" by her master.

Since Augustin Fornier couldn't "do" anything, he must "be" someone. Solange told her husband he was "a prominent colonial planter: one of Napoleon's bravest field officers."

After lifting her husband's spirits, Solange made love to him. In the afterglow, Augustin fell into deep, satisfied slumber while the sweaty, discontented Solange lay stiffly at his side. Although Ruth's regular breathing rose from the straw pallet at the foot of their bed, Solange didn't think the child was asleep.

If necessary, a pretty maidservant would fetch a good price. Yes, Ruth adored her, and, yes, she was fond of the child, but one does what one must. What had Alexandre meant when he called her "ignorant"? Of what was Solange Escarlette Fornier ignorant?

Augustin snored his unimaginative drone and wasn't up the next morning when Solange dispatched Ruth and Cook to the market and sat down to write Dear Papa! So Far Away! So Desperately Missed!

How Papa's favorite daughter had suffered. Sucarie du Jardin had been a Fornier fraud! Her husband was useless. Had it not been for Escarlette wit, they'd be trapped on Saint-Domingue at the mercy of rebellious savages! Thanks to Le Bon Dieu they were safe in Savannah. If Papa's favorite daughter had known then what she now knew, she would never have left Saint-Malo!

Solange didn't promise Dear Papa a new grandchild, not in so many words. She only suggested that Dear Papa might soon have a happy surprise! She grieved over her pawned jewelry and cobalt blue teacups but scratched that sentence out. Dear Papa would have starved before he pawned one Escarlette treasure!

There was nothing for civilized French people in this hemisphere. Might she come home?

She wiped her pen and capped the inkwell. Morning sun poured through her window. Savannah birds haggled, and camellias flaunted fat, bawdy flowers. As she sanded and folded her letter, Solange felt a little less certain of what she had written. Perhaps . . .

Troubles had come so fast and in such bewildering profusion!

A not unpleasant lassitude crept into her bones; she was safe this morning, and American songbirds were auditioning for her approval.

Solange crushed coffee beans into a muslin bag and poured boiling water through it into her cup. The rich aroma tickled her nostrils.

She reappraised matters. They were in America; she, her husband, and the child who was almost more than a servant. If they returned to France, what were their realistic prospects? Poor Augustin would always be a second son, but in Saint-Malo he'd be the second son complicit in the loss of the Sucarie du Jardin, which Solange understood would grow more valuable in everyone's mind the longer it was lost.

Negroes lived in Africa. What would happen to Ruth in Saint-Malo? When Solange's ebony companion grew into *womanhood* (Solange shuddered to think), what would Solange do? In France, she couldn't sell her.

Solange's eldest sister had married a legislator and produced a healthy Escarlette grandson. Her second sister was affianced to a cavalryman and would, in due course, produce satisfactory offspring.

While Solange Fornier was the failed second son's childless wife with an unusual very dark-skinned handmaiden.

She drank her coffee, waked Augustin, fed him a roll and an orange, and brushed flecks from his coat. She inflated his pride, insisting her hero was her Hero. "Brave men do what must be done." She kissed him on the cheek and sent him forth into the world.

When Ruth and Cook returned, they were chattering in some heathen tongue, but when Solange evinced displeasure, Ruth begged pardon very prettily.

That afternoon, Solange walked to Mr. Haversham's home, whose drawing room served (until the permanent structure could be built) as the Savannah branch of the Bank of the United States. The cherry wainscoting, florid wallpaper, and elegant ceiling medallion contrasted with the great iron safe crammed into the narrow doorway of what had been Haversham's butler's pantry.

Mr. Haversham studied Solange's impressively sealed and notarized letter of credit. "Very good, madame. Please ask your husband to come by to open an account."

Whereupon Solange laid her dower agreement beside the letter of credit.

Mr. Haversham ignored it while he explained, as if to a child, that, under Georgia law, Solange was a Fem Covert, and as a married woman could hold no property in her own name. He smiled agreeably. "Some liberal husbands accommodate their wives. Why, my own dear wife has full authority over our household accounts . . ."

Impatiently Solange unfolded and tapped the agreement. "You do read French?"

"Madame . . ."

"This attests to my right to hold property under my own name under the régime de In fiparatum de bient. Since this agreement preceded my marriage and was freely entered into by my husband, I am, under French law or the laws of any *civilized* country, a Fem Sole—exactly as if I were an unmarried female heir or widow. Should you require a translation, I can arrange one."

The banker raised a mildly surprised but not disapproving eyebrow. "Madame, not every American is a provincial. I am conversant with French legal instruments." He pushed his glasses back on his nose, and under a very large magnifying glass he scrutinized the document, its seals, signatures, and notarization. His chair squeaked when he leaned back. "Your documents are in order. Naturally I must have verification of your French balance before I advance your funds." He plucked a *Georgia Gazette* from a wicker basket at his feet and opened to the shipping register. "*L'Herminie* sails this afternoon for Amsterdam, and she's a fast sailor. We might have verification in . . . say . . . nine weeks?" He rose and bowed. "Your obedient servant, ma'am. Welcome to Savannah. I trust you will prosper here."

While Solange would have welcomed advice on how that desirable outcome might be realized, she didn't press the banker. As she strolled the broad, tree-lined, sand street in the pale November sunshine, Solange's relief that her precious letter of credit was protected in Mr. Haversham's sturdy iron safe was mixed with the apprehension a mother feels when her toddler is out of her sight.

———

Savannah's French communities were two, not one. The French "émigrés" who'd come to Georgia after the 1789 French Revolution brought wealth with them, while most "refugees" were paupers who'd fled Saint-Domingue with little more than the clothes on their backs.

In December exiles and refugees got news which was no less distressing for being expected. The news flew from the docks to the lonely settler's lean-to in the deep shadows of Georgia pines as fast as the fastest horse could deliver it. Saint-Domingue was lost! Henceforth the Pearl of the Antilles was a Black Pearl! Despite determined French resistance and terrible losses, the insurgents broke through the ring forts protecting Cap-Français and forced General Rochambeau to surrender. French officers and soldiers who could cram aboard rotting transports sailed only to become British prisoners of war; the wounded and sick left behind on the quay suffered for days before they were drowned. Triumphant insurgents renamed their nation Haiti.

That blow to French pride proved a blessing for one refugee family when Savannah's second richest Frenchman, Pierre Robillard, showed his patriotism by hiring one of the defeated army's gallant officers, Captain Fornier, as his clerk. Although Augustin's salary wasn't large, severe household economies and what remained of Mister Minnis's loan would keep the Forniers until Solange's letter of credit turned into cash.

Pierre Robillard had established himself in Georgia as an importer of French wines and those silks, voiles, and perfumes whose possession distinguished the newly rich Low Country gentlewoman from the rough-handed rustic her pioneer mother had been.

Pierre's richer, younger cousin, Philippe Robillard, spoke the Edisto and Muscogee Indian languages and assisted the Georgia legislature during Indian land negotiations—an honor Philippe mentioned too often. The cousins Robillard dominated Savannah's social season, and invitations to their annual ball were much sought after.

Georgia natives admired French urbanity but thought the new citizens too urbane, a little *too* French. The French lady's shape, so clearly discernible beneath the shimmering fabric of her diaphanous gown, may have been unexceptionable in Paris or Cap-Français, but in Georgia, where backcountry travelers sometimes encountered hostile Indians and the Great Awakening had prompted many to reexamine their (and others') sinful natures, those garments' beguiling fragility seemed foolhardy and immoral.

Despite these mild adversions, Georgians were sympathetic to the refugees' plight, and relief subscriptions were distributed by St. John the Baptist Catholic Church.

Low Country planters had vigorous, if differing opinions about the Saint-Domingue rebellion. Some claimed the slaves had been treated too harshly, others that they hadn't been disciplined enough. Although every white Savannahian saluted Mr. Henry's "Give me liberty or give me death," regarding Saint-Domingue, they believed the Jacobin passion for liberty had overreached by a country mile. Savannahians viewed the French Negroes with suspicion. Mightn't they be contaminated by rebellion? Their flamboyant dress was provocative, and some French Negroes emulated white men, even flaunting watch fobs and chains! That spring, when news came of cruel massacres of whites who hadn't escaped Saint-Domingue, many Masses were offered for their souls, and, for a time, French Negroes only appeared in their sober Sunday clothing.

Solange Fornier missed the sea. She missed Saint-Malo's promenade, where salt rime damped her cheeks and her nostrils widened to seaweed's astringent tang. Saint-Malo's cobbled streets had known the footfalls of Romans, medieval monks, and bold corsairs. Savannah was so young, not much older than the revolution of which Americans were so inordinately proud. A few offered faint praise for General Lafayette, but of the French fleet that had denied reinforcements to the besieged British at Yorktown and the French troops who'd stormed the British redoubts, Savannahians apparently knew nothing. "You were our allies, weren't you, when we freed our nation from the British yoke?"

Solange's "yessss" was remarkably like a hisss.

France had bankrupted herself supporting these ungrateful backwoodsmen, and, because of that, the spendthrift King Louis had been beheaded. But that was then. Unlike some refugees, Solange wasted no energy regretting that French help for ungrateful Americans hadn't been directed to its own rebellious colonies: Saint-Domingue in particular.

Solange exchanged her last two gold louis with Mr. Haversham. Though convinced that the Banque de France's confirmation would arrive any day—"We must be patient, madame"—he could not, in his position of trust, advance money against it. Surely the charming madame would understand his position. He deplored the turbulent Atlantic. Several vessels, including a British mail packet, had failed to arrive when expected and were feared lost. Solange's confirmation would not have been aboard a British vessel. Absolutely not! Non!

When Solange accompanied Cook and Ruth to the torchlit market building, she was overwhelmed by the number and force of so many blacks chattering away in their heathen tongues. Speak English! she wanted to shout. Or, if you must, speak French! Servants had no right to have conversations their masters couldn't understand.

And the market women deferred to Ruth, a deference that annoyed Solange. White admiration for Ruth flattered the child's owner as he who admires a Thoroughbred compliments the horse's owner. But the market women's strange deference conferred no benefits on Solange; the owner felt invisible!

Solange spoke English, but Augustin wouldn't learn the language and dismissed American ways. After his workday, he lingered with other bitter refugees in a drinking house where French was spoken, Napoleon's campaigns dissected, and the First Consul's failure to save Saint-Domingue deplored endlessly. Solange nicknamed her husband's new friends "Les Amis du France."

Although Augustin had never set a sugarcane cutting nor, indeed, ever seen cane planted, he expertly debated colonial agriculture as if his brief visit to la Sucarie du Jardin had produced bumper crops.

Augustin insisted the new Haitian government would recompense him for the sucarie. ("They stole it from us, did they not? They must pay") and to that end initiated a correspondence with the French consul in New Orleans.

Although Ruth's English was the English of the market and servants' quarters, the child was soon chattering away. While Augustin attended Pierre Robillard's customers and gloried in Napoleon's victories, Solange and Ruth explored the new world. Many mornings, just as cook fires discharged their first pungent smoke, Solange and Ruth strolled Savannah's fine French squares, discovering which elegant homes belonged to which prominent families. (Ruth, who could go anywhere and ask anything, was a fine spy.) The French woman and her Negro maid visited neighborhoods where artificers worked, animals were sold, and lumber and bricks warehoused. The rude Irishman and his brother had acquired an oxcart and an emaciated, rib-sprung ox and set up as draymen. Though the Irishman invariably tipped his hat, Solange as invariably snubbed him.

Solange and Ruth often concluded their amble at the riverfront, below the deserted promenade on the cluttered, hectic docks, where Gaelic, Ibo, and Creole dialects loaded cotton bales and indigo barrels onto big and little ships and unloaded fine goods and furnishings off them.

Without Ruth, Solange might have been mistaken for one of

the painted Cyprians soliciting dockworkers and sailors. Although some of these creatures tried to strike up an acquaintance, Solange spurned them.

Later, when there were more white faces about, the pair dallied at a small café for coffee and biscuits slathered with tupelo honey while Ruth chattered with everybody and anybody.

When they returned home, breakfast dishes and the lingering smell of tabac were her husband's remnants. Solange changed from her walking garb and dressed the child for Mass. One time she'd attended the 6:30 Mass, which served Savannah's draymen, stevedores, and laundrywomen. That Irishman approached without so much as a by-your-leave wondering how she was "faring" in the "New World" and had the effrontery to introduce "my brother Andrew O'Hara and Martha, my missus." Despite Solange's frosty silence, the man *would* presume on their brief shipboard acquaintance. Thereafter Mrs. Fornier and her maid attended the 10:30. If the 6:30 was the Irish Mass, the 10:30 was the Society. Solange didn't repeat O'Hara's mistake, nodding politely if and only if another nodded, and, in the vestibule after the service, she attended to her missal or rosary while familiars greeted each other with the ebullient chirps Savannah ladies preferred. When fine ladies remarked favorably, Ruth responded with a curtsy and "Thank you, mistress," while Solange smiled distantly.

After the 10:30, gentlefolk boarded carriages for the quarter mile to Bay Street. Solange and Ruth walked and upon arrival promenaded quietly among their social betters. Were it not for the racial strictures, Solange might have been Ruth's governess, instructing her and noting this subject of interest and that.

Those ladies Solange ignored in turn ignored her in favor of last night's scandals and the all-too-delicious anticipation of scandals to come. They were particularly interested in matters that magnified their virtues.

After their promenade, Savannahians drove home, where supper and a nap fortified them for evening soirées.

Solange and Ruth went home and stayed there. Solange would not abandon herself to anxiety. (What would they do if the Banque de France failed her? What if her precious document drowned in the turbulent Atlantic?) Although she never *priced* Ruth, Solange knew the girl would bring more than Augustin could earn in months. Dull anxiety thudded against an anxiety backdrop. Solange was waiting for her life to happen.

She lost patience with the sensitive novelists who had been such good company in Cap-Français. To improve her English, she read Mr. Wordsworth aloud until she hit upon "Fill your paper with the breathings of your heart," which reduced Solange and Ruth to giggling.

One overcast April afternoon when no ships made port and the day promised more hours than she could bear, Solange visited her husband's place of business.

Most Bay Street establishments were brick, but some ramshackle one- and two-story board houses had survived the city's fires and hurricanes. On one weathered veranda, a gray-haired ancient in frock coat and revolutionary three-cornered hat nodded at every passerby.

L'Ancien Régime, Monsieur Robillard's emporium, was tucked between a chandlery and an apothecary. When she'd passed the place, Solange had always offered a cheery wave in case someone inside were looking, but she'd never crossed the doorstep.

On this occasion, Solange wore the dull clothing appropriate to a clerk's wife, modified by Escarlette hauteur.

Ruth could wait outside. Solange was in no mood for complicated explanations, which, as a clerk's wife, she would be obliged to provide.

She paused to admire L'Ancien Régime's window: jacquard silks were draped over a gilt chair; the gold head of the cane propped against the chair was retracted an inch, revealing a bright lethal sword. Shapely crocks of emollients, unguents, and potions surrounded bottles of Veuve Cliquot against a broad fan of red, white, and blue bunting.

A bell jingled when Solange stepped into the dim interior, where a voice inquired if Madame had come for the new perfumes, which had been unpacked only yesterday and were, she was assured, the same scents favored by Empress Josephine when she and her ladies promenaded in the Tuileries.

At an altar of minuscule glass bottles, Solange presented her inner wrist to the clerk, who deposited a precious drop thereon. "The scent is inconspicuous, but, like the tuberose for which it is named, it blooms late."

When Solange raised her wrist to her nose, it was the florescence of a May morning.

The clerk was tall, balding, and wore a ruffled linen shirt and navy blue cravat. Also, he was black; more precisely, he was gray-black, as if his blackness had been bleached by too much sun. His French was the French Solange's Parisian cousins spoke when they condescended to visit delightfully quaint Saint-Malo. Solange introduced herself.

He bowed deeply. "Master Augustin has been keeping you from your admirers. I am Nehemiah, madame, your humble and most obedient servant." His second bow was deeper and more presumptuous than his first.

"My husband . . ."

"Captain Fornier attends Master Robillard, madame. They read the newspapers. All the newspapers." His head shake admired this unlikely accomplishment.

The man guided her down narrow passages between fabric trees, gold and white furniture, and artfully arranged cases of wine, to a door he opened without knocking. "Madame Fornier has this day, April the fourteenth, honored us with her gracious presence."

Solange was issued into a narrow room, whose high ceiling was somewhere above the billowing cigar smoke.

How *dare* this Negro take charge of her! In icy tones, in English, Solange dismissed him.

As if she hadn't spoken, Nehemiah lingered, to say in the same language, "Mistress Fornier, she like that tuberose. 'Deed she do."

"That'll be all, Nehemiah." Augustin found his tongue.

Pierre Robillard came to his feet, ruddy face beaming. "So good of you to grace us with your presence . . . so good." In the old-fashioned manner, he kissed Solange's hand.

The office almost had room for two disreputable armchairs, the proprietor's overflowing desk, unpacked cases, and a newspaper rack like one might expect to find in a café or coffeehouse. Intercepting her glance, Robillard chuckled. "Some men act, others think they could have done better than those who act. Though I am fascinated by mankind's wicked ways, I am too fastidious to intervene. But"—he paused dramatically—"I forget my manners." He tsked at himself. "Won't you take a chair? I understand why Captain Fornier hides you from us, but I shan't forgive him."

Robillard's excellent French explained his articulate servant but didn't entirely restore Solange's sense of order. She sank into his deep, too plush, too worn-out armchair.

When she declined a restorative, Monsieur Robillard said Nehemiah could brew tea, which she accepted, and Augustin left to set in motion.

Robillard fluttered his hands, mock ruefully. "Oh my, won't Madame berate me for this!"

"For *this*, monsieur?"

"'Tis true. 'Tis true. Madame greatly overestimates my concupiscence. Madame has convinced herself no beautiful woman's virtue is safe with me. And, madame, you would tempt a saint."

These alarming words, uttered from such beaming complacency, made Solange smile. "I understand your wife's concern, sir."

"You do?"

"Were I not a wedded woman . . ."

He sighed. "Alas, so many women are. Or they are maids with fathers devoted to the Code Duello, or their brothers can shoot the pip out of a playing card, or those ladies have lovers, or are contemplating the wimple and habit; in Savannah society, madame, the aspiring rake is utterly hobbled and nobbled. The perfidious British understand these matters so much better than we French. Fais ce que tu voudras—Do what you will—and that sort of thing."

"Shouldn't my husband be in the room?" Solange said, feeling not the slightest concern.

Robillard took her hand. His palm was damp and earnest. "Oh, my dear, I am quite harmless. Though," he added ruefully, "my Louisa doesn't think so." He clapped his hands. "That's quite enough of me. In his absence—for he rejects every compliment—let me tell you how fortunate I am Captain Fornier has entered my service."

He then offered the appraisal of her husband Solange had so hoped to create. Augustin was "Napoleon's brave captain," a "Hero of the Saint-Domingue Rebellion," and "a true gentleman"—Solange's smile faltered—"wise in the ways of the world." Monsieur Robillard noted that he himself had had the very great honor of serving under the Emperor when he was merely *Lieutenant* Bonaparte many, many years ago. "We saw no fighting, alas." His eyebrows climbed his forehead. "There *was* no fighting anywhere. Can you imagine?"

Speaking as an émigré whose long residence in the city entitled him to *some* opinions, Robillard averred that Captain Fornier's military reputation would profit him in Savannah society. "Until I came to America, I'd never dreamed there were so many colonels and majors—even generals." Robillard beamed. "Myself? I was never more than a simple soldat. Your brave Captain Fornier, madame, thank you for letting me borrow him."

Solange knew he would have kissed her hand again had it been slightly easier to bend so far.

At L'Ancien Régime, Augustin served Savannah's numerous colonels, captains, and majors. Who better to choose French wines than a French officer? And, as Solange might imagine, many American ladies were too delicate to be waited on by a Negro. Still, Nehemiah had his uses. "He checks our invoices, unpacks, and arranges goods. Aren't his displays artful? Why," the proprietor added, "Nehemiah knows our merchandise better than I do, though I shan't let him in on our secret!" He pressed a cautionary finger against his nose and winked. "Captain Fornier and Nehemiah have made Pierre Robillard supernumerary in his own establishment!"

Solange's smile drifted from amazed to admiring to amazed. Of course she didn't interrupt. Of course she didn't ask: if Augustin is so valuable, doesn't he deserve a better salary? Instead, she returned Robillard's compliments whenever she could get a word in and learned much more about his wife. "Madame, when Louisa submitted to my entreaties, she married *down!*" and even more about his daughter, Clara, upon whom Pierre Robillard doted.

As Solange departed, the proprietor pressed a vial of tuberose scent on her, asserting he was merely "gilding the lily."

Outdoors, when her mistress rejoined her, Ruth sniffed loudly and wrinkled her nose.

One cannot avoid reversals of fortune, but one needn't bow to them. Certainly, Solange did not. But she wept over her father's letter. She wept so inconsolably, Augustin fled their apartment for too many glasses with sympathetic fellow refugees, which was the sort of mistake young husbands make. Ruth never left her sobbing mistress's side. Her dark eyes brimmed as she accorded but never intruded on Solange's grief.

Charles Escarlette wrote that Solange's dear Momma had worn out her knees praying and had a two-ecu Mass said for her beloved daughter. When she read of the rebel victory, Momma took to her bed in a swoon. Charles Escarlette was so grateful at his daughter's escape he would reduce interest from 5 percent to 4 percent due for monies advanced for Augustin's commission.

He wrote his daughter that Saint-Malo had fallen on hard times. British privateers had ravaged coastal shipping, and Henri-Paul Fornier had lost three inoffensive trading vessels to their depredations. "Cannot these British pirates distinguish a merchant ship from a man-of-war?"

As a consequence, Agence Maritime du Fornier was bankrupt, and Augustin's brother, Leo, had been conscripted and was thought to be with the army in Spain.

While not so dire as Fornier circumstances (her father's satisfaction wafted from his letter as pungent as bruised mint), the Escarlettes were not as they had been. Their import-export business was reduced, and, as Saint-Malo's economy had faltered, certain loans had gone unpaid, and several investments had soured.

Doubtless his dutiful daughter would understand that monies previously advanced her were now needed at home. Although the British had destroyed peaceful commerce, they had created profit opportunities artificing for war. Charles Escarlette was negotiating the lease of a brick building, a onetime warehouse, convertible to a factory for sewing uniforms. Pursuant to this plan, he had visited the Banque de France, who informed the astonished father that under the Code Napoleon, his daughter's letter of credit could only be reassigned by that daughter, and, in any event, Solange Escarlette Fornier had already remitted those funds to America!

She and Augustin must return home immediately. Any neutral

American vessel, bound for Holland or Belgium, could pass through the British. Once they had landed, mail coaches could reach Saint-Malo in four days. Others, unscrupulous men whose names he needn't mention, were "sniffing like truffle hounds" around the warehouse, and, though Charles Escarlette flattered himself on his foresight, other merchants might reach similar conclusions about the demand for uniforms. Her father regretted that Dear Solange and Dear Augustin couldn't purchase first-class passage, but second class docked no later than first, and every penny was needed at home.

Charles Escarlette concluded his letter with expressions of parental satisfaction and affection. His postscript exuded confidence that, as a dutiful daughter, Solange would understand.

Solange understood all too well and promptly repaired to Mr. Haversham, to inquire about the Banque de France's verification.

Mr. Haversham was devastated at his impotence, but he knew nothing. He'd heard nothing. That evening over dinner he confessed to Mrs. Haversham his relief that he wasn't the person who'd occasioned Mrs. Fornier's ire.

Solange penned one letter after another but mailed none. What might her father do! What were Saint-Malo's clever lawyers suggesting he do?

She perused the shipping news the instant *The Georgia Gazette* was posted outside that newspaper's office. Other early risers who might have usurped her place were made aware that the handsome Frenchwoman's interest in arriving ships trumped any concern of theirs. Solange spent so much time on the docks she knew which pilot steered an arriving vessel by the course it chose. She waited with Mr. Haversham's clerk and the mail pouches at Mr. Haversham's when that gentleman came downstairs to start his day.

"If it were up to me, madame . . ." he said as he searched his correspondence. "Were it not for the strictures Philadelphia has put on every branch of the bank, I promise you I would abjure this tedious formality."

Solange wore a locked, minimum smile.

Not hers. Not hers. Not hers. The banker rejected the last envelope with a small frown but smiled at Ruth. "Your handmaid is such a lively child. Negroes are at their best as children, don't you think?"

Ruth found bargains at the market, and after Solange let Cook go, Ruth cooked a little.

One evening, when Augustin had drunk more than usual, he invited his friend Count Montelone to share their brown beans, rice, and okra. If the dusty old man was affronted by the Fornier offering, he was polite enough to eat all of it and the seconds intended for the next day. At some length the Count described his prominent family. When Solange admitted her ignorance of the august folk, he said, "Ah, you're from Saint-Malo, are you not?"

Although the Count never said a word to Ruth, he eyed her so avidly, the child left the room.

When Solange urged economy on her husband because almost all their money was gone, Augustin said he must be able to buy his friends' drinks as they bought his. "I am a soldier," he informed her. "Not a priest."

One morning, as a Dutch-flagged barkentine was dropping its gangplank, Ruth perched cross-legged atop a bollard, humming. When her humming suddenly stopped, Solange turned. What was Mrs. Robillard doing on the docks?

"Ah, Mrs. Fornier. So this is where you have been keeping yourself. We have missed you on the promenade. My. All these Negroes. These Irish. These, uh . . . *maritime* persons."

"Dear Mrs. Robillard. I do hope you haven't been seeking us *particularly*."

"No, no. I happened to be passing . . ."

"Are you expecting a parcel? A shipment?"

"Oh my no." Louisa Robillard laughed. "Nehemiah does our *expecting*."

Solange smiled politely as the woman meandered to her conversational destination.

"I've often noticed you at the 10:30. My dear friend Antonia Sevier says we must have been introduced ages ago, but I tell Antonia, alas, we haven't."

Ruth dashed down the wharf where a favorite pilot had a sweet for her.

"Don't you think, after so long an 'almost' acquaintanceship, we can ignore formal introductions?"

Solange would have preferred formality, but that Dutch barkentine wouldn't have her verification, and last night she'd told Augustin money was so scarce, soldier or no soldier he must be ungenerous to his French friends. "Why of course, madame. I am happy to make your acquaintance."

"How kind you are." (Meaning: "Of course you are. Your husband is our employee.")

Solange countered, "Captain Fornier speaks so highly of Mr. Robillard. 'A gentleman of the old school.'"

When Ruth came back, her attention was devoted to a large chunk of molasses candy.

"Pierre is quite taken with you." Louisa's smile was *Not* Taken. "It's easy to see why."

"As you know so much better than I, Mr. Robillard is an amiable, honorable gentleman."

"No doubt."

Given this woman's watery eyes and horse jaw, Solange thought Robillard's wife had reason to be jealous.

"My husband says Captain Fornier served with Napoleon?"

"I do not believe, madame, that any but marshals serve *with* Napoleon. Captain Fornier served *under* the Emperor."

"In his European wars?"

"Augustin Fornier was commissioned for the desperate circumstances in Saint-Domingue and earned his captaincy by exceptional valor. His promotion to Major was assured when, alas, Saint-Domingue was betrayed by the French government."

"Dear, dear. Dear Pierre would have been so proud to have a *Major* clerking for him."

Solange calculated how many days they could survive without Augustin's salary. "Our plantation, Sucarie du Jardin, had the finest, deepest soil on the island. Captain Fornier served under General Leclerc."

"That poor gentleman. To die so far away from home."

"A very great officer . . ."

Mrs. Robillard disengaged. "What a beautiful child."

Ruth curtsied.

"You are how old?"

Another curtsy. "Reckon six, missus. Might be seven."

"Well, well. Well, well."

Mrs. Robillard crooked her neck, seeking a familiar face on the promenade so far above these sordid docks. Though she spotted none of her friends, she waved as if she had.

When she pivoted back to Solange, her jaw jutted like a prow. "You are nearly as attractive as my silly husband said you are."

In honor of Augustin's pittance, Solange restrained herself. "You are too kind."

"Delightful creature. Simply delightful. You won't steal from your masters, will you, Ruth?"

"Mais non, madame."

"Speak English, child. It is a crude tongue but must be yours."

On a glorious May day, floppy white magnolia blossoms drifted onto the cobblestones and Solange's ship came in. An unimpressive, not terribly seaworthy ketch, it had accepted mail in Bruges, been dismasted off Haulabout Point, nearly swamped and very nearly abandoned.

Solange's throat was so tight it hurt to swallow. What if it had gone down? What would have happened to them?

But with sufficient verification to satisfy even the punctilious Bank of the United States, Mrs. Fornier's account was opened, and her terse reply to Charles Escarlette went by return mail.

The Forniers moved to an unfashionable house in an unfashionable neighborhood, which Solange bought outright with cash.

Her father's next letter was more politic. The Banque de France had informed Charles Escarlette his daughter's dowry was now at the Bank of the United States. What a surprise! He hadn't known the United States had a bank!

Circumstances at Solange's home were the same. He had leased the factory but needed cash to hire workers. Tailors and seamstresses were available, and the army would issue a large order. He would start with pantaloons. There was profit in pantaloons.

A notarized transfer of credit from the United States Bank must be on the outgoing tide. In anticipation, he had provided the documents his daughter's banker would require. There was a place for Augustin to sign too. Though the husband's signature was, under Code Napoleon, unnecessary, who knew what primitive laws governed Americans?

Should she wish, she could deliver the document in person. Her sisters and dear Momma have missed her so!

As a sobbing Solange tore letter and document into strips,

Ruth sang an eerie, high-pitched lament and the Forniers became Americans.

News of the family's improved circumstances somehow escaped Mr. Haversham's discreet, tightly pressed lips, and the Forniers received invitations to unimportant christenings, garden parties, and the like.

As new-minted Americans, Captain and Mrs. Fornier must attend Savannah's obligatory Grand Fete, Washington's Birthday Ball. (*Tickets one dollar. No apprentices admitted.*)

At the cold collation, Mrs. Robillard wondered if Mrs. Fornier was acquainted with Antonia Sevier.

"Isn't she a great friend of yours?" Solange spoke familiarly to a woman with whom previously every word had had to be measured. She positioned a biscuit on her plate between the sweet pickles and the drumstick.

"You have practically nothing in common." Louisa's laugh was not quite a bray. "But *everyone* knows Antonia, and you must too."

"I would be honored to make her acquaintance." Solange selected three confections, ignoring a dented macaroon. She licked her forefinger. "Tell me, dear Mrs. Robillard. Are all American balls as stuffy as this one?"

"Only the patriotic ones. You must call me Louisa. Alas, American patriotism is invariably hoarse and swathed in bunting moths have got at." Louisa cocked her head. "I'm told your Saint-Domingue balls were . . . rather . . . risqué."

"Near the end, very."

"Ah." Louisa ignored the wild boar for a tiny slice of duck. "Antonia is terribly upset about her cook. Cook's shrimp and grits are all the talk. Quite well known among us. Why, Antonia has refused eight hundred for Cook. Eight hundred dollars for a cook." Louisa grimaced. "These times. These times."

"Since I've never dined at the Seviers', I cannot comment on her grits. Doubtless her grits merit the highest praise."

"Antonia intended to invite you and dear Captain Fornier to her garden party this year. Why is it, I'd like to know, forks and knives are invariably laid at the head of the collation rather than the foot, where one's full plate needs them." Louisa paused for emphasis. "Alas, dear Mrs. Fornier, neither you nor I will enjoy those grits this year, because Antonia has canceled her garden party! Cook will *not* go to the market! She absolutely refuses! Antonia has taken strong measures"—Mrs. Robillard popped her wrist as one pops a whip—"to no avail. These days her coachman does their marketing! Overripe fruit, underripe vegetables, and everything too dear. Might we share the love seat?"

"Certainly." Solange made room.

"You know how superstitious *they* are."

"Ummm."

"Cook has the mad notion that that maid of yours (Ruth is she?) is casting the, I don't know, the 'evil eye' on her. Cook says Ruth 'sees things'—whatever *that's* supposed to mean. She claims that child is a voudou priestess." Louisa's laughter clanged like a cracked bell. "All nonsense, to be sure. Nonetheless . . ."

"Why of course it's nonsense." Solange spoke more hotly than she ought. If Solange had been an innocent, Mrs. Robillard's triumphant smile would have been cued her dangerous nonsense was in the wings.

A voudou priestess.

The next morning after the 10:30, the charming Mrs. Fornier hand-delivered the latest newspapers from a just-docked Spaniard to L'Ancien Régime, where, in due course, she made a small request to a very grand gentleman.

Resisting flattery is very much easier when one is accustomed to it, and Pierre Robillard didn't get much flattery at home.

"Anything I can do, my dear," he promised, kissing Solange's hand.

"Anything," as it turned out, was unusual but not forbidden. Although no papist himself (as he later assured his furious wife), Pierre was a tolerant fellow, and surely there were many paths to salvation.

Hence, on a lovely April morning, eighteen months after she'd arrived in America, a solemn very black child, in a white dress adorned with Flemish lace, stood before St. John's altar to be christened Ruth.

The beaming Pierre Robillard would be the child's godfather.

The Orangerie

RUTH SANG SOFTLY:

"Orange tree,
Grow and grow and grow.
Orange tree, orange tree, grow and grow and grow,
Orange tree.
Stepmother is not real mother,
Orange tree . . ."

The Robillards' orangerie was scented as if by cinnamon or nutmeg, and fruit hung like shy pendants behind sharpish leaves. Absently humming, the child traced a green-gold globe with her fingertip. Dance music was faintly audible in the narrow brick-and-glass conservatory on the south façade of the spanking new mansion. Since Louisa Robillard's young British architect didn't understand Savannah customs, this quiet meditative room faced the servant yard, where washing, butchering, and laundering got done from daylight until dusk. At peace tonight, the orangerie's windows were black glass except for a carriage house lantern illuminating guests' varnished rigs and the tiny sparks of their coachmen's cigars.

Solange sat on a stone bench, fanning herself.

Although the Forniers' improved finances had got them a house and rehired Cook, Solange understood (and often reminded her husband) money did not grow on trees, not even American trees. Keeping a carriage and coachman were unnecessary expense, and the Forniers had come to the ball in a cab.

Solange was scoring the evening thus far: had she said what she ought and, more important, not said what she oughtn't? Solange Escarlette Fornier *would* rise in this baffling, too democratic New World.

The orchestra attempted a vigorous allegro, and Solange smiled at Ruth. "Child, we are as near Paradise as we shall ever be."

The child scratched her neck. "Yes, mistress, I reckon." She didn't meet Solange's eyes. "That Count Montelone, he bein' here?"

"I haven't seen him."

"Him and Master Augustin, they friends?"

"They are more French than Napoleon." Solange's chuckle tried to enlist the child, but Ruth studied an orange as if she'd never seen one before. "He want buy me?"

"Dear child, whatever gave you that notion?"

She shrugged. A moment later she said, "I ain't goin' noplace. I wants be with you."

"If you're going to be gloomy, you can assist the other servants. Go help Nehemiah."

"Nehemiah don't need me none."

"There must be somebody who does!" Solange went toward the music.

Since Philippe Robillard was a bachelor with a bachelor's ways, the Robillard cousins' Christmas ball was at Pierre and Louisa's home, and, pursuant to Louisa's dire threats, Philippe didn't invite his Indian friends. As recompense for his perennial breach of hospitality, Philippe stationed himself at the punch bowl until he was poured into his carriage. Having not yet attained that state, Philippe and his new friend Captain Fornier reviewed injustices to Muscogee Indians, Edisto Indians, and the virtuous French planters of Saint-Domingue. Injustices were considered in detail, deplored, and toasted into oblivion.

The last of the new mansion's workmen had departed four days ago, ejected by anxious servants brandishing brooms, mops, and dusters. Pierre, Louisa, and their daughter, Clara, had spent only two nights in their new home.

Louisa was fiercely proud of it, while Pierre wondered (silently) if daring young English architects were as daring where young English architects weren't rare.

In Savannah's traditional homes (Savannah Boxes), adjacent drawing and withdrawing rooms could be opened into a continuous space for dancing. In the Robillard house, those rooms were separated by a central hall and staircase, where the musicians could be heard but not seen. As a consequence, the guests had self-segregated. Dancers, teetotalers, and old folks claimed the formal drawing room, while the young, those with weaker social credentials, and the hard drinkers congregated in the withdrawing room, whose pink valances and painted cupids were meant to please gentlewomen drinking afternoon tea. Despite her architect's strongest objections, in honor of the season, Louisa outlined the bow window with holly and hung mistletoe in the valances. This violation had so offended the young Englishman that he and his patron had quarreled and he'd stomped out, shouting, "It is no longer my work. I am not responsible!"

Louisa had presumed the Englishman's presence would ornament his creation, and that as his patron, his cachet would adhere to her. Consequently and uncharacteristically, Louisa swiftly backtracked; servants removed the offending greenery and Nehemiah was dispatched after the Englishman.

Alas, Nehemiah returned without his quarry. "He ain't want come, missus. Man be drunk and sayin' things."

"Things?"

"He sayin' you and Master Robillard, you am 'Philistines.'" Nehemiah puzzled, "Philistines like them in the Bible?"

Absent her Brilliant! Unconventional! Imaginative! architect, Louisa had the holiday greenery reinstalled and told her friends she'd let the puppy go.

The gala was as gala without him. Candles sparkling in sconces and chandeliers were amplified by wall and pier mirrors, and their flames danced the crystal rim of the punch bowl. The punch had begun the evening mild enough for a Baptist, but after many Merry Gentlemen had emptied their flasks into it, it had become heretical.

The O'Hara brothers' draying business had prospered, and they'd purchased a mercantile specializing in low-priced harness, shoddy equipage, last year's hay and dirty oats. "'Tis a profitable wee place," James O'Hara told any who'd listen.

Earlier, O'Hara had reminded Captain Fornier they'd arrived on the same boat, implying they'd had equal opportunities in the New World and now look at them. O'Hara had his thumbs in his galluses.

Augustin answered him in French.

Grinning, in Gaelic, O'Hara cursed the captain for a fool.

When the newfangled cotillion dance was announced, O'Hara and others abandoned the punch bowl for their partners.

"A French dance." Augustin refilled his cup.

Philippe said, "Unlike Americans, we French always treated the Indians fairly."

"We planters were always kind to our Negroes! How dearly French pay for misguided idealism."

Whatever this sentiment meant, Philippe and Augustin clicked glasses in its honor.

The musicians wore their masters' best cast-off finery. They grinned prodigiously, and the small woolen cap set beside them could accept any small coins white folks might bestow.

Nehemiah exited the withdrawing room, tray piled precariously with dirty glasses. To Ruth, he said, "There's more, child. Fetch many as you can without breakin' none."

Ruth folded her arms. "I ain't no servant."

"Child, you got too little to know how little you got."

In the larger drawing room, cotillion squares had formed, and the more courageous Savannahians—with laughter and apologies—executed unfamiliar steps.

Pierre Robillard introduced a younger man. "Ah, Mrs. Fornier. This is my friend Wesley Evans, who, as you might guess from his too sober attire, is a Yankee, come to us from Connecticut. Wesley was Mr. Eli Whitney's indispensable factotum. Wesley and I are to be partners—factors—in the cotton trade, an undertaking he understands better than I. Still, I shall try to understand. I shall give it my very best. I worry that my new venture will add burdens to Captain Fornier's shoulders. Where is the good fellow? He's not dancing?"

"He and your clever cousin Philippe are solving the Indian Problem."

Pierre's smile broadened. "Like a squeaking axle, that work needs lubrication."

Louisa materialized beside her husband. "Ah, the delightful Mrs. Fornier and her so lovely maid. Count Montelone has mentioned her."

That gentleman was across the room, obscured by dancers leaving the floor. "So good of you to join us tonight, Mrs. Fornier. Christmas is such a special time, don't you think? My dear

Pierre"—she took his arm firmly—"was afraid our new home wouldn't be ready, but we toiled day and night."

"Nehemiah . . ." Pierre began.

His wife patted his mouth. "Not another word about your Negro, dear. You do spoil him. I've requested the next dance be a minuet. Unlike some architects who shall remain nameless, Pierre and I cherish the 'tried and true.'"

Their host fluttered fingers over his shoulder as his wife towed him off.

The Yankee grinned at Solange. "Madame Robillard is sérieuse."

"Madame is dangereuse." Solange was surprised to mean what she said.

"Shall we quiver in fear? Must we raise fortifications?"

Solange offered her arm. "Actually, Mr. Yankee, I'd rather dance."

Evans was rangy, prematurely bald, and, as Solange soon learned, twenty-eight years old. He'd come to the Low Country with Whitney, whose cotton gin was making short-staple cotton profitable, seeking an exclusive manufacturing license.

"Unfortunately Cyrus's invention," the Yankee confided, "is clever but too simple. No halfway decent mechanic can see one operate without understanding how to replicate it. Building a gin requires no special tools, and there are no expensive 'special' mechanisms. I'm afraid my friend's cotton gin will make other men much richer than its inventor."

"You'd like to be one of those rich men?"

"Madame, I already am. Do you know these steps?"

"Sir, I am French. Or *was* French. I haven't decided what I am now."

"It is easy to be an American. Easiest thing there is."

"Yes, but . . ." She grimaced. She said, "Mrs. Sevier is energetic tonight."

In James O'Hara's arms, that lady's "dancing" might be described as "being flung about."

"I suspect Mr. O'Hara is more familiar with reels."

Solange and Wesley executed the steps to their entire satisfaction. When the music stopped, Wesley bowed and asked, "May I fetch you some punch?"

"Sir, you are sufficient intoxication. I fear for my virtue."

When he grinned, his face lit up. "I cannot promise I won't try it."

"Sir! I am a married woman."

He led her off the floor. "I am bitterly disappointed. Now, who is this beautiful child?"

"Ruth, show Master Evans your manners."

Her curtsy was perfunctory. "Mistress, that nasty Count eye-ballin' me."

"What's the harm?"

"He one of them slave speculators!"

Wesley frowned. "There are . . . unpleasant . . . rumors about Count Montelone, Mrs. Fornier. He is unwelcome in Charleston society."

"Ruth, you are perfectly safe. Fetch your master. He and Mr. Evans should become acquainted."

"Bring us a punch, while you're at it. Mrs. Fornier—may I call you Solange?"

Solange was accustomed to slower-paced men. Although she felt her horse had the bit in its teeth, she was more exhilarated than alarmed. "All these people . . ." she said. "Isn't it warm in here?"

"I'm sure we could find somewhere . . . ah . . . *cooler*."

Solange took the reins. "This is an 'unusual' house. I'm told they've done away with necessaries."

Wesley cleared his throat. "The principle has been known for centuries. Water descends from the attic through water closets and thence to the basement. The Romans knew how to do it."

"The Romans were so . . . so advanced, don't you think?"

"The Romans, yes . . ."

Biting her lower lip in concentration, Ruth balanced two brimming punch cups. "Master says he ain't comin', missus. Say he learnin' 'bout them 'noble savages.'"

"Thank you, Ruth. You may go."

Frown. "Where I go, missus?"

"Elsewhere. Mr. Evans, have you seen the orangerie?"

Worriedly, Ruth watched them depart. "Where's I got to go?" she whispered.

In the peaceful orangerie, the industrious musicians seemed a world away. "I blush confessing I'd looked forward to this evening. Mr. Evans, if Connecticut society is as tedious as Savannah's . . ."

"Worse, I believe. Very much worse. We Yankees aren't entirely sure we should be amused by our amusements." The orange he plucked may have been the fruit Ruth had been examining.

"My husband says Count Montelone is 'A True Frenchman' but failed to mention the Count's line of work. It must be profitable. Can't you buy an eight-hundred-dollar field hand in Africa for fifty?"

"Madame is a businesswoman?" Wesley flipped peels into the tub housing the tree.

"I am a lady, sir." She refused a proffered segment. "The Robillards had these trees brought from Florida."

"I don't object to any lawful trade, and under our Constitution slaving will be legal until 1808. The slave trade makes a few men rich but bankrupts more. First you buy the ship and then you must employ an experienced captain—a man with strong New England connections, that's where he'll purchase his trade goods, and even stronger connections in West Africa, where he swaps those goods for surly, unruly, unhealthy, rebellious creatures who'd as soon slit his throat as come to America. To profit, the captain must pack his cargo between decks as tightly as ever he can, which inevitably foments disease. A twenty to thirty percent loss is expected. The captain must evade pirates off the coast and the British navy in deep water. As you know, the Atlantic is no millpond, and slave ships are no more immune to storms than ships carrying missionaries the other direction."

"Slavery, sir, is necessary for sugarcane production. Rice and cotton too."

He shrugged. "That may be. I shouldn't wish to be a slave, and I venture you wouldn't either."

"Ruth is happy to be my servant."

"Ah."

"She is a curious child, and sometimes she seems . . . mysterious?"

He grinned. "She certainly doesn't want to get close to the Count."

The segment of orange Solange accepted was hot and very, very sweet.

"Excuse my forwardness." With his handkerchief, he dabbed juice from her chin.

Louisa and Pierre had quarreled. Oblivious Pierre had sparked their disagreement by informing her (as if Louisa hadn't noted the snickers at her home's "innovations"), that Mr. Haversham had asked if they'd disposed of their chamber pots, whereupon Louisa, who felt like bursting into tears, elected to assault Mr. Haversham for his well-known faults, not least his assistance to Mrs. Fornier, whose husband had no more been a planter than Louisa! and who had an "unusual" (sharp nod for emphasis) relationship with that very black child whom Pierre (yes, Louisa's beloved husband) had, in a moment of weakness and without considering his wife, accepted as his godchild before the altar of St. John the Baptist Catholic Church, despite Pierre's (and Louisa's) staunch Methodism, and where, had Pierre looked for his friends in St. John's sanctuary on that particular occasion, he would not have seen that same Mr. Haversham, who was so very, very *curious* about the Robillards' chamber pots!

While his wife caught her breath, Pierre Robillard asked his daughter, Clara, to dance, which restored Pierre's customary good humor.

Unfortunately his beaming face made his angry wife angrier. "Chamber pots! Godchild! Indeed!"

––––

Ruth slipped into the orangerie. "We go home pretty soon now, yes?"

"All in good time, dear. Please fetch us another punch."

Very reluctantly she collected their glasses.

"Go, child! You may go!"

When they were alone, Wesley Evans resumed. "Business is about putting capital to work where it may earn the most with the least risk. Ah, but I forget. As a lady you are unfitted by your finer nature for sordid commerce."

"I am a lady, sir. Not a fool."

"So." He shifted nearer. "As you may know, capital for business expansion is hard to find. Pierre is a fine fellow, but, as a partner, he lacks—how can I be delicate—passion. You may think that's an odd term for a businessman."

"My funds are with Mr. Haversham in six percent bonds."

"Commendable, I'm sure." After a pause, Wesley added, "You could do better."

––––

Louisa's friend Antonia Sevier had never been able to deny Louisa *anything,* and the delightful James O'Hara's homely wife had been shooting daggers at her all evening, and, who knows, the wife was Irish and those daggers might become real! so Antonia let her friend show off her new home's innovations. And Antonia certainly had to admit Louisa's water closet was *interesting*! What was this new century coming to? "You sit on it?"

"First, dear, you lift the lid." Her friend raised its hinged cover upright.

Antonia eyed the seat with its neat circular hole. "You sit on *that*?"

"It is a seat of ease. Like the necessary. Exactly the same."

"Then . . . ?"

"Then, my dear, nature takes its course. As you see, carded wool tufts are available for . . . uh . . ."

"Then . . ."

"Drop the used tuft into the device, then . . ."

Louisa yanked a chain descending from a varnished wooden bin overhead, and a thunderous rush of water swirled through the device.

"But where does *it* go?"

"We've a tank in the basement."

Mrs. Sevier put her hand to her mouth, "Louisa, you are so . . . unconventional."

Perhaps not the happiest choice of words. Tears welled up in Louisa's eyes. "That . . . that ungrateful Englishman. We gave him his first American commission. Our home was to be his showcase. Simple courtesy . . . Ordinary decency . . . You'd think he could have made a brief appearance tonight!"

"I think this, uh . . . *thing* is perfectly wonderful. Louisa, how I envy you. How I wish I had your courage!"

"Yes. Well. Do you wish to try it?"

Antonia giggled into her fan. "Would I were you, dear Louisa;

alas, I am merely Antonia. Surely you've tucked away a few commodes for your timid friends."

Louisa sighed. "In the small room behind the library."

The ladies exited, passing into the withdrawing room, which was so thick with cigar smoke Louisa's eyes watered. Gape-mouthed gentlemen sprawled on love seats, snoring. Doubtless, some would be here in the morning.

A long case clock struck the one o'clock hour. Antonia stifled her yawn.

Captain Fornier and Cousin Philippe hovered over the punch bowl as if it might get away. The punch had started the evening as Louisa's mother's recipe: pinkish and redolent of citrus. Now, it was shallow, dark brown, and reeked of raw spirits.

The orchestra was so . . . vigorous! Louisa heard a man's shout. Oh dear! Had the Irish asked them for jigs?

"The Robillards' Christmas ball," Louisa Robillard reminded her friend, "sets Savannah's—nay, *Georgia's*—standards!"

"Why of course it does, dear." Antonia sighed. "We are all so *grateful*."

Captain Fornier instructed the drooping Philippe about "the good earth. La Bonne Terre." The Captain crumbled invisible soil between his fingers.

Older ladies fetched their husbands and thanked Louisa.

That very black maid—Pierre's Godchild!—sat cross-legged in the window seat, half-concealed by the drapes.

Her window seat! Pierre's Godchild!

Louisa sniffed the air, and, although she would have been shocked by the comparison, she sniffed as a wolf for prey.

"Poor man," Louisa said, apparently thinking to herself. "If he only knew."

It was late, and Antonia was getting one of her headaches. "Which 'poor man,' dear? Philippe?"

"Don't be a goose. Of course not Philippe."

They passed into the hall, where the musicians offered weary enthusiasm. "Oh, to be young again," Louisa said.

"Who? Which 'poor man'?"

"Um."

"Mrs. Fornier's little maid is *so* attractive."

"Um."

"It's easy to see why dear Pierre agreed . . ." She clapped her hand over her mouth. "Dear Louisa, you were in accord with him, were you not?"

This *godchild*, that British architect, absurd water closets—all, all of it: Pierre's fault. "Poor Captain Fornier."

"What? Captain Fornier?"

Louisa's sad, philosophical headshake deplored the mischances of so many modern marriages.

"My husband's partner is a Yankee. How can he be expected to know *our* ways? Savannah ways—so tried and true."

Antonia was startled but too delighted to repress her smile. "Oh dear! Surely, you can't mean . . ."

"For the life of me, I can't think where they've got off. Perhaps they're in the library. Perhaps they are great readers. Dear Antonia, do promise you won't say a word."

Antonia's spine was stiff as sugar sculpture. "Louisa! Aren't I the soul of discretion?"

Louisa patted her friend's arm. "Of course you are, dear. Of course you are. Poor Captain Fornier. Exiled from his fabulous plantation—the Forniers had money to burn!—and now this! That innocent child in the window seat. Has she seen"—Louisa lowered her voice—"more than any child should?"

Her friend giggled. "A child is not the best chaperone!"

Louisa Robillard felt a pang of regret when Antonia began circulating through the other wives, but the pang was bearable.

———

Augustin felt eyes on him. He half-overheard remarks.

It couldn't have been the drink. Soldiers—Napoleon's officers—were expected to drink! Abjuring the ladle, he dipped his cup directly into the brown punch and offered it to his great new friend, Philippe. Philippe's eyes may have seen it or may not. He sat suddenly and heavily with open mouth and head back. Nehemiah sent for Philippe's coachman.

Now that damn child was plucking at his sleeve. "Master, I fetch Mistress and we go home."

"The hell with her," Augustin heard himself say.

"Master, we go home now."

"Who's master here?" he asked the unconscious Philippe. "Who's master here?"

———

Though Clara was old enough to put herself to bed, her parents were upstairs with her.

Taking her husband's hand, Louisa said, "How we will miss these tender moments, when our baby is grown."

Pierre squeezed her hand, relieved their quarrel was ended. But, when trouble erupted in their orangerie, the hosts could do nothing to stop it.

Do You Blaze?

I hold Wesley Evans to be a COWARD and POLTROON.

CAPTAIN AUGUSTIN FORNIER's challenge appeared in the January 2 issue of the *Columbian Museum & Savannah Advertiser*. Fornier's second, Count Montelone, posted the challenge at the Vendue House among advertisements for slave sales, races, and stallions at stud. When the Count returned to Gunn's Tavern, its habitués clamored for details—had the Yankee's friends been there to receive the insult?—to which the Count responded with his customary asperity that affairs of honor are not vulgar entertainments.

Gunn's Tavern was such a favorite with French refugees, Savannahians had nicknamed it Frère Jacques, and the Georgia-born and bred William Gunn had become reconciled to his establishment's "Frenchy" ways. Most of Frère Jacques's habitués were, like Captain Fornier, Saint-Domingue refugees, a few were émigrés, and Count Montelone, it was thought on vague evidence, had come to these shores with General Lafayette. The Count sustained himself selling horses of unknown provenance and young high yellows. He took elaborate precautions against poisoning and avoided some neighborhoods after dark. He never set foot on the docks.

Although the Count never mentioned General Lafayette, French patriots liked to ask him, "Who is the greater general? Napoleon or Lafayette?"

"Le Bon Dieu, only He knows."

The Count's reticence was clear proof of perspicacity. A few detractors mentioned the Charleston scandals, but nobody knew much about them, and, in any case, the affair had been thoroughly hushed up.

In William Gunn's tavern every French victory was vigorously celebrated. In this savage, inhospitable, and *un-French* America, these victories sustained the refugees' pride, and it was an article of faith that were it not for the damnable British blockade, every Frère Jacques habitué would return to France to enlist.

Napoleon's victories were also popular with native-born Savannahians whose commerce was disrupted by the blockade and the British habit of impressing American seamen.

A few days before Christmas, news of a great battle trickled into Savannah, initially as rumors, then as disconnected facts, and finally in flood. The earliest reports said the Prussians had defeated the French and many gloomy glasses were drained on that account. The subsequent report—not twenty-four hours later!—refilled those glasses toasting Napoleon's victory. News of the second battle—and Napoleon's second triumph—didn't reach Savannah until the new year, when Frère Jacques was already engrossed in its own scandal. Captain Fornier (a bon homme if ever there was one) had discovered his wife (a French lady of previous spotless reputation) compromised by one Wesley Evans, a Yankee newcomer. The captain had surprised the couple in Pierre Robillard's new orangerie at that gentleman's Christmas ball, a venue and occasion which sauced the scandal. Although Pierre Robillard had never set foot in Frère Jacques, he was honored there. When the Robillards dined with Georgia's Governor Milledge, Savannah's French community preened in the afterglow.

As thoroughly as they approved of Pierre, his impressive new home, and, for that matter, his orangerie, Frère Jacques's patrons disapproved of Cousin Philippe, whose advocacy for heathenish savages made other Frenchmen seem careless and sentimental.

Augustin himself remembered remarkably little of that night—just distorted and disconnected images. Solange and the Yankee had been sitting too close, he remembered that. He *thought* they were fully clothed. They were all three shouting, he remembered. He remembered Ruth hiding her face in her hands. He was struck a stinging blow on his cheek: he recalled the blow perfectly. That blow, the actual laying on of hands, had elevated what might have been a drunken shouting match into an affair of honor.

The morning after the Christmas ball, Augustin didn't get out of bed until noon, whereupon he vomited, washed his face, and ventured forth to Frère Jacques, where much misinformation greeted him. Augustin, who didn't know what to think or for that matter exactly what had occurred, shrugged. "Evans did me no harm. He is a Yankee and does not understand our ways."

Frère Jacques was divided between those who thought Augustin's indifference to insult was "très gentil" and those who imagined the blow that had reddened Augustin's cheek had struck all Frenchmen.

Sympathizers and offended alike bought Augustin drinks, and he came home late and tipsy, then went to the sideboard and poured himself a glass despite Ruth's sad expression. "You, too? Even you?" he asked.

"Master," the child said solemnly. Ruth plucked a small volume from Solange's books. "Please read to me."

In a high-pitched, slurred voice Augustin declaimed,

Strange fits of passion have I known:
*   And I will dare to tell,*
*   But in the Lover's ear alone,*
*   What once to me befell.*
When she I loved looked every day
*   Fresh as a rose in June,*
*   I to her cottage bent my way,*
*   Beneath an evening-moon.*

He closed it. "I'm in no humor for poetry." He burped a hot fluid which stung his nostrils and washed his throat with whiskey.

"Mistress don't read to me no more neither," the child said sadly.

"Well, read for yourself" hovered on the tip of his tongue. Why couldn't the child read? She wasn't as stupid as other niggers.

When Solange came into the room, her eyes lit on the glass, so Augustin emptied it. "Oh," his wife said. "You're home."

He drew himself up. "Apparently."

"Was your evening agreeable?"

Augustin tried to think of what might interest her. "The French government is demanding reparations from the Haitians."

Solange sighed.

"We will be recompensed for Le Jardin."

"Indeed?"

They hadn't discussed the orangerie, Augustin because he couldn't remember and Solange because she had been indiscreet and refused to feel guilty about it.

Ruth said, "Mistress, please read to me?"

"Not now."

"Market girl—that girl sellin' them oranges—she say Count Montelone partial to 'em. Say Count askin' 'bout me. 'Bout me, mistress."

"Go to bed, child."

"I so happy, livin' here, livin' with you and the captain. I one lucky pickaninny, yes I is!"

"Augustin," Solange asked sweetly, "can you learn *our* share of those magical reparations? Officially, I mean? Apart from thoughtfully discussing them with your drinking companions?"

"How?"

"Ah yes. That *is* the question."

Augustin poured another glass, which he offered to his wife, earning a look of icy contempt.

Ruth said, "I tries make you happy! You only family I gots."

A tremor began at Augustin's knees and climbed his frame. He shook so he could hardly get words out. "I am a la . . . la . . . laughingstock. A contemptible cu . . . cu . . . cuckold."

"Mistress! Mistress!" Ruth cried. "I opens the window. It so, so hot in here!"

"Of course I welcomed Wesley Evans's attentions," Augustin Fornier's wife said coolly. "At least he is a man."

Next forenoon, Wesley Evans was grading cotton at the Robillard and Evans warehouse when his partner appeared, dressed as solemnly as his expression. Pierre laid a mahogany box on Wesley's desk.

Wesley was telling an Up-country planter why his cotton graded poorly. "If you think you can do better," Wesley said, "there are other factors."

"Already tried t'others," the planter replied. "I'ze jest hopin' you mightn't have your eye on the sparrow today." He removed his hat to vigorously scratch his scalp. "I plumb forgot you was a Yankee."

Puzzled. "So?"

"You Yankees never take your eye off the sparrow for ten seconds. Reckon I'll take your offer."

Wesley counted out money while the planter's Negroes unloaded his crop.

When the man's wagon rattled off, Wesley turned to Pierre. "Now, what the hell was that about?"

"*That* is precisely why I have come." From his coat, Pierre extracted a folded copy of the *Advertiser*.

"I haven't time for news," Wesley said. "All the late-harvest planters are coming in. They *will* leave their cotton too long in the field and they still expect top dollar."

Robillard pushed the paper at him, tapping the advertisement.

"What the hell?"

"I cannot second you."

"Second me? For what? Because I took Mrs. Solange's hand—and was roundly cursed by her drunk husband until I slapped him sober? It was nothing. A bagatelle. Come now, Pierre. I am too busy for absurdity."

"Apparently the gallant captain is not."

Did Wesley hear a hint of satisfaction in his partner's voice? "A duel? He expects me to fight a duel? We don't fight duels anymore."

"Ah, then we unenlightened Georgians are mistaken that not long ago just outside New York City, in the very heart of Yankeedom, Vice President Aaron Burr killed Alexander Hamilton in a *duel*."

"We don't duel. It's no longer our custom." Wesley set his hat brim at a busy cotton factor's businesslike angle.

"Well, my friend. It is *our* custom. The gentleman who ignores a public challenge is . . . is . . . he is no longer a gentleman."

Wesley smiled. "Did I ever pretend I was?"

His partner looked at him sorrowfully. "However you disprize Low Country customs, my dear Wesley, we will suffer for this. Our partnership will find fewer planters willing to do business with us. Why sell your crop to a poltroon when one can as easily sell to a gentleman?"

"Jesus Christ. Je-sus!" Wesley hurled his hat to the unswept warehouse floor.

Satisfied his partner had got his point, Pierre Robillard continued. "It is our way, Wesley. You Yankees make things marvelously well. In a thousand years, we Georgians wouldn't have invented the cotton gin. We Georgians are reckless, courteous to a fault, hospitable, and, for the most part, pacific. But when my beloved daughter Clara's young gentleman calls on me, I shall make it a point to ask him: 'Do you blaze?'"

Wesley laid a hand on his partner's shoulder. "Monsieur Robillard, you amaze me. You are indeed a man of parts."

"No, sir. I was a simple soldier under the great Napoleon, and now I am a simple merchant."

The mahogany box contained a brace of plain, unengraved pistols. Pierre's finger streaked a lightly oiled barrel. "They've killed five men."

"Oh."

"Manon, their maker, has been accused of rifling his bores—imperceptible to the sharpest eye but rifling nonetheless. These pistols are from Manon's London workshop. They have hair triggers, the faintest touch sets them off. I beseech you, do not cock until you mean to fire." Pierre concluded, "I cannot second you, not against Captain Fornier. Count Montelone acts for Fornier."

Wesley groaned aloud.

"Your second must be a gentleman of equal rank."

"I am a stranger in Savannah, barely acquainted here."

"To be sure. Our seconds are the linchpins of the affair. Your man and the Count will make all arrangements, and on the day they'll manage the . . . affair. If, on that day, you are indisposed, the second may fight in your place. If you 'show the white feather,' he is empowered to cut you down on the spot." Pierre smiled. "The rules are established." He coughed. "Wesley, I have taken the liberty—"

"You've asked someone to act for me."

"Yes, dear boy. My cousin Philippe may have eccentric ways, but he is undeniably a gentleman. None will quarrel with your choice.

My cousin has never before served in that honorable capacity, but I shall school him, trust me I will. Although I cannot stand for you against Captain Fornier, I will guide Philippe."

"Philippe of the red Indians?"

Pierre flushed. "He is a student of our red brothers, to be sure."

"Jesus Christ." Wesley retrieved his hat, beat it against his leg, and hurled it down a second time.

———

Augustin enjoyed the happiness of a sailor at home after months at sea. He was neither here nor there, and, for once in his life, things seemed to be as they should be. After he issued his challenge, a great grave silence enveloped him, which only poignant or loving remarks could penetrate.

Ruth treated him as if he were gossamer, following him from room to room as if, unwatched, he might disappear. When he and Solange made love (as was only natural, only right), he could feel Ruth's eyes boring through their closed bedroom door.

The aggrieved husband didn't remember the scene in the orangerie or how compromised his wife and the Yankee had been. That didn't matter now—if it ever had.

For her part, Solange never troubled to explain, but, curiously, she seemed to love her husband, perhaps for the first time. Augustin couldn't spit in the face of his luck.

———

On the appointed morning, he awoke beside his wife to the crunch of wheels and jing-a-jing of carriage harness outside their home. A horse snorted. His wife's body was warm as new life. He started to stroke her but stayed his hand. He'd shaved last night before he came to bed. His cheek, the famously struck cheek, felt no different than the other one.

Moving quietly, he drew on his best shirt, the same ruffled linen he'd worn to the Christmas ball. The wine stains had been banished and starch applied.

Augustin wondered what remained after we were gone. He pictured waves thrown outward by a stone flung into a pond, diminishing, intermingling, lapping at the shoreline, tending to stillness.

"Je vous salut, Marie, pleine de grâces . . . Hail Mary . . ." Would he ever learn to pray in English? He'd survived Saint-Domingue when so many had not. Perhaps Le Bon Dieu had a purpose for Augustin Fornier? Augustin shrugged. Bon Dieu.

From her quickened breathing, he knew Solange was awake, but he let her pretend. His loneliness was delicious, and what more had they to say? Her love warmed him. He hadn't dared hope for so much . . . He drew on the boots Ruth had begged to polish last night and the same frock coat he wore to L'Ancien Régime. Before the pier glass, he tied his triangular cravat in a fat, flamboyant bow.

Ruth waited on the stoop. Her steady brown eyes sent shivers down his spine. He rested his hand on her head, feeling the warmth of her skull through her hair. "I shan't be long."

Unblinking gaze. "I will pray to you."

Stepping into the mist rising from the damp sand street, Augustin pondered—pray *to*?—but Count Montelone urged him to the carriage.

"You'll catch your death," Augustin advised. The Count tucked his hands into his sleeves.

They proceeded west out of the city to the Jewish Cemetery, which duelists preferred for its high dark walls, isolation, and their belief that Jews who might object oughtn't.

Not long after they arrived, as their coachman dismounted to open the door, a second coach drew up alongside. Its varnished doors bore a garish blue and green escutcheon, and its roof was outlined by serpentine undulations in the same colors. White feathers sprouting from the roof were less ghastly than the black feathers of a hearse.

"Philippe's Indian motifs," Count Montelone supposed.

Augustin's hands were so cold, he clamped them between his thighs.

Three gentlemen emerged from the Indian coach. The flash of Philippe Robillard's lucifer match set spots swimming in Augustin's eyes.

"Pardon." The Count left to confer with his counterpart. The doctor was as reserved and unapproachable as his black bag. Augustin smiled at Wesley, who shook his head ruefully.

Augustin's hands were ice. How could he pull a trigger?

Augustin went into the cemetery, where grave mounds clustered against the south wall. Apparently the Hebrews didn't believe in headstones.

As the challenged party, Evans and his second had chosen weapons and venue. Now, the Count asked Augustin what distance he preferred.

"I hadn't thought . . ."

"Are you a good shot?"

"I don't think so."

"Fifteen paces then. You may miss, but so may he. Philippe assures me Evans is no marksman."

"Le Bon Dieu."

"You will each fire once, after which, if one of you cannot continue, honor is satisfied. After blood is shed an apology may be offered."

"By Evans."

"Certainly by Evans. His blow gave offense."

As the seconds chose their principals' pistols, the rising sun limned the black lip of the cemetery wall with gold. How beautiful it was!

Montelone: "Do not cock until you are ready to fire. Cock as you raise the pistol, aim for his middle, and touch the trigger."

"Oh. So easily it is done."

The pistol was a lead lump in Augustin's hand.

At Philippe's cracked-voice instruction, the two men stood back to back, almost touching. Augustin could feel Evans's body heat. The butts of their pistols almost touched, which puzzled Augustin until he realized his adversary was left-handed. For some reason this detail made him want to weep.

One, two, three . . . paces counted as if each were an important personage. Augustin marched toward the gray-brown heap of a newly filled grave. Blackened flowers curled atop the dirt.

"Turn. Gentlemen, turn and fire!"

As he turned, Augustin smiled. What fools men are! What fools! He raised his pistol because Evans was raising his. Evans seemed smaller than Augustin remembered. Augustin's pistol lifted toward the horizontal but wasn't level when Evans's pistol produced a puff of white smoke but no explosion. The Count cried, "Misfires are the same as shots fired! Captain Fornier, you may fire!"

Still smiling at this absurdity, Augustin pointed his muzzle to the heavens. The trigger was so light it seemed to discharge by itself. The explosion was louder than he expected, and the pistol jerked at the web of his hand.

While the seconds conferred, Augustin eyed his enemy through a haze of benevolence. Good fellow! Brave fellow! The seconds approached Augustin. The Count asked, "Evans did strike you, did he not?"

Puzzled, Augustin replied, "He was holding my wife's hand."

"That is no matter. He struck you?" The Count's thin lips were noticeably blue. "Then we continue. You must meet again unless Mr. Evans consents to be caned."

"What?" Augustin frowned so hard it hurt.

The Count explained as if to a child. "Under the Code Duello no gentleman can strike another. That physical blow is, Captain Fornier—that blow is the unforgivable insult."

Philippe's face was shiny with sweat. "Mr. Evans deeply regrets his actions in the orangerie but cannot consent to be caned."

Cane him? Why should Augustin cane him? He had nothing against this fellow. He shook his head no, but the Count was adamant. "Captain, as you are a gentleman, you must blaze." He shrugged. "It need not be fatal. Blood invariably satisfies honor."

As the seconds reloaded pistols, Augustin inspected the fresh Jewish grave, wondering what the moldering flowers had been.

Philippe reloaded wearing a granite grim expression, exaggerating his smallest hand movements. He wouldn't err again. Augustin couldn't help smiling. Everybody smiled at Philippe. Philippe never noticed, and the smilers never meant offense.

Augustin sat on the grave's border stones while Evans leaned against a wall stuffing his pipe. A cigar! A cigar would taste wonderful, but Augustin's hands were shaking too much to light one.

Augustin's mind escaped to the everyday. He must ask Nehemiah to change the shop window display. He needed new socks. After this morning he would buy everyone in Frère Jacques a drink. Solange wouldn't dare object! This once, mightn't she join him?

After the seconds primed the pistols, they gravely shook hands. Evans tapped his pipe out in a shower of sparks.

We are as sparks.

The principals were told to stand where they had fired before, pistols at their sides. On command they would simultaneously raise their pistols, aim down the long sightless barrels, and fire.

"Evans might not fire." Augustin's pistol rose up to arm's length. He felt small and dirty and tired.

Deportment

THE SAME WEEK he fatally shot Captain Augustin Fornier, Wesley Evans had paid nineteen cents per pound for middling cotton. Two years later, on Wesley and the Widow Fornier's marriage day, high middling brought only ten cents. Savannahians blamed the poor prices and attendant hard times on President Jefferson, who had embargoed all American goods, even cotton, to France and England. Although both warring nations had violated American neutrality, Britain, who'd impressed thousands of American seamen, was the worse offender, and British merchant ships took the trade Americans had lost. There was smuggling and New England mills took up some slack, but Savannah cotton factors were in trouble.

Solange hadn't ever imagined Augustin might be killed: that outcome had never crossed her mind. Foolish men—like Augustin—were humiliated in affairs of honor or they apologized or at worst they received a slight, gallant wound. Men postured; that's what men do! In her secret heart Solange may have imagined brave men fighting over her was romantic, like the exquisitely sensitive novels she no longer bothered to read.

That dreadful morning, Philippe's coach brought Augustin

home. Ruth rushed to it, shrieking. Solange commanded her to stop screaming, please stop, please stop, but she didn't.

Philippe offered awkward condolences. Count Montelone assured the widow that the affair had gone off properly and honor been satisfied. "There will be no untoward questions, madame. You may rest assured." Ruth disappeared down the street, heels flying. Solange's mouth was dry and her throat hurt.

Pierre Robillard managed everything, or Nehemiah did. Solange went where they told her and sat between them in St. John the Baptist's front pew. Ruth didn't come home. Regrettably, Louisa and Clara were indisposed and couldn't attend. Apparently much of Savannah society was similarly indisposed. Frère Jacques habitués attended and the O'Haras made an appearance, but nobody followed the hearse from the church to the grave.

The third, or perhaps it was the fourth, morning afterward Count Montelone called with effusive respects.

"You knew my husband well?"

He informed her Captain Fornier had been a gallant gentleman of "the old school." Delicate as a cat unwinding a skein of yarn, Montelone said that, of course, he didn't wish to intrude but under the circumstances (her husband had been a clerk at L'Ancien Régime, had he not?) the Count wished to offer tangible assistance to the Widow Fornier. He did a little buying and selling. Mrs. Fornier's handmaid. How was she called?

Solange couldn't say Ruth's name. Naming her would declare so much more than she wished to. She shook her head. "No, monsieur. She isn't here at present."

When Montelone smiled, Solange wished she hadn't said anything. Had she run away? Might he make inquiries? He knew reliable slave hunters. Unscrupulous hunters sometimes caught and sold runaways without notifying the runaways' owners. Ladies couldn't fathom the mendacity of some men . . .

Solange found strength to say, "She is no runaway. I will not have you make inquiries on my behalf."

"Why of course not, madame. Wouldn't presume . . ."

And so on and so on, but once she had him out of the house she went to Nehemiah.

Ruth had been seen at the market, but nobody seemed to know where she slept at night. Yes, he'd make inquiries. Yes, he'd be discreet. That Count, yes, that one.

The next morning, or perhaps the morning after, Wesley's servant delivered this letter:

Dear Solange,

Please accept my sincere regrets. Your husband was a braver man than I.

Before this terrible affair I was ignorant of Southern customs. I would give anything to be ignorant still!

I know you as a sensible, virtuous woman and trust you will ignore the malicious gossip which discredits the gossipers, not a blameless lady!

As you will understand, I cannot call on you. But I stand ready to assist you materially. Nehemiah is a reliable go-between.

Like you, I mourn Captain Fornier. He held fire when he might have shot me down.

Your Obt. Servant, Wesley Robert Evans

Savannah's disapproval fell on Solange. Mr. Evans had been the challenged party, and, as every Georgia child knows: Yankees don't have good sense. The deceased captain's wife's shameless behavior had "sowed the seeds of tragedy" (Antonia Sevier's happy phrase), and wags wondered (with a lewd wink) exactly what other "seeds" had been "sown."

Savannah's better sort believed Solange had encouraged her

husband's fatal challenge to make way for his slayer, her Yankee paramour.

In dramatic contrast, Wesley Evans got the approbation accorded the gentleman who'd blazed. Wesley despised these compliments, sometimes in terms that might have occasioned a challenge had circumstances been less exceptional and Wesley not a deranged Yankee. Unwelcome compliments gave way to admiring nods, hat doffing, and knowing looks. Wesley buried himself in work. Every shipowner and planter in the Low Country soon knew him by sight. Lanterns in the R & E offices burned late into the night.

No one was surprised when a hotel porter found Count Montelone dead in his room. At first, from the anguish written on the dead man's face, poison was suspected, but the superintendent of the watch ascertained that the Count had eaten no supper that evening, contenting himself with a single orange peeled by himself.

When Ruth came home, Solange asked, "Did you know Augustin was going to die?"

Ruth wouldn't meet her eyes. "I sees some things."

"Where have you been?"

"I gots to catch my breath." Vehemently she repeated, "I gots to catch my breath!" Her icy fingertip touched her mistress's cheek. "You gonna marry that man. Yes, you is. Better be damned for what you is than what you ain't."

In due course, when Solange did marry Wesley, Antonia Sevier claimed she'd done so to demonstrate contempt for decent opinion, a notion which, in later years, Solange herself embraced because she couldn't admit—no well-bred young lady of Saint-Malo and certainly no Escarlette daughter could confess—her inexplicable, weak-kneed urgency when she and Wesley fled their wedding reception to tumble into their wedding bed.

Solange's second husband was as shrewd and determined as she, but Wesley found the humor in it. "When God looks down from

His Heaven," he said, "He sees a teeming anthill where the rich ant can't be distinguished from his servant."

"A penny is a penny," Solange sniffed. "In anthill or Heaven."

Two years and nine months after the marriage, Mrs. Wesley Evans gave birth to a healthy daughter, Pauline. The infant's christening and subsequent reception at the Evanses' residence were attended by young Savannah, uninterested in old scandals cherished by last century's grandees with that century's manners.

When Solange suggested Ruth be Pauline's Mammy, Wesley objected. "Must every Southern child have a Mammy?"

"Mammies allow Southern ladies to cosset their gentlemen," Solange said with a crooked smile no Escarlette would have approved.

Wesley cleared his throat. "Ruth is so young."

"Coloreds mature faster than whites. Ruth is a woman, not a child."

"I don't believe I've known anyone like her. Rain, sleet, high wind, good times, hard times . . . Our charming Ruth never drops her smile."

"You object?"

"I do wish I knew what Ruth was *really* thinking."

"Take it from me, dear. You never shall."

Ruth took to child rearing naturally, and Pauline's mother cosseted her husband to both parties' entire satisfaction.

———

After the embargo ("damnbargo!") was repealed, Wesley expected the cotton trade to flower, but British and American politics hindered cotton exports until 1812, when war was declared with the British, who couldn't believe the United States was no longer their colony.

Louisa Robillard and her daughter, Clara, took sick the first week of August and were buried the eighth of September 1812. The utterly devastated Pierre offered his half of R & E Cotton Factors to his partner. Thanks to the prenuptial agreement Wesley had willingly signed, Solange remained a femme sole, but she hesitated not twenty-four hours before providing capital to buy out Pierre.

Blockaded by the British fleet, Savannah languished until Andrew Jackson slaughtered Britain's Indian allies at Horseshoe Bend and, not long after, British regulars at New Orleans. The Treaty of Ghent ended the war and lifted the blockade. Church bells rang, and middling cotton rose to thirty cents.

In Savannah, hammers banged, saws rasped, and Bay Street was so obstructed with cotton and lumber wagons, society ladies promenaded on Jameson Square. The O'Hara brothers expanded their mercantile, and nobody snickered when James O'Hara bought a carriage. When Wesley offered to return Solange's investment in R & E Cotton Factors, she laughed. "Build me a house the Havershams will envy," she said. "Pink."

"Pink?"

Her mouth tightened into an expression with which Wesley was too familiar.

"Pink it shall be," he said and grimaced. "Pink?"

Although there was a continent of piney woods behind the Jewish Cemetery and new homes were rising there, society folk still built in town. Wesley bought two decrepit frame houses on Oglethorpe Square and had them torn down.

When Ruth asked, "Master Wesley, why you wreckin' perfectly good houses?" he said, "So we can be better than the Joneses."

"Who them Joneses?"

Pauline was a quiet infant and grew into a docile child, who only needed to be told what to do to do it. Even as a toddler, she was homely, though Ruth didn't think so for a minute. Ruth slept on a pallet beside the child's crib and woke to rise and banish her nightmares.

Young Mammy Ruth wore a plain blue shift and a modest, checked head scarf. She was the youngest Mammy in Reynolds Square and held her head high but didn't speak unless spoken to. Baby Pauline was always clean and properly dressed for the weather, and Toddler Pauline was so neat she almost seemed starched. Older Mammies accepted the young French Negro and opened their hearts to her. Mammy Cerise, who'd reared the Minnies' children, took a particular liking to Mammy Ruth.

Heat a cloth in melted tallow for colic.
Corn shuck tea cures measle rash.
Chinaberry's good if child passin' worms.
Child don't cry 'cause she's bein' contrary. There's somethin' wrong
*   with her.*

Little Pauline's father arrived at R & E Cotton Factors before the sun silvered the river and worked until the lamplighter made his rounds.

The Evanses ate supper with their daughter and supervised the child's bedtime prayers. Since Wesley was a Methodist, Solange, Ruth, and Pauline attended Mass without him.

Solange directed the Pink House construction. Excepting her novel color, Solange wanted a traditional "Savannah Box" and hired the elderly builder Mr. Haversham recommended. John Jameson had built a dozen Boxes and had (as Haversham noted) "made his reputation decades ago and won't hazard it. He's a worrier."

John Jameson was a glum little man who fretted about the Evanses' double lot, which was lower than neighboring lots so water must drain into the Evanses' basement. "This is the *Low* Country, madam," he reminded Solange. " 'Water, water everywhere,' as Mr. Coleridge likes to say."

Jameson admitted fashion favored the newfangled English half basement, but the traditional pillar foundation—with no basement, madam—had served for many years! Madam may not know the brick cladding she preferred was dear. Very dear. Jameson could show her any number of wood-frame survivors of mighty hurricanes! An attic cistern? Dear me! But why should Madam understand building mechanics? Savannah ladies are much too fine for such "practical" considerations. How to support such a device thirty feet in the air? A thousand-gallon cistern? Madam, a pint's a pound the world around. Yes, Mr. Jameson was aware the Robillard home had such a cistern—plus some *very* unusual plumbing. Mrs. Robillard—may God rest her, ma'am—had embraced novelty. Perhaps Madam hadn't heard about the leak ruining the plaster in the Robillards' upstairs bedroom? A room for your Mammy Ruth beside the nursery? Mr. Jameson had never heard of such an arrangement and deemed it—intending no criticism—unseemly. Mammies—as everyone knew—slept on pallets at the feet of the children's beds. A circular staircase, madam? To be sure, the circular staircase *is* traditional, but Jacob Bellows, Savannah's master stair builder, is, alas, two years deceased and the only other master in the Low Country works in Charleston. The Charleston stair builder is (Jameson lowered his voice) "a *free colored*."

"Hire a penguin if you must. I *will* have my circular staircase."

Mr. Jameson shook his head gloomily. "Madam, I don't know if Jehu Glen can be persuaded—"

"Ask him. Sir, employ your considerable charm."

Mr. Jameson, who had long abandoned any claim to that virtue, was taken aback.

Solange contained her impatience. "You can but try."

"Although Glen's a master mechanic," Jameson persisted, "he is said to be . . . difficult."

"Um."

Mr. Jameson allowed that, yes, Pink House construction could start in the spring.

Despite Jameson's concerns, a dry foundation was laid and stringers spanned the English basement. Double courses were laid to bear the attic cistern, and workmen appeared without fuss as their special skills were required. Seemingly despite its builder, the Pink House and the carriage house (presently the builder's shop) were under roof by August.

If the Pink House was ready, the Evanses would host a Christmas ball.

Solange urged Mr. Jameson to engage plasterers, cabinetmakers, glaziers, and had he summoned the Charleston stair builder and bought mahogany for the rails?

Despite Mr. Jameson's custom that finish workers never started until the mortar had cured for sixty days, three days after the gutters were hung, a small army of workers arrived in the carriage house with plaster molds, try planes, chisels, and shellacs.

On a fine September afternoon when the roses were poignant and frail, Ruth brought Pauline to the site. The workmen's busyness and jocularity fascinated her. Irishmen, free colored, and hired slaves "on the town" worked cheerfully side by side.

Inside the gaping frame where carriage doors would one day hang, Ruth perched Pauline on a sawbuck. "You see, little one. Men's doin' they work. See that man. Goodness I never seen no saw so puny. Lookin' like a doll's saw! You see men steamin' strips?"

A coffee-colored workman was adjusting wooden frames.

"You!" an Irishman shouted. "Keep your black hands off my template!"

Many workmen had outsize hands, but the coffee-colored man's hands were fine and smooth as a Master's. Ignoring the Irishman, he continued.

"Jesus, Mary, and Joseph! What are you at?"

"This ain't gonna do, McQueen," the colored man replied. "This got to be tangent. You angle way too steep."

The blond, mottle-faced man set thick hands on his hips. "Who the hell are you to be correcting my work?"

The coffee-colored man straightened as if the question deserved answering. "I been apprentice twelve years with Jacob Bellows, stair builder of Mulberry Park, Robinson House, and Blakely House ballroom. I be Master Stair Builder here. You got do as I say or get gone."

"Well now! Well now! Mr. Jameson! Mr. Jameson, sir, you're required here!"

Sawing stopped and men quietly laid down tools as the builder picked through and around stalled projects. Meantime, the coffee-colored man bent to the workbench, set his protractor, and scribed an arc on a board.

Jameson ran a hand through his hair. "What's this? What's this? Can't we work without disputation?"

"Mr. Jameson, sir. This nigger is telling me what to do. This *impertinent* nigger."

Indifferently, as if in another room, the coffee-colored man scribed a second arc. Ruth heard his pencil scritch on the wood.

A workman farted, and his fellow punched his arm.

Jameson's smile wasn't quite sure of itself. "Mr. Glen?"

"Sir?" He laid his pencil beside his instrument before turning.

"McQueen, here—"

"'The workman is worthy of his hire,' Mr. Jameson. Be he not? McQueen won't do what I tells him do. McQueen more bother than he worth."

"Jehu—"

"Mr. Jameson, Savannah got plenty mens needs work. I need men to do what I say 'thout back talkin'."

"This nigger—"

Jameson opened his purse to count coins. "Your wages."

"You'd let a white man—"

"Mr. McQueen, I have need of a stair builder. Jehu Glen is English trained: the best in the Low Country."

"Well, I'll be. I'll be a . . . a son of a whore!"

McQueen may have instigated mayhem as he passed behind the stair builder bent to his work, but others had his arms and McQueen contented himself with spitting into the sawdust. Jehu didn't look up.

Ruth whispered, "You seed that, Baby Pauline? Does you believes what we seed?"

The stair builder inclined his ear to Jameson's quiet admonishments but didn't stop what he was doing. Jameson perhaps wanted to say more but turned to the others. "Is today the Sabbath? If not, perhaps you will continue your work."

Walking home, Ruth hummed a tune she had heard somewhere a very long time ago. Next morning in Reynolds Square, Mammy Cerise heard her and frowned. "Don't you be hummin' Rebellion song," she said.

"Rebellion song?" Ruth asked.

"Don't you be hummin' that!"

Ruth frowned.

Mammy Cerise whispered, "Don't you know you hummin' Haiti uprisin' song? White masters plumb hates hear that song."

That afternoon, shaded by a parasol, Pauline napped outside the carriage house.

Jehu Glen was the most beautiful creature Ruth had ever seen. Where had the man been born, what had shaped him? His movements were economical and swift. Sunbeams touched his arms gold as his wood plane made curls. When he shaved his arm hair to test a chisel's edge, Ruth wanted to cry, "Watch out! Don't go cuttin' youself!" She wondered if Jehu's dramatic test of each razor-sharp blade meant he was as aware of her as she was of him.

She came back the next day and the day after. One time, when Jehu was in the house, she touched a plane blade and sliced her thumb, which she popped into her mouth, sucking hot, sweet blood.

Another time she slipped a curl of cherrywood into her apron, and its faint cherrywood tanginess scented her pallet that night.

Other Mammies brought their charges to the grand house a-building. Older children made scrap lumber forts and fleets.

Mammy Cerise had heard about the free-colored stair builder. "He daddy, he white man. He buy heself a pretty servant girl and not long afore one thing lead to 'nother. When baby growed, Glen set him free and 'prentice him to an Englishman what build all them big Charleston town houses. When Englishman die, that Jehu boy set up on he own. He think high of heself."

Ruth smiled. "He do."

"That boy so cheap he make a half cent beg for mercy. Sleep on bench in the carriage house 'cause he too cheap to rent heself a room."

"He practical. He savin' to get married."

"Girl, don't you go slippin' down carriage house after dark."

"I ain't never said nothin' to the man, Mammy Cerise. Nary word."

———

Solange thought Wesley was working too hard, too long hours, and one October evening over supper she said so. She also thought he was drinking too much but didn't mention that.

Wesley ran his hand over his eyes. "All these fresh-minted factors and buyers, naturally they all need to 'see me' or 'buy me a whiskey' or 'sit down to (ha, ha) pick my brain'—learning a business I understand and they do not. The Up-country planters are swamped with novice factors offering prices that don't allow anyone to profit."

"Perhaps you should do a little less. Delegate more of your duties."

"In this boom, anyone worth hiring is in business for themselves."

She changed the subject. "Our little Mammy is smitten with your stair builder."

He relaxed. "He's not *mine,* dear. I wouldn't know the man if I saw him on the street. He's Jameson's perhaps, or, since you are in charge, I suppose he's yours."

"Jehu is free colored and very much his own man."

He shrugged. "Ruth is how old? Fifteen or so? Old enough to jump the broomstick if she wishes."

"It's not gone so far as that. She's mooning over the man, that's all."

"Then we'll cross that bridge when we come to it." He raised his glass. "Two more years of good times, and I'll have a competence for you and Pauline."

"Only Pauline?"

He frowned. "What . . ."

"You are to be a father again, my dear. If you don't work yourself to death first."

He offered his arm. "Dear, dear Solange. Let us go upstairs and celebrate."

———

Ruth and Pauline began taking supper at the carriage house, where plasterers were preparing molds and Jehu Glen assembled sections of his curved staircase.

One afternoon, when all the others were busy in the house, Ruth tiptoed so close she could smell his sweat.

The stair builder didn't look up from the rail he was sanding. "Inferior mechanic got no business takin' pay. That man no better than thief."

"Oh." Ruth backed away.

Another day, Ruth offered Jehu their dinner basket. "Eat some," she urged. "We gots plenty."

Expressionless, Jehu picked through the basket she'd carefully assembled, taking a chunk of jack cheese and an apple, which he munched as he passed into the house, grumbling at plasterers whose scaffold was in his way.

For three days Jehu accepted Ruth's food without thanks and without quitting work. The fourth day, a slow Saturday, he returned her basket. "Who you, girl?"

Ruth said.

"You one of them French Negroes?"

"I was a baby in Saint-Domingue."

"Huh."

Next Monday, dust motes floated in the sunlight of the carriage house and Pauline was napping with her mouth open. Jehu tightened clamps and laid glued pieces on the workbench. "Tell me, girl," he said. "Jameson pays me a dollar a day. What I worth to that man?"

"Jehu . . ."

"Is I worth more or less than a dollar?"

"Worth a dollar, I 'spect."

His smile barely lighted his face. "Workman figure if he pay a dollar, he worth a dollar. Why in tarnation would Jameson hire man weren't worth no more'n he was payin' him? Jameson got to get more for my work than he payin' me, else why not do it heself? That extra money go into he Capital."

"I didn't think—"

"Course you didn't. Course not. You don't worry 'bout no money. Servants don't got worry 'bout money. Free men gots to worry 'bout it. 'Deed they do."

Jehu spoke about "Capital" like "Le Bon Dieu" or "United States of America." Jehu described "Capital" like Masters describe a beautiful lady or a fast horse. Jehu had four hundred and seventy-one dollars Capital. He owned chisels and planes and try squares and plumb bobs and the walnut toolbox he'd made himself. He slid open velvet-lined drawers like each drawer had a name. That toolbox had pride of place on his workbench, and every evening he dusted it, last thing. Touching a perfect dovetail, Jehu informed Ruth, "Before you a 'Master' you got to make a Masterpiece."

Jehu's Capital was in Mr. Haversham's safe, where nobody could steal it, and one day soon, he'd use his Capital to set himself up as a builder, just like Mr. Jameson. He'd hire coloreds "on the town" 'count they'd work for less and wouldn't sass like free coloreds or Irish. With lower costs he could charge less for his work, and whites would naturally *have to* hire him.

Jehu pursed his lips. "Preacher Vesey say my notion ain't gonna work. Vesey say white man ain't *never* let no black man get up. They's afeared. Tell me, girl, you think white folks afeared of us?"

"Sure they is." Ruth's blurt surprised herself and she covered her mouth.

He dismissed that. "Well, they ain't. Ain't no Negro got no army, nor navy, nor no big guns. Ain't no black man own no white man, that for sure."

After work and on Sunday afternoons, free coloreds and Irish drank in sailors' taverns on the docks, but Jehu never went with them. "Man can't hang on to his Capital never gonna amount to nothin'," he told Ruth.

Ruth was Jehu's only friend in Savannah, and he named only

Vesey in Charleston. Denmark Vesey was "just a rough carpenter, don't you know? Ain't no master mechanic. He fine preacher, though, breathing with tongues of fire, yes, he do. When he preach, you can feel Hell heat!"

For the first time in her life, Ruth dreamed about living with someone besides Solange. But she couldn't. Solange was expecting another baby, and Ruth would be Mammy Ruth to both children. That's how things were.

Ruth wondered what she'd earn if she were *paid* to be Mammy. Would Solange want a Mammy if she had to pay, or would she care for her babies herself?

Jehu's dreams were as beautiful as the man himself. Charleston was rich as Pharaoh, and a man like Jehu . . . why, a man like Jehu could set up his own shop just like his friend Denmark.

Although Mr. Jameson fretted prodigiously and kept his workmen at it from "can (see) to can't," by the second week of December the Pink House wasn't ready and the furniture Solange had ordered from New York City hadn't arrived at the docks. Wesley seemed almost relieved. "A Christmas ball would have been a very great expense."

"Expense?" Solange frowned. "Wesley . . ."

"I, for one, am grateful we shan't be bothering."

"This year."

"Of course, dear: 'This year' . . ."

For two decades, Savannah dames had thrust eligible daughters against Philippe Robillard's bachelorhood. Some of the repulsed declared that any male who could resist such beautiful, gracious, *suitable* girls must be a little *unusual,* and much was implied by that bland description.

Without prior announcement and to general consternation, the wealthy Philippe suddenly married a Muscogee Creek woman said to be a princess of that savage people. Dames whose daughters had been spurned thought she'd damn well *better* be a princess.

No gentry attended the wedding, to which only Cousin Pierre and several Muscogee kinsmen had been invited. After the ceremony, the wedding party repaired to Pierre's home for sherry, with which the Muscogee were apparently unaccustomed. One was spotted spewing into Pierre's rosebushes as Nehemiah helped others into Philippe's carriage for return to their camp.

The next day Pierre made an incautious jest about "fearing the loss of what hair I have," which was elaborated upon—with extravagant miming—in Savannah's best withdrawing rooms. Antonia Sevier insisted that prior to Mr. and Mrs. Philippe Robillard's Christian nuptials an altogether pagan ritual had been performed at the Muscogee encampment.

Curiosity about the Muscogee princess was intense, and though calling cards accumulated in Mrs. Robillard's hall salver, she was never "at home."

Pierre Robillard claimed his cousin's bride was a woman of considerable charm, but, despite rather unsubtle prompting, he never elaborated on that. "Cousin Philippe is a happy man. Finally, my dear kinsman is 'in his element.'"

After its decade-long absence, the Robillard Christmas ball had become a legend; an icon of "Old Savannah," when every lady was gracious and every gentleman blazed. Savannahians weren't disappointed when the Evanses' invitation failed to materialize and the Robillards' did. Invitations were signed by Philippe and Pierre, and underneath the cousins' signatures was a squiggle which might have been a Muscogee bird though nobody knew which bird exactly.

———

None of Savannah's leading citizens had been in Philippe's mansion since his mother's funeral feast twenty years ago, and everyone was eager to see what the Muscogee princess had made of her new home. Sentimentalists hoped it had been restored to the grandeur it enjoyed during the Revolution, when it had served as General Howe's headquarters.

In happy anticipation, gentlefolk had their carriages revarnished, glittering jewelry emerged from strongboxes, and Savannah's seamstresses worked their fingers sore creating ball gowns from the latest Paris patterns. Curiosity met Speculation in every withdrawing room; neither was sated, both invigorated.

Solange handed their invitation to her husband. "She may be a Princess, but her penmanship is deplorable. Any child could do better."

"What does Dr. Michaels say? Should you be attending balls in your delicate condition?"

Solange pouted. "He says I will deliver a healthy happy baby. He urges more exercise. This isn't the dark ages, you know."

Did Wesley hear? He was so distant these days. "It's a busy time for the firm. Planters . . ."

"Darling Wesley!" She took his face between her palms. "It's Christmas!"

"Afterward it'll be the Washington's Birthday Ball and all those damnable patriotic toasts, and then—"

"Can we not enjoy one another?"

He surrendered. "My dear, of course we can . . ."

———

Philippe Robillard's wood-frame house stood at the north corner of Broughton and Abercorn Streets. Two hurricanes and a citywide fire had destroyed most of Savannah's frame houses, but battered, gray, and askew, this house had endured. Fashion had deserted the neighborhood, and when Philippe's mother passed, even her staunchest friends expected Philippe to find a better address.

Carriages began arriving at eight. Flaring torches illuminated servants directing these conveyances and assisting elderly guests up Philippe's steep yellow stone steps. The double doors were so brightly lit from the hallway behind, Nehemiah's familiar features couldn't be made out as he greeted newcomers and forwarded them to Philippe's surly Muscogee coachman, who snatched their wraps. "Evenin', Miss Solange, Master Wesley," Nehemiah said. "We doin' our best. 'Deed we is."

Philippe's bachelor abode hadn't been feminized. Older guests recalled the drawing room wallpaper whose colors had been brighter twenty years ago. Younger ladies envied their elders' weak eyesight, which couldn't quite identify what was dwelling in the high, dark cornices.

Ladies spotted the mop strings caught on furniture legs but didn't drop a conversational stitch as they wiped their chairs before sitting.

Balsam, mistletoe, and holly writhed along the chair rails, and a grand festoon of Spanish moss drooped from the chandelier.

Antonia Sevier wondered, "Isn't moss sacred to the savages?"

In the drawing room too full of his parents' last-century furniture, Philippe (who had already drunk more than wisdom prescribed) presented his Princess. "This is my darling wife, Osanalgi. Mrs. Haversham, Osanalgi." He chuckled. "Call her Osa as I do."

The woman's hair was very black, very shiny, and chopped off. Her fussy ball dress had been sewn for someone whose flesh didn't crawl at its touch. Osa's smile was pasted on, and her eyes skittered.

"The Muscogee are Georgia's first citizens. There are eight . . . perhaps *nine* subtribes depending on how we reckon them."

"Why, Philippe, that's fascinatin'. Mrs. Robillard, you *must* tell us all about it."

"Yes," Osa said but no more.

So her guests moved on.

Philippe had banned the stodgy, old-fashioned, happily familiar minuet, and when his musicians struck up the new (and some said indecent) waltz, Philippe and his bride sailed onto the floor so lost in each other they didn't hear the whispers behind fans or see the uncharitable winks.

Pierre did a cousin's duty, working dance after dance through the widows and spinsters. Some ladies, who had known better days, lingered at a buffet their fastidious sisters avoided despite Pierre's assurances no savage delicacies were concealed beneath the gumbo's dark red roux.

Still, strong punch lifted spirits, and soon enough, despite the waltz steps they must learn as they danced them, their silent Muscogee hostess and dour coachman, Philippe's guests began to feel something like Christmas. They'd wanted to meet the Princess? Well, now they had. Might as well make the best of it. Havershams mingled with Seviers, Minnises with O'Haras.

Their servants celebrated in the basement. Mammy Cerise had appointed Mammy Antigone to tend the children in the nursery, and the coachmen had picked an unsociable fellow to stay with the horses.

The kitchen was brick nooks and candlelit crannies beside a tall fireplace where a kettle burbled cheerfully. Pierre Robillard had entrusted Nehemiah with a cask of Madeira. Seated at the head of a long plank table, Mammy Cerise kept a hawk eye on it when Nehemiah was about his duties, nodding when a tin cup might be charged, coughing disapproval when a cup had been charged too often.

The dispenser of the Madeira hadn't stinted herself and pressed Ruth about Jehu and private matters Ruth wouldn't have confessed to anyone. Mammy Cerise knew how young girls are. "I was one myownself."

"Please, Mammy Cerise!"

"We just the same, child; all us womens needin' love."

Mammy Ruth fled to the nursery, where Pauline was building a block tower, which other children were as earnestly dismantling. Mammy Antigone waved off Ruth's offer to relieve her. "I reckon I stays here with the children. I likes children better'n grown-ups."

Ruth hoped Mammy Cerise's curiosity would have moved on to someone else's secrets, but armed with Madeira and memories of what she'd got up to in her girlish days, Mammy Cerise went at Ruth again. "That Jehu shrewd. He make enough money one day for a wife 'n' childrens. Might even buy he own house live in."

"Might be he do."

Mammy Cerise smiled as if she'd got to where she'd been heading all along. "Jehu talkin' 'bout that Vesey? Preacher Vesey?"

"Say he strong Christian man."

"Um-hum. Um-hum. Vesey free colored like Jehu. Won Charleston lottery and bought heself free. He say God give him the number. Vesey"—Mammy Cerise lowered her voice to a rumble—"he—"

"He what? I goes to Mass every morning. Me and Pauline always be goin'."

"Vesey ain't no Catholic man, honey. He *say* he for the colored man!"

Ruth's faint smile deferred to her elder.

Mammy Cerise's eyebrows knotted. "I doesn't know, child. I just don't know. That what worry me." She poured Ruth a half cup of Madeira.

"I don't drink . . ."

"Then it time you start. There ain't so many good things in this world. Childrens, a good man's lovin'"—she poked Ruth in the ribs—"and this here. Sometimes I thinks it the best. For certain, it nearest to hand."

But Ruth didn't like the taste, and soon as Mammy Cerise wasn't watching she set her cup down. Some Mammies were laughin' and carryin' on, and what if their childrens need them?

Master Wesley was red faced, laughing with Master Haversham and Master Pierre. Mistress Solange and Mistress Antonia were talking close like they'd been best friends *forever*. Ruth tugged Mistress Solange's sleeve. "We go now, missus? Li'l Pauline need go home."

"It is Christmas, child. Surely I'm allowed to forget my cares one night a year."

Ruth couldn't think what cares Mistress Solange needed forgetting. "I bein' with Miss Pauline," she said. In the nursery's ancient love seat, two sleepy toddlers nestled against Mammy Antigone, who opened one eye in a slow wink.

Ruth sat in the corner with her back against warm chimney bricks and slept fitfully, waking each time a Mammy collected her charge. When Nehemiah shook Ruth awake, her mouth was parched and her eyes felt like she had sand under the lids.

Nehemiah passed the sleeping Pauline to Ruth in the entry hall. Since Philippe was unable to do so, Pierre Robillard said good night to his cousin's guests. "Mrs. Evans, so good you condescended to attend. Philippe was so gratified you and Wesley could grace our little fete." He whispered, "Philippe says the Evanses are 'the cream of Savannah society.'"

Having heard Pierre apply that happy compliment to others, Solange smiled. "Our hostess?"

Pierre looked around. "Perhaps she's . . ."

When Solange returned to the drawing room, two drunks were sleeping in chairs and the bearded fellow curled in a corner was protesting to his servant, "Doan' wanna go. Sleep here."

Mrs. Philippe Robillard's hands were wrist-deep in the gumbo, and roux dribbled down her ball dress. She dropped something—a shrimp? sausage?—back in the tureen. Her eyes tried to bolt.

"Why," Solange said to the girl, "why, you are . . ." Solange touched her own pregnant belly. "As am I."

Impulsively, Osa snatched Solange's hand. "We talk?" she said. "We talk?"

Fighting the urge to wipe grease from her hand, Solange inclined her ear. They spoke for ten minutes—two expectant mothers—until Osa stopped trembling and her eyes quieted. When Solange said she must be going, hospitable Osa dipped a bowl into the tureen and offered it to her guest. Delicately and deliberately, Solange extracted a single gray-brown shrimp with her fingers and made every show of enjoying it. Osa beamed.

"We are both refugees," Solange told her. "Savannah can be so cruel." She wiped her fingers on the tablecloth. "Refugees must become who they weren't."

Ruth carried Pauline to the carriage. Since Wesley was very drunk, Solange laid Pauline on the front seat, and Ruth climbed up top beside the coachman. Ruth wasn't tired—not one bit. The winter stars were so bright.

The next morning their house was cold until Mammy Ruth laid a fire in the withdrawing room. Cook made oatmeal. Solange came downstairs yawning. Her hair was unkempt, she hadn't scrubbed her face, and last night's makeup was smeared like—Ruth didn't giggle—a red Indian's war paint. Solange appropriated Ruth's oatmeal and demanded coffee—"boil chicory in it"—and the morning paper.

Solange was on her second cup when she snorted, tapping a black-bordered advertisement. "Dear Mother of God." She shook her head, incredulously.

Aloud, she read the president of Haiti's advertisement offering free land to any American free-colored craftsmen willing to immigrate. "Oh, dear me. Dear me, Ruth. Must I suppose you and your master stair builder will go to Haiti?"

Ruth smiled. Almost. "Thank you no, missus. I Mammy Ruth Fornier. I American."

Solange rubbed her forehead. "Yes, I suppose you are." She folded the paper and laid it down. "She is intelligent, you know."

"Miz Robillard?"

"She doesn't have a doctor. Her people don't have them—not our sort of doctors, anyway. Philippe is no help. I shall ask Dr. Michaels to call on her."

She turned to Ruth ferociously. "You see how cruel people are? How terribly cruel? Osa is the wife of the richest Frenchman in Savannah. Yet how the grand dames are chuckling this morning over their tea and toast! Princess Osa. 'Poor, poor Princess Osa. Uncouth and so *Indian*!'" She brushed a wisp of hair off her forehead. "My precious Pauline. How will she behave when she's Osa's age? Will she be out of step, eccentric, a figure of mockery? Or will my daughter be one of those fortunates who set the tone for others?"

Ruth told her Mistress, "Mammy Cerise say we all needs love. Love be-all and end-all."

Solange dropped her forehead into her hands. "Mammy Cerise! Mammy Cerise! The fount of good taste and deportment! Oh, dear me. Oh dear!"

"Missus, what else—"

"Pauline will not be a servant, Ruth. She will not care for another woman's children. She will marry someone with a good competence or expectations of getting one. My Pauline and"—Solange touched her belly tenderly—"this little one will live happily among their peers, knowing the benefits of civilization, providing charity to those less blessed. Pauline must be herself, but she must not stand out—as poor Osa does, as I did when I arrived on these shores. How they whispered: 'Poor woman! One more "tragic" Saint-Domingue refugee!' They whispered until I had my money."

"But, missus. You always stands out."

With a gesture Solange dismissed that compliment. "Mammy, I must inform you of the rules—nay the *commandments*—of polite society." She bowed her head as if in prayer. "To be someone"—she searched for words—"one must first *appear* to be someone. Osa's father is a potentate. Therefore, he acts like, dresses like, and speaks like his savage subjects expect a potentate to act. Do you understand?"

"I ain't never seen no poooot . . . I ain't seen none, missus."

"Ah, but you have. When Wesley wobbles downstairs, he won't seem like a potentate, but he'll be one before he goes out to pursue his affairs. Mr. Haversham—in his very expensive, very plain black suit—he's a potentate. And Pierre Robillard, despite his fusty ways and mannerisms—he's one too. They are potentates because they match our notion of what such should be. As Pauline's teacher, you must be alert to those marks that distinguish a young lady from the mere woman or"—she winced—"the slattern or slut. Those distinctions are as important as they are fine. Those fortunates with good breeding and refinement are distinguished by their deportment."

"'Deportment,' missus?" Although Ruth didn't know what it was, she would heed and obey.

———

Solange was too shrewd to ignore handwriting on the wall. A prominent cotton factor, first cousin to Mrs. Sevier on her father's side, was found dead in his office, having murdered himself with a dose of bitter arsenic dissolved in a glass of very old, very fine bourbon. High middling brought four cents a pound—if a buyer could be found. A full-task field hand, sound and obedient, could be had for four hundred dollars, half what he would have fetched last year. The riverfront was cluttered with cotton, like so many moldering snowbanks, abandoned when Up-country planters had failed to sell and gone home.

Perhaps because she didn't want to think about those snowbanks,

Solange read to Pauline (who listened when her doll or kitten didn't positively require her attention) and to Ruth, who was fascinated by the confident proscriptions of the little etiquette book.

"The lady does not speak about herself. She lets others praise her."

"What if she done somethin' special?"

"'By inquiring, others may learn of our achievements.' Pauline, you must avoid popular phrases. 'You may rely upon me' is a sure sign of the cheat. 'To be brief . . .' predicts long-windedness. And 'Without boasting . . .' a braggart."

Every winter day rain kept Pauline indoors, Ruth brought out the etiquette book.

"'In the event a lady hears an indecency, she must promptly interrupt, rebuke its utterer, and, if he cannot be checked, the lady is free to depart with her dignity intact. A younger lady's chaperone can be expected to intercede, if indecency is merely indelicacy.'"

And so forth.

Wesley ate dinners with his family and was tender to Solange and Pauline but afterward returned to his office to sleep, joking that his presence "keeps the bailiffs away."

Ruth slept badly. Too much mist hanging over the family and too many spirit voices.

As if deportment could improve the price the mills paid for cotton and drag cotton piles from the promenade, Solange continued her instruction relentlessly. " 'The lady must vary her dress lest idlers amuse themselves by confusing their description of her dress with her person. In dress, society applauds the woman who is in no hurry to follow fashion yet adopts the démodé when her betters do.'"

"You mean she dress like all them other ladies do."

"Precisely. 'The young lady's dress must be modest in form and ornaments lest her suitors conclude that she loves luxury.'"

Over supper Wesley said, "Haversham is calling in loans. It's not his idea. Credit him for that. But he's Philadelphia's dogsbody. Still it's a damn, damn shame."

"Isn't the Bank of the United States supposed to lend? To encourage commerce, I mean."

Wesley's smile was knowing and bitter. "Six months ago, any man able to cast a shadow in bright sunlight qualified for a loan. 'Sir, is that *all* you need?' A man's good reputation and credit meant nothing. The bank financed silly fellows who undercut honest men. Now the bank wants the silly fellows to pay up. Since they cannot pay, *their* disaster becomes *our* disaster."

The next morning Solange explained why an unmarried lady must not eat too much. " 'She must not be deemed too lusty in her appetites.'"

"What if she hungry?"

"A girl may have appetites. Indeed, she *will* have appetites. But she must *not* acknowledge them. Suitors don't think respectable girls have appetites, and only reckless girls will disabuse them."

Solange noted the O'Haras' prosperity in these hard times as an object lesson. "Prudence, Ruth, is the lady's mightiest tool."

Pauline didn't pay much attention, but Ruth was an eager student. She'd usually figured things out for herself, and being taught was a rare pleasure.

———

Wesley hadn't been to the Pink House in the new year.

When Solange told Mr. Jameson to abandon work on it, he objected, saying sixty days would see it finished.

"I can pay your last bill," Solange said. "But no more."

Jameson told her the attic cistern, though installed, had not been plumbed, the chair rails weren't attached in the central hall, the circular staircase lacked balustrades, handrails, and varnishing. In short, the Pink House was incomplete.

Solange found a smile. "As you say, sir. But we no longer have means to complete it."

Mr. Jameson sputtered angrily. He inquired if she'd given a thought to the workmen he had assembled, men who like himself had families to support.

"You can reassemble them when times improve," she said.

This pregnancy was more disagreeable than Solange's first, and spring rains often kept her indoors. One overcast day when Solange visited Pink House, workmen were disassembling scaffolding as Jehu stacked lumber in a decrepit wagon. Gloom descended on Solange so profound she slumped on a nail keg, clinging to consciousness.

When she opened her eyes, Jehu was standing before her. "You wants water, missus? Somethin' I can do?"

"No, no."

"Mr. Jameson don't come round no more. You want I fetch Master Wesley?"

"No, I'll be fine. Dizzy, that's all."

He helped her up. How her back hurt. How glad she would be when all this was over.

Jehu cleared his throat. "I been meanin' talk to you, missus. 'Bout that Ruth gal."

"Not now," Solange said. "Not now."

———

Three days later, Sunday morning amid the clamor of church bells, Nehemiah stood on her front stoop with his hat in his hand and an expression on his face she'd never seen before. He was bursting with news he didn't wish to deliver. After he did so, he helped her into the house, where Solange fainted.

From the Factors' Walk forty feet above him, Wesley looked like a dead blackbird with his cape wings flared across wet cobbles, a blackbird that had flown into window glass and fluttered dying to the dock below.

"It were terrible slick, missus," Nehemiah excused Wesley's fall. "Why nobody hardly keep their feets. Wet cotton waste slicker'n axle grease."

Clumps of the worthless stuff cluttered the walk, the stairs, the gutters: it was everywhere. The river roared, smashing dirty spume against the docks. Wesley had never been still. The people circled quietly around were not as still as Wesley now. Where had Wesley's motion gone? Solange crossed herself. Could Methodists go to Heaven? She'd never thought about that.

"How?"

"No one saw, missus."

A spectator spotted Solange and Nehemiah on the Walk, and the circle opened to accord the new widow a better view. Solange began shuddering and was grateful when, of its own accord, her shuddering stopped.

"Does missus wish to . . . ?"

These stairs, these docks; how many hundred times had she descended without once noticing how loudly, how jarringly the gulls screamed? When Solange let go the handrail, her hand ached.

Men removed hats and, with murmur and rustle, stepped aside. Wesley's poor head was turned unnaturally, and his hair had fallen over his eyes. His cheek lay in a pool of dark fluids.

After a time, Nehemiah took her arm. What would Ruth think? And poor Pauline? And who was Widow Solange? Desperately, she gripped Nehemiah's kindly arm.

———

Pierre's new carriage delivered Solange, Pauline, and Ruth to the Methodist Chapel. Perhaps at Pierre's direction, they passed down Abercorn Street, where the floppy crepe badge on Philippe Robillard's front door mourned Osa's stillborn baby. There'd been no Catholic funeral. Some said the baby had been buried by the Muscogee.

Pierre had hired the coffin maker and Pierre handed out funeral favors before the service: black kid gloves for the ladies, dark handkerchiefs for gentlemen. The mourners were Pierre's friends and businessmen Solange barely knew. In their pew, black-clad Philippe and Osa pressed against each other. The O'Haras stood in the back of the church.

Solange's mind flitted from the flowers on the altar to the preacher's velvet-faced gown to the smell of beeswax candles. She could not imagine tomorrow. Wesley and Solange: their *is* had become *was*.

At the graveside she gave Pauline a rose to lay atop her father's coffin, and Ruth slipped something wrapped in blue cloth among the flowers. Solange dribbled sandy dirt onto the box.

The sky was the color of Spanish moss.

Back in Pierre's carriage, the stink of newly tanned leather and neat's-foot oil made Solange sick. She swallowed. The knotted black lace of her mourning dress stretched like anchor cables across her bulging belly.

In Pierre's home, men and women she knew and didn't patted her lifeless hand and offered condolences. Why should she believe them? Their beloveds still lived! At least the O'Hara brothers didn't offer to touch her. "It is sorry we are for your trouble, ma'am."

The drinkers drank, the hungry lined the buffet. Philippe was dumbstruck: his grief for his stillborn child superseded. Two other guests were in full mourning; others wore mourning bands, still other gentlemen had mourning badges in their lapels. Antonia Sevier embraced her. Hadn't Antonia recently lost a sister? Those who'd come to mark her Wesley's death were a headland toppling yard by yard, beloved by beloved, into the sea. The brandy Nehemiah gave her tasted like water.

Ruth was feeding Pauline cake and protecting her from effusive adult condolences that left the child sobbing.

Solange's eyes leaked.

What was she to do? What to do? She had always *done*. Something. She had always *done* something.

Everything was blurred. Why couldn't she see through the damn mist?

She snatched Pierre Robillard's arm. "Pierre, dear Pierre. You must help me. I must sell the business."

He patted her hand. "Yes, dear Solange."

"Soon I shall need money. With Wesley gone . . ."

"Poor Wesley, my dear, dear friend." Pierre sobbed. He extracted an oversize handkerchief from his sleeve and honked into it. Solange flexed her very empty hand.

"Pierre. You must help me sell Wesley's business."

"Ah, dear. Oh, my dear . . ."

Solange fought the urge to comfort him. Pierre was so *helpless*. Mr. Haversham offered his condolences. His wife stood at the door waiting to go. Wasn't Mrs. Haversham wearing a mourning brooch? A favored cousin? Solange had heard something . . .

Mr. Haversham's face was gray, and his formerly corpulent cheeks hung from his cheekbones like a hound's. His eyes were shot red, so bright red they must be painful.

"So kind of you to come," Solange said.

When they'd gone, Solange asked Pierre, "Mrs. Haversham's cousin?"

"John Whitemore, yes. John was one of General Jackson's volunteers. His war wounds . . ."

"We are all mourners, everyone here . . ."

Which thought refreshed Pierre's tears.

"Your dear Louisa, precious Clara. You must miss them so."

"Oh, I do! How I do!"

"Pierre, I must sell our house. I'll move into the Pink House."

"What?" He wiped his eyes.

"I cannot afford two domiciles."

"Dear me. Dear me, Solange. But your Pink House isn't finished!"

"The plumbing isn't, but I have lived all my life without it and can manage perfectly well."

"The bedrooms?"

"Unfinished. But the roof is new, the exterior complete; doors and windows installed. Why, I even have a fine mahogany circular staircase. At any rate, part of it . . ."

Whereupon they both wept for beloveds lost and sweet dreams come to naught.

————

Early next morning, Nehemiah arrived with wagons and O'Hara men to move Solange to the Pink House. She, Ruth, and Pauline rode with the first load, and Pauline ran through the big empty rooms, sorrow forgotten.

O'Hara's men set couches and sideboys in the withdrawing room. The unfinished withdrawing room would be Solange's bedroom, and Ruth and Pauline would share the smaller room meant to be Wesley's office.

"Master Wesley, he be laughin' now," Ruth opined. "Seein' Pauline and me in here!"

"'Laughing!'" Outraged. "Why, how do you mean?"

"Oh, Master Wesley like things separate. He business *stay* at he business. Now we be snorin' in Master Wesley business." Ruth chuckled.

"How do you know what Wesley thinks—thought?"

Ruth went to a glass-front china cabinet being carried carelessly and answered, distracted, "Oh, I talks to him. Talks to Master Augustin too." To O'Hara's men she said, "Careful that! That glass!" Her eyes flashed. "They cares 'bout you, missus. Both you husbands lookin' after you."

Solange felt a curious luminescence at the edges of her eyes and the stillness that presaged a fierce headache. She swallowed bile. More cheerfully than she felt, she said, "We will be happy here. After I sell our other home we'll manage quite well."

Spell broken, with her customary cheerfulness Ruth replied, "Yes, missus. I sure you will. You has and you always will." She wiggled a finger at the men. "Have a care with that. It ain't yours and you ain't got money to pay if you busts it."

Solange's familiar furniture was adrift in the much larger room, and her carpets were islands in seas of yellow pine floor. The thought "We'd have been happy here" popped into her mind, uninvited, and she blinked it away, ordering O'Hara's men to move her four-poster (*her* bed not *their* bed) against a different wall.

Ruth took Pauline for her nap.

Somewhat later, Solange was sitting on that bed with thoughts chasing their tails when Ruth returned, upset.

"What now?"

"Missus. You got come the carriage house. Please come."

"But . . ."

"Somebody gots talk to you. Waitin' in the carriage house."

"Later, Ruth. I need to rest. Tell whoever it is to come back later."

"He can't! He goin'!"

Solange saw two shimmering Ruths side by side, separating and reblending. She feared she might throw up.

"Very well. If it's so desperately important. Fetch me a glass of water."

While Ruth did as bid, Solange went to the carriage house. Its empty doorframe pulsed. Its unwashed windows gleamed balefully.

Jehu Glen was sharpening chisels at the empty workbench. *Rasp, slick, rasp, slick, rasp, slick.* He dripped oil onto the stone.

"Why are you here? Hasn't Mr. Jameson paid you?"

Jehu jerked around suddenly, *too suddenly,* and whipped off his hat. "Sorry, missus, I didn't hear you slippin' up on me. These chisels Sheffield steel and gots be looked after." He caressed a wooden haft.

Solange felt like screaming. She licked dry lips. "You're finished here."

"Yes, mistress. I comes back when you wants your staircase complete. Only lack a fortnight."

"Not now."

"Yes, missus, I knows. Staircase complete anytime. You say and I comes."

"Jehu, I am feeling unwell and you must go. Now."

"Mistress Evans, I can't go till I put proposition to you. I been waitin' this whole day."

"Your proposition . . . it . . . it will wait."

"No, mistress, it can't no more. I done loaded my wagon, bought my mule, and I ready to go. I ready yesterday."

Solange felt coolness on the back of her hand. Ruth had brought water. She lifted the tumbler to her lips and swallowed.

"I bought the lumber Mister Jameson ain't need. Pay good money for walnut and cherry in Charleston." Jehu shook his head at that astonishing fact. "Got Mister Jameson's sale bill right here."

Solange saw writing on the paper he produced from his vest pocket. She recognized Mr. Jameson's signature.

"I sorry 'bout Master Evans. He were"—he searched for a word—"he were right kindly."

"Yes, he was."

Jehu set his hat on his head but snatched it off as if his hand had betrayed him.

Ruth said, "Jehu . . ."

"I want marry Miss Ruth."

Solange clamped her eyes shut but reopened them when she began to sway. "You wish to jump the broomstick. As Ruth is my servant and you are free colored, that presents difficulties we can resolve when you return to the city."

"I ain't comin' back." Then, brightly, "Till Mister Jameson send for me. Mighty fine staircase, missus. Only lack a fortnight."

Solange handed Ruth the empty glass. "Later," she said. "Come back later."

"We ain't jumpin' no broomstick, missus. Me and Ruth marryin' in church. Stand up front of everybody. Till death us do part."

"That won't be possible. Ruth is my . . . Ruth belongs to me."

His eyes were so hot, so determined! Jehu's face blurred, and Solange heard his voice as if underwater. "I good with my hands."

Solange thought, stupidly: Oh. You're good with your hands.

"But I ain't no kind of talker."

Solange thought: Indeed.

He said, "I buys Ruth. I got money."

At her side Ruth whispered, "Go ahead, Jehu. Show Missus your money."

Ruth—her Ruth—was a shape, a black blurry shape. Solange needed a cool dark place. The Pink House windows didn't have curtains. There were no dark rooms where she could lie down while Ruth laid a cold cloth on her forehead. "Tomorrow. I'll consider this tomorrow."

"Missus Evans, all this rain bringin' the rivers up and I got go. I goin' with or without Ruth. Ruth say ready money welcome today."

The man untied a leather purse from his belt, laid it on the bench, and carefully counted ten-dollar gold eagles, eight stacks of five. He squatted to eyeball each identical stack, containing not one more or one less. "Might have give five hundred last year, but prices down and four hundred's more'n fair. Just last evenin', girl like Ruth—though not so fetchin'—brought three hundred at the Vendue House. Four hundred more'n fair."

Solange croaked, "Ruth?"

Ruth squeezed her hand hard. "You been good to me, missus. I gonna miss you and Pauline. I wants go. I wants be Missus Jehu Glen."

Solange howled, "But who will take care of me?"

Who You Pretends You
Is, You Comes to Be

AS SUNRISE GILDED the marsh grass, a lanky coffee-colored man and a very black woman departed Savannah on the old King's Highway. She perched on a tool chest in a decrepit wagon beside odd lengths of cherry, walnut, and mahogany lumber. The man led the aged mule, who was much inclined to balk.

Ruth marveled at spring flowers, tiny frogs peeping, big frogs croaking, and all those birds darting and swooping over cattails and oat grass. Ruth knew just how they felt because that's how she felt!

The King's Highway wasn't fit for a king; it was a narrow sand track with shelly intervals and planks or logs laid down where small streams crossed. Sometimes Jehu had to roll up his trouser legs and wade, dragging the hee-hawing mule.

They moved onto the verge for other wagons, riders, and a coffle of twenty-two coloreds chained single file behind the slave speculator dozing in his saddle and brought up by the driver, a burly Negro whose bullwhip rested upon his shoulder. The coloreds didn't see Ruth and Jehu or the marsh birds or the cattails. They saw the switching buttocks of the speculator's horse or the back of the colored in front of them. Their feet swished in the sand and their chains clinked and somebody's breathing was loud and raspy and somebody else was whimpering.

When they passed they took the light with them, and Ruth didn't look around for a while. She heard the thud of their mule's hooves and the tiresome predictable squeak of an ungreased axle. The sky had turned gray, the marsh stretched to flat horizons, and those darting birds were killing and eating every creature they could. Ruth shivered and drew her shawl close.

They continued along until dusk, when they stopped, shared a loaf of bread and a chunk of hard cheese. Jehu unhitched and hobbled their mule, and they bedded down under the wagon. Jehu was too tired to talk and Ruth too afraid. One misspoke word might permit anything. Anything! She wrapped herself around Jehu's back, tucked her knees into his hollows, and slept.

Next forenoon, the pilgrims arrived at the broad reach of Port Royal Sound. A distant dot eventually became a ferry under a yellowed triangular sail. The ferryman shouted instructions from his chair in the prow to two shirtless coloreds, whose ripped trousers snickered at modesty. The ferryman spat the stub of his cheroot into the water as the helmsman quit the rudder to dash forward and secure the craft to its floating dock.

Swiftly, the captain stepped ashore demanding papers. "Caught me four runaways last year." He ran his finger down Jehu's certificate of emancipation. "Fifty-dollar reward for the full task hand, thirty for the house slave, twenty for her whelp. Course"—the man admitted gloomily—"I had to share with the slave catcher, but 'twere found money. Nobody wanted the old runaway, so he died on me. Slave want be prudential when he run off lest Master don't want 'em no more. Wench, you 'mancipated too?"

He studied Ruth's bill of sale. "Huh. You a Master now? Master

Jehu Glen?" The ferryman cackled. "This landin's prime for catchin'
runaway niggers. Only place to cross Port Royal Sound in a hundred miles up or down 'less'n you swim like a fish." Pleased with a
familiar phrase, he repeated, "Like a *fish!*"

Jehu's face betrayed nothing, but his eyes never left the captain's
hands with the precious papers, which meant who he and Ruth were
in this heartless world. Finally, the ferryman rolled them carelessly
and pushed them at Jehu, who refolded each to its original creases,
laid one atop the other in his oilskin wallet, and returned that wallet
to the inner pocket of his leather vest over his beating heart. He
said, "Me and Missus needin' cross, Master. What you fare?"

He rubbed his jaw, considering. "Dime each. Two bits for your
wagon and mule."

"Master, that's half day's wages."

The man grinned. "Like I told you. Hundred miles to the next
crossing."

A Savannah-direction dust cloud became a redheaded drover
with twenty black and tan Aryshire cattle.

The captain greeted the drover familiarly. "Calm today, Tom," he
said. "Not like last time."

"Master . . ." Jehu said.

"Back for you all soon as ol' Tom's acrost." He chuckled. "*Provided* you got my forty-five cent."

"Oh, I gots money. Master, they's plenty room . . ."

The captain cackled. "Yeah. But these damn Aryshires are par-
tic-ular." He guffawed, but the redheaded drover seemed embarrassed.

The cattle lowered their heads and objected to the slick plank
footing, but the drover was everywhere with his lash and they were
soon aboard.

The sail was swivel-screeched around, and the younger colored
flipped hawsers off the stanchions and trotted to the rudder, where

both men waited until the current captured the craft before they grunted into the rudder, using it as a sweep to set course.

Jehu perched on the wagon as the ferry beat back across the sound. When Ruth put a hand on his shoulder, Jehu said, "Not now."

They shared a heel of bread. They grazed the mule. They waited as the sun marched toward Savannah and dipped into the marshes. Clouds of mosquitoes came out of nowhere. Shrill marsh birds feasted.

A buggy with a black-clad driver and woman appeared. Ruth guessed he was a preacher. The driver never spoke, and when the woman spoke she leaned in to whisper. Maybe, Ruth thought, he ain't no preacher. Maybe theys runnin' off! The notion cheered her. A shabbily dressed farmer appeared with two shoats on ropes. The farmer leaned against the preacher's buggy, and the white men talked.

As the ferry neared their shore, Jehu cast a casual eye for travelers who could displace them but didn't say anything to Ruth, and, though Ruth checked herself, she didn't say anything either. The ferryman bit Jehu's silver two-bit piece before ushering them aboard behind the preacher, the farmer, and his shoats. The breeze was light, and the boat drifted a good while before its triangular sail popped and filled.

Jehu stayed in the stern with the ragged coloreds. The older man cackled at something Jehu said. The preacher and the woman conversed. A shoat snuffled and grunted. The young colored steered while the elder wrapped his arms around his knees and dozed. The western shore flattened into a line while the eastern acquired detail.

The sun was a yellow band when their wagon squeaked onto dry land. "You in Carolina now," Jehu said.

"Same like Georgia," Ruth said. Same palmettos, same live oaks, same sandy soil, same drooping moss.

Atop a low rise, candles gleamed in windows of the Shellpoint

Inn. The preacher turned over his rig to a colored boy and escorted the woman inside. The farmer and shoats trudged up the road. Jehu went around back, where Cook said they could sleep in the barn for a dime plus a half dime for fodder. Two cent for a bowl of ham and beans. They set the bowl between them and shared, one spoonful at a time. Jehu made sure Ruth scraped up the last bite.

A nighthawk swooped through the lamplight when Cook opened the kitchen door. Clatter of cook pots. Somebody sayin' something in there.

Jehu unhitched their mule and hobbled him where he could reach hay and water. Dim light peeped through unchinked logs. The mule snorted his muzzle into his water pail.

There was no sign coloreds had slept here before, but that didn't mean anything. Coloreds don't own anything to leave behind. Jehu carried his tools and toolbox into a horse stall. He laid their blanket atop hay tumbling out of a manger. He peeled off his shirt. In the faint light his skin gleamed like wet steel.

Jehu looked at Ruth. "You mine now. I does anything I wants with you."

She stepped into his broad smile.

She said, "Oh, Master. Don't you do it to me! I never knowed no man afore."

She said, "Oh no, Master," when his fine hands freed her breasts.

She said, "Yes, Master," when he entered her.

———

Charleston was like Savannah but richer, busier, and blacker. The city sprawled athwart the narrow peninsula where the Ashley and Cooper Rivers met, and ships docked, undocked, raised sails, made bow waves, and did all those things big and little ships are supposed to. Charleston's town houses were larger than Savannah's, but, excepting White Point, Charleston had no beneficial public parks or squares. The principal avenues were north to south, and White Point on the tip of the peninsula was almost the only place in Charleston where, since coloreds were forbidden, there were more whites than coloreds. Charleston's white masters were more arrogant than Savannah's and quicker to use a cane or bullwhip.

Sensitive white masters could send disobedient servants to the workhouse to be whipped. Since the workhouse had previously been a sugar warehouse, they were sent "to get a little sugar."

Jehu sold his lumber, wagon, and mule and rented a two-room shed behind a rice factor's warehouse off Anson Street. In each room a window without glass or shutters let breezes through, and the roof was in shadow during the hottest hours of the day. Ruth made Jehu remove his shoes outside the wood floor she scrubbed until it was glass smooth and bleached white. She painted the doorframe and windowsills blue so spirits couldn't pass and hung oakmoss, yellow dock, and mayapple to flavor the air (and keep Jehu's mind fixed on the woman it ought to be). At sunset, when the breeze came off the river, they ate rice and beans or fried greens, sometimes with a scrap of salt pork. Jehu likely took a drink of whiskey then, only one, but Ruth never did. It was their chance to talk, but they didn't say much.

Jehu had more work than he could do. His staircases and cabinetwork had won him a reputation, though his customers boasted Jehu was "the Englishman's apprentice."

Jehu had spent most of his Capital buying Ruth. Sometimes he wondered if he should have offered less.

"What I worth to you?"

"I didn't mean nothin' by it. Money make money if you use it proper."

"I ain't never seen money do nothin'. This ten-cent piece, it just lay there. 'Dime, you gets up and sweeps my floor. You can't? You can't?' I reckon I gots to sweep myownself."

"Capital," Jehu lectured, "make a man free. Got enough Capital we eat meat every night. Was Capital rented you this place."

Giggling, she climbed into his lap. "Here I is."

Ruth found work at a market stall selling produce. She'd forgotten her childhood languages but not how to drive a bargain.

When she turned over her small earnings to him, Jehu said, "We pretend you Jehu's slave but we know whose slave is whose, don't we, girl?"

Most of Charleston's light-skinned free coloreds worshiped with whites at St. Philip's Episcopal. Their Brown Society initiation fee was fifty dollars, and they paid dues too. Some owned slaves; a few wealthy Browns owned a dozen slaves.

Like most coloreds, Jehu and Ruth attended the African Methodist Episcopalian church on Cow Alley in the north end. It was a big new building, whitewashed inside and out; you didn't want to rub your Sunday best against any wall because green lumber was still leaking pine pitch through the whitewash. The benches were backless and the pulpit unornamented, but Jehu Glen had made the front door of best cherrywood which the preacher, Rev. Morris Brown, locked and unlocked with a big iron key.

Reverend Brown had been a free-colored bootmaker before he heeded the Lord's call and went north to Philadelphia to be instructed and ordained. Brown's thriving church married, buried, and blessed as well as offering Bible studies for servants who couldn't read the Book themselves and Sunday school for their children.

Founded by free coloreds, well-known craftsmen, the African church was clear proof that Negroes could advance in this world and be equal in the next.

The African church was the only place in the Low Country where coloreds could gather without whites present, the only door they could lock. The Brown Society and the Cow Alley church were the poles of colored society in the thriving port city of twenty-three thousand.

Ruth's church friend Pearl joked, "You gots what you s'posed to have and most I s'posed to have too." There was some truth to that. Pearl's small face lurked under her kerchief, and she was straight up and down flat, like a boy. She'd been born on the Ravanel plantation, "back when they was plantin' indigo. Before the rice come, you know," and the daughter of a house servant became a house servant herself. "Missus Ravanel, she don't favor town," Pearl told Ruth. "But Colonel Ravanel do. So we town mostly. Colonel Ravanel famous for he horses!"

Mrs. Ravanel needed a Mammy for her young Penny but didn't want to buy one. "What if Mammy no good? Ain't like good Mammy come to slave market every day. What if Mistress buys Mammy what says she do arything but can't *do* nothin', what Mistress do then? Got to sell her on, and, in the meantime, what about Miss Penny?"

"Why ain't you Mammy?"

"'Count I don't like childrens. Childrens botheration!"

"Why you tellin' me?"

"'Count Missus Ravanel, she lookin' to hire a Mammy. She can fire ary Mammy don't work out, which ain't near the trouble of sellin' one. Wasn't you a Mammy once?"

Ruth laughed. "I Mammy Ruth afore I be Missus Glen."

"You ain't Missus Glen yet." Pearl giggled. "You livin' in sin."

"For now," Ruth corrected.

Frances Ravanel hired Ruth on Pearl's recommendation. Penelope (Penny) Ravanel was two years old and "troublesome," but Ruth took to the child. "You and me ain't so different, honey. We ain't listen to nobody 'cept our ownself," Ruth told her. Which, while not strictly true about Ruth, was certainly true about Miss Penny.

Jehu wasn't altogether pleased by Ruth's new employment. "You a servant again!"

"You makin' two dollar every day you work. Missus Ravanel pay me fifty cent. We keep eatin' like we been eatin' and pays our rent and don't buy no whiskey nor tobacco . . ." She paused.

"Go on."

"We can live on my salary and yours can be Capital."

"What about the church?"

"Half dime for the collection every Sunday."

"I thinks about it."

Ruth knew what thinking was needed had been done.

Colonel Ravanel had fought under Andrew Jackson at the Battle of Horseshoe Bend, and, though Colonel Jack never hid his light under a bushel he never boasted about that. Most Low Country planters had evaded the war, and, as one of the few Low Country heroes, Jack had been invited to stand for the legislature.

He laughed it off. "You don't want a senator who knows as much about horses as I do. He might gallop off."

When Governor Bennett himself made a plea, Colonel Jack told him, "We slaughtered those Indians like hogs in a shambles. I don't reckon slaughterin' qualifies me to make laws."

Since Jack's wife, Frances, often tempered the colonel's moods and tongue, James Petigru said, "Too bad Frances can't stand for the legislature in Jack's place," a remark which made the rounds.

Jack's refusal and contempt for "the shambles" eroded what goodwill his heroism had brought, and he was never asked to stand for office again.

Jack didn't care. He was happiest when riding or training or betting on or buying or racing horses, and some said, "The only human Jack Ravanel ever liked was his wife," adding, "Lucky for Jack his wife is Frances."

Frances was one of those fortunates who could don dignity or discard it as easily as she changed hats. Her perfect deportment at St. Philip's or the Bay Street promenade dissolved into girlish laughter at her husband's rude, fond jokes, and she allowed Jack's sly caresses when she thought the servants weren't looking.

After feeding Jehu his two eggs, oatmeal, and the heel of yesterday's bread, Ruth walked to the Ravanel town house to dress and feed little Miss Penny. At noon, while the child napped, Ruth brought Jehu his dinner bucket. Amid aromatic shavings and the pungency of hoof glue, John ate his cheese and apple while Ruth wondered how Le Bon Dieu could have blessed her so.

One day, as Jehu wiped his mouth and picked up his tools, Ruth told him she wanted to be a married woman when the baby came.

"Why . . ." Jehu said. "I . . . Baby?" He lifted Ruth to her feet and embraced her, just her torso, leaning away from her precious belly.

Jehu asked Denmark Vesey to stand up for them at the wedding. Decades ago, Denmark had been Captain Vesey's cabin boy (some whispered the handsome boy was more than that), but Vesey sold him to a Saint-Domingue planter. Upon arrival at the plantation, the boy exploded into the Falling Sickness: thrashing about, raving, frothing, spitting, and biting so vigorously the disgusted planter returned him to the ship for full refund.

Despite that inauspicious interlude, the boy recaptured the captain's trust, learned to read, and eventually became captain's clerk. When the captain retired from the sea to establish a ship chandlery on East Bay, Denmark Vesey performed the duties a white manager might have. "1884," Jehu enthused. "1884 was the lottery number God say Denmark play. Girl, you know how much Denmark win?"

Ruth, who'd heard this story before dutifully asked, "How much he win?"

"Fifteen hundred dollars."

"So much as that?"

"Denmark buy himself free. Nobody 'mancipate Denmark Vesey. Denmark Vesey make heownself free."

"Vesey wife, Susan, she free? His childrens?"

"Denmark could live anywhere," Jehu said. "Anywhere in the world. Go to Liberia or Haiti or Canada . . . could quit the Low Country, go Philadelphia. Ain't no slaves in Philadelphia."

"He wife and childrens go too?"

"No, they don't. Denmark ain't goin' 'count he *won't*, and they ain't goin' 'count they *can't*!"

The sixty-year-old, very big, very black carpenter taught Bible studies in his home Tuesday and Friday evenings.

Reverend Morris Brown, Cow Alley church's *ordained* preacher, was brown like Jehu. What hair Brown had jutted behind his bald pate braced against the wind even when there was none. Brown was slightly deaf, and sometimes, despite his polite nods, he didn't understand what was said. Brown's gentle Christian eyes focused on the newer, loving Testament while Vesey, Brown's unofficial counterpart, rarely strayed far from the harsher, older one.

Masters, even conservative Masters who distrusted *any* Negro gatherings, found no harm in Brown and as Christians hoped to meet the preacher and their other servants in Paradise, where they might need them.

The beaming Reverend Brown married Mr. and Mrs. Jehu Glen before his congregation and asked God to bless their union. Ruth had never thought she could be so happy. She floated light as a feather.

Ruth's blue shift was worn loose so her belly didn't get married before she did, and Jehu was very much the Master Stair Builder in Colonel Jack's cast-off frock coat and the top hat a horse had mashed. Ruth had bought Jehu's white linen cravat with the wedding pennies Mrs. Ravanel gave her.

Beside her at the altar, Pearl clutched the wedding ring Jehu had hammered from a Spanish silver coin. Denmark Vesey loomed over Jehu like Goliath. After Pearl passed Jehu the ring and Jehu put it on Ruth's finger (it was so heavy!), Preacher Brown said they were wed and Jehu could kiss her, which Jehu did while Denmark Vesey spoke up: "This here man and this wife, they be one and God wants they stay one. No man, whether colored or free colored or Master, can tear them asunder."

Preacher Brown wasn't the only grown man who gave Denmark Vesey space. The man's gray hair was clipped short, but his size and full gray beard made him look like Abraham or King Saul or some other Bible ruler. When Vesey approached, some whites crossed the street rather than step aside for him.

As Mr. and Mrs. Glen came down the aisle Gullah Jack, the voudou man, clapped hands and danced around them, crying, "God has made them one. Spirits blessin' this union. Spirits pourin' down love!"

The couple paused while Gullah Jack rattled his gourd rattle. He shook it at Ruth, and his eyes popped. "Who you, woman? Who is you belong to?"

Ruth clasped Jehu's arm. "I his now. Ain't you heard?"

As if Ruth had answered a question he hadn't posed, Gullah Jack held his stare until folks got restless and Preacher Brown said, "Jack! That's enough!"

Jack blurted, "Woman, you knows what I talkin' 'bout! You 'n' the spirits knows," and whirled away.

Jehu squeezed Ruth's hand to bring her home.

Vesey murmured for their ears alone, "Gullah Jack, he got Power but ain't got good sense."

Jehu and Ruth smiled. Vesey clapped Jehu on the shoulder and confided so the whole congregation could hear, "You got you a good man. Jehu, he brown enough for the Brown Society, but Jehu, he is black as me."

His eyes skipped over his listeners. "Browns, they got too much to lose."

Ruth said, "Denmark, why you carryin' on, on *my* wedding day?"

He laughed a big man's laugh but didn't leave it be. "Browns hopin' to fade into white men. Put on white man's habits, white man's business, go to church at St. Philip's with the whites. They up there in the garret—all the coloreds is—but goodness me, why make a fuss 'bout that! Why ob-ject they can't walk down the aisle and testify they love for Jesus. Don't ob-ject ownin' a few coloreds neither. Course them they owns, they Black colored, not Brown colored. Brown coloreds fade till one day they ain't got no more black and they white as snow."

Jehu was agreein' with everything the man said, so Ruth jabbed him sharp in the ribs to remind him why they'd come. Out of the corner of her eye Ruth saw Preacher Brown depart almost like he was slipping away.

So she pulled away from her husband and his friends to her woman friend Pearl, who hugged her (carefully) and said Ruth was the most beautiful bride ever been, and Ruth smiled because she knew it was true.

Pearl introduced Ruth to Thomas Bonneau, whose face and hands had been roughened by sea salt and weather. His smile gleamed.

"I seen you at the market afore. You that fisherman!"

"Oysterman mostly, but I do know where flatfish like to hide. I sees you too, Miss Ruth. Hard not see girl like you."

"Thomas!" Pearl warned, then giggled. "He pretend he wild, but Thomas tame as tame."

"You the onliest one ever tamed me," Thomas testified.

Pearl said, "Look at you: 'Mrs. Glen.' That who you be."

"I been Ruth long time. Don't remember who I been afore."

———

Wispy clouds decorated the indifferent sky above coloreds taking refreshment in the yard outside the Cow Alley church. Mr. and Mrs. Glen sat on the stoop beside Thomas Bonneau and Pearl.

"Jehu," Ruth whispered. "I feel so *important*. Like I a queen or something."

"Thomas, ain't you gonna introduce me?"

The brash boy was a year or so younger than Ruth. He was brown and beautiful.

"This boy Hercules. Boy fancy heself a horseman."

"'Fancy myself,' fisherman?" Incredulous eyebrows and a flashing grin. "One day I win the Jockey Club stakes. You can bet on it!"

"Bet I knows one nigger thinks too high of heself."

"Course I do. Course I do! Girl, now we properly 'quainted, I propose you leave off bein' married to that carpenter and run off with me. We go north and seek our fortunes."

Ruth couldn't help smiling. "I married *today*! Don't you think I could stay married for a little while?"

"I give you one week." Hercules raised a finger in the air. "Afore I comes for you!"

Coloreds in spotless, perfectly ironed Sunday Best congratulated the young folks starting their family in a *Christian* manner, praying the couple'd be lucky, that their children would survive infancy and not be sold away and thus be able to comfort them in their old age. That's what, in their innocence and knowledge, they wished for Jehu and Ruth Glen; they prayed Le Bon Dieu would favor them.

———

Sometimes officers of the watch sat in back of the Cow Alley church while Reverend Brown preached of Jesus' love and great patience and the rewards of eternal life to come, but no whites came to Denmark Vesey's Bible studies.

Three weeks after Jehu and Ruth's wedding, Pearl followed her friend out of Denmark Vesey's Bull Street house. Ruth fanned herself. "Ain't Charleston ever cool? I can cut this air for pudding."

"Honey, it ain't hot. It's you."

"Uh-huh. If I wasn't . . . It too darn hot to think!"

"It were warm inside."

"He all the time preachin' Moses. Moses! Moses! Moses! Lord, I wish I could read myownself! What that ol' Moses got to do with coloreds? Catholics got Mary lookin' out for us and Saints, and voudou got spirits lookin' out, but here be Moses, Moses all the time and all the way!"

"Denmark fine preacher."

"Oh, he am. But sometimes I wonderin' why he don't buy he wife and take he family north. Why he don't think more 'bout them. I thinkin' he don't care 'bout nothin' but Moses!"

Pearl changed the subject. "When baby come?"

"Soon's she want to! When you marryin'?"

"She?"

"She. When you 'n' Thomas marry?"

"Soon as Thomas save enough to buy me. Mistress Ravanel let me go for two hundred."

"Two hundred dollars?"

"Says she'd 'mancipate me herself, for no money, but Colonel Jack, he didn't get his rice winnowed proper and fetched a poor price, then he went and bought heself 'nother fast horse, which cost a pretty penny."

"Missus Ravanel got a good nature."

"Colonel not bad neither," Pearl confided, "'cept when he drinkin'. When Mistress ain't to home and Colonel Jack drinkin', I props a chair under my door latch. I gots to smile when Miss Frances get on him. Big war hero, colonel of infantry, and that gal run up one side of him and down t'other. Colonel Jack drop his head like a little boy. Let's go back inside. Ol' Moses ain't gonna hurt nobody. He been dead long time."

Ruth said, "I gets to thinkin' 'bout them Egyptians. They wasn't so much different than Moses's people. Maybe some of 'em had laid down with Moses's women, maybe some Israelites laid down with Pharaoh women. But Le Bon Dieu, He 'hardens Pharaoh's heart,' so Pharaoh, He can't let Moses's folks go. He can't 'cause Bon Dieu won't allow it! Le Bon Dieu harden Pharaoh heart and Bon Dieu send locusts and them plagues and finally he kills all the firstborn sons of the Egyptians and Pharaoh own son. So Pharaoh heartsick and let Moses go. Pharaoh glad be shut of 'em. So Bon Dieu He harden Pharaoh's heart *again* and send he soldiers chasin' after 'em. They gallopin' along pretty good and come to the sea, which Moses has divided. Wall of water on one side. Water on t'other. General, he say 'Forward!' and they got to obey, so they gallop twixt two walls of water though they horses afeared and snortin'. I s'posed to feel glad them Israelites safe on t'other side, but sometimes, Pearl, I feels like them Egyptians do. Like them water walls gonna come crashin' in on me."

"You afeared havin' a baby."

"'Deed so. Ain't never had no baby afore."

"Me neither. But if no woman never had no baby, you and me wouldn't be breathin' this air what is thick enough make a puddin' of."

Ruth chortled and they went back to the Bible study, Denmark Vesey, and Moses.

———

Unlike most of the Charleston gentry, the Ravanels stayed in sweltering Charleston all summer, although, taking the commonsense precaution, Jack never visited his plantation from sunset to sunrise. Everyone knew that yellow fever killed at night.

The Ravanel town house had a cook but no butler or coachman, and Frances's young friend Eleanor Baldwin Puryear urged Frances to buy more servants. "Why," Eleanor said, "how can you *ever* entertain?"

Young Mrs. Puryear was convinced her inherited wealth wasn't a sign of the Creator's favor. It was proof of His appreciation.

"Entertain?" Frances sighed. "We entertain at the Jockey Club more Saturdays than I'd like. Dear Eleanor, a fast racehorse costs far more than its jockey."

Eleanor's husband, Cathecarte, wrote poetry, and the *Charleston Courier* had published several odes to his wife (tastefully disguised as a Greco-Roman goddess). These poems made Eleanor blush, and she "barely glanced at them," though she could recite any of them by heart.

Cathecarte sometimes appeared in a bright purple cravat and was so proud of his tailor-made Charleston Rangers militia uniform he wore it to every social gathering. Mrs. Puryear—though presently childless—had opinions on child rearing, which she offered Ruth when that servant brought Miss Penny into the withdrawing room to amuse Mrs. Ravanel's friends. Ruth nodded and smiled. "Yes, Mistress Puryear."

After a particularly vigorous peroration, Miss Eleanor finally departed, despite Frances's "Dear Eleanor, would you deprive us of your company so soon?" Once Frances closed the door behind her friend, she slumped against it, sighing. "I must remind myself: Eleanor means well."

Ruth couldn't contain her giggle, which infected Penny and then her mother, and the three laughed until they clapped hands over their mouths.

In January, after the rice crop had been sold and plantation Negroes issued their yearly clothing allotment and enjoyed their day-long Christmas revels, their Masters came to town for the gayest social season in America. The Jockey Club and St. Cecilia Society balls were bracketed by grandees' soirées, sometimes two or three in the same evening. Gossip was fattened by intrigues, rekindled rivalries, rivers of whiskey, and Low Country prickliness, which readily became affairs of honor. Horses raced every day but Sunday, and ruinous wagers were unexceptional.

Jehu chafed. Those who could afford his work were partying. Their homes were busy with comings and goings, and no grandee welcomed the workman's necessary disruption. At some sacrifice to dignity, Jehu found day work at "on-the-town" wages, fifty cents a day unloading lumber on the Ashley River docks.

Enfeebled Middleton Butler, the indigo planter and Revolutionary War patriot, rarely left his King Street town house. In late February, after planters returned to their plantations for spring planting, he hired Jehu to replace the house's chair rails and wainscoting.

Ruth was so heavy that delivering Jehu's dinner bucket to the Butlers' was hard work, and Frances Ravanel suggested Jehu might carry his own dinner until the child was born.

"But, Missus," Ruth said. "I likes watch him eat."

That particular Saturday evening Jehu had just come home and Ruth was laying out their Sunday clothes when she hunched over and groaned, "Baby comin'."

Jehu had been thinking about the Philadelphia preachers who were to speak at the Cow Alley church tonight, and he blinked and gaped at his wife. Ruth was wet as if she'd peed herself. "Oh," Jehu said. But he ran into the street for a cab, and not long afterward Jehu Glen was banging on the door of the Ravanels' kitchen house. A shutter opened overhead and Pearl poked out her head. When she saw who it was, she clapped her hands, and her feet pattered down the stairs. Jehu carried Ruth upstairs onto Pearl's bed.

"Put down rags for to lay on," Ruth whispered. "I leakin'."

"Don't you fret, honey," Pearl said. "We gots soap."

Mistress Frances dispatched Jehu to the Butlers' for Dolly, the midwife (and some said voudou priestess). In the cab Jehu framed questions, but Dolly's snappish demeanor kept them unuttered.

Pearl's small room was full of women who treated the Master Stair Builder like a bulky, unwanted piece of furniture.

Pearl said, "Whyfor you standin' round? You want get in the way while you woman howl?"

Ruth said, "Jehu, go to you church service. You been wantin' go. I fine. Miss Frances and Pearl and Dolly takin' care of me."

Yes, Jehu wanted to stay, but when he left that women's room he felt very free.

———

Ruth's cheeks and forehead glistened with sweat. Dolly put her mouth close to Ruth's ear. "You sees things, doesn't you?"

"Sometimes," she gasped.

"Sometimes I sees 'em too. Baby be fine."

"I believes you. But I feared."

"Sure you is. Arybody be."

All the women prayed, although Frances Ravanel wasn't quite sure she and the colored women were praying to exactly the same deity. They waited. Mistress Ravanel had her fancywork basket, and Pearl watched every flick of the tiny needle. Pearl wished her fingers weren't so thick and opined only white ladies were fine enough to make fine stitches. Mistress Ravanel just smiled.

As flat gray predawn light seeped through the small window, they washed Ruth, rubbed oil on her belly and aching breasts, and covered her with a clean, patched linen sheet. Mostly they discussed the seasonality, variety, and condition of produce and fish available at the market. But sometimes they veered off the safe subjects, and Pearl, who could be indiscreet, mentioned the terrible accident, "right on Meeting Street so late Saturday night it weren't Saturday no more, 'twere the Sabbath morning!" when the very drunk young Master William Bee had trampled his body servant, Hector, under his horse's hooves.

"Terrible tragedy." Miss Ravanel assigned the incident to "Acts of God" quicker than Pearl might have wished. Pearl had strong opinions as yet unexpressed.

They braced Ruth while she squatted on the chamber pot, which Pearl carried to the necessary in the yard. Frances Ravanel read comforting psalms, and Dolly recited psalms she'd memorized. It grew lighter, and they heard Cook rattling around in the kitchen and the whoosh as she got the fireplace going. Pearl went down to fetch hot tea. The tip of the teapot spout was broken, so tea dribbled when she poured. Missus Ravanel got the mug with the handle. When Ruth's breasts got hot, hard, and painful, Dolly milked her into a bowl. They washed Ruth's face and propped her up so she could drink water. They gave her a leather strap to bite when the pain was bad and daubed her sweat. When the baby's head emerged, Dolly tugged gently until she could hook a finger into its armpit and the baby came in a rush. Pearl was wide eyed. Dolly cleaned out the tiny mouth and wiped the nose, and the red-smeared chest filled like a balloon for an angry "waaaa," a sound they found exquisitely beautiful. Dolly snipped the cord and wrapped it in a scrap of blue cotton while Mistress Ravanel pat-washed the baby's confused red face. Baby waved her fists and scrunched up her face. Dolly set her on Ruth's teat and tipped Ruth's nipple into her mouth, whereupon a jolt near as powerful as first breath surged through the infant: first nurse.

Pearl and Dolly and Mistress Ravanel grinned like fools. Ruth's smile was weary and peaceable. "Name come to me," she said. "She be Martine. Baby Martine."

The sun was well up when Pearl and Mistress Ravanel emerged

into the yard, where the laundress stirred a steaming cauldron and a stable boy admonished a horse he was feeding. Pearl raised her skinny arms over her head and stretched.

Mistress Ravanel said, "The colonel should come home tomorrow. Probably we'll own a new horse or two." She rolled her head, cracking it on her neck stalk, and flexed her fingers. "Penny will be wondering where I've got to. Pearl, please collect Ruth's husband. After Dolly goes home, you and he can tend Ruth. Sometime today, when you get a moment, change my bed linens."

"Yes, mistress."

Frances Ravanel hugged herself. "The sweetness of God."

"Yes, missus."

After her mistress left, Pearl harked for Martine's cries, but the baby was quiet. Pearl's excitement buzzed on the surface of her weariness. She was eager to give Jehu the news. On this soft, quiet Sunday morning, there were too few coloreds on the street and they were wary, so Pearl became wary herself. She stopped a woman she knew. "Been birthin' a baby all night. What wrong?"

In hushed swift detail, Pearl heard how, near nine last night, with services just commencing, the Watch busted through Jehu's cherrywood door into the Cow Alley church and arrested everyone.

Though there'd been a city ordinance forbidding colored gatherings between sunset and sunrise, it hadn't been enforced. Visiting Philadelphia preachers, Reverend Brown, Denmark Vesey, Jehu Glen, and a hundred forty others were locked up in the workhouse.

"Oh my," Pearl said and hurried back to the Ravanels'. She waited as long as she could to tell Ruth her husband was in jail.

The Charleston City Council sentenced Reverend Brown and four free-colored elders to either "one month in the workhouse or leave the state." Brown and Vesey chose prison. The Philadelphia preachers were deported to Philadelphia.

Ten congregants, including Jehu Glen, were sentenced to pay

five dollars or receive ten lashes. Jehu told the bullwhip man, "I got new baby girl, so five dollars ain't mine to spend."

"Uh-huh," he said, uncoiling his lash.

Until their Preacher was released, Sunday morning services were led by deacons, and, as soon as he could work again, Jehu repaired the church door.

Things returned to normal, and Charleston enjoyed a quiet summer. Sunday afternoons when the weather was fine, the Glens escaped the city's heat on Thomas Bonneau's skiff. Although the skiff smelled mightily of fish, with Martine in her arms Ruth felt rather grand as the tiny craft slipped through barkentines, ketches, schooners, and all manner of boats, some of which had crossed oceans. The current bore them downstream to the property Thomas Bonneau's white father had deeded him. Thomas Bonneau was as proud of his rocky half acre as if it were a Master's demesne, and, after he tied up, Thomas helped Jehu and Ruth and Pearl onto his dock. "Welcome to my home," that's what he said each time.

Thomas lived in a fisherman's shanty, but a more substantial dwelling was a-building. The four friends burned oyster shells and crushed them before mixing them with sand and water to form the tabby walls of a small square house. "This house be livin' hundred years," Thomas boasted. "Not wind nor tide nor hurricano gonna bring Bonneau house down."

"Hundred years," Ruth said. "Can't 'magine so long."

"My staircases . . ." Jehu began, but Ruth's flashing grin turned his brag into a smile.

While her parents worked and laughed, Martine lay under a palmetto in the fine cradle Jehu had made. Martine was a burbling, contented child.

The stripes from Jehu's whipping laddered his sinewy back. "Only part of Jehu Glen what's white," he joked.

At noon Ruth provided greens and Pearl a loaf of bread to go with Thomas's catch. After they ate they paired off in the lazy afternoon. Thomas and Pearl slipped into the grove behind the new house while Ruth and Jehu sat on Thomas's dock, dangling feet in the cool water as aloof calm sails passed in and out of Charleston Harbor.

"You ever want be somewheres else?" Ruth wondered.

"Ain't got no name 'cept here. Low Country builders heard 'bout Jehu Glen."

Ruth said, "I don't reckon how white folks can give children over to a Mammy. Ain't no finer creature than a child."

"'Count children ain't Masters yet. Children too puny swing that ol' bullwhip."

At Jehu's words the sun that had been shining so brightly dropped behind a cloud.

———

Workdays, Ruth carried Jehu's dinner bucket to the Butler job and brought Martine for her daddy to admire.

Old Middleton's nephew, Langston Butler, would be Master when Middleton died and supervised the plantation and most doings at the town house. Had it been up to Langston, he wouldn't have hired "an overpaid craftsman to rip out 'perfectly suitable' pine wainscoting and replace it with 'very dear' cherry paneling topped with Honduran mahogany chair rails. His uncle Middleton could be 'whimsical.'"

Jehu, Ruth, and Martine often ate with Hercules, sitting on overturned buckets in the yard. Hercules was Middleton's son, but nobody said so. His mother had been sold away after the boy was weaned—some said to Georgia, some Alabama. "Master Langston, he yearnin' for that old man die. Each day pass with he uncle breathin' 'nother day wasted. That how Langston reckon. 'Twere I Master Middleton"—Hercules dropped his voice—"reckon I'd be suspicious 'bout arything Langston give me to eat." He gave his listeners his broadest, most innocent wink. "If you gets what I means."

Servants see what we don't conceal from them, because if we must conceal our secrets, servants wouldn't be our inferiors and deserving their state. Hercules described Langston Butler's ambitions candidly in terms that would have concerned the young Master if a white man of equal rank knew as much as Hercules.

"Master Langston gonna turn us topsy-turvy. Master Middleton like spend money. Onliest thing Master Langston spend money on is horses, and he ain't same like Colonel Jack. Colonel Jack, he *like* horses. Master Langston, he buy horses 'count that's what Low Country gentlemens do."

Langston Butler detested his uncle's profligacy and neglect of Broughton, their Ashley River plantation. Langston sought to expand rice production, but when he made an offer for adjacent Ravanel acreage, Colonel Jack asked, "Your uncle Middleton knows these plans?"

Middleton didn't—which Jack knew perfectly well, and it can be admitted Jack enjoyed Langston's discomfiture. Hercules said, "White men greedy. They was black theyselves till greed bleach 'em white."

Jehu agreed. "Master Langston askin', how much this wood cost? What you gonna do with leftover? So I leaves all them worthless scraps in a heap. He can do with 'em what he wants."

Hercules laughed. "Cook usin' he fine cherrywood cook supper."

Ruth said, "Man always sayin' how this one and that one cheatin' him, you know he cheater. He warnin' like scorpion wavin' he tail."

"Girl?" Hercules grinned. "Who put them ideas in your pretty head?"

"What make you so saucy?"

"'Count I is. They don't send me for sugar 'count I knows how talk to horses."

Ruth thought Hercules was just struttin', the way beautiful young men do, but Jehu got jealous, so they stopped eating in the yard.

Master Langston Butler excused Hercules's sauciness but sensed something in Jehu he didn't like. He inspected Jehu's work closely and suspiciously. "Ladies will use this room."

"Yes, sir." (Jehu hated calling any man Master.)

"They won't remark poor workmanship, but I will." On his knees, young Master Butler shuffled along the wainscoting, tapping spots where the varnish seemed slightly shinier and trying to get a fingernail under where the chair rail fit. He stood and brushed his trouser knees. *Whish, whish, whish.* Butler's smile made Jehu want to ask, "What you want from me? Why you botherin' me?" but of course he couldn't.

"Your work is almost as good as an Irishman's."

Jehu couldn't help himself. "Colored man want to hold his head up too."

Young Master Langston grinned at a grown man his own age, a master of work Butler couldn't do; a man with a wife and an infant and a good name. His grin was to let Jehu know that should Langston Butler strike him down—perhaps with a fireplace poker; that very poker so near his hand—or took a pistol and shot him dead, the only consequences of Jehu's death would be blood mess on the parquet and the inconvenience of dragging a dead nigger's body into the street.

Despite Butler's awful grin, Jehu licked his lip and repeated, "Colored man want to hold his head up too." When Jehu's words just hung there, suspended in air, he joked, "Least as high as an Irishman's."

Later, when Jehu recounted that conversation, Ruth shivered. "You can't be saucy, Jehu. You ain't his uncle's bastard, and you got no way with horses. You everything to me and Martine."

Jehu clinked coins in his pocket. "Man paid me, didn't he?" he asked. "Fair and square."

————

After Thomas Bonneau bought Pearl from Mrs. Ravanel, Pearl worked for her former mistress for twenty-five cents a day. When Reverend Brown married Pearl and Thomas, Frances Ravanel attended the service but didn't stay for the fete.

Legal emancipation wasn't easy, but Colonel Ravanel helped Thomas Bonneau emancipate his bride. When Pearl asked Jehu why he hadn't emancipated Ruth, Jehu joked, "Can't deplete my Capital."

For nearly a month, Ruth denied him the marital bed until her own needs made that impossible.

"Whereas the great and rapid increase of free negroes and mulattos in this state by migration and emancipation, renders it expedient and necessary for the legislature to restrain the emancipation of slaves . . . Be it therefore resolved, by the honorable, the Senate and House of Representatives now met and sitting in General Assembly that no slave shall hereafter be emancipated but by act of legislature."

SOUTH CAROLINA LEGISLATURE, DECEMBER 20, 1820

On Meeting Street, with carriages backed up behind him and angry drivers shouting, Hercules gave Ruth the bad news. He took off his hat and didn't flirt. Martine asked, "Momma sick?"

Supper that night was silent. Walking to Bible class at Denmark Vesey's, Ruth didn't talk, and when Jehu reached for her hand he couldn't catch it. Vesey's small frame house was quiet. No coloreds lingered outside, except Gullah Jack on the stoop whittling.

"Nice night," Jehu said.

"'Lessn the watch come by." Jack wiggled thick comical eyebrows. "'Lo, momma. Spirits been askin' after you."

Ruth set her lips and brushed past. Blankets draped the doorframe and windows, and too many bodies jammed the small room. Jehu and Ruth found floor space in the back. It was close, hot, and airless.

Denmark Vesey's Bible was propped up on a stool, and Vesey's lips moved as he read silently. Ruth wondered why some folks' lips moved when they read and some folks' didn't.

Some wore caps or kerchiefs. Some heads were bare, shiny or dull, black, bald, or gray. Ruth thought: them which ain't free can't never get that way.

She was still puzzling when Denmark Vesey set his finger to mark his place and spoke. "Behold, the day of the Lord cometh, and thy spoil shall be divided in the midst of thee." He tapped the page with a thick workman's forefinger. "You think Zeachariah talking to us niggers? You think God look down and see how much spoils niggers got? No, He ain't talkin' to us; He talkin' to the Masters. 'Behold the Day of the Lord cometh.' How you gonna prepare for that day? You gonna stand in the way or give it a hand? 'Behold the Day of the Lord . . .'"

Despite the fug and hot, rebreathed air, Ruth felt a chill roll down her shoulders. The Day of the Lord.

Denmark Vesey perused, tracing sentences with his forefinger. "Behold," he whispered.

The room was so quiet his whisper slipped among them like an old friend. "Tell me, brothers . . . How many you bows to Master in the street? How many you?"

Some looked down. Some looked off. "So: none of you bows to Master?" He licked his lips. "That the truth? Now you knows and I knows White Masters cruel drunks, fornicators, and unbelievers. You and me knows they is. But you bows to them anyway because—I reckon—they better'n you. Hmmm." He set a thoughtful forefinger to his chin. "Mercy! Coloreds worse than fornicators and unbelievers and cruel drunks. I 'spect you all damned. You on the road to eternal damnation." Mock amazement flickered across his hard-used black face. "Jesus Christ, he savin' the Masters but he ain't not botherin' 'bout you.

"That Master you meets on the street, do he note you bowin' 'n' scrapin', or do he pass by like you was no more'n a hitching post or a horse apple in the dirt?

"Raise you hands. How many of you bow? How many steps into street let Master pass?"

Martine wiggled in Ruth's arms.

"Worse than anything the Lord hates a liar!"

Heads lowered as if they had nothing to do with the hands they raised.

Mock surprise. "Why that's most all of you. Well, well . . ." Vesey's smile was a fond uncle's. He read silently, lips moving, tapping the text before he looked up, apparently surprised to find so many people in his home. "How many you 'colored gentlemen' pretend you dumb as that old milk cow Master has you to milk? How many womens roll you eyes and sighs and say, 'Master, I just colored girl, this too hard for me understand'?"

Murmurs and humming as if inside a beehive, loud with beating wings.

"How many you teach your childrens: 'Master ask you somethin', you drops your eyes 'n' look at your toes. If you know answer, give it. If'n you don't know, answer anyway! More niggers get whipped for not knowin' than for bein' mistook.' You tell your children: 'Don't look up at that white man, and whatever he do, don't dare sass.' How many you?"

He removed his glasses and rubbed the bridge of his nose. "Mommas and papas, how many of you say that?"

Thomas Bonneau got up to say, "Childrens get hurt if they doesn't."

"Ah, Mister Bonneau. Happy to hear your Biblical interpretations. But you right, the Master, he got the slave block and he got the gun and the workhouse and Mr. Bullwhip. But 'Behold, the Day of the Lord is comin',' Mr. Bonneau. Behold . . ."

He closed his big fist and stared at it. "I been carpenter long time. I builds plumb and level, same as ary white. I knows how to hang a plumb bob or check a level. That brown-skinned nigger there, Jehu Glen, he the best stair builder in the Low Country, better'n ary white man. You know it, he know it, white man know it—why Jehu got to bow on the street?

"You heard 'bout that Thomas Jefferson—White Master were President? Well, he were. President of all these United States. Last week I workin' on Master Bee's piazza 'count them walls rottin' from inside out! White carpenters run Bee's guttering inside them walls; inside 'em 'stead of outside! 'count that how Thomas Jefferson done it. And I bet you a dime Thomas Jefferson's walls rottin' too. Ain't one Low Country nigger carpenter so stupid he put guttering inside the walls, where guttering get plugged up and you can't unplug it. Take a white man do that!" He shook his head sorrowfully. "Sometimes, I think Masters should be bowing to *us*."

Laughter started as a chuckle in the back of the room but was deep throated before he silenced it. "I was tearin' guttering out so to put it on the outside where a man could get to it if it clogged, but old Master Bee's servant, Archimedes—you all know him: brown-skinned man goes to that St. Philip's Episcopal. Archimedes fussin' at me. 'You don't want do that,' he say. 'White man put it there. Must be right.'

"Gutters can't leak because a white man hung 'em?

"Mercy!

"Archimedes, he start out same as you 'n' me. He get he first learnin' on he Momma's knee. Afterwards Master tell him so and Master tell him such. Master tell Archimedes, 'You don't know nothin', and who argue with Master, who got all them guns and workhouses and bullwhips!"

He paused with the air of a man possessing the truth and whispered, "Because you Master don't make you right! Because you slave don't make you less'n a man!"

Vesey lifted his eyes to the low plank ceiling as if he wasn't talking to them, wasn't talking to anyone in the room. "I will not step into the street for ary white man. You knows I won't. Twict I been sent for 'taste of sugar.' Twict I felt that old bullwhip.

"But I ain't stupid and I ain't lazy and I ain't no boy. I'm a man in my prime." His laugh was a snort. "Well, maybe a *little* past my prime."

Chuckles at Vesey's self-deprecation. Some cramped muscles shifted, and an old man coughed.

He pointed his forefinger like Moses's staff. "You can't pretend to be a boy 'thout becomin' a boy. You can't pretend to be stupider than the white man 'thout becomin' stupider than what the white man is. Who you pretends you is, you comes to be.

"The nigger what bows to the Master on the street, who acts the fool, who forgets who he am, that man a slave." He shut his Bible. "He deserve to be a slave!"

He whispered into the silence, "The Day of the Lord is at hand."

They slipped out by twos and threes. Around the corner, Thomas Bonneau grasped Jehu's sleeve. "We gots to pretend. We don't pretend, we whipped or worse. Sometimes I think Denmark Vesey tryin' to get us killed."

Jehu replied, smugly Ruth thought, "Who you pretends you is, you comes to be."

Thomas Bonneau let go Jehu's sleeve and studied his face before nodding slowly and not angrily. The Bonneaus never returned to the Bible studies or the Cow Alley church, and the Glens never again sailed in Thomas's skiff or ate together, and the Bonneaus completed their tabby house without their help. Sundays after church Jehu, Ruth, and Martine ate on the riverbank, though never on White Point, where only white folks could go.

———

The social season that winter was disappointing. Money was tight and rice prices poor. The Ravanels had less work for Ruth. Although Frances Ravanel recommended her to Mrs. Puryear, after a lengthy interview Mrs. Puryear offered suggestions on how Ruth might economize. "One needn't eat beef every supper," she advised. "Torn socks can be mended." Although Middleton had asked Jehu to draw up plans for renovating the Broughton farmhouse and Jehu had spent weeks doing so, Langston Butler decided against the project and, as work had not been commenced, paid nothing. When Jehu objected, young Butler told him he might be rehired when rice prices were better, if he stopped whining.

No work meant more Bible classes, and Jehu often didn't come home until after midnight. The Watch came to know the Bible students by sight and didn't demand their passes.

Hercules didn't go. "That Vesey, he got too much reasonin' for me," he told Ruth. "What he say be right what but it be wrong too. 'Sides, I got me colt to train; he gonna be a bell ringer."

"Hercules . . ." Ruth wanted to talk about it.

"I mean this colt, he special. It's like him and me, we was born twins."

Pearl came to childbed in February. Ruth, Dolly, and Mrs. Ravanel managed the birthing, but Pearl's infant died within hours. Ruth and Pearl's intimacy died with the poor thing. Pearl quit the Ravanels and moved across the river to her tabby house. Ruth hardly ever saw the Bonneaus anymore.

The late-night Bible studies were too much for Martine, so Ruth and her daughter quit going.

Not many women had attended, and Ruth was the last. Jehu was relieved. "Bible learnin'," he said, "is for men."

When Jehu came home so late, Ruth pretended she hadn't waked. She pretended she didn't hear Jehu pacing and muttering in the other room.

But she was grateful for her husband's return, which broke her familiar dream of crouching inside a manioc basket with blood seeping through weave.

Churchgoing Shoes

THE SUN WAS high in the sky, the better produce had been sold, and stall keepers were loading to go home.

Ruth had her eye on a plump yam earlier buyers had overlooked. Sometimes good produce was hidden by worse; sometimes a stall keeper held a fine yam back too late. Ruth's yam was without blotches or tine scars. It had been dug properly.

"You best make up you mind." Empty baskets were already stacked in the stall keeper's wheelbarrow. "It sundown afore I gets home."

"How much you askin' for that puny, unripe yam?" Ruth inquired for the third time.

"Half dime."

"I can buy better'n that for half dime."

The stall keeper yawned and tapped her mouth. She set her basket of unsold peppers atop the empty baskets.

"It's hard times, Missus," Ruth said. "My man ain't worked since afore Christmas. I got two cent for your yam."

Pursing her lips, refusing to meet Ruth's eye, the woman placed three unsold cabbages in the pepper basket, reshuffling so the peppers were on top. She added two less desirable yams. "I gots to push this barrow up the road home and push it back afore daybreak. This here yam be just as good tomorrow as today. Come morning, fine yam fetch a dime. I gots children and a hungry man. You don't buy yam, maybe I cook it myownself!"

Ruth fingered the pennies in the pocket of her apron. Boil it up, dice it for Jehu and Martine, and eat the skin and clingings herself. She craved that yam.

So she didn't turn at the shout. Shouts is shouts. But a scream snapped her head around. Scream was the Dread she'd been expecting. Dread am Come! Dread be Here Today!

Dread was a white rider galloping full tilt down the aisle between the stalls. When his horse jumped a barrow, a hoof clipped it, barrow upset, and red potatoes spinnin' and rollin' on the cobblestones. Coloreds dashing for safety. A drover jerked a mule bucking in his shafts and kicking the wagon box: *crash-thump*.

The horseman had his horse's mane in one hand and his saber in the other, and he was galloping straight at Ruth as if she were the very one he'd come for. Almost too late, he slammed heels into his stirrups and hauled his reins, and his fat white horse dropped onto its haunches and stopped. White boy on a fat white horse. The horse was sweat-slaked, the rider's eyes were wide and unfocused. "Ho!" His screech started high-pitched and cracked. "Ho! Return to your Masters! Ho! Governor Bennett's orders!"

His green Charleston Rangers jacket was one button misbuttoned, and the bird-handled pistol in his sword belt was perilously ready to leave its nest. "Return to your Masters!" he screeched again. "Any niggers found on the street will be considered fair game!" He stood in his stirrups to wave his sword over his head.

Ruth's stomach lurched, but she produced a smile. "Young Master Puryear, how you been?"

Cathecarte Puryear glowered as if a secret had been betrayed.

"I Ruth, young Master, Miss Penny Ravanel's Mammy."

He didn't hear. Perhaps he couldn't. His eyes roamed everywhere and nowhere. His white knuckles gripped the hilt of a bright saber, which yearned for flesh to bite. In an awful monotone he asked Ruth, "Why do you wish to murder us?"

"Murder you, Master? I hardly knows you."

"I've been a good Master," Cathecarte insisted. "I never, never sent a servant for 'a little sugar.' I never have. I never took any nigger wench against her will." Sweat glistened on his cheeks. The curved tip of his saber flicked like a serpent's tongue. Ruth felt emptiness at her back like a cool breeze. The stall keeper had abandoned her barrow and vanished.

Ruth daren't take her eyes off the young militiaman. His fat horse was careless with its hooves, but Ruth daren't back away.

"Ho!" Cathecarte Puryear shouted to the empty market. "Return to your Masters!"

Wheelbarrows lay overturned. A droverless mule had dragged his cart where he could nibble spilled beans. Palmetto fronds drooped in the heat.

Sweat escaped Ruth's armpit and trickled cold down her side. "Some trouble this mornin', Master Cathecarte?" she inquired brightly.

"Trouble! You goddamned right!" (Reflexively) "Excuse my language." He sheathed his sword, took a deep shuddering breath, and quoted, " 'A soldier braves death for a fanciful wreath . . .' " His fingers wandered over his misbuttoned jacket. "Return to your Master," he said calmly.

"Mistress Ravanel?"

"Who? To your damn Mistress, whoever she may be. Any nigger found on the streets is liable to . . . liable." He unbuttoned a button and rebuttoned it.

"You gonna have to start from scratch, Master," Ruth said.

He looked at her but didn't see her.

"The buttonin', I mean. You gots do 'em one at a time, bottom to top." Her hand snaked out to take that plump yam and jam it in her apron. "I done paid for this," Ruth lied. "This am my yam."

"A yam," he said. After a moment he mused, "On this day, in solitary grandeur, a yam . . ."

"Master?"

"Poetry. The sublime Byron as corrupted by a humble Charleston poetaster."

"Master, you don't got be afraid. I ain't gonna hurt you."

He shook the cobwebs out of his head. "You? Hurt me? 'All we see is but a dream within a dream'? Go. My patience has limits."

Apron rucked up to her hips, Ruth dashed across town fast as she could, and she wasn't the only runner. Blacks and whites fled public places. Saddled, bridled horses were dragged into stables, doors slammed behind coaches, shutters pulled shut, and doors double-bolted.

The yam would feed her family, and Ruth still had two pennies and a half dime. Ruth fought a strong urge to discard the yam. Yes, she'd stolen it, but that stall keeper wasn't coming back. She'd abandoned her barrow, hadn't she? Ruth might have stolen more, but she hadn't. Ruth turned in to Anson Street. The yam in her apron pocket was guilty-heavy as a brick.

She wouldn't name the Dread. The spirits had warned Dread was coming, but she hadn't heeded. Now she murmured, "We get by like we always has," but her mouth was dry as dry bones.

Ruth hesitated at the door. Her own door! Sun had cracked the blue paint around the doorframe, and chips flaked off. Why had she neglected to renew it? She choked down a moan and leaned her forehead against warm, rough wood.

Her hand balked at the latch. In her entire life Ruth had feared nothing more than opening her own front door. Dread was waiting inside.

Sun streaming through the window formed a yellow-white rectangle on the far wall. Jehu sat with his back in a corner, head lowered into his hands. Martine was clamped to her father's knee.

When her eyes met her husband's, Ruth wanted to flinch. Tears spewed.

"All us coloreds," Jehu said dreamily. "Goin' out free. Think on it, darlin'. My own shop. Might be I'd hire a 'prentice. Rich folks in Haiti got to have staircases too, don't you know? No more bowin' and scrapin' 'count he white and I nigger. White man and colored man just the same. Good worker gets ahead, lazy man fail." Jehu paused and in Denmark Vesey's familiar voice said, "We is goin' out free."

"Oh, Jehu," Ruth said. "But you is free."

"'Free colored' ain't free. We gonna rise up like Moses and board ships like Noah's Ark and sail on down to Haiti. All us coloreds, black and tan, gonna be *free*. Behold the day of the Lord cometh . . ."

"Who you kill?" Ruth whispered.

"Masters same like Pharaoh: Pharaoh ain't gonna let Moses's people go."

"Mistress Ravanel? Colonel Jack?"

"I knows where Langston Butler sleep."

In a rush Ruth laid their cook pot, forks and spoons, tin cups, Martine's other shirt, Jehu's church jacket, and her church shoes on a blanket she rolled and tied. "You carry Martine. Got to leave your tools."

"No!" he shouted. "Took me six years gather them tools, and I ain't leavin' 'em."

"We sure as hell ain't leavin' Martine!"

When Martine whimpered, Ruth kissed the top of her head. "Honey, you soppin'. I swear Papa ain't been carin' for you."

Jehu's eyes were blank, as if he didn't know who Ruth was.

She managed a smile. "Sweet man, we gots to go. We gots get out of Charleston. We gots to run!"

"But, Ruth," he explained patiently, "we can't run. Gullah Jack come by just now. Somebody done *informed* the Masters, and they called out the militia, and militiamen guardin' city gates. Denmark, he try to run but couldn't get out. We catched, Ruth. They done catched us."

She wanted to slap his face. "You never even been to Haiti. I has!" She found a clean nappy. "Honey, I changin' you and then we gonna eat a fine yam."

In a softer voice Ruth said, "Clay pot can't wrestle iron pot, Jehu. You already free. Why you doin' this?"

The man she loved said, "I couldn't pretend no more."

———

Sunday, they didn't go out to church and Ruth cooked horse oats. Jehu couldn't eat, so she saved his bowl for later.

Jehu honed his chisels and plane blades. Martine clung to her momma; hot, sweaty, and afraid. When Martine finally dozed off, Ruth walked across town; she was the only colored on the street. Although militiamen eyed her suspiciously, she walked fast with downcast eyes, and they didn't stop her. She breathed easier after she slipped through a familiar alley into the Ravanel yard. She rapped on the back door.

Maybe they hadn't heard. She knocked louder.

After a long time there was a footfall, a rustle, and a metallic click. "Who is there?"

"I Ruth, Colonel Jack. I needs ask you."

The door opened just wide enough for Colonel Jack's red-streaked eye to examine her. When he was sure Ruth was alone, he opened the door and lowered the hammer of his pistol. "Ruth."

"I need talk."

"Yes? What might we talk about?"

"Reckon you knows."

"No, I don't 'reckon' I do. I am told our servants planned an insurrection. I believe they planned to murder us in our beds. Perhaps you've heard something about that?"

Ruth nodded numbly and lowered her head for his reproach. Instead, he sighed, shook his head, and ushered her inside. "Goddamned fools. In God's name, what were they thinking?"

The boot room was crowded with hunt jackets and riding boots, and it smelled of leather dressing. Colonel Jack swigged from a flask and breathed fumes on her. "Secrets aren't secrets if more'n one man knows," he said as if instructing a child.

"What will—"

"Oh, they'll be hanged. No doubt about it. Can't go round murdering Masters, you know. Frances and Penny don't venture out, and I go nowhere without pistols. Cook's father, Jarod, was my manservant in the war, but I've locked her in her room and we dine on tinned biscuit. Who can we trust, Ruth? Who? Why are you here? It's not safe for any colored to be wandering about . . ." Colonel Jack gasped. "Dear God. Not your Jehu . . ."

"Colonel Jack . . ."

He held up a hand for silence. "You mustn't. Please don't say anything you wouldn't want a judge to hear."

"But, Colonel . . ."

"Ruth, you're a fine Mammy. Frances sings your praises. Yes, I know, I know . . . But don't put me in a position . . . I cannot be put in a position where—"

"Master Jack, what I gonna do?"

Colonel Jack took another swig, wiped the flask's mouth, and offered it to her. "Best cure I know."

Ruth blinked. "I took the pledge, Master. I temperance."

"Barley does more than Milton can to reconcile God's ways . . . Ruth, I am sorry if . . . No! Don't tell me. There's naught I can do, and I do *not* wish to know!" He wore a lopsided smile. "Since you're here, would you . . . ? Penny is frightened out of her wits . . ."

In the stifling family room, little Penny ran to Ruth and clung to her legs. The shutters were bolted, curtains drawn, and the room stank of a chamber pot wanting emptying. Clothes, dirty and clean, festooned every chair, and Colonel Jack's sword belt and musket lay atop the table.

Frances Ravanel's eyes were red from crying.

"My Jehu—"

Colonel Jack snapped. "Not one more word."

"I—"

"You, Ruth? Surely not you!" Frances gasped.

"No, Missus, I didn't . . . No, I didn't know nothin' 'bout 'nothin'." She wailed, "He never tell me!" Of its own will, Ruth's forefinger twirled a curl of Penny's hair.

"Aren't they Christians?" Miss Frances said. "I told Jack they are Christians and they wouldn't . . . So many whites leave town in the hot months. The Bees are in Southern Pines, my cousins are in Table Rock, North Carolina, so many friends are gone. Do you think the plotters counted on their absence? How clever! Who would have thought illiterate coloreds could concoct such a plot? Or might wish to? Didn't their plot originate in a Christian church? I suppose they were *trying* to be kind: if they rose up when most whites weren't in Charleston, they'd have fewer to . . . murder."

"Missus—"

"Governor Bennett's Rolla; do you know Rolla?"

"No'm. I mean I seen him at church, but we never talked."

"Rolla serves Governor Bennett. Were it up to Jack, our social life would be nothing but racetracks and the Jockey Club, but sometimes I do like to get out, and dear Jack obliges me. Rolla has served me at Governor Bennett's dinners. 'Have more this ham, Missus Ravanel, you always partial to it.' Governor Bennett is fond of Rolla. He considers Rolla part of the Bennett family! When Rolla was arrested, he confessed to his part. Apparently . . ." Mistress Ravanel frowned. "Apparently Rolla is fond of the governor, because Rolla said he couldn't kill the governor with his own hands. He would have asked another plotter to kill him."

The Ravanels were immobilized by amazement. To think. Such a thing.

Ruth whispered, "I never . . ."

Frances used her handkerchief to dry Ruth's cheeks. "I am carrying my second child. I didn' tell you because . . . because . . . Didn't you suspect?"

"No, Mistress."

"I have miscarried twice. I would dearly love to give Penny a sister or brother to play with. I wonder who was designated to murder Penny and me."

"Yes, Mistress." Ruth's hand fell dead at her side, and Penny put her thumb in her mouth and started to cry.

On July 2, Peter Poyas, Ned Bennett, Rolla Bennett, Betteau Bennett, Denmark Vesey, and Jess Blackwood were hanged.

Days passed. Long days passed. Ruth sold her wedding ring for food. Martine didn't whimper or fuss. They didn't go out. They spoke in whispers.

Jehu told Ruth, "Some men never learn what they's cut out to be. I'm lucky." Ruth went into the other room so he couldn't see her cry.

Without speaking of hope because it was too tender, they were starting to hope.

Though militiamen patrolled the streets and the Cow Alley church was locked, the river plantations were back at work. Trunk gates had been raised and rice flooded for the sprout flow. The market reopened, though Charleston Rangers patrolled it and coloreds bought or sold and didn't linger.

Tuesday, they came for Ruth's husband. Although the door was locked, they kicked it in, passing through the blue doorframe as if it didn't matter. Seven white men, armed with swords and pistols: afraid of one unarmed Negro. Their leader demanded, "Jehu Glen?"

"Jehu Glen, stair builder."

"Why should we give a damn about that?"

Jehu's head raised, and for one proud moment, he was her Jehu again. "'Count I do."

When they took her Papa, Martine sobbed so helplessly Ruth thought her heart would break. "You gots to smile," she said. "World treat you better if you smiles. You got to hide whatever you truly feelin', child. They kills you if you don't smile."

That night, while the moon was high in the sky, Ruth left Martine asleep and slipped across Charleston to the Butler yard. Horses snored or shifted their hooves in the stable. Ruth creaked a door open on narrow stairs climbing into darkness.

The moonlit upper room was studded with men sleeping on straw mats. "Hercules?" she whispered.

The nearest sat up, chest gleaming in the moonlight. "Damn, boy," he grumbled. "Now you womens comin' in here!" He lay back with a grunt.

A shape became Hercules, naked except for the rag clutched before his loins. "Damn, gal."

"I . . ."

"I hear 'bout Jehu. I sorry."

"He just wanted—"

Hercules snapped, "We all wants!"

She nodded to the sleepers. "Please."

He followed her down into the moon-drenched yard.

She searched Hercules's face for the impudent boy, but that boy was gone.

"I ain't got nothin' for you, Ruth. You gots to sell Jehu's tools . . ."

"Jehu'll need them when he come home."

Hercules blew a puff of air through his lips and said, "I got two bits hid. I fetch it."

As he clumped around, someone whined, "How's a man to sleep in this damn commotion?"

Another voice said, "Close the goddamned door. Night air bring fever."

When Hercules came down again, he wore ragged britches. "What you heard?" Ruth asked.

"They hanged Preacher Vesey, Peter Poyas . . ."

"I knowed that. Arybody know that. What you heard?"

Hercules paused. "White folks afeared. Don't know who was for Vesey and who wasn't. They afeared. Master Langston, he sleep with pistols by his bed. He done told me 'bout pistols so's I could warn off ary nigger what wants kill him." Hercules's unexpected boyish smile. "I says, 'None of us want kill Master Butler. We satisfied niggers.'"

"What you heard?" Ruth repeated.

"In the sugarhouse they askin' who else was with Vesey. Most don't talk. Vesey never say one word. Peter Poyas said nothin' though they whipped him till he couldn't stand. Gullah Jack says arything they wants hear."

Muggy and hot. A night bird called. Fireflies blinked cheerless messages.

Hercules said, "Might be they sell some of 'em 'stead of hangin'. Master Langston say hangin' coloreds same like hangin' money."

"What was they thinkin'? They surely wasn't thinkin' 'bout my Martine nor none of they wives 'n' children. They surely wasn't."

Hercules shrugged. "Me, I likes horses."

On July 12, Jack (Gullah Jack) Pritchard and Monday Gell were hanged.

Ruth did not know if she dared wear shoes. Her plain churchgoing shoes were sober as Sunday morning but . . .

Her small wood crucifix: she knew better than wearing that. These days, Charleston was not a good place to be a Negro Christian.

Many Masters had been uncomfortable with their slaves' Christianity. Yes, they wanted them weaned from heathen superstitions, and as confessing Protestants Masters believed every Christian should be able to read his Bible, but literate Negroes were dangerous.

A few devout planters overcame their fears, but most contented themselves by preaching to illiterates. A favorite text was St. Paul's: "Servants, be obedient to them that are your Masters according to the flesh, with fear and trembling, in singleness of heart, as unto Christ."

Philadelphians who'd encouraged Reverend Brown's Cow Alley church were (as the Charleston Courier noted), "Philanthropic and openhearted white clergy who excited among our Negroes a spirit of dissatisfaction and revolt." Low Country Masters breathed easier when that Cow Alley church was torn down.

In less fearful times, Ruth's church shoes (and her crucifix) would have signaled the docility Master Butler expected. Though she couldn't scrub off her black, scrubbing proved her desire to do so. Ruth's white blouse was starched stiff as a board, her checked kerchief was spotless. Her full skirt was mouse brown, and she was barefoot. Bringing Martine was chancy—what if the child acted up? But Mercy would be summoned by the child, and Ruth's only hope was Mercy. No matter if young Master Langston Butler hadn't had one single merciful thought in all his days. No matter what *HAD* happened! Only mattered what WOULD!

Coloreds couldn't testify *for* other coloreds, only *against* them. Although most of Vesey's conspirators kept silent, Gullah Jack hadn't been the only man who named others to avoid the hangman.

Ruth hated those men worse than she hated the men who'd hanged Vesey and would judge Jehu this very morning.

Since Ruth couldn't testify before the court, she'd testify outside the court! Martine was scrubbed to a fare-thee-well and her hair plaited in neat cornrows. Whites thought a black in fine clothes was insolent, but Martine was charming. White men could whip a colored man bloody but be charmed by his child.

They waited just down Meeting Street from the Butlers' front door. Martine sat on the curb instructing her rag doll, Silly. Yesterday, Ruth overheard Martine warning, "Silly, be good! Bad niggers hanged!"

The brick sidewalk held the night cool though the morning sun scorched the sky. Inside town houses, servants went tiptoeing from room to room, closing sunny shutters and opening shady ones to catch the errant breeze. What would white folks do without us? Ruth wondered. Who would open and close all those shutters if we wasn't here to do it?

He'd be coming pretty soon. He wouldn't be late. Important Masters would wait on Langston's uncle Middleton, but his unproven nephew must be on time.

Ruth didn't think he'd remember her, though she'd often been in his house with Jehu's dinner bucket. She mustn't think of Jehu or she'd start crying.

Martine sang to her doll: "la, la, la." Ruth felt as if her soul had dried to a nubbin.

Butler materialized so swiftly, it was as if he'd always been there.

In a blink, Ruth's quarry had arrived! "Martine." Her daughter stuck her thumb in her mouth. "Don't forget Silly."

The Young Master wore a conservative frock coat and tight gray trousers. He consulted his watch.

Hercules had promised he'd be five minutes late. He'd kissed Ruth's forehead. "I trainin' Valentine for the Jockey Club races, and I the only one can handle that horse. Master Langston wants to beat Colonel Jack's horse. He'll figure I on purpose late, but he won't whip me until the race. If he wins, he'll forget 'bout that old bull-whip. If he don't, I gets whipped whatever I done for you." Hercules shrugged. "I gets you five minutes, Ruth. Make the best of 'em."

When Ruth fronted him, Langston Butler looked through her as if she was glass. Ruth blurted, "Master Butler!"

When he didn't respond, she babbled, "Master Butler, I Ruth, Jehu Glen's wife. I don't reckon you recollects, but I been fetchin' Jehu's supper when he doin' your fine withdrawing room. Master Butler, you tryin' my Jehu in court today."

His eyes were cold and flat like a snake's. He looked her all up and down. He frowned. Was his frown for her bare feet?

Ruth begged, "Jehu Glen good husband, Master. He li'l Martine papa. Jehu try to do right, but that Vesey . . . that Vesey . . ." Ruth shook her head disgustedly. "Vesey make Jehu crazy. My Jehu, he scared plumb to death of that old man."

The Young Master clicked his watch shut and examined the corner where his carriage must appear.

"You knows my Jehu, Master. He makin' you chair rails. He makin' you plans for you plantation house. My Jehu valuable nigger, Master. Was you to sell Jehu, I believe he'd fetch seven, might be eight hundred dollars. I know he done wrong. I ain't askin' you let him off. No, sir. No, sir. But he worth eight hundred dollars, Master. That's what I'm askin' you, Master. Sell him. Don't let eight hundred dollars go to waste."

As if touched by her plea, young Master Butler reached down to tip her chin, and hard blue eyes searched scared brown ones. "If I am late to court, I will have you whipped for your trouble." His soft voice was the hardest thing Ruth had ever heard. Despite the sun burning her shoulders, his voice made her go cold.

The clatter at her back was Hercules's carriage. "Ge'e up, you scamps!" like Hercules was mad at the horses for makin' him late.

Desperately, Ruth lifted Martine, as if her living child was an argument. "She love her Papa," she begged. "Her Papa all she got."

Martine was startled into silence. Then she wailed.

Disgust rolled over young Master Butler's pale white face. "If your husband is valuable," he said, "think how much more valuable you are: a breeder with proof of fecundity at your side."

Ruth gasped. Langston Butler set his foot on the step and glanced up to let Hercules know he hadn't been fooled.

He closed the door and smiled down at Ruth. "Your husband— Jehu? Didn't he want to hold his head up high?" He nodded. "I believe we can arrange that."

As he drove off, Langston Butler was chuckling.

For years afterward Ruth wondered what she might have said to make things turn out different. Maybe she should have worn her churchgoing shoes.

Martine

On July 26, Mingo Harth, Lot Forrester, Joe Jorre, Julius Forrest, Tom Russell, Smart Anderson, John Robertson, Polydore Faber, Bacchus Hammett, Dick Simms, Pharaoh Thompson, Jemmy Clement, Jerry Cohen, Dean Mitchell, Jack Purcell, Bellisle Yates, Naphur Yates, Adam Yates, Jehu Glen, Charles Billings, Jack McNeil, Caesar Smith, Jacob Stagg, and Tom Scott were hanged.

"WE IS PUT asunder, honey. Ain't no helpin' it," Ruth told Martine. Her daughter wore the best rags Ruth owned, and her shiny hair was braided with green ribbons, for which, last night in the slave jail, Ruth had bartered her supper. "You so pretty, child," Ruth advised. "They gots see how pretty you is. My Martine. They gonna love you just like I do. New Mistress gonna love you to pieces."

With other slaves Ruth and her child waited on the wooden platform next to the stairs of the Exchange House, Charleston's customs house and post office. Horses would be auctioned after the slaves. Diverse merchandise—halters, saddles, hand-cranked grain mills, small tools, and two bright green portmanteaus—would be sold last.

In the morning of the same day Jehu was hanged, the Watch knocked politely on Ruth's broken blue door. Charleston's prudent authorities meant to recoup expenses and confiscated Jehu's tools, Jehu's slave, and her get. His planes, chisels, and measuring implements were sold to a builder, and Jehu's human Capital was delivered to the workhouse for auction.

Ruth concealed her father's fate from Martine but imagined it whenever her tired eyes shut.

The authorities were determined to have an exemplary hanging, and since the gallows couldn't accommodate twenty-four men at once, they were marched to the long stone wall which had protected the city from the British in 1812. Twenty-four hemp ropes were dangled over and attached behind this wall before the condemned mounted low benches in front of it. A rowdy mixed-race crowd pressed against the militiamen as the executioner adjusted nooses. When he kicked the benches away, the drop was insufficient to break necks and twenty-four men began strangling. Most danced, kicking, twirling, and convulsing. Bacchus Hammett lifted his knees to shorten his agonies, and the executioner dispatched several lingerers. Jeremy Clement's young son, Cicero, tried to run to his father, but Cicero was kicked by a militiaman's horse and died later that evening.

———

Ruth's auctioneer, a bearded gentleman in linen coat and spotless broad-brimmed hat, perused sale documents while his merchandise was inspected by buyers and the idly curious. At one planter's request, a young Negro jogged in place, rotated his arms, and squat-jumped to demonstrate his fitness for field work. The young brown-skinned woman next to Ruth bared her teeth and turned this way and that. When a young fellow told her to raise her shift, the auctioneer interrupted, "You buyin', son? Or just want a free peek?"

The auctioneer stacked his papers, cleared his throat, and began his chant. "Now this boy gonna make you some *money*! That's M-U-N-Y: *Money!* This boy can plant, weed, harvest, and thresh. He come from Anderson Plantation, so he knows everything there is to know about Carolina Gold rice."

Ruth felt nothing. Unlike Hell, this day would end.

After the field hand and light-skinned young woman were sold, the auctioneer's helper pulled Ruth and Martine onto the block. Although Ruth had *belonged* to the Forniers, the Evanses, and Jehu, she hadn't really *belonged* to them. She'd been Ruth or Mammy Ruth, which wasn't the same as *belonging to*. Now she was simplified.

Just twenty feet from Ruth and her daughter, a planter entered the Exchange House. He'd be checking a manifest, filing a deed; perhaps he had a letter to mail. He didn't notice them. If Ruth called out, he might be startled or annoyed before he continued about his business. Ruth, Jehu, her beloved Martine: how had they existed? If not in men's eyes, had they shared a small, unassuming place in Le Bon Dieu's heart?

The auctioneer continued, "Gentlemen, I beg your best attention. I have a house servant for sale! Twenty or so years, in tip-top health, an experienced Mammy and housemaid, compliant and hardworking. Gentlemen: she cannot read a seditious word in any language! Not a sick day in her life with a child of five years at her side. The child is well nurtured, has no scars or sores, and her mother's a proven breeder. One or both; how much for the pair? Two hundred and fifty dollars; very well, sir, two fifty to begin. Mr. Smalls has bid two fifty. Truly, gentlemen, she's a bargain. Two fifty? Look at these eyes, examine her straight limbs. Shall I say two sixty? Picture this young woman, uh, *cleaning* your bedchamber."

A ripple of knowing laughter.

"You sir, I have you! Two sixty, I have two sixty. Do I have two seventy-five? Gentlemen, this is a five-hundred-dollar wench if I ever sold one! Now! Two eighty for the best Mammy in the Low Country? Think how your dear wives will thank you for her services!"

His emphasis on this last word rekindled knowing laughter, which some Christians thought in dubious taste.

"Must I sell them for two hundred eighty dollars? Three hundred. Thank you, sir, I have three hundred . . ."

A rustic stepped forward. "She's one of Vesey's devils. Her own husband was hanged Tuesday last. This slut been lying aside him plottin' to cut white throats! Her 'n' him 'n' Satan Vesey. Sir, you reckon my wife'd thank me for clasping this viper to the snow-white bosoms of our innocent babes?"

In the back of the crowd, cheerful horsemen arrived. More interested in bonhomie than the auction, one drained his flask; another clung to his saddle as a precautionary measure.

The auctioneer snapped at the rustic. "Sir! If you please! I have three hundred . . ."

"The hell you have!" the high bidder cried. "You never said she was one of Vesey's!"

"Sir, I have auctioned two score loyal servants caught up in that desperate business. All were thoroughly examined and proved ignorant of Vesey's plot. Left to their own devices—without agitation—our Negroes are happy and respectful. This woman has served fine families in Savannah and Charleston. She is no Judas! No women was involved in Vesey's plot. How could they be? Are not women the weaker vessel?"

The three-hundred-dollar bidder turned his back and walked away. One of the newly arrived horsemen dismounted to shake a pebble out of his boot while his friends offered advice.

The auctioneer had met the "Vesey objection" before. He pursed his lips. "Woman, turn away and remove your shirt."

Ruth's shirt slipped off, light as the faintest breeze. The slaves facing her stared at their feet.

"You see any scar on her back?" the auctioneer asked. "Has she been whipped? No! And I'll tell you why. Because her man was a rebel but this woman knows her place! Face forward."

Young boys giggled. Someone guffawed.

"This wench may not be light enough for the fancy trade, but I have been told by sophisticated gentlemen that blackness cannot be seen in the dark. I had three hundred. I begin anew. Have you two fifty for this young nigra with youngster at her side. Two fifty? Do I hear two fifty?"

"I'll give you forty for the whelp," the interfering rustic sang out. "My cook lost hers and I despise her whinin' 'bout it."

"I have forty, forty. You in the back, sir. Will you go forty-five? Forty it is then. Sold to number sixteen. Sir, my associate, Mr. Mullen, will take your money and provide your bill of sale."

Ruth's hand was entirely numb, so she didn't feel Martine's hand pulled out of it. She didn't hear Martine's wail. She didn't see her go. Ruth had deportment: what she didn't touch or hear or see or feel wasn't.

A moment of blackness, a few seconds dead, her heart scarred forever; that was all there was to it.

A white man hollered, "It's noon, Mr. Smithers! I've come to buy me a horse. When's the goddamned horses?"

"Patience, Jack. I'll sell the niggers, then the horses."

"What the hell! What the hell!" Colonel Jack dismounted and pushed toward the block. "Smithers, you double-dyed son of a . . . Ruth! By God, it is you! What the hell is going on?"

Ruth whispered, "Martine."

"Well, I'll be damned. I'll be damned. Does Frances know 'bout this?"

Ruth shook her head.

Jack opened his pocketbook and thumbed through his money. "Smithers, how's my credit?"

"Jack . . ."

"How much I owe you?"

"You haven't settled for that bay mare. Remember? White fore-leg. Nor that black colt you bought in December. Jack, you know and I know you stole that colt."

Jack jabbed a finger at his chest. "Steal a colt? Smithers, you namin' Jack Ravanel: horse thief?"

Jack's friends laughed, and the fellow holding Jack's horse volunteered, "Be damned if you ain't, Jack. Damned if you ain't."

After more back-and-forth, it was established that Jack's credit was unacceptable until back payments were received, or unless a lien was recorded on certain rice lands, in which case credit would be willingly, nay gladly, reinstituted by Smithers and Sons, auctioneers of slaves, horses, and general merchandise.

"Frances would kill me," Jack said.

Ruth wondered how many words there were and why there were so many.

Colonel Jack worked his horsey pals with entreaties and assurances. He invoked Frances.

Normally, the $217 Jack put together wouldn't buy a young woman with child, but the woman was tainted, the market glutted, the auctioneer wanted to get on, and the child sold separately.

———

Seventy years ago, Jack Ravanel's great-grandfather Nathaniel put his profits from the deerskin trade into indigo land beside the Ashley. Jack's grandfather Josiah was eighteen when he was killed in a duel, and his brother, William, planted rice on the Ravanel lands and built a rambling cypress farmhouse on high ground across the river. Carolina Gold was light, shippable, and kept forever. Napoleon's and Wellington's quartermasters poured money into the Low Country, where newly rich planters gilded their carriages and demolished their grandfathers' workaday farmhouses for "plantation houses" in the Georgian style. The Ravanels were content in their rambling, unfashionable cypress farmhouse between the river road and the river where it was tucked under the back slope of the bluff, and storms howled over harmlessly. While Jack reveled in town with his horsey friends, Frances preferred to be where, as she said, she could hear the birds and termites singing. The family rooms were cheerful with knickknacks, and the dining room wall was covered with Creek Indian blankets in vivid red, green, and orange patterns. Though eighteen full- and half-task hands toiled across the river in Jack's rice fields, only Cook and Mammy Ruth lived in the house. Jack's stable boys and jockeys slept in the annex of a twelve-stall stable.

Colonel Jack was neither a keen nor a careful planter and treated his Negroes as he had white militiamen. Consequently, they worked well under Jack's eye but tended their own gardens, hunted, and fished when Master was away. Jack's friends recommended overseers, but one was too slack, the next too strict, and none lasted for more than a month or two.

Since Jack was often away buying horses, Frances and her daughter, Penny, were each other's best company.

When Jack arrived with Ruth on the back of his horse, his eyes were tight with headache and Ruth was gray as mop water. Her wan smile was terrible.

"We bought us another servant," Jack said. "I know; I know I shouldn't, but how could I let Ruth be sold away?"

"Sold away? Sold? Where . . . ? Of course you couldn't, dear Jack. Come inside, Ruth, you are exhausted."

Penny, who'd rushed out to greet her Mammy and her friend Martine, stuck a thumb into her mouth.

"Fine house," Ruth managed.

"It's an old ruin, but it's home." When she shot a questioning glance at her husband, Jack's frown warned her not to ask about Martine.

Ruth sat stupefied on a front porch glider until Penny found her way into her Mammy's lap, and, after a long time, Ruth stroked her hair.

That night, kneeling beside her bed, Penny prayed that Martine would be well and happy. Ruth's eyes caressed the child so fiercely and tenderly, Frances couldn't look.

In the morning, Jack left for Beaufort, where a widow might be selling her husband's horses.

By week's end, Ruth was able to sleep, sometimes for thirty minutes at a time.

Jack was brave enough to face bullets, but not this. When Colonel Ravanel wasn't traveling, he stayed in town.

Ruth did everything Frances asked as she melded with her drab brown shift and worn green kerchief. Not infrequently Frances would look up and wonder when had Ruth come into the room and how long had she been sitting there.

She invited no remark, and when Frances tried to converse, Ruth's wan smile stifled it as a blanket smothers fire. Only Penny mentioned Martine, in the child's bedside prayers. Though neither grown-up remarked, they would have noticed if one night Penny forgot.

Fever was often fatal to Low Country newcomers. Native-born whites and coloreds—whose forebear knew the fever in Africa—often contracted the disease in milder form. They'd all had it at one time or another, and two or three days' distress until the fever ran its course was what Frances expected one morning when Penny couldn't get out of bed and her forehead was on fire.

Ruth dosed her with quinine bark tea and a decoction of radish leaves, and for three days Penny improved. Next day, when Frances thought Penny would leave her bed, her daughter complained of headache and the fever was back. By nightfall the child was so weak she had to be carried to the chamber pot.

Frances sent for Jack and the doctor. "Fever is particularly dangerous for children," the doctor said, telling them what every Low Country parent knew.

Penny lay in bed burning up. Her mother, Ruth, and Jack took turns bathing her with cool cloths.

After a long night with his child, Jack found Ruth sitting blank faced in the kitchen and burst out, "Prime young woman can't just quit. Frances needs you, Ruth."

Ruth's eyes were murky and flat.

"God damn it!" Jack whispered his shout. "Penny needs you!"

Ruth smiled her too-familiar awful smile. "Oh, Colonel Jack. Is so many needs me."

———

Her parents or Ruth were at Penny's bedside day and night, and if their prayers didn't cure the child, something did, because come December a pale-faced Miss Penny Ravanel enjoyed a quiet Christmas and a new rocking horse she named Gabby.

Jack returned to town for the races, where Langston Butler's Valentine defeated the favorite and Butler brought Valentine's trainer into the clubhouse, where James Petigru toasted him. "Coloreds understand horses better than we because coloreds have animal natures." Hercules was not a social success. A black man, even the jokey horse trainer, made other Masters uneasy, and Master Butler sent his servant back to the stables.

Jack returned to his plantation for the planting and was underfoot in the house. He told Frances he felt like an "extra teat round here."

"If you were 'round here' more frequently, perhaps you'd be a more necessary appendage."

Frances joined Jack's laughter.

He nuzzled his wife's neck. "Our house has never been so gloomy. Why aren't we happy. Is it Ruth?"

"It hasn't been a year since Ruth came to us. She does more than I ask and never complains. Penny adores her. Our daughter reads to Ruth every night."

"Yes, but . . ."

"Our friends hanged her husband and sold her child."

Jack shrugged. "Vesey would have murdered every white in Charleston. He would have murdered Penny and you."

"Martine?"

"Madame, that was regrettable but has ever been so." He offered Frances a glass of sherry which she refused, and she refused her husband as well.

———

Heavy spring rains drove the Ashley out of its banks. Levees were breached and trunk gates washed away. Jack worked to exhaustion until he heard of a Virginia stallion who was six seconds faster than Valentine in the mile. He kept on with the repairs for three more days. Plantation work undone when Jack left would remain undone.

Penny wouldn't let Ruth be. "Ruth, do you see those ducks? Why do they fly in a V?" "Ruth, if Gabby was a real horse, how fast would he be? I *know* he's not a real horse, silly!"

As her mother had read to her when she was small, before she said her prayers Penny read to the silent black woman at her bedside.

"Farmer Meanwell, the father of little Margery and of her brother, Tommy, was for many years a rich man. He had a large farm, and good wheat fields, and flocks of sheep, and plenty of money. But his good fortune forsook him, and he became poor. He had to get people to lend him money to pay the rent of his house, and the wages of the servants who worked on his farm.

"Things went on worse and worse with the poor farmer. When the time came at which he should pay back the money lent him, he was not able to do so. He was soon obliged to sell his farm; but this did not bring him money enough, so he found himself in a worse plight than ever.

"He went into another village, and took his wife and two little children with him. But though he was thus safe from Gripe and Grasp-All, the trouble and care he had to bear were too much for the ruined man. He fell ill, and worried himself so much about his wife and children that he grew worse and worse, and died in a few days. His wife could not bear the loss of her husband, whom she loved very much. She fell sick too, and in three days she was dead.

"So Margery and Tommy were left alone in the world, without either father or mother to love them or take care of them. The parents were laid in one grave; and now there seemed to be no one but the Father of orphans, who dwells beyond the sky, to pity and take care of the homeless children."

Penny snuggled deeper into her bed. "Mammy, how does God let such things happen!"

For a time, Mammy couldn't speak. "It just a book, honey. Folks put all manner things in books what never happened."

"But they *can* happen, can't they?"

Like someone reciting a half-forgotten poem, Ruth whispered, "You so pretty, child . . . They gots see how pretty you is . . . They gonna love you just like I do."

After a deep silence, Penny decisively closed her book. "Kiss me, Mammy. Give me good dreams."

———

Although Frances made inquiries, Martine had not been sold into genteel circumstances. Apparently Martine's purchaser was an Up-country farmer unconnected to Low Country kinship circles.

Frances's inquiries bore fruit one August noon when songbirds panted and no shade was deep enough. Sweat dripped onto the letter from a third or perhaps fourth cousin on her mother's side who sent most affectionate regards and hoped to visit should they ever stir from their dullish Up-country homestead to the grand and wicked city she'd heard so much about. Sweat blurred the ink, and Frances set the letter on the rattan table beside her glass of tea. Before Frances could decide—anything—Ruth came onto the porch. "Penny nap for little while."

Frances met her servant's eyes unflinchingly. She touched the note.

Ruth's gaze attached to the folded paper as if it were Christ's dying promise. "Martine . . . ?"

She had her answer in Frances Ravanel's face. "Oh, I knowed it, missus. I knowed my Martine dead. No baby livin' long without she Momma. Babies in terrible rush get back to Heaven. Only they Mommas can keep 'em here."

When Frances stood to embrace her, Ruth raised a hand. "No, missus," she said. "Ain't nothin' I be needin'. I don't want for nothin'."

"Ruth, I'm . . ."

"Yes, missus. I thanks you so much. I reckon we both is."

The rest of that summer, the broad hospitable porches of the old farmhouse offered airless heat and sorrow.

———

One morning so early Frances was still in her robe, a great hallooing proved to be patrollers returning Jack's runaway jockey, Ham, and expecting a libation with their fifty-dollar reward. An annoyed

Frances fetched both. After their second brandy, guffawing and friendly, they offered to chain the runaway. Perhaps they should take him for a little sugar?

"I don't believe that will be necessary."

The patrollers rode off into the sun's hot hard eye. "Why, Ham?" Frances asked. "Haven't we treated you fairly?"

"I reckon."

"Then why? Damn it! You will answer me!"

"Master Butler, he sellin' my Martha south. No tellin' where she goin'."

Two months before, Ham had jumped the broomstick with a Broughton Plantation house servant. "Master say Martha 'sassy' so she goin'. Do me how you will, missus. Whip me or sell me or anything. My heart broke and I wants to die."

Frances lost patience. "How dare you think you're the only one with a broken heart!"

———

Jack bought four Tennessee horses and sold them for profit. He didn't know why he bothered with rice. He wasn't no damn planter. Yes, he'd cross to the plantation first thing tomorrow. Yes, he'd hire a good overseer. Yes, he knew some of his trunk gates still needed repair. Yes, he'd talk to Langston about Ham's woman. "I'll talk to him. It won't change his mind, but I'll talk to him."

"Perhaps you can buy Martha."

Snort. "Langston will want more than she's worth. More than she'll fetch from the slave speculator. We don't need any more servant problems."

"True, Jack, but when you do find your great horse, you'll want a jockey to ride it."

Jack bought Martha, and Ham promised he'd win his next race, sure. Jack could bet on it.

Ruth was all the time smiling. Her bones jutted her skin, and her breasts shrank and disappeared. She walked as if walking hurt her, but she was all the time smiling. She said the most cheerful things in a voice as dead as dead can be. Mistress and servant inhabited the same house like strangers. They devised patterns so they didn't encounter each other. One day, Frances lost patience. "Ruth, you must eat. You need your strength. Penny needs your strength."

With her cheerful, ghastly smile, Ruth said, "Or what, Missus? You sends me for a little sugar? Missus, I gots too many on the other side. I lonesome."

———

Jack was somewhere in North Georgia when Penny's fever came back. The doctor said, "She has the great advantage of youth" and "Most unusual." Ham drove Frances to Broughton Plantation, where she found Dolly nursing in the infirmary. Frances was blunt. "Mammy Ruth wants to die."

"Le Bon Dieu want Mammy Ruth?"

"I suppose . . . I suppose we'd have to ask Him."

Impatiently, "No, missus. We asks spirits so they asks Le Bon Dieu. They interferes for us."

Frances thought Dolly meant *intercedes,* but perhaps not. "Can you . . . ?"

Stoutly, "I good Christian, Missus. I don't heed no conjurin'."

"My Penny . . . I . . ." As if someone else, some spirit, spoke in her voice, Frances said, "If Ruth dies, my daughter will die. I know that as fact."

In the end, Dolly sighed and said she'd do what she could.

Ham drove the woman into town for certain purchases and borrowings and they didn't return until dark. With a pungent, nose-wrinkling flour sack of mysterious bulges tucked under her arm, Dolly asked Frances, "You wants to help?"

This gap-toothed smiling woman chilled Frances Ravanel's Protestant soul.

"I needs someone help."

"Ah . . . why not Ham? One of your . . . your own."

"Ham." She dismissed the man. "Ham want love potion. That only thing he want. Make he wife act the fool."

After Ham's unfoolish wife, Martha, closed the door behind the two women, Frances, who sometimes drank a glass of sherry at Christmas, filled a tumbler to the brim with the dark sweet whiskey Colonel Jack brought from Kentucky.

The second tumbler shut her ears to the very odd sounds behind that door, which as a Christian she didn't want to think about, neither the singing nor the chants nor the multiple voices.

She betook herself to Penny's bedroom and fell asleep in the chair beside her daughter.

The morning sun tinted the river mist pink, and a beam found the window of the old farmhouse. Frances jerked awake to touch her daughter's cool forehead. Penny's blue eyes opened wide. "Momma? Water?" Frances poured from the pitcher at her bedside and helped Penny drink.

"I had the strangest dreams . . ." Penny said. "But I can't 'member . . ."

A tear tracked Frances's cheek.

She helped her daughter into a clean nightshirt. "Whew." Penny giggled. "I smell bad!"

Frances opened the shutters to the river breeze. "I'm so grateful," she said.

Penny made a face. "Why are you grateful for that?"

"We'll get you washed after a little while."

Frances took a pot of tea upstairs and knocked on Ruth's door. She heard a rustle inside. A grunt. Feet hit the floor.

Dolly's shirtwaist was pulled out and her braids were undone.

Her face was soft, as if she'd spent the night making love. Behind her, the room was dark with drawn curtains and shutters. Odd things hung from wall sconces, and Dolly smelled powerfully of pungent, musky spices. Frances couldn't tell whether one woman or two lay in Ruth's bed. "It be 'nother morning, don't it," Dolly announced. "Missus, you ask Ham drive me home? I too tuckered walk."

"Ruth?"

"Oh, Ruth she just need say good-bye. We can't let 'em go, withouts we say good-bye. That tea for me?"

Dolly took the tea and closed the door. Her mother helped Penny onto the porch, where Cook brought Penny's oatmeal, which she ate as if nothing had ever tasted so good.

They watched the morning for an hour or two, and it didn't escape them, not a single minute.

Ham hitched up to drive Dolly home.

Ruth came out, rubbing her eyes like she'd had the deepest, happiest sleep. "'Lo, Miss Penny. How you?"

"I feel awfully weak."

"I weak too. But I cares for you now."

"Ruth, will you take breakfast?"

Ruth nodded. "Miss Penny?"

"I couldn't eat another bite!" Penny proudly announced.

But the child sat with them while Ruth ate and barges loaded with unshocked rice were poled up the river to the winnowing mill. Birdsongs punctuated the boatmen's solemn chants.

"It is all so ordinary," Frances said.

"There's ordinary 'n' ordinary," Ruth replied, helping herself to another hoecake.

"What . . . ?"

"All my days spirits been askin' after me, but I runs from 'em. I ain't no African, I christened at St. John the Baptist Catholic Church."

"I hadn't known . . ."

"I never like Gullah Jack, but Dolly fetch Jack talk to me. Jack don't want me up there bossin' t'other spirits round. I gots stay here for a spell."

"Then thank God for Jack."

"Gullah Jack no better spirit than he were a man." Ruth took a breath. "Reckon I live long as childrens need me. Mammy do what needs done."

———

Higher rice prices swelled the purses of good planters and poorer alike. Jack bought three horses, one on the heels of another, and paid top dollar, but, despite Ham's best efforts, each horse came in second when it was important to be first.

Jack tried to buy Hercules, who'd trained some of the horses who'd beaten his, and to this end he spent hours listening to old Middleton Butler's reminiscences of traveling with the South Carolina delegation to the constitutional convention. "I have the honor of being the patriot who kept slavery in the United States Constitution," Middleton averred. "The Yankees needed South Carolina's votes. Tom Jefferson, aloof and so very proud of his learning; John Adams and his harridan wife; oh yes, they all deferred to Broughton Plantation's humble rice planter." Middleton cackled and coughed until he was red in the face.

Langston invariably saw Jack off. "Uncle'll never sell Hercules, and neither will I," he declared.

"We'll see, won't we?" Jack replied cheerfully.

While Jack flattered Middleton, Ruth and Penny visited the stable yard, where Hercules flirted with Ruth.

Hercules told her, "Ruth, I think we be good with each other."

She said, "I had me a man. I don't ever want 'nother."

It wasn't so much what she said as how she said it. Hercules drew himself up, whistled, and, though he kept flirting, he didn't mean it the same.

Frances Ravanel gave birth to a son, an active, colicky child who wailed for his mother's breast even after he was fed.

"Baby Andrew, you gonna be a terrible man," Ruth said. "But the womens gonna love you."

Middleton died without succumbing to Jack's blandishments. Though his heir sold two hundred slaves to satisfy his uncle's creditors, Hercules was not among them. Two months afterward, Langston married fifteen-year-old Elizabeth Kershaw, who, as William R. Kershaw's sole heir, was as rich as she was plain. Elizabeth produced an heir ten months after her nuptials. The Negroes made much of the fact that the firstborn son was born with his caul in his fist: a powerful if ambiguous portent.

Things went on as they do for planter families, their excitements and travails dictated by crops, storms, and the vagaries of distant markets.

When Penny was seven, she had another bout with fever, but it came and went after thoroughly frightening her parents.

It was the middle of August, and nobody could remember such a rainy summer. Langston Butler came by, and he and Jack sat on the porch talking for an hour.

"What was all that about?" Frances wondered.

"Our fields down by the river—those fields where Great-grandfather grew indigo—Langston claims 'Dear Elizabeth wants them.' Apparently Elizabeth has a mad notion she and Langston would picnic on the riverbank." Jack snorted. "Come live with me and be my love, and we will all the pleasures prove, that valleys, groves, hills, and fields, woods or steepy mountain yields . . ."

"Thank you, Jack. What does Langston really want?"

"Langston's ambitions are actually quite limited. He only covets 'what's adjacent.' I've already sold more land than I should. I wish you managed our business affairs. You're more sensible than I."

"Jack," Frances said, "you have made me very happy."

"I never could figure what you saw in a horse-crazed, worn-out soldier like me."

"Whatever else you may be, Jack, *worn-out* is not the word I'd choose."

———

In the Low Country to say a man was a poor rider was to say he was a poor sort of a man. Thieves were jailed, horse thieves were hanged. Horses raced at road junctions, livestock markets, political and patriotic celebrations: wherever horses and betting men came together. The largest and grandest races were at Charleston's Washington Racecourse during Race Week, which attracted fine horses, jockeys, owners, and spectators from the South, the West, and even Yankeedom. New York papers advertised "excursions for ladies and gentlemen" with swift passage on an up-to-date vessel, deluxe accommodations in Charleston, and precious tickets to the Jockey Club grandstand for the important matchups.

Wagering was passionate and purses stupendous. Langston Butler's Valentine was expected to repeat last season's win.

That fall, Jack was drinking in the damp, unhappy clubhouse of the Knoxville racetrack. Despite pouring rain, the race had been run as scheduled and the horse Jack had optioned fell, crippling his black jockey. The horse was shot even before the jockey (who was blamed for the accident) was dragged off the track. Glum Jack Ravanel perched on a stool watching drizzle through a rain-speckled window whose broad sill held his cigar and tumbler. Rain lashed the clubhouse, and a smoky fire added that reek to the funk of wet wool clothing.

Jack owed so much, and this year's rice crop was worse than the last. He swirled the dark liquid around as if wisdom might manifest herself in the fumes. Horses, horses, horses.

At a table inches behind his back, two locals were speaking confidentially. "I'ze told you about Red Stick."

"Well, I guess you have." A whisper was very faint. "Jesus Christ. Four miles in eight minutes ten."

"Junior says Andy's gonna sell him."

"Oh yeah. You bet. Horse like that."

"Ain't I Junior's cousin, ain't I? Wasn't we tads together down on Mutton Creek? Not many knows 'bout ol' Red Stick. Andy plays his cards close to his vest."

As if alerted by Jack's stiffness, the other said, "Hush now, Henry. This ain't neither time nor place."

Two days later, Colonel Jack Ravanel trotted up a lane between blooming cotton fields and surmounted the rise above a two-story brick home, more farmhouse than the mansion of a Southern grandee. After the boy took his horse, Jack was welcomed in the entry hall by a buxom Negress. "I'ze Hannah, sir. Can you tell me your business or who you be?"

"Colonel Jack Ravanel. I served with the general."

"Oh, he be glad see you, sir. Have a seat, sir. General Jackson always got time for he old soldiers."

Jack didn't wait long. Jackson was a short, wiry man whose head was too big for his body, which had—as he said—been "kicked about." The general carried two bullets as duel mementos, and not two years before, he'd won election to the Presidency of the United States but been cheated out of it. He never once complained.

"Why, Colonel, Colonel Jack Ravanel. So good. So good. What brings you up from that Carolina den of iniquity?"

"I am a reformed man, General."

"You haven't taken 'the pledge'?"

"I'm reformed, General, not dead."

"Then you must try my whiskey. Come into my office."

In that small room, Jackson introduced Jack to Mr. Harmon of New York and Mr. Fitzhugh of Virginia: his "advisers." Jackson's whiskey was as excellent as the conversation was restrained. The presentation gold sword on Jackson's desk had been awarded by the Tennessee legislature to their major general of militia.

Jackson's advisers yearned to be giving advice; their faces glowed with the need.

Jack said, "General, there are many very fine horses along the Cumberland. I believe you own most of them."

"I keep a few that are no better than crowbait." Jackson bared his teeth in a grin and turned to the New Yorker. "Do you know horses, Mr. Harmon?"

The Yankee pursed his lips impatiently.

"What a shame. Colonel Ravanel, if you've come to see horses, I'd prefer to show them myself, but these gentlemen won't be put off. If you don't mind . . ."

Hannah sent a boy to fetch Overseer Ira Walton, who arrived in a dust cloud of hurry. The overseer was annoyed at being plucked from the cotton harvest.

As they rode to the stables, Walton asked Jack how he could get a crop with coloreds who had no respect for the white man. "You cannot coddle niggers, sir," he said. "General Jackson's harvest must be shipped on time. No coddling, sir." Walton's eyes swiveled to every unfinished task and every scant deviation in what seemed to Jack to be one of the tidiest, busiest plantations he'd ever seen. At the stables, the overseer cried, "Dunwoodie! Get out here, you rascal! A Negro shoeing a horse didn't look up, but a light-skinned colored stepped out, shading his eyes against the sun. "Master Walton, how can I serve you?"

The man's words were deferential, but something in the tone . . .

"Show Colonel Ravanel our horses," the overseer snapped. "I am presently occupied."

"Why sure you am, Overseer. Don't know how no crop get made 'thout you."

Unsmiling white face, smiling black face; the white man cursed, jerked his horse's bit, and spurred toward the work.

"Ol' harvest needin' plenty 'tention," Dunwoodie said solemnly.

"The prudent overseer is a pearl without price," Jack said as solemnly.

"Well then, Master Colonel Ravanel, whyfor you here? What can I show you?"

"I wish to see Red Stick."

Dunwoodie whistled soft and low. "That one."

"I believe he's fast."

"Oh, yes, sir. He fast."

"But . . ."

"Ain't no buts 'bout it. Red Stick fastest Thoroughbred I ever seed, and the general don't keep no slow horses."

"But . . ." Jack invited.

Slow smile. "Might be you see for yourself. Might be you don't. He in back pasture with our geldings."

Chanting field hands scythed and shocked hay in the field beside a meadow of beautiful horses.

"How happy they are," Jack said.

"Red Stick he aggravate Bertrand and Bertrand chase after him and Red Stick let him almost catch up, almost. Bertrand fall for trick every time."

Some horses are so beautiful they are profound. The sun glistened on Red Stick's back.

Swallows swooped and dipped for insects the hay cutters dislodged. A field hand started a call, and others responded, a duet as sorrowful and ancient as their work.

RUTH'S JOURNEY

Then the horse turned his head, snorted, and charged the men at the fence. He came with hurricane force, all thudding hooves and fluttering mane until Jack understood he wasn't going to stop and cocked to jump for his life when Red Stick dropped onto his haunches and *did* stop. Dust, manure, and grass clumps in Jack's face. Jack sneezed and found himself staring into two limpid brown eyes inches from his own: "Who you?"

Red Stick was a roan with black mane, tail, and fetlocks. Slender neck, perfect balance, high-set tail, gentle croup, stout cannon bones, flaring nostrils, and wary intelligent eyes.

"He sayin' hello," Dunwoodie said.

"Hello." Jack rubbed the great brownish red nose, and the horse snorted, tossed his head, shook himself, and ran to the others, kicking his heels. Jack was smitten. His heart beat like a young man's, and it was hard swallowing. "Four miles in eight minutes ten."

"Clocked him myself."

"Out of Bertrand."

"By Trifle."

"Why in God's name does the general wish to sell him?"

The colored man made a face. "He don't hardly."

"Then?"

"General Jackson busy right now 'count he means to be President. He ain't havin' no time for no horses." Dunwoodie smiled. Colonel Jack swallowed. Sweat started under his arms.

"Red Stick broke to rider or chaise." Dunwoodie snorted. "Chaise! Might as well hitch Mr. Congreve rockets to it."

Colonel Jack Ravanel whispered, "He'll fetch a pretty penny."

Dunwoodie grinned a hard grin. "Oh, yes, sir. For sure he will."

———

Alone after the political men had departed, General Jackson poured Jack more of his "very pleasant" whiskey but neglected his own glass. "Ah, Colonel. So you've seen him. I am the most reluctant seller in Tennessee. That horse will make a man's reputation. But, if I'm to make my home in Washington, my dear Rachel believes our Chief Executive cannot be connected to horse racing. I mean that as no aspersion, sir. I have loved the sport of kings since I was a young lawyer starting out. To please Rachel, I will sell Red Stick. But not to just anyone. That horse must go to a man I call friend."

When Jackson named his price, Jack flinched.

"Colonel, Red Stick will, not can, *will* win races. He is the fastest animal in the South."

"You've priced him as such. Where I'm from, some plantations would fetch as much."

"Well, sir. If you're not interested . . . I do hope you will honor us with your presence at dinner. We have an excellent cook." Jackson rose to offer his hand.

"You will take my note? I will have your cash before the end of the month."

"Certainly I will take your note, Colonel. We have served together."

———

One week and two days later, Jack Ravanel alighted from a chaise in his farmyard.

"He's skittish, Ham." Jack snubbed the traces to the hitching post. "Start getting to know him by rubbing him down. Right here. Take him to his stall after he's used to you."

Jack stretched. What a fine day! Jack Ravanel was no damn rice planter making his livelihood driving slaves through the mud. How could a man be good at work he despised? Horses—there was nothing small or petty or mean-spirited about horses. When a fine horse came thundering down the track, it was as if he himself, Jack Ravanel, was in that horse's body, straining, gladsome, and magnificent!

His homecoming had been delayed by negotiations with Langston Butler, who was, Jack thought, the only man he knew who was already damned.

"Bucket of water and just a taste of oats. Just a taste, mind. Let him get used to you. No sudden moves."

Frances stepped onto the porch. "Hello, Jack. I expected you yesterday."

"Business in town." He bounded up the stairs. His kiss tasted her reserve.

"Have I seen that horse before?"

"He was General Jackson's. The general wouldn't have sold him but . . ."

"I see. Penelope was ill again, but her fever broke yesterday and her appetite returned. Mammy doses her with Jesuits' bark. A bitter necessity, I suppose."

"Andrew?"

"Is troublesome. Very much your son, Jack."

"With none of your sweet nature."

"Very little"—she avoided his embrace—"but he is lovable."

"Like his Poppa." Jack preened extravagantly.

She laughed. "Yes. I'm afraid so." She shaded her eyes and sighed. "Your new horse is magnificent."

"Come race season, he'll earn back his price."

Frances raised an inquiring eyebrow he feigned to not see. In the family room, Mammy was helping build Andrew's alphabet-block castle. Penny rushed into her father's arms, and Andrew, not to be outdone, toppled his construction to hug his father's legs.

Frances eyed Jack strangely. "They are beautiful too, you know."

"I know they are. Believe me, I do." Jack squeezed Penny until she giggled. "Mammy, how are you faring?"

"Master Jack, when you gonna stay home, take care of business?"

"My business is where I lay my hat. I *have* been doing business."

"Humph. Come on, children. Time for you nap."

"Oh, Mammy, please!" Penny cried.

"Put Andrew to bed, Mammy," Frances said. "Penny can stay for a while." She waggled a finger. "Just this once!"

Although clearly she believed herself too old for such a task, Penny picked through tumbled blocks to lay out H-O-R-S-E. "She didn't fall far from the tree." Jack chuckled.

"While you were gone, dear, Mr. Bell, our rice factor, delivered his reckoning."

"Which we'll pay as soon as the crop is sold."

"Bell said he had considered our crop in his reckoning and that our balance is overdue."

"Dear Frances. I've been talking business with Langston Butler for two days, and, I confess, I haven't stomach for more."

"Jack, I'm afraid it may be time to sell Langston his wife's picnic spot. Our debts—"

"What a prize you are!" Jack cried. "You anticipate my every move!"

Half smile. "Langston?"

"We are signed, sealed, and attested."

"So you will deal with Mr. Bell?"

He waved negligently. "After race season I will be pleased to satisfy Mr. Bell."

"But, Jack, if you already sold . . ." Frances's mouth formed a silent O. "Jack, you didn't! That parcel is our best land. Where will you pasture our horses?"

"Red Stick's grandsire, Sir Archy, earned seventy thousand dollars in stud fees. He'll buy our pastureland back."

Choked voice. "How . . . how much . . ."

"Dear, our home is your responsibility. In business, I must be free to act as I see best."

"Jack, you didn't . . ."

Jack Ravanel fled his distraught wife for the library, where he pushed a stack of bills aside to reach the decanter. The whiskey went down smoothly but struck his gullet like a bomb. Jack's hand shook.

At his desk he pawed papers as a dog scuffs dirt. Red Stick would earn thousands! He was a horseman, he'd never pretended to be a planter. Mud. Negroes. Heat. Mosquitoes. Unenlightening, ugly, tedious mortality.

He drained his glass in four hard swallows and poured a second. He heard the jingle of traces and Frances's distracted "Hold tight, dear." His wife's alarmed "Hey!" followed by the skitter of iron horseshoes jerked him to the window with his heart in his boots.

———

Some said Jack was drunk when he reached the wreck. Certainly he was very drunk soon afterward and remained in that condition through Frances's funeral. Nobody could get near him, and Cathecarte Puryear, who rode out to the Ravanels' to take matters in hand, suffered bruising when he was thrown down the stairs. When Penny expired three weeks later (and, given the severity of her injuries, expiration was a mercy), Penny's very young brother and his Mammy represented the Ravanel family at the funeral. "Perhaps Jack is sick," Mrs. Puryear suggested.

"He is as sick of life as life is sick of him," Cathecarte (whose bruises had purpled magnificently) pronounced. "The man was a fool to buy that damn beast and more fool to let his wife drive it."

"I shouldn't have cared so much if Jack had been killed," Eleanor averred. "Jack would have brought it on himself."

Cathecarte said, "He should shoot that damn horse."

Many of Charleston's better sort held the same opinion, and a certain tale—which may have been apocryphal—caused more than one well-dressed shoulder to shudder.

It seemed William Bee was in the deed room of the Exchange House when Jack appeared asking for Ravanel deeds, including the deed for the indigo land he'd recently pledged to Langston Butler.

Conversationally, Jack wondered if William had plans for Race Week.

As politely as possible, William Bee noted that some might think three months a curiously brief mourning period.

Jack's eyes were bloodshot as bullet wounds. "Mourning?" he puzzled. "You didn't know?"

"Know what, pray?"

"Red Stick didn't have a scratch on him."

Which anecdote cemented respectable Charleston's disavowal of Jack but amused the racing crowd.

Some said Jack should have shot that horse. Mammy knew Jack couldn't bear one more loss.

———

Cathecarte Puryear called Red Stick "the devil's horse," but his nickname didn't stick.

Eleanor Puryear observed that the Ravanel household was now Jack, his infant son, Andrew, and a comely, young colored Mammy.

Although some found Eleanor's suggestion distasteful, others imagined all sorts of goings-on, which would be revealed, "my dears," in good time. "All in good time!"

Flash sports and dubious gentlemen gravitated to Colonel Jack's town house, where they'd drink, talk horses, and be bawdier than at home. Once, only the once, a young man bawled, "Nigger, fetch me a glass!" and Mammy informed him, "I little Andrew's Mammy. You want some low-natured slattern do your biddin', I reckon you best brings one."

No slatterns appeared. Although sports drank at Colonel Jack's and wagered and swore great oaths, they entertained their slatterns elsewhere. Some joked about Mammy, and others winked or glanced knowingly, though never when or where Jack might see them.

Two days after Frances Ravanel was buried, Langston Butler moved his rice hands onto the indigo land. He waited a month after Penelope was buried to ask Jack his price for what else he owned on the west bank of the river.

Jack said, "You ain't satisfied, Langston?"

"Colonel, I didn't ask you to buy that brute. Nor did I quarrel with Mrs. Ravanel. I admired Frances and certainly didn't suggest she chance herself and her daughter to a horse she couldn't hold. I am told your creditors are impatient, and I am willing to buy certain of your properties. I will also make an offer for your horse. Red Stick can't hold a candle to Valentine, but I have no unfortunate history with the"—Langston paused to savor Cathecarte's phrase—"devil horse."

Jack's tired eyes narrowed. He took out his flask, unstoppered it, and drank. Without offering it to Langston, he tumped the stopper home. Jack said, "The Washington track, four miles. Three thousand says Red Stick beats your damn cart horse."

"Five thousand. Against your remaining rice lands."

"I suppose your word is good?"

"If necessary, my Second will assure you it is very good."

———

Neither the Ravanel farmhouse nor town house had air enough for Mammy's grieving. Little Andrew kept asking when his mother would come back. He couldn't understand she was gone. He wailed when Mammy was out of his sight, and Dolly made up potions so he'd sleep. Mammy slept no better than the child but wouldn't take anything.

That winter's Race Week was notable for its paucity of scandals—which disappointed Charleston's grande dames, who envied Savannah kinswomen their happy disapproval of the wickedness of a certain rich Frenchman. In Charleston, alas, although young men drank themselves into a stupor and pursued young maidens into improper bedrooms, none of the malefactors were prominent.

Constance Venable Fisher pronounced scandal's death sentence: "But, nobody *knows* them."

The only *interesting* talk was the matchup between Colonel Jack Ravanel's Red Stick and Langston Butler's Valentine for a huge purse held by the respected advocate James Petigru. Jack was popular with young gentlemen, Langston approved by their parents. Families were strained by the rivalry and thousands bet.

Both horses were famous. Red Stick was from the newly elected President Jackson's stud, and Valentine was out of the famous Lady Lightfoot. As it happened, the horses were distant cousins.

A very few planters stayed on their plantations to prepare for planting, but most and all the most notable were in town. By noon last night's revelries had been recounted in Charleston's withdrawing rooms by tsk-tsking ladies. Wednesdays and Fridays, the town was at Washington Racecourse before noon.

Mammy couldn't think why she'd ever liked Charleston. She'd be walking down any old street when a blue doorframe slapped at her. The rasp of a carpenter's saw could bring tears to her eyes. So many faces from the Cow Alley church. That church was an empty lot now, and those familiar faces hurried by without greeting. Coloreds who still went to church sat in St. Philip's garret behind the Browns. Mammy wouldn't. Couldn't. The market was the worst. That quick shape ducking into a stall . . . who . . . ? A laugh of purest delight? Behind that stall keeper's legs, who . . . ?

The Butlers were in town but not at home. At Broughton Plantation, Hercules was preparing Valentine for his big race while Dolly added herbs and potions to his rations.

The Ravanel town house was quiet until noon, when Jack rose up and Ham shaved him. Attended by a cloud of bay rum and last night's soured whiskey, Colonel Jack and Ham went uptown to the racecourse, where a trusted cousin and his pistols had spent the night outside Red Stick's stall.

Jack directed Red Stick's exercise, feed, and training to bring the horse to just shy of peak performance. Ham tasted every bucket of Red Stick's feed, and a second armed Ravanel cousin attended the horse when it grazed the meadow behind the course.

At Bonner's saloon tent, Jack drank with friends until the early hours, when they'd repair downtown to Miss Polly's, where Jack spent liberally but never took a Cyprian upstairs.

Often, the night's survivors found their way to Jack's to greet the sunrise from his piazza. When two of Miss Polly's Cyprians trooped along, they were evicted. While Jack's companions grumbled, Mammy said, "Your baby son here, Master Jack. Baby Andrew don't need seein' all this."

Andrew clung to Mammy's legs. When she tucked the boy back in bed, Mammy murmured, "Womens always takin' care of you, honey. Don't you fret 'bout no thing."

Come Race Day, jockeys led beribboned prancing Thoroughbreds up Meeting Street, and Mammy watched from the piazza with Andrew in her lap. It was chilly, and Mammy's shawl was wrapped round her shoulders. "Child, I'm thinkin' you be famous with horses one day. Them horses got plenty to make right for you."

"Momma?"

"Yes, child. You Momma lookin' out for you. Might you can't see her, but she lookin' out."

A tear rolled down Mammy's cheek. "Your Papa bet everything on that darned Red Stick. Everything he got and prolly what he ain't got. Might be you Momma watchin' after Colonel Jack too. I pray she am."

At noon sharp, stewards chivied spectators off the track. The rail was three deep at the start line, and well-positioned saloons did a land-office business. At the finish line, planters drank champagne or rum punch while touts cried the odds. "One to two on Orbit." "Four to one on Mister Sully's Fancy Foot!"

Six horses lined up for the first one-mile race and four for the next. Only Red Stick and Valentine ran in the fourth and final at five o'clock.

In the clubhouse afterward, Wade Hampton paid his wager and offered a toast, "To Red Stick and Old Hickory. We may have lost one hell of a horse breeder, but we've gained a great president."

"General Jackson!"

"Red Stick! Huzzah!"

Since Cathecarte Puryear had pocketed three hundred dollars on the race, he forgave Jack. "Red Stick," he enthused, "has utterly redeemed himself."

Langston Butler sent Hercules for a little sugar.

The winter sun set, and lanterns illuminated the Jockey Clubhouse, where Colonel Jack bought round after round. Although Jack never said what he'd paid for the horse, it was widely assumed that Red Stick more than doubled his purchase price.

In gathering darkness, jockeys rubbed down their mounts and led them quietly down Meeting Street to home. Their manes were uncombed and ribbons torn or lost; their legs were bandaged and sore.

Ham tugged his Master's sleeve. "Master Jack: Red, I rubs him down good. You want I should leave him in the stables or walk him home?"

"Saddle him. A ride will clear my head."

"Master Jack, I takes Red home myself, puts him up. I sleeps in next stall."

"Ham, you tellin' me what to do with my own horse? Keep that up and before long niggers tellin' white men what to do."

Everybody laughed at Jack's absurd conceit. To take the sting out of his words, Jack patted the jockey's shoulder and gave him a gold half eagle. "You rode well today. Still want to run away?"

Ham, who'd ridden the ride of his life, looked down and scuffed the ground, which provoked more amusement.

"Go home. Patrollers stop you tonight, say you the fella rode Red Stick to glory."

Jack bought one last round before he walked the exhausted Red Stick down Meeting Street to his town house.

Mammy was in the family room sewing when Jack's key scratched at the lock plate. He stumbled in, tossed his hat on a bench, and grinned.

"I heard what you and that horse done," she said.

"Are you congratulating me?"

"Andrew, he say he prayers and go to sleep. I guess I can sleep now."

"Langston Butler was furious."

"We ask to love our enemies. Some enemies harder love than others."

"I reminded Langston his loan bought Red Stick." Jack lifted his flask to his lips without result. With one eye squeezed tight, he inspected the flask, recapped it, and tossed it beside his hat. He lurched to the sideboard to pour a tumbler and after deliberation poured another for Ruth.

Startled, she said, "Master Jack, you *know* I temperance."

"Just this one time. To celebrate our victory over Butler."

She brushed it off. "Master Jack, I didn't do nothin' 'bout that.

'Twas you horse beat he horse. I don't got no horse. Don't want no horse."

He set the tumblers down and sat beside her too close. "Ruth, I've been so lonely since Frances died."

"I reckon."

He put an arm around her shoulders. "Ruth, you lost your spouse too."

She shrugged his arm off and stood. "Master Jack, I ain't Mrs. Jehu Glen no more. I ain't even Ruth. I'ze Mammy! I was Miss Penny's Mammy and I be young Master Andrew's Mammy. That who I is!"

He got to his feet, weaving. "Ruth, you . . . you're comely, a comely young woman. Whole damn town thinks you're my lover."

She backed against the sideboard. "Well, I ain't!"

"Must I remind you who . . . who's your Master?"

He groped at her breasts. "A peach," he said. "A luscious black peach." He added, "I *will* have you." He jerked her blouse, and her breasts fell free. "My, aren't you the pretty girl."

"Master Jack . . . *MASTER JACK!*"

He clamped her head so he could kiss her. "So lonely . . ."

She struck his skull with the heavy crystal decanter, and he wobbled and backpedaled into a love seat, which upended with a crash. Master Jack Ravanel sprawled on the floor with his left leg draped over the upset furniture. With her fingertip, Mammy dabbed a blood drop from the decanter's glittering crystal and absently put her finger in her mouth.

Then came a frightened cry. Andrew had been startled awake, and his wail was becoming a howl.

"The apple," Mammy noted, "never fall far from the tree."

That night she dreamed about a manioc basket.

Saturday forenoon, three of Jack's young friends came calling, but Mammy informed them through the closed front door that "Master Jack ain't seein' nobody. He ain't fit be seen."

They surmised, chuckled, and joked, but went away.

The older friends who arrived to congratulate Jack were rebuffed with the same information.

Jack limped into the kitchen half past three. He drank long swallows from the pitcher, covered his mouth, looked around desperately, and spewed into the dry sink.

Mammy took Andrew to the nursery while Cook cleaned up the mess. "Don't you worry now, honey. Your Daddy ain't hurt heself, he just drunk too much."

"I know," the child said.

———

Mammy found Colonel Jack in the darkened drawing room beside a pitcher of cool water and a tumbler of whiskey.

He considered rising but contented himself with a pitiable smile. "Mammy . . ."

"Yes, you done did what you think you done and you ain't doin' it no more. As for me, I am called away. I don't know why I called, but I is. You gonna write me a pass so I get bought by someone won't do what you done and are gonna do again sure, next time you drunk."

Colonel Jack Ravanel said more than he wanted to, but each word fell from his lips with a thud. He didn't want to lose her, but he already had.

Advantageous Connections

ANTONIA SEVIER BURBLED, "How Louisa would have loved this day!"

Solange, who was rarely startled by Antonia's *unique* views, felt her armor slip. "She'd be glad to see her husband marry another woman?"

"Oh, do hold still. How can I pin this collar if you keep wriggling like a fish? Of course Louisa would be pleased. You will make her dear Pierre so happy."

"Wasn't Louisa terribly jealous?"

"Why, of course she was! But that was when she was *alive* and could do something *about* it!" Antonia stepped back for a better look and set a finger to her chin. She tugged a sleeve. "You should have worn the blue tulle. I preferred the blue tulle."

"Be that as it may, dear Antonia, I didn't."

Antonia stuck out her tongue.

"We must make do with what's on hand: a thirty . . . uh . . . plus widow who is somewhat enceinte but making the best of it."

Despite her belief that "forty . . . uh . . . plus" would have been nearer the mark, Antonia dutifully clapped hands. "Indeed you *are* making the best of it, my dear. Oughtn't we hurry? Everyone will be waiting."

"Let them wait. They're enjoying a *delicious* scandal." Solange sighed theatrically. "Dear friend, if my wedding only brought out true friends, there'd be me, Pierre, the girls—and you, dear Antonia."

Antonia Sevier, whose privileged position inside the scandal had opened Savannah's finest homes, demurred. "Dear Solange, you have so many advantageous connections."

"Sans doute that is why so many offered help after poor Wesley died. If it hadn't been for the few dollars I concealed from his creditors, my babes and I would have been destitute."

Pauline, the elder of those babes, stormed into Solange's bedroom. "Maman! I cannot find my earbobs."

"Then," her mother informed her, "you must do without them."

"Maman! One of Jameson's filthy workmen has stolen my earbobs. Our home is destroyed! I will not go without my earbobs!"

"As you prefer."

"Maman! It is your wedding day!" She eyed her mother's slightly protuberant belly. "Or ought I say *our* wedding day?"

Expressionless, Solange slapped her daughter. "Do find your jewelry." Relenting slightly, she added, "You have such pretty ears, darling. You must set them off."

Rubbing her cheek, Pauline departed and soon after could be heard downstairs. "Eulalie, if you have misplaced my earbobs, I shall pinch you until you shriek."

"Ah, children," Antonia breathed. "Such a blessing. My own infant daughter . . ."

Pauline was correct: the unfinished mansion she'd known was changed beyond recognition. The drawing room was now a lumber pile, and its canvas-covered window openings provided light without a view. One mounted the circular stairs one third of the way with the help of varnished balustrades, the next third were unvarnished, and the upper third and stair rail had not yet been installed. Mr. Jameson had promised renovations would be finished *before* the wedding. Ah, well. Builders are the most deceitful of men.

Antonia had envied Solange's maternal remonstrance and sighed dramatically. "Our Mammy indulges little Antoinette's every whim! But what to do? My daughter is so *attached* to the creature!"

Solange suggested the fault might lie in her friend's management. "Mammies provide the affection for which mothers haven't time or inclination. I dislike my daughters and fully expect to dislike"—she tapped her belly—"Baby Ellen. Men are far more amusing than the consequences of their attentions."

Mrs. Sevier tapped her friend on the arm. "Tsk!"

"How is my face?" Solange turned it this way and that.

"You make a beautiful bride."

"Practice, my dear, makes perfect." She called, "Eulalie, Pauline. Must your mother become an honest woman without you?"

———

Pierre Robillard was conservative by inclination and habit. One could set one's watch by him. Mornings, he arrived at L'Ancien Régime at nine o'clock precisely, when he'd peruse newspapers over coffee and the day's first cigar. If some mischance delayed his newspapers, he reread old ones. After the affairs of the world had been reduced to ink, Pierre went through his business correspondence and accounts until noon. Supper was noon to two, dinner at seven. Although many Savannahians didn't sit down at table until 9:00 P.M., Pierre Robillard was abed by then.

So why was this paragon of predictability standing outside St. John the Baptist Church, surrounded by chattering Irish and clutching an enormous orange blossom bouquet? Pierre Robillard didn't really know how he'd come to be here or who he'd become.

Pierre Romeo? He had served with the much lamented Napoleon Bonaparte in the Emperor's first command! Orange blossoms?

"You be fine, Master," Nehemiah whispered.

How had he, a mature widower blessedly free from domestic disturbance, with a satisfactory competence and so very many friends, been caught in the net of desire?

Pierre Romeo? Captive of Love? Dear, dear . . .

O'Haras, O'Hara wives, O'Hara children, and O'Hara grandchildren surrounded the groom, while Pierre's peers, those (or the grandchildren of those) who'd once groveled for invitations to Robillard balls, hid inside carriages lining Drayton Street. Pierre felt a decided urge to give each varnished conveyance a sharp thump. What a boy he had become!

Solange Evans had reignited fires Pierre'd thought long dead. Louisa—and how he'd loved dear Louisa—had acquiesced to his mild spousal desires; Solange had fanned decidedly unspousal desires to a blaze that consumed him, Pierre blushed to think, sometimes twice in one night. Even on this sacred and very public occasion, Pierre Robillard felt an unseemly stirring in unholy regions. Protestant Pierre Robillard had even consented to be married in a Roman church and raise his children as Catholics. Unthinkable, Pierre thought with a broad smile.

"You be fine, Master," Nehemiah said. As resplendent in his Master's discarded frock coat as Pierre was rumpled in his new one, Nehemiah's solemn phiz insisted on the dignity of the occasion.

The prophet wrote: "Learn to do well; seek judgment, relieve the oppressed. Judge the fatherless, plead for the widow."

It took Pierre some time to get around to it.

Wesley Evans was killed too soon after Louisa and Clara's passing, when Pierre couldn't help anyone. At Wesley's funeral, when Solange asked him to repurchase R & E Cotton Factors, the grieving Pierre assured the widow he was content in the import business, where Nehemiah did all the work. Solange didn't seem to appreciate his little joke.

Then, just as Pierre emerged from mourning, his cousin Philippe died, and, to Pierre's dismay, his cousin had named him executor.

Although Philippe had introduced his Indian bride to Savannah society, he hadn't carved out a place for her, and places for an exotic Indian princess were fewer than they'd been. Gold had been discovered in North Georgia, and settlers poured into Muscogee lands, which became towns and counties and plantations. The Indian Princess who'd been regarded with equanimity and curiosity became uninteresting and odd.

Even so, Savannah was a friendlier city than Charleston, and had Philippe's bride been more personable, she might have found friends. Her stillborn infant would have garnered sympathy, and Philippe's wealth excused her unconventionality. Alas, Osanalgi was quite shy, and, after her Indian kin quit Georgia, she shut herself up in Philippe's quirky, gloomy mansion. Those who did call never found her at home.

Philippe's advocacy for Indians embarrassed those who'd profited by Indian evictions, and, after the Treaty of Indian Springs, the legislature never again sought his opinion. Philippe devoted himself to cataloging his collection of Muscogee artifacts and corresponding with the Columbian Institute for the Promotion of Arts and Sciences in Washington, D.C., to find them a permanent home.

Osanalgi might have been seen more often had anyone been really interested in seeing her. Philippe's coachman brought her to the pine forest at the edge of the city and collected her at dark. Market hunters on uninhabited Fig Island mistook her for a runaway slave and were disappointed when their captive earned them no reward.

In March, Savannahians turned out to welcome the Marquis

de Lafayette, the aged Revolutionary War hero. The Jasper Greens brass band did enthusiastic justice to "La Marseillaise," and Philippe presented the marquis with a Red Stick war club as a memento. Osanalgi wasn't present and, had she been, couldn't have prevented the chill Philippe caught, which occasioned his demise two weeks later and Pierre's sudden immersion in his cousin's affairs. Although Philippe's wife attended his burial, she was heavily veiled, and some whispered she'd slashed her cheeks in a pagan mourning ritual. Pierre arranged the funeral and burial. The reception (which the widow didn't attend) was at Pierre Robillard's home.

Pierre, Nehemiah, and Mr. Haversham spent weeks sorting out the estate. Philippe's deeds to farms in Normandy and government bonds in various amounts were found in the unlikeliest drawers and files. A portmanteau unopened since Philippe arrived in Savannah decades ago contained clear title to a Martinique plantation worth fifty thousand. The secretary of the Columbian Institute was interested in Philippe's collection if—and only if—it was properly cataloged. "We have a great number—nay, a superabundance—of uncataloged Indian artifacts."

Pierre didn't know Osanalgi was missing until a week had passed, and when he discovered her absence the executor's first response was more annoyance than distress. The Muscogee coachman knew more than he'd say, but no threat or promise persuaded him to divulge Osa's whereabouts. One morning, six weeks after her husband's death, Osanalgi reappeared with a newborn in her arms. Osanalgi's devotion to her baby was fierce and unyielding.

Pierre hadn't known she was carrying a child, but, whatever his private reservations, he treated young Master Philippe Robillard as his cousin's son and heir.

All bad things must come to an end, and one winter afternoon Pierre and Nehemiah finished consolidating Philippe's assets into a trust to be managed by Mr. Haversham's bank and the two emerged from Osanalgi's awful house warmed by self-congratulations. Pierre rubbed his hands together. Soon it would be Christmas.

In that spirit, impelled by the most genial Chri tian motives, Pierre dismissed Nehemiah to walk home alone, and, since he was passing, he'd call on his old partner's widow. It was too late for supper and too early for dinner; Pierre wouldn't strain Mrs. Evans's hospitality, and there had been some good years at R & E factors. Very good years.

His hostess welcomed him into a house that had gone unfinished for a decade. The family lived in the finished part—the first-floor drawing room and family room, where exposed lath rose from unvarnished wainscoting to a yellowing plaster ceiling. The beautifully shaped staircase lacked balustrades and rose to a second floor whose condition Pierre could only guess at.

No fire burned in the cavernous fireplace, and Solange's daughters kept their cheap coats on. (Importer Pierre had an eye for fabrics.) Pierre took a wobbly chair, whose rungs were snugged with leather laces, for which the lovely widow apologized. "I have sold the good furniture," she confessed. She added, "We bivouac in an unfinished Versailles. I should never have let Wesley start building it."

Despite that bleak room, conversation proceeded apace until Pierre uttered that most conventional of platitudes with the most conventional of sighs. "God's ways are inscrutable, dear Mrs. Evans. We must accept what we can't understand."

"And why is that?"

"Madame?"

"My husband slips on a scrap of cotton waste and breaks his neck. Your Louisa and darling Clara, who've survived many fever seasons, unexpectedly succumb. That we cannot do anything about these tragedies is perfectly apparent. That we must accept them as part of some Divine Plan is disgusting."

Pierre gaped: was the woman a freethinker? Her guest's discomfort didn't check Mrs. Evans's excursion into the unconventional when she blamed her Dear Departed for her present penury. "That the cotton business was overextended was evident to anyone with eyes to see. Indeed, sir, you had slipped that trap. But Wesley ignored logic"—she made *logic* seem like bad temper wielding a bullwhip—"and forged ahead. Sir, persistence in bad judgment ever makes matters worse!"

"Maman," Pauline warned. "Please."

"I trusted Wesley! I did not know!"

Pierre tried to forgive her, him, and everyone. "How could you, a woman . . ."

"Pah! Who ever said the ability to bear children forecloses intellect?"

Pierre's own intellect was completely overwhelmed. He made his excuses, and on his way out discreetly slipped a double eagle under the dusty visiting card tray.

Half a block down the street, the coatless Solange caught him. "Sir, I believe you forgot this."

"Madam?"

She thrust the gold coin at him. A prudent woman, and he knew Mrs. Evans to be such, could feed her family for a month! "But . . ."

Her temper cooled. "Dear Pierre. Sir. You meant nothing amiss. You have a kind heart. But you must be aware how your generosity might appear to gossipmongers."

———

As it turned out (as Pierre thought, ironically), to avoid titillating society they had scandalized it. The next time he visited the widow, Nehemiah carried a heavy basket of provisions, a custom he repeated every two weeks. As weather warmed and they could sit outside, Pierre's visits became less duty than pleasure, and one afternoon he visited without Nehemiah (over that worthy's objections). Not long afterward, he visited later, much later, after Solange's children had been put to bed.

He had thought himself no longer capable of rapture. He had thought his fingers and lips would never again trace the scented contours of a woman's skin. That grateful mindlessness of thrusting into the light!

Solange might have wept or accused her seducer, but she did not. She stretched luxuriously. "I had forgotten what pleasure can be. Thank you, dear, sweet Pierre."

Which was when Pierre Robillard, who was quite old enough to abjure love, heard its summons loud as a clapper striking a bell.

He hired workmen to finish the Pink House and commissioned Thomas Sully, whose portrait of Lafayette was widely admired, to capture Solange's likeness.

Three months of careless bliss, tainted only by Pauline's disdain. (Eulalie, the second child, was too young to make judgments.) The four took Sunday drives and picnicked on Fig Island. With no regard for discretion, Pierre, Solange, and the children visited friends' plantations as a family. Father John dropped by L'Ancien Régime to inquire about Pierre's intentions.

"Intentions?" the befuddled Pierre replied.

"I cannot absolve Mrs. Evans if she means to continue in sin."

"Sin?" It had never occurred to Pierre that love *was* a sin.

When Solange told him he was to be a father again, Pierre was delighted. His life was opening like a spring flower. "Marry me," he said.

"No," she said.

Pierre was flabbergasted beyond speech. His jaw dropped. His face went from pink to scarlet. "But . . ."

Solange laughed merrily and kissed his forehead. "Certainly I will marry you, dear Pierre. You are the gentlest, most amusing man in the world."

"Hmmm. I thought it was my strength, my dominating presence, my service with Napoleon. My brute force . . . ?"

She giggled like a girl.

Savannah loved the wealthy, amiable Pierre, but, as Solange's pregnancy became unignorable, gossips resurrected memories of Solange's first marriage and the duel that ended it. Mrs. Haversham dubbed Solange the French Widow, and despite (or perhaps because of) a certain lethal spider, the name stuck. When a prominent, well-bred, painfully homely spinster complained, "That woman has buried two husbands, is she now to get a third?" her remark was quoted around town.

Although Pierre was happily deaf to such remarks, Solange was not, and, of course, Nehemiah heard every aside white folks whispered as well as secrets whites did not tell but every Savannah housemaid knew.

An embarrassed and aggrieved Pierre came to Solange. "Dearest," he said, "apparently there's been offensive talk."

"Don't you dare take exception. I've surfeit of the 'field of honor.'"

"Dear me, no. I mean I wouldn't. I mean, I would but . . ."

She hushed him with a fingertip upon his lips. "Pierre, when was the last time Philippe's widow was in society?"

"I couldn't say. Although my cousin introduced her, the poor woman didn't . . . she . . . it was excruciating. Poor, dear Cousin Philippe. He believed Indians had lessons for civilized men!"

"By some measures, she and I are alike."

"You? You two?" Pierre continued as if Solange hadn't spoken. "Her competence is in good hands, and she lacks for nothing. She adores her child. Sunday mornings, when all are in church, she walks Little Philippe through the city. Osa, the toddler, and that coachman. They don't return anyone's greetings."

The boy's saturnine features and high cheekbones hinted of his mother's people. His blue eyes, as cold as a winter sky, were his father's. "Philippe is a handsome child," Pierre said. "My duty . . . I fear I have not performed my full duty to him or his mother."

"You shall have your chance. Pierre, I want Osa to give me away."

"Osa?" He imagined the wagging tongues of Savannah's scandalized society. He could almost hear the mosquito whine of their gossip. Fortunately, Pierre's face was perfectly shaped for an impish grin. "How kind . . . How kind you are, my dear."

"And those Irishmen you sometimes do business with?"

"The O'Haras? Their younger brother has arrived from Ireland. Supposedly Gerald O'Hara's even shrewder than his brothers."

"Invite them. Wives, brothers, children—all the Fenian kit and caboodle."

Pierre's grin broadened. "But, dear Solange, all the best people— why, they'll be *scandalized*."

Solange's grin was as small and wicked as his was good humored. "That, my blessed husband to be, is my intention!"

———

But on his nuptial morning, with spring flowers flowering and gladdening the air, surrounded by chattering Fenians while his peers hid in their carriages, Pierre Robillard wondered how wise they'd been to snub people unaccustomed to snubs. A vague, brave, rather-be-anywhere-but-here smile clung to his lips. A rumpled, unshaven Irishman stuck out his hand. "You'll be the lucky groom. May you have children and your children have children."

"Thank you."

"Gerald O'Hara, sir. Formerly a merchant in my brothers' firm, but as of last night at four thirty-seven, not long before this blessed—this very blessed—sun decided to rise, I became a planter."

Fuddled, Pierre couldn't help asking, "So early?"

"No, sir. So late! At the hour when the rooster is clearing his throat and drink numbs the wits of the gambling man."

Gerald O'Hara, new-minted planter, was shorter than Pierre by six inches and resembled the bird he'd just mentioned. His broad, happy face was empty of guile and so flushed with the conviction that the world, as a matter of course, would share his joy that, despite Pierre's dreary ruminations (perhaps because he'd tired of them), Pierre asked, "Have you been to bed then, Mr. O'Hara?"

"No, sir. First because I would not (because I was playing cards) and then because I dare not (because I was winning) and then because I must not because a gentleman, having sacrificed the contents of his wallet, laid the deed to an Up-country plantation on the cloth and was urging me to wager against it. I had nines over jacks, a full house, and I believed he held a straight, though in cards, sir, one may be mistook."

Pierre, who hadn't wagered at cards since he was Napoleon's soldier, agreed.

Gerald's brother James intervened. "Boyo, it is Master Robillard's wedding day, sure it is. God's nightgown! Don't bore the man with your goings-on."

None of Pierre's *finer* guests had set foot outside their carriages. Well, then. Perhaps he'd marry without them. Pierre said, "I have some difficulty with your brother's accent, James. But I relish his tale."

"It is just two hundred acres," red-eyed Gerald continued as if no objection had been raised. "Being Irish, sir, I've ever dreamed of 'a bit of land' of me own. Nothing grand, mind. Land where neither king nor grandee could expel me or mine."

Gerald described his deed in surveyor's detail. ". . . and five hundred from the white oak at the corner to the Flint River. Isn't that a grand name? Hard as flint, but soft as water. I cannot wait to see it."

"Flint River . . ."

"'Tis Up-country, mister. The lottery of Cherokee lands. Some was won by honest settlers, others—as I gather 'twas the case here—by speculators seeking not land but only the profit to be made off it.

"I come, Mr. Robillard, from a country where men squabble over a few yards of dirt that grow nothing better than potatoes. These Indian lands have never known a plow! They will grow anything!

"I shall name it Tara, sir. I name it for that grand and great place where reigned the Irish kings."

Overwhelmed by the little man's bonhomie, Pierre took Gerald's hand again. "Sir, I congratulate you. It is good to become a king!"

The Irishman's face was alight with good humor. "Faith and it is that. For yourself, your honor: may the most you wish for today be the least you receive."

At the dismounting step, Philippe's son tumbled out of his father's disreputable coach, banging his ankle on the stone and setting up a howl to gladden any savage.

The boy was dressed unexceptionally in short pants, shirt, and felt hat. His mother wore a beaded red and green headband, and a necklace of some sort of animal claws above what may have been the same gown she'd worn to the disastrous Christmas ball so many years ago.

Pierre hurried to her, extending his hand. "Osa! Osa! So good of you . . . So very good . . ."

Nehemiah collected the howling child, who thumped his ears just as the bride's carriage turned onto the street and gentlefolks' carriages disgorged their contents.

As they neared the melee, Antonia Sevier asked Solange, "You seem so distant, my dear. Regrets?"

"One does what one needs do."

"Of course, but . . ."

"Pierre is honorable. Perhaps too honorable. He hasn't a devious bone in his body."

"But?"

"Dear friend, there are no buts. I have no reservations. We will be happy together, my Pink House will be completed, my dear daughters"—the younger daughter smiled, the elder exhibited repugnance for noisesome remarks coming from such a being as her mother—"will enjoy the advantages two parents provide. We will be happy. Do you hear me, Pauline? We *will* be happy."

Pauline glowered at her gloved hands.

Antonia gasped. "Mrs. Haversham, Mrs. Lennox, Old Birdy Prentis—why, *everyone* is here."

"My dear Antonia," her friend replied. "Of course they are. Savannah has come to wash the soiled dove."

———

A beaming Father John greeted the wedding party while Nehemiah clamped the squalling child's arm. Young Master Philippe gasped but stopped howling.

His cousin's widow, Osa, offered Pierre a tentative smile, but Pierre's eyes couldn't leave his bride. He bowed to kiss her small hand, and his besotted eyes met Solange's amused ones.

Solange said, "Shall we go inside?"

The wedding party was followed by Savannah's young mayor, William Thorne Williams, the Havershams, and other dignitaries, who demonstrated by insistent chatter that neither the occasion nor St. John the Baptist was more important than they. After those they privately called "the nobs" made their entrance, the O'Haras took the three back pews.

———

Osa performed her modest duties creditably while her son rattled the pew door, which Nehemiah had providentially locked.

Mrs. Haversham murmured to Mrs. Sevier, "That boy is more savage than his mother."

Mrs. Sevier whispered, "He is uncommonly beautiful in repose."

"Which is when?"

Holy matrimony proceeded to its customary destination, and Pierre Robillard kissed his bride with enthusiasm that might have fetched applause in a less formal setting.

Pierre held Solange's arm as if his bride were life itself, and the couple led the procession into a fine morning and wedded bliss.

When the party appeared, coachmen quit gossiping and hurried to their Masters' conveyances.

Arms crossed beneath her breasts, a modestly dressed black woman waited at the foot of the stairs.

"Why . . ." Solange gasped.

"Good morning, Missus," Mammy said. "I wishin' you every happiness."

"But, Ruth . . ." Pierre began.

Pauline burst past the couple, crying, "Mammy! Mammy! Mammy!"

At which Eulalie—who had never met this woman—burst into tears. Father John asked, "Is there something you want, dear woman?"

"I wants come back," Mammy said. "Master Pierre and Missus Solange needin' they Mammy now."

Jammed behind them in the aisle, important necks craned and impatient questions were asked.

Hugging the sobbing Pauline and speaking past her, Mammy said, "I wants come home."

The Gift of Prophecy

"POOR CHILD GOT no teat to suck and no Momma love her. Just look at you, Miss Ellen Robillard. All scrunched up and you head squoshed where Doctor clamp it. Your Papa wouldn't have no midwife, wouldn't tolerate none. For rich folks it's modern times. Master Pierre hire himself a prime 'fizz-i-shun.' That man studied doctorin', can't say how many years he studyin'. Enough so man what never had no baby he ownself nor never catch one knows better'n any nigger midwife who done had babies and catchin' 'em for years. Doctor man studied 'bout babies—why he even been to Philadelphia!

"Miss Ellen, you was still considerin' should you come to the light or should you not, just takin' your sweet baby time. But Doctor Man impatient. Might be other babies needin' him or might be he had somewheres important go. Well, he fetched you with he shiny clamps and your Momma bleed like a butchered hog. Honey, I seed enough of blood, I don't want see no more."

The Pink House shivered to an old man's tremulous shriek.

Mammy rocked little Ellen, shushing, shushing. "Nehemiah, he findin' you a wet nurse, and soon you be suckin' and warm. Miss

Solange hold you onct 'fore she go to them spirits. You Momma smile at you, Baby Ellen. I seed it!

"Your Papa, he don't know what. He find love when he don't hardly think he love no more, and now love took away. Master Pierre he whipped and wonderin'. Master Pierre already lost one wife and child afore Miss Solange. Now she gone too and Master Pierre thinkin' there ain't much reason for livin' on when livin' hurt so. Sometimes, Little Miss, sorrowin' am the onliest thing what am."

The doctor bustled past the woman and baby. He paused, maybe to say something, or examine the infant one last time, but with an oath he clattered down Jehu's beautiful stairs.

Although Mammy was expected to use the back stairs with the other servants, some mornings before the white folks were up and about, she visited those stairs to touch a mahogany stair rail she'd seen Jehu fashion. That wood was slippery as water and turned like an invitation.

Baby Ellen lay in her lap, light and heavy. Her breathing was soft and strong.

"Baby, I reckon Miss Solange my Momma too. I knowed her all my life, and I reckon, weren't for Miss Solange, I wouldn't be holdin' you today. I don't recall hardly nothin' 'bout my born Momma. Sometimes, so faint it like she in a faraway room, I hears her sayin' *'Ki kote pitit-la?'* which was a game we play. *'Ki kote pitit-la?* . . . Oh, where is that child?'* Where is that child?" Momma ain't never come to me like Martine or Gullah Jack or Miss Penny or them other spirits, but she speak sometimes. I 'spect my born Momma love me, but she don't come. My Jehu, he . . . he don't come neither. Spirits busy doin' spirit things. They's different rooms where them spirits be and they comes and goes. Might be one day Missus Solange come too. But might not. Might be she busy tendin' Martine."

She adjusted the infant in her lap. "Your Momma kind when she remember to be kind and she wouldn't never have sold me 'cept

I wanted sold. Reckon she loved me after her fashion. Miss Ellen, listen to Mammy talkin' foolishness . . ."

Mammy kept an ear cocked for Nehemiah and the wet nurse. The infant had only one suck before her Momma's teats went cold.

Mammy was tired past tired. "All them you loves gonna die, child. Every one of 'em. If Le Bon Dieu smile on you particular, you die afore they do. That the truth, child. Everybody know it but nobody wants hear it 'count hearin' don't make nothin' no better. Some things hearin' 'bout make things worse. Ain't like dyin' is some newfanglement nobody ever heard nothin' 'bout afore.

"Sometimes I can see things. Didn't want to, didn't ask to, and wish I didn't. Seein' never did me a lick of good. Before you born I seed Mistress Solange like she got a mist round her; she blurred, not sharp like rest of us. Should I told her, 'Mistress Solange, you ain't long for this world'? How that help arything? How that make Miss Solange's last days better? Might be she knows anyway but not sayin' herself. Sometimes folks do. Might be she ready to go."

The sobbing Pierre efmerged from his wife's chamber. He stared at Ruth's lap as if his infant were an unwelcome stranger.

"Mammy . . ."

"Master Pierre."

"I . . ."

"We gonna miss her terrible. Miss Solange in the Kingdom this day."

"Oh, God!" A sob racked the man, and he stumbled off.

Mammy touched the soft blue-veined hollow throbbing atop the baby's head. "How can it help us knowin' when our lovelies gonna die? We knows they is, and we knows grievin's worse than dyin'. Don't need know when. After you gone, you with the spirits and spirits ain't grievin'. Martine ain't grievin'. Martine ain't . . ."

Mammy bent to kiss Baby Ellen. "We got to act like what ain't true is, that we gonna live long and be happy, that tomorrow be sunny, never no hurricano no more. Them hurricanos, they thing of the past! You be happy, Miss Ellen, you gets 'vited to balls and picnics, all the fetes. People see you bein' happy and figure, 'Maybe I'm wrong. Maybe Miss Ellen knows somethin' I don't. Maybe my lovelies ain't gonna be laid under the cold ground. Maybe my lovelies be the first since Jesus live long as they wants to.' Little Missus, you got to pretend. Pretenders welcome everywheres. Got to pretend get from one day to the next." Mammy dabbed her eyes. "We dependin' on pretendin'."

The babe's life pulsed under her hand. "Reckon, after today I be pretendin' again, but not today. Can't rightly bear no pretendin' this day."

Mammy's tears fell onto the baby's blanket. "Little Missus, world didn't start when you did. It been here awhile. Bein' Miss Ellen Robillard gonna be troublesome. You got two sisters what's older, and they gonna boss you like you was one of they doll children. They gonna do that, sure as you're lyin' here. Master Pierre—you see how he look at you? Ary time he look at you, he don't see the woman he loved. He learn to love you, sure he will, but in the very back of he mind be dark corner where you Momma's gone and you ain't.

"Savannah folks: they gonna remember you killed your Momma. Likely they never say nothin' to your face, but they looks at you and remember your Momma, always so sharp and so gay, and they thinkin' five-pound baby Ellen ain't no fair swap for Mistress Solange. No, they ain't gonna say it outright, but they thinkin' it. Until those who knowed you Momma is gone theyselves, they thinkin' you killed her. No, 'tain't fair. 'Tain't fair! Fairness what preachers bother about.

"'Tain't fair they thinkin' little child killed her Momma, but they thinkin' it—can't help theyselves—and directly you see in their eyes, they blamin' you for somethin' and you ask, 'What was it I done?'

and directly you hits on the answer. Might be you thinkin': why, that ain't so. I never done no such a thing. Prolly you buck and jibe. Might be you fight back, but their eyes don't change and after time you start thinkin', maybe I din't mean kill her, but 'twas me done it, and you take that lie on yourself. Can't help youownself. Might be none of us can. We comes into the world the way it am, and we gots make the best of it."

The child fussed and burped but didn't wake. The front door opened quietly, and Nehemiah and a young woman mounted Jehu's stairs.

Mammy said, "If Le Bon Dieu and the spirits will it, we find some happiness on this earth. You ain't got no Momma, but you got you a Mammy. And, honey, I reckon I gots me a child."

Lives of the Fathers, Martyrs, and Other Principal Saints

The passions are not to be stilled by being soothed: whatever is allowed them is but an allurement to go further and soon makes their tyranny uncontrollable.

THE REVEREND ALBAN BUTLER

ELLEN ROBILLARD WAS a quiet child in a quiet household. Her first word was *Mam*, which Mammy told everybody was Ellen's attempt at *Mom-ma* because the child missed her Momma so much. Others failed to spot any special affection for a dead mother whose place had been usurped by her Negro servant.

Ellen's oldest sister, Pauline, was fixed on marriage and saw the child, when she saw her at all, as a distraction. Mammy blamed Pauline's imperfect deportment for the caliber of her suitors: the second sons of rich planters or first sons of unsuccessful ones. Absent Carey Benchley's greening stovepipe, fusty frock coat, and short boots, one could be forgiven for mistaking the man's shrillness for a nervous woman's. Having been "saved" at a camp meeting,

Carey expressed conventional moralisms as if he'd invented them.

Pauline was engaged to become Mrs. Carey Benchley.

Her younger sister, Eulalie, had deportment but was dreamy. When Mammy caught Eulalie reading a novel—Mr. Dickens's *Oliver Twist*—she warned the child that no Georgia gentleman would marry a girl who was smarter than himself.

Pauline couldn't marry Carey until her father emerged from deep mourning, but Ellen was walking and talking when Pierre's tailor delivered his third successive black suit. A year later, when Ellen began to read, Nehemiah quietly exchanged his Master's black mourning garb for slightly cheerier purple. Pierre made no objection. Indeed, he may not have noticed. Soon afterward Mr. Carey Benchley and Miss Pauline Robillard were married in the Baptists' new church on Chippewa Square. While the family pew was nearly empty, the rest of the church was packed with Pierre's friends, grateful he was out and about. Antonia Sevier, in purple for her husband, who'd passed eighteen months before, was particularly amiable. At the City Hotel reception, Pierre was disappointed by the teetotal punch and didn't stay as long as Mrs. Sevier had hoped.

That next Saturday, although Mrs. Sevier arrived at Pink House without invitation, she and her daughter, Antoinette, were admitted. Mrs. Sevier told Pierre that children of similar rank and heritage must naturally become friends. Despite this indelicate push, the girls did become fond of one another, although Antoinette was as quick and disrespectful as Ellen was quiet and obedient. On the Seviers' third visit, while the girls were admiring Ellen's French porcelain dolls, Antoinette announced that she was thirsty and commanded Mammy to fetch water. Mammy replied that any healthy child could walk downstairs, go to the well, and wind the windlass. That evening Antoinette informed her mother that Pierre Robillard owned an impudent Negro. Determined that Dear Pierre should enjoy the best service, Mrs. Sevier informed Pierre that absent a Mistress to discipline them, his servants were assuming more than servants' due.

While Pierre let this pass, Nehemiah and Mammy didn't, and though Mrs. Sevier did her best, the blossom she hoped might set delicious fruit withered. Pierre was often out when Mrs. Sevier called, and her visiting card (corner turned up to indicate delivery *by her own hand*) vanished between the card tray and Pierre. Her sincere, much-labored-over letter—Had she committed some offense?—elicited no reply.

Weekday mornings, Ellen's Mammy and Antoinette's Mammy brought the girls to Reynolds Square. One morning, Mrs. Sevier rose earlier than her custom to come to the square and demand of Mammy what, *exactly*, was going on.

Alas, Mammy was so *stupid*, so completely *oblivious* of her Master's intentions and affections. The following Sunday, the resourceful Mrs. Sevier attended services at the South Broad Street Presbyterian Church, and, after its painfully Protestant service ended, she waylaid Pierre, and that amiable, slightly befuddled widower discovered a previously unknown intention to escort the charming widow to the mayor's reception for Governor Lumpkin Saturday next. In the intervening week, despite unpleasantness about certain overdue bills, Antonia's seamstress delivered a new gown with gigot sleeves. To set it off, Antonia purchased a hat with egret plumes.

When Robillard's carriage didn't appear at the appointed time, Antonia presumed a harmless misunderstanding and proceeded to the reception, where she told Mayor Gordon her escort had been delayed on business, only to sit through the three-hour affair without him.

Thenceforth, she snubbed the baffled Pierre, who believed Antonia had canceled their engagement. Hadn't he heard so from Nehemiah's own lips? Pierre never deciphered the angry glares and pregnant silences Antonia Sevier directed at him.

Six months later, Antonia Sevier married Mr. Angus Wilson, and Pierre sent them a rather nice silver cream pitcher, which gift was never acknowledged.

January 30, 1835, was consequential nationally and for different reasons in the Pink House as well. On that date in Washington, D.C., an unemployed housepainter, one Richard Lawrence, failed to assassinate President Jackson, and in Savannah, Georgia, little Ellen Robillard tugged the Reverend Butler's *Lives of the Fathers, Martyrs, and Other Principal Saints* off the shelf. That book would have greater influence on the child than the assassin's misfiring pistols had on Jackson. *Lives of the Saints* became "Miss Ellen's Book." She toted it around like a favorite doll, poring over stories and lurid pictures. Young Mistress Ellen spoke about St. Teresa, St. Agatha, and St. Margaret as if they were real folks on the other side of town.

When Ellen asked whether her mother, Solange, might be recognized as a saint one day, Mammy said, "Sure she will, honey. You Momma was the bestest saint ever been."

Although she never spoke against Miss Ellen's book, Mammy didn't favor it. All those pictures of saints stuck full of arrows or 'bout to be cut to pieces or set upon by wolves—anyone who knew just how much blood could pour out of one poor human body couldn't have made those pictures, that's what Mammy thought. Anyway, those saints didn't look like people stabbed with arrows or 'bout to have their heads chopped off; they looked like they were whiskey drunk or maybe they was halfway to Paradise already. In her whole life, onliest man Mammy ever saw lookin' like Miss Ellen's saints had been Denmark Vesey.

Desiring to Die for Faith was foolishness, but not Everyday Foolishness. It was one of those Honorable Foolishnesses Mommas praised to their children all the while praying their babies wouldn't try it out for themselves.

Mammy warned Ellen, "Ain't no use bein' poor and good. Cheerful face get you arything you gots to get."

———

Ellen Robillard became a Saint-in-Waiting. On her own, without consulting her father, she approached Father Michael for confirmation instruction. Though the good father was busy with a flood of Irish immigrants and a handsome new church a-building, Ellen's childlike eagerness to explore her faith invigorated his own, and unless he was called away to a sickbed or deathbed, Father Michael was available to the sincere little girl Mondays and Thursdays after dinner. Pierre set a good table, and two nights a week, the Father dined at the Pink House.

If Pierre ever regretted the promise to Solange to rear their child in the Catholic faith, he never said so, and Father Michael was so learned and kind, Pierre looked forward to the priest's regular appearances.

———

Savannah's French community was smaller than it had been, Frère Jacques was once again Gunn's Tavern with an Irish clientele. Pierre's compatriots spoke with the Low Country's languid soft r's. As French influence diminished and cotton wealth grew, Savannah's appetite for French silks and wines and fashions grew too, and under Nehemiah, L'Ancien Régime's able manager, Pierre's business flourished.

When Father Michael told Pierre his daughter might have a vocation, her father chuckled. "Oh, Mammy won't like that. She believes all young ladies are incomplete until they wed young gentlemen."

"Mammy . . . ?"

"Runs our household, don't you know. Orders me about like I

was *her* slave. When I balk, Nehemiah has 'a little talk' and I'm soon toeing the line again."

"But you . . . you're Master here."

"So I am," Pierre said complacently.

When Antoinette snickered at Ellen's invitation to join confirmation class, their friendship ended.

Antoinette befriended Philippe Robillard, whose mother had reared the boy, it was said, "like a wild Indian." (When Pierre offered advice and help, his cousin's widow slammed the door in his face.) Young Philippe didn't attend church. "Apparently," one grande dame sniffed, "the Sabbath is just another day to that boy."

The unexceptionable Franklin Ward began calling on Eulalie.

Because Mr. and Mrs. Carey Benchley came to town for Saturday market and stayed over at the Pink House, the couple were present when Franklin called. Since Mr. Ward was a Millerite, the Baptist Benchleys subjected the earnest young man to amusing gibes. Franklin Ward's father and uncle had been Yankee physicians, and Franklin had been fixed on that vocation until he was influenced by Reverend William Miller's prediction that Christ would return in the flesh between March 1843 and October 1844—dates devised by scrupulous calculations from certain prophecies in the Book of Daniel. Carey Benchley had never heard anything so risible, and if, during the week, he thought of an amusing question, he was bound to pop it Sunday. "When Jesus comes again," Pauline's husband asked, "who's gonna drive him around? Who's gonna cook for him?"

Another time Carey guffawed, "Why you courtin' Eulalie anyway if it's all gonna be over and done?" He repeated, with satisfaction, "Over and done."

Although Franklin Ward reprised Reverend Miller's thinking

and provided corroborative essays by prominent theologians, Carey and Pauline enjoyed many a joke at Eulalie's suitor's expense.

Ellen listened more attentively. That Christ should bring the corrupt, ungodly world to an end certainly seemed plausible.

They were living through, Franklin Ward explained, the "tarrying time."

—————

Eleven months before the soonest date for the world to end, Ellen put away her catechism and *The Lives of the Saints*. She trumped up reasons why Father Michael should no longer be invited for her instruction and the dinners the good father and Pierre so enjoyed. When the priest asked when Ellen wished to be confirmed in her faith, the young lady was desperately vague.

Mammy didn't need the laundrywoman's report to know what had happened.

"Child," she said when they were alone, "you ain't cheerful like you been."

"What's to be cheerful about? My life is mean, small, and dull. I've no friends, really . . ."

"Nary one?"

"You don't count." Reluctantly she added—for Ellen was always truthful, "You are more than a friend."

"You changin', that's all. Honey, you a woman growed."

"I do not wish to be a 'woman growed.'"

Mammy grinned. "Well, you ain't gonna be no man. You got the Jack, and every moon Jack, he come visit you."

Mammy gave Ellen soft cotton napkins. "Pin 'em in your drawers and change 'em much as you needs. Leave 'em in that covered pail next the back door. Keep pail covered. Your daddy don't want to know 'bout it."

Ellen's face twisted. "Oh, Mammy! Do I have to?"

"Yes, child. I reckon you do."

She wailed, "I'm so dirty!"

Mammy didn't smile. "You ain't dirty, child. What's happenin' was meant to be. Happen to your Momma, happen to me. You gets used to it."

"I'm so dirty," she whispered.

A month or two later, Antoinette Sevier reappeared. Skinny, thin, and pale, she knew not to sass Mammy but sassed her anyway.

The two girls resumed friendship as if there'd been no breach, and Antoinette's friends became Ellen's. Balls and picnics and racecourses and sailing filled her days. Often Ellen stayed over at Antoinette's home, and before long Mammy didn't know whether to set a place for her at table or not. Ellen accepted Mammy's cautions and reproofs with her head cocked as if evaluating novel, dubious propositions.

Early one Saturday, returning from the market, Mammy jumped to the curb as Philippe Robillard's carriage clattered by. Miss Antoinette Sevier was sprawled across Philippe's lap, and both were laughing.

Children. When Mammy pictured how they were, what they thought, what they cared about—it all seemed as remote and ethereal as the plump clouds overhead. Mammy tucked her market basket under her arm and marched home, where Nehemiah was at breakfast.

Nehemiah didn't want to know. "No colored ever gained nothin' by white disgrace."

"That Miss Antoinette, she goin' round without no chaperone," Mammy insisted.

Nehemiah took a cautious spoonful of hot oatmeal. "Not our bother. Not our bother to any degree."

"Wherever that child be goin', she ain't be goin' alone," Mammy predicted unhappily.

Mammy blamed Miss Antoinette for unpleasant changes in Ellen's appearance and behavior. Miss Ellen's posture drooped, and the child who'd been meticulous and neat became flamboyant and not at all tucked in. The thoughtful replies Mammy was accustomed to became vague, uninformative mumbles. The child who had taken to deportment like a duck on a June bug had abandoned it.

One hot summer night, startled wide-eyed and heart-pounding awake by a dream, Mammy slipped into Miss Ellen's disordered bedroom and sat on her empty bed until the downstairs clock struck thrice and a carriage drew up out front. Silence. The coachman popped his whip, and it rolled away. Key in the door, footfalls tiptoeing up Jehu's stairs. The child eased her door open and whisked inside.

"G'mornin'," Mammy said.

Through the window, the moon cast a pale swatch on the far wall. Caught in that light, Miss Ellen wiped her mouth and tugged her shirt collar straight. "I . . ."

"Don't lie me no lies, young Missus!"

Ellen kicked her slipper into a corner, where it thumped the wall. Her other slipper followed. "Tell me, Mammy. Do you think the world is going to end? Antoinette says it won't, but Philippe believes it will. We humans have done so many wicked things, wouldn't the world be better without us?"

"Le Bon Dieu . . ."

"Do speak English, Mammy. You mean God. He who has His eye on the sparrow."

"God see what we do, and what God don't see, you Momma do."

"Sorry. I don't seem to recall that lady."

"Miss Ellen . . ."

"Mammy, if you dare interfere, I shall . . ."

"What you gonna do to me, miss? What you gonna do ain't been done worse afore?"

"Mammy . . . I just don't know. I don't *know* anymore."

Stiffly, Mammy got to her feet. Her knees were bothering her.

"Take care, young Missus. You ain't so bad as you wants to be. You ain't got it in you."

———

Nehemiah wouldn't tell Pierre. "What Master Pierre gonna do?"

"He can talk to her."

Nehemiah nodded. "What good that gonna do?" He cleared his throat. "If she was colored, be something we could do. Colored girl, we could hang bells round her waist so we catch her slippin' out, or we can chain her ankles so she too hobbled to run."

"Or send her for 'a little sugar,'" Mammy suggested.

"But we can't. That girl goin' to the Devil, but she goin' at her own pace and in her own time, and, Mammy, there ain't one thing in the world you nor me can do 'bout it."

They didn't tell Pierre.

When Eulalie's Franklin called, Pierre joined them in the drawing room beneath Solange's portrait until the Benchleys came down, whereupon Pierre escaped for his Sabbath nap. At dinner Pierre drank a bottle of claret and Nehemiah helped him upstairs. When old friends called, Pierre greeted them amiably but after a half hour begged forgiveness and repaired to private quarters. Pierre Robillard's grip was very much loosened, and if that amiable, distracted gentleman noticed the changes in his youngest daughter, he didn't remark them.

Ellen didn't lack respectable suitors. Moony-eyed Robert Wilson—son to that steamboat captain. Mammy found Robert on the front steps one morning—crack of dawn—hoping Miss Ellen would come out. And Gerald O'Hara kept calling with flowers, candies, all sorts of small gifts. True, he was an Irishman, but he was a respectable Irishman!

Respectable, Philippe Robillard was not. He was a scandal.

Wasn't his fault, Philippe had no Mammy to rear him and plenty money to go wrong. Before he was out of short pants, his mother stopped taking Philippe to St. John's. Other parishioners, who hadn't enjoyed the boy's kicking, screaming tantrums, were glad to see the back of him. By fifteen, Young Philippe had gone through five tutors, including a Boston Yankee.

Savannah market was happily scandalized by the young Master. When there were no new outrages to deplore, they recollected old ones: how Young Master Philippe rode a fine horse to death or how he'd insulted a nun and "that scamp sent Charles workhouse be whipped 'count Charles didn't get scuffs out his boots. Scuffs is leather cuts. Charles didn't cut scuffs in, how he gonna get 'em out?"

As the Robillards' chief house servant, Mammy expected deference and small courtesies. "Fine green turtle. I know how Master Pierre like his green turtle, so I been keepin' this fella back special, Mammy."

Mammy did not expect impertinence, but one morning, Mammy Antigone (whose white folks lived on the trash side of Jackson Square) confronted her. "You Miss Ellen, Mammy Ruth. She carryin' on outrageous with that Philippe boy. Outrageous! Miss Ellen scandalizin' you!"

"Distress for Robillard family is you?" Mammy retorted. But sharp retort cannot hide truth.

As a child, Miss Ellen had snubbed Philippe. She wasn't snubbing him now.

Mammy Antigone put her hand on Mammy Ruth's arm! "You done everything you could, girl. Bless your heart."

Mammy shook that hand off like it was a snake. Mammy Antigone feelin' sorry for Mammy Ruth! How dare she!

Miss Eulalie was still in curlers when Mammy burst into her bedroom. "I hearin' 'bout Miss Ellen," she said. "Folk's talkin'!"

Eulalie smiled a dreamer's smile. "Philippe and my sister are very much in love. Everyone says so."

"*Everyone* do?"

"It is so *romantic*."

"You only want what you ain't got. If you got it, you wouldn't be wantin' it."

A blind woman could have seen trouble coming: Miss Ellen's moodiness, her indifference to favorite pastimes, her superior, cunning air—as if she had some secret nobody else was wise enough or good enough to know. Like many before her, Miss Ellen thought she'd invented love. She wore "I'm in love" like a placard.

Young folks think love is as simple as the sunrise and plain as the nose on your face. They hope to melt in their lovers' eyes.

Mammy knew love is never simple or plain, and can be worlds of hurt. Miss Ellen was fifteen. Ripe enough to fall in love. Who she was in love with was the problem. Anybody but Cousin Philippe! After a night when the spirits wouldn't stop chatterin', Mammy went into Ellen's bedroom and shook her awake. "What you up to with that boy? You scandalizin' Robillard family."

Although Ellen's eyes were tinged with red and her hair was mussed, she rose, drew on her robe, sat down at her dressing table, and patted powder on her cheeks.

"I got to tell Master Pierre, honey. You leavin' me no choices."

Ellen's shoulder dipped in a shrug so slight it might have been overlooked.

Mammy waited until Master Pierre made his toilette, was shaved, and had breakfasted on a coddled egg and a small cup of bitter chicory coffee. When Mammy told her story, the anger, distress, and concern flitting across Pierre's face reminded her of the godparent he'd been so many years ago. But the lightning passed and his face subsided into an old man's soft folds. "Young folks will be young folks. Not much we can do about it."

"You ain't gonna do nothin'?"

Pierre's shrug was wearier than his daughter's and no more helpful.

The twelfth of March was the soonest date Reverend Miller's dire prediction might be realized, and Savannah's young sports vowed to celebrate. Antoinette Sevier suggested, "With so little time left to live, shouldn't we live it?" Mammy wanted to wash the child's mouth with soap.

When Mammy prepared ambush by the back door, Ellen slipped out a window. When Mammy waited at the stable, Miss Ellen's lover came to the front door. Mammy ran into the street in time to see Miss Ellen and Philippe on his horse, her hair loosed, arms wrapped tight around him as his stallion galloped down the street.

Mammy understood how a girl like Ellen might sacrifice herself, her virginity, and her reputation to a scoundrel provided that scoundrel was beautiful and perfectly in the moment, alive. Understanding didn't mean she'd let it happen.

———

Midnight, March 10, Mammy banged on Nehemiah's door. "Bring the coach round," she commanded. "Hurry. It am Miss Ellen and that boy. Miss Eulalie knows what theys up to. 'Tweren't no secret to Miss Eulalie!"

"I ain't doin' no such a thing," Nehemiah said. "This white folks doin's. Not for you 'n' me."

She said, "You don't come, I tell spirits you doin' wrong."

Nehemiah said, "I don't believe in them African spirits." He dressed and hitched up the carriage.

———

Farnum's Tavern had been a respectable two-story farmhouse twenty years ago. The red lantern in its window paled in cold moonlight.

Tucked under unpruned live oaks, its broad veranda was fronted by a row of bleached casks. Unusually handsome horses dozed at the familiar hitch rack. Farnum's Tavern was where flash sports came to play.

"Around back," Mammy commanded. "Ride me round back."

"I ain't waitin' for you!" Nehemiah whispered.

"Yes, you is. I fetchin' Miss Ellen. We needin' you bring us home."

"I don't see her."

"Course you don't. Miss Ellen, she inside!" The wheel ruts in the yard lacked shadows or depth in the pale light. Outside the back door, Mammy hitched up her skirt and murmured a prayer. So many ways this could go wrong.

Thumbing the latch, she slipped into a filthy kitchen. Arms crossed, a scar-faced mulatto dozed against a scummy sink, whose drainboard was heaped with unwashed tankards. His eyes snapped open. "Who you?"

"Mammy Robillard. I come for Miss Ellen."

The man raised his hands as if deflecting a blow.

Behind the taproom door, she heard men laughing. Mammy tucked her starched blouse and straightened her red-checked kerchief.

"Le Bon Dieu preserve me," she prayed.

Smoking lanterns illumined splotched plaster walls. Mismatched tall and short candles marched raggedly down a long table. The air was a fug of stale tobacco smoke and spilled whiskey. If Farnum's Tavern were, as some Baptists claimed, Satan's Entry Hall, Satan needed a new housekeeper.

Young Masters in various stages of drunk sat along the table. Mammy Ruth knew them. She'd known them as children.

She should have been surprised to see the man presiding, but she wasn't. She was heartsick.

Philippe Robillard sat beside Colonel Jack, and Miss Ellen was pressed against Philippe like a second skin. His top hat askew and his ruffled linen shirt open to his navel, Philippe was a beautiful ruin. On her pale brow, Miss Ellen wore a circlet of delicate pink camellias: a bride's circlet. Miss Ellen's eyes were dull. Youngbloods will continue too long and too late, until what had been bright and hopeful with the sunset and the first glass has died.

"Fetch us a tankard, wench!" In the shadows Colonel Jack hadn't recognized her. "Savannah niggers slower'n my piss water."

"They were quick enough until Philippe caned our waiter," young Master Billy Obermeier objected. "Niggers have limits. Man can't push them too far."

Absently but tenderly Philippe patted Miss Ellen's hand. "Are you performing my wedding, Jack? Or must we wait until you drink the last of my wine?"

Colonel Jack Ravanel grinned. "Perform, Philippe? Tonight?" He scraped his chair back, stood, and beamed on the company. "Dearly beloved . . ."

"I ain't your beloved, Jack," young Master Fleet objected.

"More's the pity, Jimmy," Jack leered.

Billy called, "Wench, where's those damn tankards!"

Mammy stepped into the light. "I ain't no wench, and you already drunk aplenty. An' you, young Master Fleet: what your Papa think if he sees you now?"

Colonel Jack gasped. "Ruth!"

"I Mammy Robillard now, Colonel Jack. I comes to fetch Mistress Ellen home."

Philippe lurched to his feet. "You forget yourself, nigger."

"You gonna cane me, Master Philippe? You gonna beat me till I faint? What your poor Momma think of that? Miss Osa, she never cause nobody no harm. What she think of these shenanigans?"

"Ruth . . ." Colonel Jack began.

"I young Mistress Ellen Robillard's Mammy. This suppose to be Miss Ellen's weddin? Where her guests? Where her family? Where the churchhouse? Where the preacher? Is you, Colonel Jack? You repented and confessed your sins and got yourself ordained so you can tie the knot what no man put asunder? God be praised! Miss Ellen, them saints of yours; what they think of these goings-on? What Jesus Christ think? You think He nailed Hemself on the cross so young masters could drink and fornicate?"

Philippe shrugged off Jack's restraining arm. "I'll sort this out," he said and fronted Mammy.

Mammy gave not one inch to the young white master. "Young Master Fleet," she called past Philippe. "What you gonna tell your Papa 'bout tonight? He gonna be so proud? And you, Master Obermeier, three weeks after your Papa pass to his Heavenly Reward and you Momma sorrowin' and grievin'. You think your Momma smile when she hearin' what you done tonight?"

"I never . . ."

"You never said no neither. You never said 'Don't mock God!' He been here tonight, what would Papa Obermeier thought?"

Miss Ellen restrained Philippe's arm. Her tiny hands forestalled him. "Darling Philippe, she is my Mammy!"

Whiskey fumes clung to the young master like morning fog. "Nigger!" he bleated as if the word explained everything anyone might want to know about her.

"Master Philippe," Mammy said quietly, "I knowed you when you in nappies and you was a troublesome child! But you was lovable. You always been lovable, and I reckon Miss Ellen loves you tonight. But you ain't in nappies now: you a man! One day, be important man; governor, senator maybe. You gonna want this *affair* knowed then?" Mammy mimicked Langston Butler's Low Country drawl, 'Philippe Robillard? Oh—that fellow! Didn't he marry in a tavern?' You want that name for youself? You want that name for Miss Ellen?"

Colonel Jack's guffaw broke the spell. "My God, don't I love a fiery woman!"

Coolly, Mammy replied, "Yes, sir. I reckons you do. Least, you tries to. But I got to ask you, Jack, I fathomin' your heart"—the candles fluttered and popped—"what would Miss Frances have said 'bout these goings-on?"

Jack's forehead furrowed into knots and he swallowed. He dragged his sleeve across his eyes. He lifted the bottle to his lips, and his Adam's apple bobbed. He wiped his mouth and set the bottle down. "I believe that's enough for tonight, gentlemen. The cock will soon crow. Philippe, let me pour you a nightcap."

The young Masters sat stiff as statues while Ellen unpinned the flower circlet and laid it on the table. Absently, she patted it. "It is awfully late, gentlemen," she said. She smiled at Philippe. "Good night, my darling."

Miss Ellen Robillard didn't speak another word that night. She wept all the way home.

Hardening the Heart

THE FESTIVAL CAKE was a shambles.

Eulalie Robillard happily picked through the visiting cards guests had left that afternoon. Some had been Master Pierre's émigré compatriots—solemn and considered—others L'Ancien Régime customers. Eager young bachelors, including the persistent Gerald O'Hara, had called on the one day of the year Savannah's great homes admitted anyone who knocked. Eulalie's Franklin Ward had come early and stayed late. Exhibiting an uncharacteristic holiday spirit, Carey Benchley hadn't joshed Franklin—not even once—about the end of the world.

Nehemiah's tray was loaded with empty tumblers, half-empty teacups, and overflowing ashtrays. Eulalie ran her finger over Franklin Ward's engraved card, and Nehemiah pretended he didn't hear her whisper, "He loves me, he loves me not, he loves me."

Six o'clock in chilly Savannah, Georgia, Sunday, the first day of the new year. Outside drawing room windows, the lamplighter was illuminating Oglethorpe Square. Redolent with perfume, tobacco, and whiskey but empty of guests, the withdrawing room was reverting to familiarity. Master Pierre had gone to bed. These days Pierre avoided all but obligatory social occasions.

Miss Ellen had managed hostess duties while Mammy and Nehemiah fetched drinks, teas, and Cook's holiday dainties.

Now, when the pull bell clanged, Nehemiah didn't bother concealing a yawn. "Goodness me. Who can that be?" he inquired of no one in particular.

Eulalie preceded him into the hall, where she returned the visiting cards to their tray. After a glance in the pier glass, she patted her hair into place before settling in the hall chair, where she took up a *Godey's Lady's Book*.

Nehemiah's bow as he opened the door would have seemed less than perfectly welcoming only to those who arrived during polite visiting hours. "Good evening, Madam. Mercy!"

Osa Robillard's black hair had been jerked out in clumps. Her slashed cheeks oozed dark blood. Her eye sockets were guttering fires.

"Why, Mistress Osa! Do please come in. May I fetch tea? Something stronger, perhaps?"

She held a small packet in her trembling hand.

"Do come in, Mistress. Please take a seat in the drawing room whilst I summon Master Pierre . . ."

Eulalie set her magazine down. She gaped.

Nehemiah said, "Weren't you intendin' to retire, Miss Eulalie?"

Eulalie promptly did.

Nehemiah found the reassuring smile one reserves for unpredictable people. "I must insist, Mrs. Robillard. Come inside the house. Please."

Immobile as the wooden effigies with which tobacconists promote their wares, Osa Robillard was caught between the last cold light of a winter evening and the warm glow of the Pink House's holiday candles. Nehemiah tried a new tack. "You've something for Master Pierre?"

She shook her head sharply.

"For . . . ?"

"For her."

"Madam?"

"Her. That girl. Philippe's woman."

"If you're thinking of Miss Ellen, Miss Ellen hasn't seen your son since he left Savannah." Nehemiah searched for a commonplace. "Young love rarely runs smooth."

The Indian woman waited still as death, until Nehemiah took her packet.

"Are you sure you won't come inside? You . . . I . . . Master Pierre . . . Thank you, Mistress Osa. Wishing you a happy and prosperous . . ."

When Philippe's mother was gone, Nehemiah bolted the door, ran his thumb over the packet, and muttered, "Oh, dear me. Oh, dear, dear . . ."

. . . I regret to inform you that your son has met an unhappy end. Some months ago when Mr. Philippe Robillard arrived in New Orleans, he was too familiar with pursuits older, more prudent gentlemen avoid. With his considerable means, the young man attracted associates with similar inclinations.

The young man chose me as his confessor. Though he did wicked things, Philippe didn't have a wicked heart. To this day I believe had he known what was acceptable to his Maker, he would have embraced those practices as easily as the familiar sins he busied himself with. To me, who became his friend (perhaps his only true friend), Philippe seemed curiously innocent—no more responsible for his acts than wild animals in the forest. Philippe's soul was

turning to the light, and his Faith in God's goodness remained
strong. He was shot in a quarrel over cards, and, thanks be to God,
he lived long enough to repent his sins and receive absolution.

Philippe wasn't given time to become the man he would have
been. I shall pray for him and for you in your sorrow.

Yours in Christ,
Fr. Ignace, Cathedral of S. Louis, New Orleans

The packet contained four of Ellen's letters and a miniature of
Ellen Robillard painted only last year.

———

Mammy said, "I knowed it. Just looking at that boy, I knowed.
Young Master Philippe too beautiful to live." She stuffed everything back in the packet and, sick to her heart, trudged up Jehu's
stairs to give Miss Ellen the news.

———

Mammy didn't talk much that long, long night. Sometimes she
held her child. Sometimes she washed the child's face. What Ellen
said that night, her cries and the terrible words she uttered, were
never repeated by Mammy and won't be repeated here. Ellen's soul
flowered that night as her old soul died in agony, recriminations,
and tears.

———

As sunrise lightened magnolia leaves from black to green and a
valiant songbird attempted a brave hesitant twitter, Mammy wiped
Ellen's tear-streaked face. "Honey, yes you can go numb, but goin'
numb ain't different than lyin' down and dyin'. Miss Ellen, don't you
never harden your heart. They folks in this world, folks right here
in Savannah, Georgia, who done lost everyone they loved. Them,

even them what has lost everything, they gots to get to doing, same as they loved ones was still here. They gots learn to love again. They gots open they heart. We don't know—none of us knows—what sorrows gonna trample us. But we ain't put down on this earth for to buck and jibe. We gots bear our burdens and don't pass them on to nobody else. Want to or don't, we gots get up and be doin'."

After a time, Miss Ellen blew her nose and opened the French doors. Soft, scented Southern air slipped into the room, washing the bitterness away. One brave bird became a choir. Miss Ellen sat at her dressing table and brushed her hair.

"Please lay out my gray outfit," she said, dabbing color onto her wan cheeks. "Mammy, have Nehemiah bring the coach around. I shall call on Mr. O'Hara."

"Miss Ellen . . . visitin' a gentleman! At this hour!"

Ellen turned to take her servant's face in her hands. "When I accept Mr. O'Hara's proposal, he will forgive the unseemliness of the hour. And, Mammy—you must not question me. Never again,"

PART THREE

The Flint River

How Me and Pork Get Lit Afire

NEHEMIAH ASKS ME, will I jump the broomstick with him? He say Master Pierre need us take care of him. What about Miss Ellen, I say: who be carin' for Miss Ellen, married to that Irish O'Hara and goin' Up-country, where there snakes and gators and red Indians and every kind of nastiness waitin' for a nice Savannah girl like her? Nehemiah say Miss Ellen old enough get married, she old enough take care of herself. Master Gerald take care of her. Master Gerald cunnin'. He win at cards and now he win Miss Ellen. I say I don't hold with cards; cardplayin' Devil's Work what get young Master Philippe killed. Nehemiah, he say, young Master Philippe be Satan's problem now, and I say, who you be judgin' him? and Nehemiah say, he 'most ruin Miss Ellen and break he Momma heart, and I say, Nehemiah, I thought you was a Christian.

He say, be that as it am, will I jump the broomstick with him? Now, Nehemiah a good man. He been doin' Master Pierre's business so long, it like he Master of that store. But I been marry and 'tweren't no broomstick neither. Weren't no Master take up some old broomstick for we hop over when Jehu and me marry. I marry by a real preacher, in the AME Christian church in Charleston with Le Bon Dieu and all He spirits watchin'. I married Jehu till death do us part, and death didn't part us neither. Jehu and me, we still married afore Le Bon Dieu and all them gone on afore. I didn't tell Nehemiah that. Nehemiah don't know 'bout suchlike and likely give me sass. I tell him I goin' with Master Gerald and Miss Ellen and that snooty boy, Pork, Up-country and we make new lives there on Master Gerald's plantation, where we be happy 'n' blessed. Nehemiah say it ain't gonna be no different Up-country than right here in Savannah, but I tells him sure it am. Ain't it a different place? Ain't we startin' over? You distress 'cause I ain't jump the broomstick with you.

So he say he gonna miss me and his life never be good when I gone, and I think maybe he say that first when he ask might be I answers different but probably not.

Miss Ellen never say one word more 'bout Master Philippe, not after she come back from seein' Master Gerald, nor that afternoon when she and Master Pierre in the drawing room and Master Pierre ask his daughter what she thinkin' for to do. Miss Ellen say she got it in her mind to be a nun. Mistress Solange, she was Catholic and Miss Ellen reared Catholic, but Master Pierre ain't. He thinks Catholics got to bow down to Pope in Rome. Now, Master Pierre tell Miss Ellen she shouldn't go off and be no nun. She don't argue back. She just sit there lookin' sad but like she mind made up.

That evenin' after supper, which nobody ate not a bite, Master Gerald comes to Pink House and Nehemiah show him into the drawing room, where he sit on one of them tall stiff chairs. He wearin' his black suit. He black top hat in his lap.

Master Pierre come in and Nehemiah fetch a decanter and glasses and Master Pierre offers Master Gerald a drink and Master Gerald say, "Just a finger," which is a test, I 'spect, 'count of him bein' Irish. Master Gerald thank Nehemiah, meanin' he can leave, which he do, but him and me stay outside door overhearin'.

They talkin' 'bout the weather and they talkin' 'bout cotton prices and they talkin' 'bout who gonna be next president and whether Texas gonna be took into the Union. Then Master Pierre jerk open the drawing room door, but me and Nehemiah hears him tiptoein' and has made ourselves scarce.

Mistress Ellen in her bedroom with that old *Lives of the Saints*, which she has plucked out of the closet I guess. I ask her do she want tea and she say she don't. I want say more but she don't want hear nothin' so I goes to the kitchen and drinks tea myownself.

When bell jangles in the kitchen, me and Nehemiah returns to drawing room, where them gentlemen is standin' up like they has decided where and when they gonna duel. Master Gerald, he red faced, and Master Pierre saggin': old and tired. He ask me fetch Mistress Ellen.

Miss Ellen come down Jehu's stairs, pretty and proud as one of them French queens goin' to the guillotine. Master Pierre want get everything done and over with, and in the drawing room with me and Nehemiah pretendin' we is wallpaper, Master Pierre he ask Miss Ellen do she want marry Gerald O'Hara. Master Pierre start to call Master O'Hara "this Irishman," but he got deportment, so he choke them words down. Miss Ellen white as winding sheet and her lower lip tremblin' and she lookin' miles past them gentlemen, might be all the way to young Master Philippe and Mistress Solange and the other spirits. Miss Ellen Robillard say, "I will marry Mr. Gerald O'Hara."

That were the end of that.

Next day, Miss Pauline come to Pink House throwing a hissy. She stomp upstairs into Miss Ellen's bedroom and tells her sister how she can't marry no Irishman, which make Robillard family look low-down in the eyes of everybody what matters. Since she marry Carey Benchley, Miss Pauline go to Baptist church five days a week. Miss Pauline ask her sister how she gonna meet her Maker married to an Irishman. Miss Ellen am Miss Pauline baby sister and she not so big and she ain't hardly got no reputation left 'count of carryin' on with young Master Philippe, but she say she will marry Gerald O'Hara and she thank Miss Pauline to watch out for sheownself, 'stead of meddlin' in other folks' business.

Miss Pauline holier than Moses, but Miss Ellen shootin' fire out her eyes and won't hear no foolishness, so Miss Pauline she start snivelin' and sayin' how she don't want nothin' but what best for her baby sister and she and Master Carey gonna pray for her every day. Miss Ellen say what prayin' needs done, she do it sheownself!

Miss Eulalie protest too, but she hypocrite. Miss Eulalie pretend she shamed 'cause her sister marryin' Irishman but if whole truth told, Miss Eulalie can't wait for Miss Ellen be out of Pink House, farther the better! When gentlemens come Pink House, ain't no Miss Ellen to look at, only Miss Eulalie.

Master Pierre glum. He friends come round with they hat in they hands. Everybody tiptoein'.

Miss Antoinette come to Pink House. She smilin' and she pert but she pantin' like dog sniffin' new bone. She say she Miss Ellen's friend. Say she Miss Ellen's *oldest* friend. They has known each other since they was childrens. Miss Antoinette has all kind of idea 'bout Miss Ellen's weddin'. Miss Ellen, she thanks her for stoppin' by and thanks her for offerin' help and thanks her until Miss Antoinette understands Miss Ellen sayin' no thanks. Deportment a two-edged sword.

Master Pierre mopin' round 'count he lose he favorite daughter, and me too. But come wedding day, he he old self. It a pretty spring day, sun shinin' and everybody happy see young folks marryin'. At St. John's, French folks and Master Pierre's friends on Miss Ellen's side the aisle and Irish on Master Gerald's. Me and Pork and Cook and Big Sam up in the garret. Afterwards the white folks go down to the City Hotel, where they get drunk and happy so they forgets which am Irish 'n' which French.

If Miss Ellen's sisters thought she was lowerin' herself marryin' that Irishman, they was mistook. Master Gerald weren't French and he didn't have no deportment, but he were a sight better husband than Philippe would have been. Better cardplayer too. Master Philippe, he drink whiskey and play cards 'cause that's what Low Country gentlemens do. Master O'Hara, he doesn't drink only a little bit when he playin' cards and mostly he win. Cards 'nother business to him. A while back he wins Pork, who s'posed to be the most finest gentleman's gentleman in Savannah. Couple years after Pork, Master Gerald wins a Up-country plantation from a speculator who got it in the land lottery.

After Master Gerald gets Tara fixed up nice, he comes to Savannah with Pork and Big Sam, Tara Plantation foreman. Master Gerald come to fetch himself a wife, best wife he can, who was naturally Miss Ellen. My Mistress were the "most eligible" maiden in the Low Country.

For a wedding present Master Pierre Robillard give Mrs. Ellen O'Hara her momma blue French tea set and me. I reckon I the only woman in the whole world been a wedding gift twict.

———

After they wedded, Master Gerald a whirlwind and Miss Ellen keeps with him. When Pork drag he feet they leave him behind. They buyin' necessaries for the Up-country, which ain't civilized. Now she married woman, Miss Ellen practical. She asks Cook what pots and pans she should buy and asks me 'bout what babies got to have. She blushes when she ask so I guess her and Master Gerald bein' friendly.

Pork say Tara got big kettles for scalding hogs and boiling down syrup and apple butter but ain't got nary small pots and pans nor roasters. It ain't got nary loom nor spinnin' wheels nor carding combs. It got no herbs, powders, nor potions. It got axes and saws aplenty, but Master Gerald carve he roast with he belt knife.

Tara need salt, barrels, and casks. Tara need bedclothes and lamp oil and lamps. Tara need everything what makes plantation civilized!

Miss Ellen buy cottons and woolens and best thread and English needles. Master Gerald buy calf hides for traces and shoes, ox hides for hobbles and harness. He buy a big iron screw for he cotton press and a three-piece plow what am the first three-piece plow ever get to Savannah. Master Gerald poke through cotton seed like he ain't seen no cotton seed afore, he pokin' and sniffin' and peerin' and askin', and he put seed in his mouth and taste afore he chooses. He buy a roan mare for Miss Ellen and a sidesaddle with roses stamped into the skirts and carpet where she sit. He buy house servants for plantation house. Big Sam, he load servants and all them goods into three wagons and they sets off Up-country.

Morning after they gone, we say good-bye to Savannah. Good-bye, Customs House. Good-bye, St. John the Baptist. Good-bye, Oglethorpe Square. Good-bye, Pink House. Good-bye, Jehu staircase.

Master Pierre, them Benchleys, Miss Eulalie, and Nehemiah at the railroad depot see us off. Miss Pauline, she informin' she sister how to dress and how to behave and how to brush she hair. Miss Pauline ain't got deportment, but she think she do. Miss Pauline tell Miss Ellen how to travel on the railroad, though Miss Pauline never been on no train sheownself. Master Gerald actin' like goin' Up-country pulled by a smokin', huffin', puffin', hissin' steam engine is the naturalest thing in the world.

I smell whiskey on Master Pierre but don't say nothin'. When we 'bout ready to get in the train, Master Pierre walk Master Gerald down the platform where rest of us can't hear. I 'spect Master

Pierre sayin' how Master Gerald got to take good care of his daughter, and I 'spect Master Gerald promise he goin' to. Nehemiah ask I should write him. I never told him I can't write nor read neither. I kiss Nehemiah like he were my husband.

I thinks how many peoples I knowed I ain't never gonna see no more and gets to cryin', and Master Pierre is red faced and waggles he hands like he do when he don't know what else. It's for Miss Ellen to say, "Time we get in the car. Time and the Georgia Central Railroad won't wait."

Railroad train is an engine car and a wood car up front and a passenger car and three empty freight cars after. We climbs onto the passenger car and the train conductor has me and Pork to sit on the very front bench. The steam engine is puffin' and shiverin' like any minute it gonna explode, and I reckon that's why coloreds is up front.

Master Gerald and Miss Ellen ain't finished sayin' good-bye to the Robillards when comes a jerk near to snap my head off and a whistle screams hurtful and then a second jerk, which yanks me forward, and another jerk into the bench and we is rollin'! Nehemiah and Miss Pauline joggin' alongside. Miss Pauline got last advices for her sister.

Pretty soon Miss Pauline drop back and Nehemiah too. Goodbye, Savannah! Good-bye, Bay Street! Good-bye, Everybody!

We cross canal basin and swamp and we gets to goin' faster and I learns why we up front: black smoke and hot cinders find us afore they find white folks and they cinders aplenty and they hot as hornets!

I dabbin' all over myself with my kerchief so I don't burn up!

When wind blows crossways, smoke gone. Train rattlin' and clatterin' and I sees Pork's mouth movin' but can't hear one word. Swamp grass a-whizzin' by. We goin' faster'n fast horse! We goin' faster'n Lucifer when he tumble out of Paradise, and if this train quit it tracks we surely gonna meet Lucifer or Jesus: one or t'other. Betwixt dabbin' cinders I got death grip on my bench. Little black holes burnt in my new shift!

Forenoon, train come into a town and stop. Miss Ellen says we is halfway to where we goin'. Halfway plenty for me. Train don't fuss Miss Ellen none. Her duster has holes burnt and her hair a mess, but Miss Ellen ain't fuss.

Master Gerald, he laughin' an' carryin' on. "Grand!" he say. "God's nightgown! Isn't this grand!"

He go on 'bout how world changed now, how railroad gonna change everything. Master Gerald say folk gonna stop fightin' each other 'count we closer and people gets to know each other.

Master Gerald proud like he invent railroad hisself, and I ain't got heart to say sometimes we fight 'cause we already know 'zactly who the other is.

My hands sore from grippin' my bench and my knees knockin'. I glad turn my back on that train!

We is in Louisville, which wanted be Georgia state capital but didn't get to be. Town's near pretty as Savannah. Wide streets and big houses and fancy carriages and hundreds of cotton bales piled up for train. Across the street from train depot is this big hotel with white pillars and shaded veranda, and Master Gerald, he pick Miss Ellen up and totes her up the front steps past all them folks on the veranda, who is clappin' they hands. Miss Ellen, she 'barrassed as can be. Master Gerald ain't got deportment. Deportment don't mean nothing to them Irish!

Pork walk me round back to the hotel yard, and whilst Pork washin' at the pump I come into the kitchen house, where Cook and her maids gettin' supper for white folks. Directly Cook gives me a mess of greens.

After a time Pork come in too, fussin' like always. Pork a "gentleman's gentleman." Onct I ask Pork why ary gentleman needs a gentleman if he am one heself and Pork get huffy. He tell me if I got to ask I'll never understand, which am one of them things men say when they got nothin' to say.

After the white folks gets they supper, kitchen quiet and Cook and me goes outdoors, where ain't no hot stoves. Cook says she been at hotel since she pickaninny and hotel never been busier. White masters cotton rich and they buyin' 'spensive horses and house servants.

I tells her we is goin' Up-country but can't say how far. She say Up-country planters swears and drinks and whips they servants for no good reason. I say I never seen Master Gerald with no bullwhip, and she says I ain't Up-country yet. She says bein' Up-country coarsens ary Master so he don't know who he is nor what he doin' no more. Up-country Masters worse'n savages. Pork has ate he supper and is stuffin' he pipe and he say he has known Master Gerald many a year and only onct did he take a whip to a colored and that nigger deserved it. Pork strikes his lucifer and I sneeze at the stink and he light he pipe and puff like a railroad engine. Pork say, Master Gerald hate to whip a horse, and if he don't whip no horse, why he whip a man?

Cook say many a Master kinder to he horse than he coloreds. She know one Master come to this hotel many a time and he sob like a baby when he horse break it leg and he gots shoot it. Very next day he whip a colored boy, ain't sixteen, until boy couldn't stand on he feet no more.

Pork say Master Gerald a kind Master. Field niggers take advantage of him. Don't take advantage of Overseer Wilkerson, no sirree. Pork so smug so I asks who hire overseer and who give overseer run of the plantation. Pork pipe smoke set him to coughing. He tell Cook Tara Plantation just as civilize as Louisville. Cook snort and won't hear 'bout that.

That night I sleeps in kitchen house and Pork sleep in hall

outside Master and Mistress door. Pork 'customed to sleep foot of Master Gerald's bed, but them days gone!

Pork distress next mornin' 'count Master Gerald shave himself 'stead of waitin' on Pork bring hot water and soap and brushes and neckcloth and strop like he do. Mistress Ellen she quiet like always but smilin' like she got some secret nobody else got. We quit hotel for train, which different train from yesterday but smoke just as stinky and cinders just as hot. Masters got no sense. When you can ride or walk without cinders in your hair, why pay good money burn yourself up?

Train was quicker'n lightnin', but we didn't get to where we was goin' until evenin', which was Macon. Pork been to Macon afore and knows all 'bout it.

Today, Master Gerald don't tote Miss Ellen into the hotel. Likely Miss Ellen has say somethin' to him. Today Master Gerald got deportment.

Pork ask me walk to livery where Master Gerald have he horses. I say I seen enough stables last a lifetime and Pork say he show me somethin' I never seed. Past the livery we comes to old stone house with wooden house built atop. Last summer's weeds standin' round and door barred and boards fallin' off it. I say what this? Pork say it a fort. I say I don't care 'bout no fort. He say, it fort for when the Indians come. I looks round and say what Indians? Pork say they gone. Been drove away but I show you where they been. We walks to a hill like a big green hoecake and Pork say this where Indians bury they dead.

Might be. Hoecake hill was hummin' like beehive when spring locust flowerin'. Pork don't hear hum, but I does. Pork never sees the mist clutchin' at that Indian hill in the sunset, but I do. I shivers and tells Pork I seen enough Indians and I cold. We goes back to the hotel. Pork sleep outside O'Hara door that night too, which he don't like better'n he done afore.

There ain't no more railroad for us. No more stink, smoke, and fire. I say huzzah. Hip-hip-huzzah. Master Gerald want me and Pork ridin' horses while him and Mistress Ellen ridin' the buggy, but I say I ain't never seen no colored woman on no horse and I ain't gonna see one this day. Horses ain't no good for nothin' 'cept killing folks.

Master Gerald he get red faced and say he's had enough of insolent servants and where his bullwhip and I say he bullwhip in the whip socket where arybody got eyes can see it, so Master Gerald say him and Pork ride the horses and Mistress Ellen and me in buggy.

We side by side. Miss Ellen drivin'. She were babe in my arms. I first person to carry her. Miss Ellen tellin' me 'bout red dirt. She been studyin' up. Red dirt can grow cotton, yes it can! Miss Ellen sayin' how Up-country ain't Savannah, and how glad she is we comin' to Tara. She sayin' we gots to count our blessings and I say yes'm and yes'm and my won't that be nice, but everything changed betwixt us. She Mistress now and I Mammy. Same like she never lay in my arms and I never changed her nappy. I gots to smile and like it 'cause that how it am.

We comes to the Ocmulgee River, where ferryman know Master Gerald and they talkin' 'bout Up-country happenin's. Ferryman ask buy buggy horse and Master Gerald ask what horse pull the buggy and ferryman say, "Niggers can walk," and laugh fit to be tied. Pork don't laugh. I don't laugh. Master Gerald, he don't laugh neither.

All that mornin' was up one hill and down t'other. Piney woods all round. Piney woods droop over the road and not lettin' no sunlight through. I so cold I wraps my shawl to my neck. I ask Miss Ellen is there Indians in the woods and she say don't be silly and I say I ain't silly if they is Indians in the woods and they scalps and murders us. Every few miles some track veer off into piney woods. Somebody live in there, which don't make me feel no better. Sometimes we pass by fields which is red dirt without nothin' growin' in 'em. Master Gerald all the time pesterin' us, "Is dearest Ellen comfortable," and she smile at him and say she just fine. We rides into smoke, gettin' so thick I sneezin', which is trees field hands burnin' from clearin' land. Them Up-country coloreds stare at us like they never seed nobody in their whole lifes.

Midday, we eats some cheese and some biscuit, and when we sets off again, Pork is drivin' the buggy and Miss Ellen ridin' with Master Gerald. They falls back for a long time, and when they catch us pine needles am stuck to Miss Ellen's clothes.

We comes into a small town I never did catch the name of. It were rough but had a hotel for the Master and Mistress. Mister Hitchens owned hotel. He name on it. The kitchen coloreds was friendly and fed Pork and me fatback and greens. They ask us a hundred questions 'bout Savannah because they never been nowhere civilize.

Another weary day travelin' up and down hills. Piney woods sparser and I sees a plantation house now and again. Sun droopin' and turnin' river gold when we fords the Flint River. The road climbs a hill and Master Gerald standin' in he stirrups pointin' and I sees a roof through the trees which is Tara we comin' up on.

Them fields we rollin' past am Master Gerald's. Last year's trash been turned under and plow furrows neat and straight. We comes around so the sun at our backs and we trottin' betwixt cedar trees, some big round as I am. Master and Mistress gallop on ahead. Pork says Master Gerald always gallop when he comes home, like he afeared Tara not be there no more.

Big white house on a hilltop with a commotion out front where coloreds comin' round and greetin' Master Gerald and he bride. Pork and me drive round back to the stables. Pork shouts "Toby!" and this spindle-shanked boy come runnin', takes the reins, and ask Pork how Master Gerald get Tara new Mistress and what sort of

Mistress she am though how Toby know Tara got new Mistress I don't know.

Pork say what Master do or don't do is for his gentleman's gentleman to know but ain't no business for no ignorant stableboys. I reckon Pork still smartin' 'bout sleepin' outside Master's door.

Toby say he been prayin' for Pork's safe return, which make Pork sorry for what he say, but he can't 'pologize 'count he gentleman's gentleman. I 'splain I is Miss Ellen's Mammy and she good and she kind. Toby, he bow from the waist just like Masters and say, "Welcome to Tara, Mammy."

Toby tells what happens whilst Pork gone, what field hands doin' and what house servants up to. Pork, he don't want to hear 'bout none of it. Afore they come to Savannah, Master Gerald done made Pork driver of the house servants. Driver tells servant do this, do that, go here, go there, but Pork don't want be no Driver. He happy be gentleman's gentleman and don't want drive no stableboy nor no milkmaid nor no housemaid nor no cook nor no scullery nor no farrier nor no coachman. Pork glad Master Gerald gots heself a wife for to drive the coloreds. Now Mistress Ellen drivin' house servants and Pork get back to doin' what he knows.

Pork put on mournful face when Toby say coloreds whipped while Master Gerald off in Savannah. Phillip and Cuffee whipped 'count Overseer Wilkerson, he drunk and he whip them boys for no good reason.

Pork ask what Toby want him do 'bout it. Whipped boy can't get unwhipped, can he?

Toby says there don't be no 'scuse them boys whipped. "No 'scuse at all."

I leaves them gabbin' and goes into Tara House, which has it kitchen inside. Me, I like kitchen out-of-doors, where it ain't so hot in summer and if it catch on fire don't catch house on fire.

Tara kitchen newer'n Pink House kitchen, but ain't enough

pots cook proper meal and sink's filthy! Ladles and stir spoons and whisks in a jumble in one drawer when drawers either side ain't got nothin'! Tara got one of them newfangled step stoves, but don't look like it never used. Cook pots on that stove been sittin' there so long they rusty. Cook been cookin' in the fireplace like folks in olden times.

'Spect I speak to Cook. 'Spect I speak to scullery maid too.

Down Tara hall is little room what got papers heaped on a big old table like where Master Pierre lay bolts of cloth. There a whiskey decanter and some dirty glasses on a shelf. Hanging on the wall is a picture of a foggy meadow which didn't 'pear be red dirt Georgia so I reckon it Irish.

Chair rails paint chipped, they's hand marks on the plaster and spiders favorin' everywhere light don't get to. I 'spect I speak to housemaid too. Staircase golden oak straight to second-story landin' with nary curve. Good-bye, Pink House!

Plenty jubilation out front; coloreds carryin' on like they do. Master Gerald Home! Master Gerald Home! Hip-hip-huzzah! Ain't nothing happier or foolisher than coloreds carryin' on!

I comes onto front porch, which got swings and rockers so wore I figure porch where Master Gerald mostly been livin'.

Master Gerald, he beamin' like a damfool. Miss Ellen askin' the pickaninnies who they am and how old they is, and even the shy ones answering back. Miss Ellen set one on the buggy seat and sure it wouldn't do until they was every one of 'em in the buggy just like they was white folks with somewhere's to go.

Big woman in a filthy apron might be Cook. Toothless woman, so old and crippled she can hardly hold herself up, she might be housemaid. Tara Plantation only got two house servants not countin' Pork? I thankin' Le Bon Dieu Big Sam bringin' servants for Tara House!

White man gallop up, scatterin' dust 'n' coloreds. He toss reins to a boy and jumps down. He pluck hat off to Master Gerald and bow to Miss Ellen sayin' how honored he is, so on and so on. Man don't talk like folks. Talk like Yankee. Overseer Wilkerson long and slick like string beans fried in lard.

Coloreds' faces tighten and pickaninnies creep out of buggy. Master Gerald askin' Overseer how things am whilst he gone and don't notice tight faces, but Miss Ellen, she sees 'em. Miss Ellen don't miss much.

Overseer Wilkerson claps boy on he back sayin' how Cuffee got "bit in his teeth" while Master Gerald away but Cuffee a good nigger now, and Cuffee flinch but he nod and grin and say how he seed "the error of his way" and won't backslide no more, no sir, no more.

Back of my head like voice comin' from 'nother room I hears: "What you pretend you is, you comes to be," but I don't want hear that voice, I despise that voice, and I shuts my ears.

Hand touch mine. You wouldn't know what Miss Ellen meant with that touch, but I do.

Overseer makin' it sound like Master Gerald should have stayed on Tara Plantation 'stead of runnin' off to Savannah chasin' a wife. Overseer didn't never exactly *say* that, but it what he *mean*.

After Master Gerald hear nothin' burned up nor flooded nor blowed down nor die, he don't care what Overseer say. Master Gerald he push he chest out and he lookin' round like this is where Le Bon Dieu lives, right here on Tara Plantation. Overseer Wilkerson talkin', tellin' everything he do big 'n' little till Master Gerald break in on him. This woman, he tells him, is Mammy. Been with Miss Ellen since she were born.

Overseer mouth slow from canter to walk and say how Georgia coloreds are "gratifyingly loyal." I don't know nothin' 'bout that. Overseer, he say how he overseein' *all* coloreds on Tara Plantation. I'm gonna 'ject but Miss Ellen squeeze my hand and says, "Thank you, Mr. Wilkerson. I'm sure you'd manage the house servants better than I, but they are properly the Mistress's duty and henceforth I'll direct them. Surely you have enough to do supervising our field hands."

Overseer can't do nothin' 'bout that. Deportment knife so keen you don't feel it goin' in.

How Me and Miss Ellen Bring
Deportment to the Up-country

UP-COUNTRY WEREN'T ANYTHING like that Louisville cook say. The closest town were Leaksville and got two stores, a smithy, a tannery, a saloon, a cotton gin so planters who don't own one can gin they cotton. Leaksville got a Baptist church with a garret for coloreds and a school and a racetrack, where folks sell pigs and chickens and mules and slaves Saturday mornings and race they horses Saturday afternoon. Railroad tracks down the middle of Broadway street, but weren't never no trains. Railroad gone bust afore it get to Leaksville and grass growin' twixt the tracks. Weren't no wild Indians Up-country, and Up-country Masters weren't no different than Savannah Masters. Some better, some worse; most middlin'. Tara Plantation beside the MacIntoshes, who Master Gerald don't care nothin' about, and the Slatterys, who is purely white trash, and the Wilkeses downstream on the Flint River. Wilkeses' Plantation is Twelve Oaks. Twelve Oaks Plantation house all of one piece. Ain't one room added nor subtracted since Twelve Oaks built. Twelve Oaks fancy as the Pink

House. It even got a curved staircase, though not so fine as Jehu's.

Wilkeses comes from Virginia, which was higher'n comin' from anywheres else, and Wilkeses got a rose garden and schoolin'. Master John Wilkes smilin' and nice as a summer breeze but mostly he don't say nothin'. Like he house: he big and quiet and got too much money ever talk 'bout it. He don't chew no tobacco nor spit. He horses might jump a fence if he ask 'em but generally he don't. He speak so soft other Masters drops they voices. When he tell a joke he doin' everybody a favor.

Master John got more deportment than arybody 'cept Miss Ellen. Other planters looks up to Master John and want to know how he do things. Even Master Gerald ask, though most times Master Gerald do what he was gonna do anyway. Mistress Eleanor Wilkes pretty but got fast nerves. 'Twere Miss Eleanor 'splained Up-country deportment. Up-country, Miss Eleanor tell Miss Ellen, is "vital," meanin', I 'spose, Miss Eleanor be apologizin' for Up-country when she visit Boston or New York.

Twelve Oaks got a room for books and nothin' else in it!

Young Master Ashley Wilkes already got near as much deportment as he father. Young Master Ashley go with Master John to cotton sales and racetrack and barbecues and Georgia legislature, but Young Master ain't altogether *present*. Young Master Ashley more like spirit than young man! When them other boys huntin' or fishin' or ridin' or fightin', Ashley Wilkes readin' he books. He findin' everything he need in them books!

Soon as Miss Ellen at Tara Plantation, Up-country folk calls to meet wife Master Gerald catched in Savannah. Pork serves 'em whiskey and I serves 'em tea or cool water or sassafras drink, but nobody get past front porch, which is where all visitin' done. Miss Ellen don't allow nobody set foot inside Tara House. Master Gerald peeved. I 'spect the first man and wife disagreement them two had was whether folks come inside Miss Ellen's house afore she get it ready or whether Tara still Master Gerald's house, where folks come in any old time they wants and don't wipe they boots. Naturally Miss Ellen gets her way.

Tara Plantation Master Gerald's delight. He take Miss Ellen round showin' her everything. He show red fields waitin' be planted and he show her cotton press and 'splain how new screw he bought in Savannah be better'n old screw, and Master Gerald cuss Big Sam for not bein' here yet, though Sam can't hardly be 'count we come on the train and Big Sam comin' with wagons. Master Gerald 'pologize for cussin'.

Master Gerald show Miss Ellen cow barn and horse barn and milkhouse. He brag on Tara spring, which am "sweetest spring this side of Limerick," which am in Ireland. Miss Ellen says, "How wonderful!" and "You have done so much in such a short time." And Master Gerald swells like one of them hog bladders children blow up at Christmastime.

Suppers is grits and burnt greens and fatback. Miss Ellen don't say nothin', but it don't get past her.

Miss Ellen perk up when Master Gerald takes her into little office off the hall. He point to heaps of papers, callin' 'em "plantation records." Miss Ellen itchin' get her hands on them records I can tell.

Overseer big boots come thumpin' down the hall and he crowd into office without no by-your-leave. 'Cept for removin' he hat, he take no notice of Miss Ellen.

Overseer got field hands clearin' a field in the woods beside Tarleton Plantation, and most stumps pulled out and burned up. He got hands readyin' horse tack for plantin', and didn't Master Gerald buy new three-piece plow? How his ignorant field hands gonna understand new plow?

Master Gerald laugh and say if he can understand it, anyone can. Overseer bite his lip and ask what was wrong with old plow and Mister Gerald ain't so friendly as he been and he say how we all got to make changes for more cotton production and keep wire grass down, which he has seen greenin' in some fields which wasn't greenin' afore he went Savannah. Master Gerald don't say as how Overseer should have hoed wire grass, but that what he's meanin'. Master Gerald like to laugh and act the fool and get red face 'bout what don't matter a hill of beans, but when things do matter and Master Gerald get that Irish look in he eye, best jump.

Overseer Wilkerson say he hoein' wire grass and hoein' be finished directly. He say a field hand, Prophet, too sick to work so he borrows Dilcey from Twelve Oaks. Dilcey give Prophet potions so he be workin' tomorrow. Overseer Wilkerson catch Phillip stealin' ham hocks out the meat house. Phillip pry up a board and put it back after he comes out, so no tellin' how long he been stealin', probably afore Master Gerald left for Savannah. Overseer would have whipped Phillip but Master Gerald home now.

Master Gerald don't want whip nobody, and Miss Ellen she lookin' at him like he best not. Master Gerald ask why Phillip stealin' from meat house if he got enough to eat.

Overseer fidget and say all coloreds thieves. Can't naturally help theyselves.

I'm thinkin' Overseer cut rations so he can sell what the coloreds 'sposed to eat. All overseers thieves. Just can't help theyselves.

Might be Master Gerald think so too 'cause he tell Overseer fix board in meat house and leave Phillip to him. Phillip got slow wits but he a good cowman. Cows come in like dogs when Phillip call.

Overseer Wilkerson say he got bills discuss with Master Gerald, intendin' Miss Ellen and me to leave. Master Gerald harrumph and tell him Mistress Ellen doin' Tara accounts henceforth.

Mistress Ellen smile and say Overseer bring bills and receipts to her. Henceforth.

Overseer don't favor that.

Miss Ellen say she's glad to take on some of Mr. O'Hara's burden and how Overseer Wilkerson gonna find her easy to work with which we all knows ain't gonna be so.

So Miss Ellen, she Tara Mistress, and Overseer got no more to say. Henceforth.

Miss Ellen, she ain't lyin' 'bout carryin' her share. Three days her and me goes through that house top to bottom, pokin' into nooks and crannies which rats know better'n Tara housemaids.

It a fortnight and a day afore Big Sam gets house servants to Tara. Miss Ellen look 'em over good and is they well and do arybody teeth hurt? She take 'em to the little whitewashed cabins in the Quarters, where they gonna live, and 'splain they get their rations end of every day 'cept Sunday 'count they get two days' rations Saturday night. Tara wagon leave for Leaksville Baptist Church Sundays at nine, and after they come home they can tend they own gardens and such. Miss Ellen say, "Mammy will answer your questions," and make herself scarce.

Them Savannah niggers distress. Roads rough, they didn't like sleepin' out, didn't care for they food, and don't like no Up-country, which ain't civilize. Where our market? they ask. Colored got to have a church and a market. They 'feared of Indians and snakes and bears. I say I ain't seen none. They say this ain't Savannah, and I say any fool can see that. Two womens sold away from they husbands, so I say there's nothin' arybody do 'bout that. Get yourself 'nother husband you want one. Young gal starts cryin', so I ask how foolishness make ary things better. Can't undo what's been done. They should be glad they at Tara, where Master Gerald don't favor no bullwhip and Mistress Ellen got a kind heart. They get enough to eat and no work on Sundays 'lessn it's plantin' or harvestin' time, and Master Gerald, he buy niggers but he ain't never sold none. I asks, arybody have children sold south? Two women has. I says no childrens sold south here on Tara. One more thing, I says: ain't no white man creep into the Quarters after dark for you or your daughters. Miss Ellen, she Catholic, and Catholics don't hold with such goin's-on. That's what I told 'em. I told the truth.

The scrubbin' we done—weren't no end to it! Miss Ellen and me and housemaids Teena and Belle starts in the attic, where there wasn't nothin' 'cept for leftover shingles, and through the trap into Master 'n' Mistress bedroom, which we take every scrap of furniture out afore we scrubbin' the walls, which is painted wood, not paper like Pink House. Girls beat that rag carpet for an hour get dirt out, and Miss Ellen wash the windows sheownself. Bedroom got French windows onto a balcony so you can look over Tara lawn to the river. Miss Ellen say, "Oh, Mammy! It's so beautiful!" I glad see her glad.

Other bedrooms been used by visitin' Masters who don't go home after John Barleycorn invite 'em stay. We find stinking leather breeches stuffed under a chifforobe, a sweaty sock amongst dust balls under the bed, and a gold toothpick in a crack between floorboards. Master Gerald say: "Begorra, Hugh Calvert was lookin' for that pick. Drunk as a lord Hugh was. Drunk as a lord."

Miss Ellen's smile kill his.

No furniture nor rugs or nothin' in the middle bedroom except curly pine shavin's nestin' in the corners since Tara House built. "This will make a fine nursery," Miss Ellen say.

Cuffee done paint Tara horse barn, so Miss Ellen fetch Cuffee out the fields where he been pullin' stumps. Cuffee glad for a change, but Overseer fuss to Master Gerald 'bout Miss Ellen interferin' with field hands and Master Gerald tells him how bride got to be give she head and Overseer keeps on fussin' but Master Gerald ain't listenin' no more.

Miss Ellen 'struct Cuffee mash curds for milk paint, and he ask where am the colorin', and she has brought pigments from Savannah: blue and green and gray and red. She want sky blue in the nursery with French gray moldings, and if Cuffee do good where callers ain't gonna see it, he can paint downstairs after it cleaned. She ain't decided every room, but the hall gonna be squash yellow.

Master Gerald, he ridin' his fields and overseein' his overseer and he callin' on his neighbors, and eventide, Master Gerald rides over Twelve Oaks to set on the veranda with Master John and drink whiskey. Master Gerald, he stretch out he boots and him and Master John, they talk 'bout which horse gonna win Saturday and cotton crop and whether federal government "annex" Texas to join Georgia and South Carolina and all them other United States. Then they drinks another whiskey.

Sometime Master Gerald come home singing and Toby got to help him off his horse. One time he sleep in the stable 'count of he don't want distress Miss Ellen. Come morning she pretend she don't know he weren't sleepin' in their bed. "Dear Mister O'Hara," she say to him, "you're up so early. You must learn to take your ease now and again."

Master Gerald hang he head.

Master Gerald, he don't object 'bout nothin' we doin' to Tara House, and when arybody ask him he say, "Ask Miss Ellen . . ." like he glad have *that* off he hands.

But he not glad come home and see his favorite old chair in wagon headin' to the Quarters for Big Sam to set in it. He and Miss Ellen, they have words, him red in the face and her talkin' quieter whilst he talkin' louder.

"Mr. O'Hara," she says, "you'd usurp your Negro foreman's chair. And sit in it?"

Which settled that. Miss Ellen had new chair made for Master Gerald which wasn't coming out at the seams and new chair had all four of its feets, but Master Gerald said it weren't so comfortable as the old one.

Miss Ellen, she send a young girl to study Wilkeses' kitchen. Wilkeses' cook know how to make them things fine white folks likes to eat, and Master Gerald's cook is good enough for a bachelor, but folks be visitin' now Tara got itself a Mistress.

We get after Tara kitchen with scrub brushes and buckets and lye soap. Newfangled step stove am rusty where pots been sittin', so Teena blacks it. In pantry, flour moldy, table salt rock hard, and tea leaves in tin so long time they crunch twixt fingers. Pantry ain't got what Miss Ellen need, and most of what it got only fit for hogs.

Miss Ellen smile bright. "I'll inspect the meat house later." She turn to Cook. "The key?"

Cook give Miss Ellen that key like it her own baby child.

Next morning, Miss Ellen puts on her hat and I puts on my Sunday kerchief and Big Sam drive us into Leaksville. We got to tie up behind Kennedy store, 'count they's men layin' track and sleepers down Main Street. Somebody done bought railroad and is layin' track to Atlanta, where other railroads already am.

Miss Ellen march right into Kennedy store, and I come behind.

One nigger sweepin', another layin' out new flour sacks. Master Frank Kennedy, he fidget. He running he hand through he hair and pickin' at he hand and he cheek. He so glad make Mrs. O'Hara's acquaintance and arything he can do . . .

But when she say she sign every store order here on out, he balk like a Carolina mule.

"Overseer Wilkerson . . ."

"Is in our employ."

"But he . . ."

"Mr. Kennedy. You have so many of the goods we will require, I am reluctant to take our custom elsewhere."

It sinks in she mean what she say, and Master Frank smile big like he in love. He bows to Mistress. "Mrs. O'Hara, the Kennedy store is grateful for your continued custom. Will you need an invoice with every order?"

"That would be best," Miss Ellen says. "More businesslike, don't you think?"

Me, I never guessed Miss Solange's shrewdness run in the blood.

Leaksville ain't Leaksville no more. It called Jonesboro today, but it same town it been.

———

Miss Ellen write Master Pierre: send Savannah wallpaper. Four of us scrub and sand and patch the drawing room walls, but paper get to Tara afore we finish. Miss Ellen, Teena, me, and Pork, we tote them rolls into the drawing room and unroll to see what Master Pierre and Nehemiah pick for us. Paper is tiny tangled red flowers on tan. Don't look like no flowers I ever seed, but Miss Ellen approves it.

Me and Miss Ellen ain't hung no paper afore, but Pork has. Pork mix up wheat paste and lay up canvas atop the wood walls so seams don't show. Miss Ellen got the surest hand, so she trim wallpaper strips afore me and Teena lay 'em up. It devilish gettin' 'em neat round the fireplace and windows. When we got the whole room papered, we got some left, so Miss Ellen cuts a border like crown molding at Pink House. When Master Gerald allow into room, he right glad. He crowin', "Even John Wilkes hasn't anything so fine!"

He hang he picture of a green Irish meadow over the mantel and say, "Now, Tara's home!"

By now it's September and Miss Ellen startin' to show. She want ask the neighbor ladies for tea. Master Gerald say teas be for Savannah, Up-country has barbecues and dancin', but Miss Ellen say, "Mr. O'Hara, I need to pamper myself."

He swoop her up in he arms but set her down quick, sayin', "What was I thinkin'. Faith, what was I thinkin'?"

So Miss Ellen, she write notes to ladies invite them to Sunday tea, which nobody ever heard nothin' about afore. Up-country planters 'customed to goin' everywheres together. When aryone go to a barbecue, everybody go: childrens, babes, spinster aunts, grandmas, and they coloreds too. So when Miss Ellen invite ladies come get 'quainted, half the county come to Tara. Mistress Ellen greet 'em on front porch and invite ladies inside, but don't invite no husbands nor childrens, and the coloreds wander round back to the Quarters.

Master Gerald fuddled: all them white folks standin' round with nothin' for 'em. He decide mens go huntin' while me and Dilcey watch the childrens.

All the gentlemens gallops off, and Dilcey and me take our ease on the porch. Oldest childrens nine or ten, youngest still crawlin' and tastin' the dirt they gets on they hands. Boyd and Tom Tarleton make up games for boys to play, and Cathleen Calvert am queen of the girl children. Two-year-old Tarleton twins chasin' little colored Jeems fast as they can toddle, and Joe and Alex Fontaine playin' a game with sticks. When enough childrens together they make a government and take care of theyselves until they wearied and crossways.

Dilcey got Indian blood. Her hair straight and so black it purple. She got sharp nose and tight mouth and sharp cheekbones. She calls sumac "qua lo ga," but whatever it called, it the tea what cure fevers. Voudou Catholic and Cherokee spirits different, but Cherokee get to be spirits when they dead same like voudou.

After children wearies, we marches 'em to the kitchen for a sugar cookie. Then we lays 'em down in the nursery. Dilcey say she watch 'em, so I goes downstairs, see what the ladies up to.

Them ladies in withdrawing room drinkin' tea and eating Cook's beaten biscuits with honey. Cook beat those biscuits forever! She roll 'em out and beat 'em until what can be squeezed out been squooze.

They drinkin' out Miss Solange's blue cups. Mistress Ellen has the cup with broken handle sheownself.

Teena wearin' clean dress and white apron and standin' with she hands gripped behind she back case ary lady be needin' somethin'.

Mistress Eleanor Wilkes been Savannah and Boston and New York. Her and Master Wilkes buy paintings and books. They been educated.

Miss Ellen ain't done of these things and ain't got any of these things. She a young woman married to an Irishman and carrying Irishman's baby. But ain't so many ladies in the Up-country they can put on airs.

Master Gerald has bragged on her so ladies knows Miss Ellen ain't Irish sheownself, she French. Her Papa served under Napoleon and her Momma escape from Saint-Domingue. They know Miss Ellen Papa rich. Though the Up-country ladies like Master Gerald, Irish am Irish and French French, so the ladies figure Miss Ellen marry down. Mistress Calvert was governess to Hugh Calvert children until old Mistress die and she marry Master Hugh. She a Yankee. Yankees clip their words like if they opens their mouth too long somebody snatch they tongue.

Aside her on the sofa is Old Miss Fontaine, who is Grandma Fontaine, snorin' with bubble of spit on her lip. When she see me see, Young Miss Fontaine dab Old Miss spit with handkerchief.

Miss Ellen askin' 'bout birthin' without 'pearin' to really care about no birthin', no, no; but she don't fool them ladies. Mistress Munroe say how last child nearly kills her and six childrens enough for any woman to bear, and Miss Beatrice Tarleton brags she pops out eight like a brood mare. Nothin' to it if the stallion ain't too big. Ladies smile at that, and Old Miss wake up and guffaw. Teena bring the teapot round and fetch Miss Eleanor more sherry. So nobody notice she onliest one drinkin' sherry, Miss Eleanor ask if Henry Clay ever gonna get chance be president, and Miss Munroe, who am miffed at this turn in the conversation, say if presidents came to childbed they'd do things different, and every lady agrees with her.

Miss Eleanor give me a "Who you?" smile, and Miss Ellen say I her Mammy and been "with her" forever. Miss Ellen tell how Miss Solange first husband rescue me from Saint-Domingue rebels and Maroons, and Miss Eleanor say, "First husband?" with she eyebrow raised, and Miss Ellen say, flat out, she Momma had three husbands.

The ladies digestin' that when Miss Tarleton laugh and say, "Usually husbands bury their wives. Your mother must have been tough as hickory to outlast three."

Miss Ellen say, "I regret I never knew my mother. My father, Pierre Robillard, keeps her portrait draped in mourning to this day."

Some ladies murmur approval, but Miss Tarleton say, "I hate mourning. Why waste a year of life mourning someone who cannot possibly know you're mourning?" She see on my face I don't agree and ask, "Mammy?"

'Tweren't my place socializin' with white ladies, so I tells her, "Mighty thin wall twixt them's livin' and them's dead," and leave it at that.

"Rescued from rebels and Maroons," Miss Eleanor say. "How fortunate for you."

I say, "Yes, ma'am," without really knowin' what I yessin'. White ladies wonderful at questions which ain't got no good answers.

Miss Calvert say, "Saint-Domingue—what a terrible, terrible tragedy. Wasn't it very rich at one time? One hears very little about Saint-Domingue nowadays."

"It's called Haiti now," Miss Munroe say.

Miss Eleanor sniff. "It will always be Saint-Domingue to me." She turn to Miss Ellen. "How are things in dear Savannah? The gaiety, the balls, the French cuisine . . . Savannah's such a *continental* city."

Other ladies used to Miss Eleanor carrying on suchlike and don't make nothin' of it.

Mistress Amy Hamilton be Master Wilkes's sister-in-law. She

in black mournin' for her husband but carryin' he child. Miss Hamilton say Atlanta growing fast.

"It will be a very, very long time before Atlanta is truly *continental*," Miss Eleanor say.

Other ladies feelin' sorry for Miss Hamilton for carryin' baby with she husband dead, so nobody say if Atlanta *continental* or not. Old Miss tells 'em, Atlanta used to be Terminus—the end of the railroad line. Nobody lived there.

Mistress Hamilton say, "Well, if Atlanta isn't *continental* it is *cosmopolitan*."

I thought them two names for same thing, but I can't read.

Mistress Beatrice Tarleton snap her finger at Teena, who start for the teapot till Miss Beatrice waggles her finger, no. Teena fetch Miss Beatrice glass of sherry, which she raise in toast to Miss Eleanor, who is pretendin' she ain't had four glasses already so don't toast her back.

Ladies in hoopskirts, except Miss Beatrice in tweed ladies' ridin' britches and a jacket which is hardly big enough keep her warm and boots halfways up her thighs. Pork already warned me 'bout Miss Beatrice. Miss Beatrice ain't got deportment.

Miss Beatrice rather be with men jumpin' they horses over fences and knockin' top rails off so the cows stray and coloreds got to go out and catch cows and put rails back up again.

Fairhill Plantation far side of Tara woods. They clears Fairhill when Creek Indians still about and Tarletons sleep with doors barred and loaded muskets beside they bed. Tarletons first settlers and got the best soil. Master Jim, he richer than Munroes or Wilkeses or Calverts, so no matter what Miss Beatrice wearin', the ladies say "how good" and "that's true" to her 'pinions.

Miss Beatrice strong medicine. Miss Ellen don't care for her much, but I do. Like Miss Solange, when she think somethin' she spit it out 'thout botherin' where it lands or on who.

The ladies tryin' think what to say next. They has admired Tara's "ren-a-sonce" (Miss Eleanor called it). They has got acquainted with Miss Ellen, and since she ain't had baby yet, they ain't got baby to talk about.

Miss Eleanor has got herself another sherry and is talkin' 'bout New York City, which is grander'n anyplace other ladies ever been to. Miss Tarleton jumps to the window. "Oh, look, there's the gentlemen, now. Gerald *will* lather his horse."

Ladies don't say they is, but they glad husbands ridin' in so's they can collect they children and coloreds and get on home afore dark.

Teena has got bored with bein' lady's maid and is restin' her butt against the new wallpaper, scratchin' herself where she shouldn't.

How Jesus Don't Come
but Miss Katie Do

MILLERITES FIX ON the twenty-second day in the tenth month in the Year of our Lord eighteen hundred and forty-four for Jesus come. Gonna be angels and trumpets and flamin' chariots with wheels made of eyes and pillars of fire and all manner of bother. Millerites never say whether Jesus come from Lovejoy way or Fayetteville way, so nobody know which way be lookin' nor did Millerites say 'zactly when: somewhere's betwixt sunrise and sunrise was close as they come to it. Unbelievers and backsliders lookin' over they shoulders in them days.

Master John and Master Gerald scoffin' at Millerites 'count most am Yankees and when did Yankees know anything? But Master Hugh Calvert, he 'blieve might be somethin' in it. Them Millerites read up on Book of Daniel and sat down and figured until they was blue in the face. Master Hugh say, "Very clever men made those calculations." Some of Master Hugh's coloreds start to takin' fits, so Master Hugh sits 'em down and says he just foolin'. Sun gonna rise day after tomorrow just like it always done.

When September get to October, they's a chill in the air and leaves turnin' quicker'n usual and woolly bears ain't got no red band and Master Gerald ain't scoffin' so loud. Master Gerald mostly figure he know more'n Master John 'count of Master Gerald play better cards and better rider and grow better cotton, but these days Master Gerald thinkin' might be somethin' in them books Master John set such a store by. Master Gerald, he rides to Twelve Oaks ask Master John could it be true, world gonna end? Master John laughs and claps Master Gerald on the back and says he gladly loan him thousand dollars to be repaid with fifty percent interest day after Millerites figure world end.

Tell the truth? Master Gerald don't want fret 'bout Miss Ellen and baby, so he fret 'bout world endin' instead. Lesser fret.

Master Pierre writes Miss Ellen letter. Master Pierre give me greetin' from Nehemiah. Franklin Ward and Eulalie believe them Millerites has got it right, and nowadays the Benchleys ain't laughin' so loud. Master Pierre say Franklin and Eulalie tiresome 'bout Jesus. They don't give away they money nor nothin', but come sunset October 22, they gonna be down at the church, way up in the belfry so they can see them flamin' chariots with eyes in they wheels afore arybody else.

Me, I didn't figure Jesus comin'. If He gonna take us, how come we ain't no mist round us like folks what is bound to pass? I don't see no mist round nobody 'cept Old Amos, who born in Africa and can't rise up off his pallet no more. Ain't no mist round Overseer Wilkerson, who got to be very first sinner Jesus rebuke.

Miss Ellen don't pay Millerites no mind. Jesus comin' or He ain't. She powerful sick mornings and can't eat more'n a bite, and she fret how Tara get on while she lyin' in with baby. Tara linen closets so full, you couldn't squeeze a silk handkerchief in; smokehouse hams and bacon counted and Pork holdin' the key, Cook instructed every supper Master Gerald is to eat for a fortnight. When all that done, Miss Ellen lie down and summons Dilcey.

Master Gerald want fanciest Atlanta doctor birth he baby, but Miss Ellen ain't havin' none of it. She want womens: me and Dilcey and Miss Beatrice, 'count Miss Beatrice birth so many foals and babies.

That get Master Gerald's Irish up, and he say Miss Ellen more precious than any colt ever been foaled, and when Master Gerald hears what he sayin' heownself he say, "By the blessed Virgin, I will not lose you or our baby!" Master Gerald say he gonna call on Old Doc Fontaine, and Miss Ellen lift her chin and say, "Mr. O'Hara. A male doctor killed my mother with his arrogant science and masculine impatience. The proper wife defers to her husband, as I have and will. Not, however, against her Christian conscience nor when birthing the child she has carried since conception."

Master Gerald sputter and balk but red leakin'; out of he red face and directly she kiss he cheek and say, "I know you want the best—the very best—for me and our baby. But, darling, you must trust me in this."

I 'spect I know much as Dilcey do 'bout curin' folks, but not 'bout fetchin' babies. Dilcey and Miss Beatrice, they sits next childbeds afore and one woman is like the other's hand.

Miss Beatrice, she wash she hands and pat 'em dry and lift up sheet which coverin' Miss Ellen's parts and peer close and say, "Not yet, Ellen. Rest as best you can." And she leave the room and I hear her say to Master Gerald, "Leave your wife to us, sir. You've contributed everything any man can."

Mens shouldn't come too close womens brought to childbed.

Daybreak next, Miss Katie Scarlett comes into this world. She weren't no Jesus, but prolly she was more welcome than He would have been.

Goin' home to Fairhill Plantation, Miss Beatrice jump every fence, which would have been fine if Dilcey hadn't been clingin' for dear life behind her. Old Doc Fontaine come see Miss Ellen after baby was born. He say he often doctor behind Miss Beatrice and Dilcey. Doc say they never lost no Momma nor no baby neither. His son, Young Doc Fontaine, don't hold with midwifin'. Young Doc "scientific" and suchlike. Old Doc satisfy with what works.

Like all papas, Master Gerald wants a son, but first time he picks up baby Katie and feel her warm self, he love her. From that moment, Master Gerald would have laid down his life for Miss Katie Scarlett O'Hara. 'Twere Master Gerald what named her, Katie bein' his mother's Christian name, and Scarlett his granny's family name. Master Gerald like to say, "Martha Scarlett never traveled fifty miles from Ballyharry in all her born days. Now her namesake's in America!"

Old Doc Fontaine say Miss Ellen rest in bed for a fortnight, but day after baby born she up and doin'. I bury Miss Katie's cord outside kitchen door so Tara be Katie Scarlett's home evermore.

Some folks say babies, they come into this world like a bolt of cloth. They say baby somethin' you can cut and stitch and hem into what you want: apron or headcloth or frock coat, but I'm here to tell you that ain't so. Baby got most of who she gonna be as old, old woman when she first open she baby eyes. Some baby quiet. Miss Katie can't lie still: tiny feets and hands all the time goin'. All babies greedy, Miss Katie grab ahold of Momma's teat and don't let go! Won't take no wet nurse neither. Dilcey find a fine young colored got more milk'n ary baby need; you think Miss Katie satisfy? She bawl and carry on and she ain't gonna take that teat if she starvin' to death!

Master Gerald say, "Once one has had the best . . ." Then he get red face and say, "I mean . . ." and can't think of *what* he means, but I believe Master Gerald *proud* how Miss Katie refuse that poor girl!

When she gets to crawlin' round, she means go forwards but her arms and legs drives her back till she bump up against somethin' and can't get nowhere. She get mad at herself for what she doin' and squall until I picks her up and sets her in middle of the floor and she looks at me like she's a-comin' and goes backwards again and her little lips start to tremble and nothin' ever been so wrong in the wide world as her not goin' where she want go. She don't blame me nor do she blame her Momma. Miss Katie mad at sheownself. She already know feets and arms, they's her servants and gots to do what she say, not t'other way round.

Papas forget 'bout babies once they's named. They think namin' biggest thing and Papas got other big things need done.

Master Gerald and Master John Wilkes against we goin' to war with Mexico but most Up-country folks favors it. Master Jim Tarleton in the Georgia legislature and he say America got "Manifest Destiny," which mean takin' everything what ain't nailed down.

Come July, Miss Katie gettin' round better, she scoot round the kitchen garden when I weedin', and soon enough, Miss Katie walkin'. When Miss Katie fall she bawl but gets right back up again.

When Overseer Wilkerson take Tara cotton to Jonesboro for to sell, Master Gerald go with him. Might be Master Gerald fears Overseer gonna take cotton money, run off to Texas, and make new life for heself.

After Master Gerald got he cotton money in Master Kennedy's safe, he watch the racin'.

All Masters favor horse racin', young Masters and old Masters too. Wagons and horses and shanks mare comin' to Jonesboro Saturday mornings, sell they cotton, they hogs, or they coloreds and buy what they needs, then they races till it too dark to see who wins.

Sometimes little Miss Katie and me come too and Overseer gots take us home afore racin', and he smile when Master Gerald tell him go, but ain't no smile goin' home.

Noon race is two-horse, two-miles twixt famous horses from hereabouts, some far as Macon. All the gentlemens studyin' horses and jockeys and got 'pinions, and racetrack 'pinions ain't cheap. Might be Jonesboro not grand like Charleston, but Saturday night some mens go home and hide they faces from they wives and childrens. Master Gerald, he holler and cheer but he never bets. "Faith and I should wager on another fellow's horse?" He raise he eyebrows when he say that.

After noon race, Masters go home and racetrack is for overseers and poor whites. Some hires colored jockeys. Oh, them jockeys think high of theyselves! But white men ride too except in the mule race.

Coloreds 'lowed bet on mule race, and if they ain't got no money, they bet they hats or coats.

Don't understand gamblin'. Life am dangerous and we don't know certain we gonna see sun rise tomorrow. Why men got to bet their coats, I don't know. Salt poured on salt don't make it no sweeter!

Miss Katie's first word was "Ma . . ." which she say to me one morning in the nursery, but her second word was "Pa . . ." which she say to her Papa when he put her to bed. I let Master Gerald think he the first word his daughter ever say to the world. He tell everybody!

Cotton prices poorly, so Master Gerald he push on Overseer Wilkerson and he push on the coloreds to work harder'n what they done and God help poor colored man waste arything, whether it scattered seed or ill-picked boll or broke harness snap. Harder they works, lower cotton price drop. They's money in cotton business, but harder you works, less you makin'.

Second baby, Miss Susan Elinor O'Hara, take her middle name from Miss Eleanor Wilkes, only spelt different 'count of Master Gerald didn't want be beholden. Miss Suellen, for that's what we gets to callin' her, were as quiet and sunny as Miss Katie busy and didn't see no difference twixt wet nurse teat and Momma's. Miss Suellen weren't particular.

Masters talkin' 'bout Mexican war. First time America ever invades ary other country. Afore now, we's the ones bein' invaded. Masters struttin' like they're a better country since they invade somebody like British and French been doin'. Master Jim Tarleton say war bound to drive up cotton prices, war be good for planters.

"Bad for our sons," Master John Wilkes say.

They's twict a day trains to Atlanta. Gamblers buy a dollar ticket come for Jonesboro races.

Me and Miss Beatrice and Miss Ellen sit with Dilcey while Dilcey have her baby, Prissy, and Miss Ellen birth her third girl child, Caroline Irene, who is colicky. She fuss and cry and nothin' satisfy her. I don't get no sleep till she six months.

For Christmas, Master Gerald take whiskey cask to the Quarters and some coloreds get ravin' and Miss Ellen tells Master Gerald he married with three childrens and he don't need no coloreds pukin' and fallin' down. I don't say nothin'. Don't got to. Master Gerald know how I feels!

Miss Katie favors Mistress Solange. She ain't no pretty child except for her eyes, which are green like spring leaf. Whatever her smile be sayin', her eyes be thinkin'. From the start, Carreen be serious like her Momma be, and I pray nobody don't give her no big book of saints to study up on.

If I doesn't know where Suellen come from I couldn't figure who her people am. Suellen sneaky like neither her Papa or Momma. I reckon she come from somebody way back, maybe Solange's granny or Granny Scarlett O'Hara's papa. Sometimes when Suellen sly without no need, I almost see old woman in old-timey clothes slippin' round.

Sometimes Miss Katie do somethin' or hold her head cocked

like she do and I can almost hear Miss Solange fussin' at Master Augustin 'bout money or somethin', but when I looks at Suellen, I sees that old woman in old clothes and halfway wish old woman speak her piece.

Everybody happy when Mexican War finish. White folks always excited go to war and glad when it over. Master Gerald's Savannah nephew Peter, he fought with the militia and got to be an officer and Gerald's friends talked about buyin' Peter a commemorative sword, but nothin' come of it.

One mornin' when Big Sam shinglin' our tobacco barn, Master Gerald climbs onto rooftop 'count there ain't nothin' he like better'n overlookin' Tara, admirin' he fields and he woods and he crops and he barns and Tara House and meat house and everythin' he got.

When Master Gerald hear voice sayin' "Papa," he look quick but don't see child in the lane nor the wagon yard nor stable nor anywhere until he turn round and he eye pop out he head 'count Miss Katie on the ladder tippy-top reachin' out so's she can climb on the roof, which is terrible long way from the ground. Later Master Gerald tells Miss Ellen, "Holy Mary, Mother of God! My heart near stopped!" He speakin' soft to Miss Katie while he easin' down until she wrap she little arms round his neck. Big Sam go down ladder first and Master Gerald after case Miss Katie slip her grip. When Master Gerald reach the ground and let her down, Katie gigglin' like it the most fun any child ever have! Master Gerald knees knockin' together and he gots sit down!

When Master Gerald tells, Miss Ellen face go white and she want to know who was watchin' Miss Katie and Teena sent out to the milkhouse and Rosa brought up to Tara House as housemaid.

Not long after, it evenin' and fireflies sparkin' and I hear hummin', one of Master Gerald's Irish tunes, and I peeks into hallway and there they is, Master and Mistress in each other's arms and they dancin'. That were the happiest they was ever to be.

We Grievin'

THEM DAYS SEEMS like I everybody's Mammy: Master Gerald, Miss Ellen, Miss Katie, Miss Suellen, Miss Carreen, Pork, Rosa, Cookie, Little Jack tryin' be a house servant, and them coloreds come to kitchen door 'count somebody sick or been cursed or need a herb to help they man love 'em. Mammies gots to see and Mammies gots to know. Masters can believe arything. Master Gerald think he a foot taller'n he be, and Miss Ellen think she less'n what she am. Mistress Beatrice think she boys grow up just fine without no Mammy and Momma more with she horses than she sons. Mistress Eleanor believe settin' silver proper am good deportment, and Master John, he think he can do right and mind his business and read he books and nothin' terrible ever happen to Twelve Oaks nor to them he loves.

Mammies gots to see and Mammies gots to know. We don't know, we can't do, and Mammies got to do. We can't hold with no foolishness.

Mammies don't got to say what they know. Plenty times Master Gerald ask me 'bout this colored or that colored and I shakes my head, pretendin' I don't see nor hear no evil.

293

Ol' Denmark Vesey half right 'bout pretendin'. Fool pretend he know more'n he do, Mammy pretend she know less. I knew what I knew and never told a soul. What I wasn't 'sposed to see I doesn't, but arything I wants to know I know. Mammies gots to know.

Mistress Ellen all the time callin' on sick folks and old folks and in Baptist church every Sunday, though she ain't Baptist, and afore supper she gather children and house servants around her for prayers.

Masters celebrate after President Taylor elected 'count Taylor be Southern; he own a hundred coloreds and he fought them Mexicans. Masters think General Taylor 'zactly like them though they never fought no Mexicans theyownselves.

Miss Ellen got Overseer Wilkerson dancin' to *her* tune, and when bills come due, Miss Ellen pays and cash comes in she count it and she study every cotton and tobacco receipt and sale bill for every calf, hog, or lamb go to market. With her half glasses on her little face, Miss Ellen so serious she affrights Overseer, who don't dare cross her.

Although sometime Miss Ellen sick and sometime she stretch and groan and press hands to she back, she carry child like 'tain't nothin' and she don't take to bed until womb drop two hours before her water break.

Master Gerald gots himself a son! In he delight he pour Old Doc whiskey and Miss Beatrice whiskey and Pork whiskey and even pour me a glass, though I teetotal. He bounce baby—which he ain't done with none of the girls—and he lift blanket be sure he a he. Miss Carreen too young know what goin' on, but Miss Suellen she come in to kiss baby on he head. Miss Katie, she don't come in the room. She sit on porch swing and swing so hard chains rattle.

After Master Gerald see Miss Ellen and baby thrivin', he gallop to Twelve Oaks and Fairhill with he whiskey bottle and don't come home till dark and he singin' 'bout some "minstrel boy to the war is gone," which were a sad song which Master Gerald sing like a glad song. Pork helps him upstairs to sleep in bedroom t'other end of the hall.

Little Master Gerald gurgle and rock in he cradle, but all the time mist hangin' round heself, which I pretends I don't see. Mammies don't say everything they see.

Tara Christmas be gala that year. Master Gerald makes the punch heself, and Mistress Ellen drink tea with lady friends in withdrawing room across the hall. Men singin' carols and clappin' each other on the back, and Master Buck Munroe cursin' the Yankees like he always do, but Zachary Taylor in the White House and it Christmas, so Buck Munroe curses drowned out by masters singin' "God Rest Ye Merry, Gentlemen." Ladies sing "Little Town of Bethlehem." Mistress Beatrice drinkin' tea with ladies but prefer be in other room drinkin' whiskey with men.

Ten o'clock I brings the children down, and all the ladies admirin' Baby Gerald, and Miss Katie she climb in Master John Wilkes's lap and don't want come out. Master Gerald carry Baby Gerald round askin' do they see how alike they be.

"He appears to be even shorter'n you are, Gerald," Master Jim drawl, and Master Gerald's ears gets red.

Little Master Gerald, he play and gurgle like babies do, and if he sees mist round him he don't care, and I s'pose I wish it away because I'm startle as arybody when I wakes middle of that night to a low sound, I never heard the like. I jumps up to Little Master Gerald cradle. He dead. Baby still warm, so I talks to him and prays for him and begs spirits give him back to us, but mist goes away and Little Master goes away too. I beg Miss Frances and Miss Solange and even Martine why they takes him, but they don't say nothin'.

'Twas hard go down the hall to Master and Mistress bedroom.

Hard to rap on they door. I don't got to say nothin' once Miss Ellen see my face. She lift up poor little Master Gerald in she arms and rock him and sing him a lullaby.

Tara carpenter, Elijah, make a small cedar coffin, which smell so fine in the morning air when we and the neighbors standin' next the grave. Master Gerald brought a Catholic priest out from Atlanta do the buryin'.

We set back. We all set back. Master Gerald don't ride over to Twelve Oaks no more, and Miss Ellen take to starin' off like she could see into spirit world where her baby am.

But it plantin' time and seed got to get in the ground and Master John Wilkes come down with fever, so when Master Gerald ain't at Tara, he at Twelve Oaks plantin' Wilkeses' crop. He gone mornin' to night, and he come in after dark and don't wash afore he sets down on the porch, where Miss Ellen waitin' supper. He drink water straight from the jug and pour jug over his red face and hands, and Master Gerald say, "You know, Mrs. O'Hara, if John dies I b'lieve I'll make Eleanor an offer for that river field of his."

Miss Ellen shocked, then notice his mouth twitch and them two laughin' was the finest sound I heard that spring.

By July, though he weakly, Master Wilkes healed and things most back to normal. Every Sunday, Miss Ellen and Master Gerald visit Little Master's grave under the cedars.

Master Gerald weren't no Master back in Ireland. I heard 'em tell Miss Beatrice closest he gets to horses was "the tail end of a plow pony," but Gerald were Master now and 'tweren't plow horses he ridin'. Master Gerald's mares stand for Miss Beatrice stallions. Him and Miss Beatrice outbid each other when special fine horse sold at Jonesboro track, and when horse don't turn out good for one, it sold to the other. There nothin' Master Gerald like more'n jumpin' fences. Fences twixt Twelve Oaks and Tara on ridgetops where horse can't jump good 'count he climbin', them top rails knocked off so regular Master Wilkes's servants stack spare rails up there don't need tote 'em so far.

_____

Pretty soon Miss Ellen showin' again. Oh, they careful of her. I never seen no folks carefuler. Mistress couldn't ride and didn't walk 'thout Pork at her elbow, and Mistress buggy horse swapped for Old Betsy, who can't run away 'count she too *old* run.

Miss Eulalie Robillard send wedding invitation, she marryin' Dr. Franklin Ward of Charleston, but Miss Ellen can't travel so far.

Miss Katie, bored and she ain't be bored 'thout mischief, so Master Gerald grateful Miss Beatrice teachin' he daughter to ride.

Toby drive us to Fairhill at daybreak 'count Miss Beatrice like to start early. When stableboy bring out pony for her, Miss Katie say, "No."

"You needn't be afraid, Katie," Miss Beatrice say. "Pinky is mild as milk."

Well, nobody gonna say Miss Katie O'Hara afeared. "He's a . . . a . . . midget! I will ride a real horse."

"Oh?"

"Like Papa ride."

"I'm not sure you're ready for Gerald's mount just yet." Miss Beatrice laughin' at her, and no day in she life do Miss Katie tolerate bein' laughed at.

"Like Papa ride," Miss Katie say, and when Miss Beatrice don't go get horse she want, Miss Katie climb back in our rig and fold her arms and say Toby take us home.

Miss Beatrice really laugh then, like she never seen nothin' like Miss Katie. "Child, you're sure you're a girl? You're more boy than my brood!"

"I am a girl," Miss Katie says, so high-and-mighty it sets Miss Beatrice off again. She bent over laughin'.

"I swan," Miss Beatrice say. "Have you seen the like!"

Miss Katie looks her up and down cool as you please. She say, "My father promised me you would teach me to ride. I am gravely disappointed."

"Well," Miss Beatrice say, "I'm not the one to disappoint a green-eyed girl. Billy, saddle Trinket. Short stirrups."

The horse is old and solemn, and he seen childrens afore. Almost see him thinkin', Not again! but he stand still while Miss Katie set her foot in Miss Beatrice hands and climb atop.

She terrible small sittin' up there higher than our heads. Miss Katie lookin' round like world look different where she am now. I sees her thinkin' that. Horse snort and lower he head for Billy rub his nose. Miss Katie not like that and jerk the reins so Trinket raise he head up and shake it, janglin' he bridle, and he snort and prance his front feet.

"Miss Katie," Mistress Beatrice said, "as you wouldn't wish Trinket to be a little girl, you must not try to be a horse. You must let Trinket be what he is, and, so long as that doesn't interfere with your wishes, you'll allow him his little pleasures. As a rider, you are a twosome, no longer a lone-some." Pleased with what she say, she say it again. "A twosome, not a lone-some."

She attach a rope to bridle and Trinket walk round in a circle, he big feet stirrin' up dust.

Well, horse ain't gonna kill her, which the best I hopin' for. When we comes home and her mother ask Miss Katie how her horse lesson go, Miss Katie say, "I am a twosome, not a lone-some," like that were something big.

Horses and me don't see eye to eye. I figures horses one of them "necessary evils." Coloreds be jockeys and stableboys and they saddles and brushes and feeds them horses, but coloreds don't owns 'em. Horses same like plantations: horses for white folks.

Soon's I sees horses ain't gonna kill Miss Katie, I stops goin' with her. Carreen and Suellen need Mammy more'n she do, so Miss Katie go to Fairhill by sheownself, and pretty soon she stayin' there all day.

Round Christmastime, Miss Suellen get the pox, so naturally her sister get it too. Miss Carreen won't stop scratchin' herself until we wraps her hands in cotton batts, and she cry until her eyes swelled, she so frustrate. Master Gerald goes to Atlanta buy presents for he girls and comes back with oranges, which I ain't seen none since Savannah.

Come February, Master Hugh Calvert riled 'count Southern gentlemens done met with President Taylor up in Washington and President Taylor tell 'em if they secede from the Union, he lead troops against 'em heownself. Master Hugh so hot under the collar it take three drinks of whiskey settle him.

In the spring, Miss Ellen brought to childbed, and Dilcey come and Miss Beatrice and me. We don't feel good 'bout this birthin', so we talkin' 'bout arything else; Miss Beatrice goes on and on 'bout Miss Katie and her horses.

Baby born twenty minutes after water broke, slips out slick as grease. He dead. He gots red hair. Somethin' ain't right with he little fingers and toes, which I sees when I wash him for he coffin, but I don't say nothin' 'bout it.

I don't know why Master Gerald name him Gerald. To me, second baby always be Red.

Baby laid down in the shady spot beside his brother. Tara go on. Not long after Red born, President Taylor falls over dead. They ain't no wars. Cotton prices holding up. We grievin'.

Next winter Miss Ellen showin' again, but nobody say nothing 'bout it like words am curses.

Gerald O'Hara born on a bright Saturday in September. It ain't got cold yet. Miss Ellen, she labor for an hour and out he come. I cuts the cord but don't bury it outside kitchen door 'count of baby born with all he toes and tiny fingers like Red ain't got but he got mist same like first Gerald. Miss Ellen, she tired but smilin', and I can't say nothin' 'bout no mist so I gots pretend I happy as a fool. Dilcey, she gives me the eye like she see mist too. She Cherokee woman. No tellin' *what* Dilcey seein'.

Next morning after Gerald born, comes Nehemiah letter sayin' Master Pierre Robillard done pass. In he dyin' breath Master Pierre send he blessing to Miss Ellen.

Master Gerald, he take letter into Miss Ellen bedroom and close the door. Hour later, he come out and say Miss Ellen restin' and I brings tea and teapot and Solange blue cup.

After all these years, Miss Ellen still got young Miss Ellen eyes. We weepin'. I sits tea tray down afore I drops it 'count tears. "Oh," Miss Ellen say.

"Honey . . ."

"He . . ."

"'Deed he is. Master Robillard, he . . ."

"Mammy, he's gone. How I wish . . ."

So I says, "Master Pierre glad 'bout baby, Miss. He so glad." Which was hard sayin' 'count mist liftin' off Little Gerald lyin' aside her. I hate that mist. I want bat it away!

Miss Ellen so wearied she can hardly keep her eyes open, but she say we goin' Savannah soon as Baby Gerald can travel, and I say yes'm. What else I gonna say?

Miss Ellen ask me tell the childrens they gonna visit Savannah, but I reckon I forgets to.

Miss Beatrice give Miss Katie a colt of her own, so Miss Katie ain't got no time for no baby brother. Suellen and Carreen want see baby, but I don't 'low it.

White folks fightin' the Crimea, which is somewheres in Europe, and when childrens eatin' supper Master Gerald 'splains the Crimea to them 'count he don't want talk about the third Gerald, who wastin' away not born a week. Miss Ellen can't do nothing 'bout it. Young Doctor Fontaine, he can't do nothin'. Dilcey herbs do nothin'. I mix sulfur 'n' lard and dab it on my finger to give him suck, but he too puny.

Miss Ellen sleepin' when baby die. Baby Gerald tuck under her arm with he little mouth open. I close he blue eyes, but when I tries slip him out Miss Ellen sit bolt upright and snatch. She knows better, and she hands drop like leafs in the fall. She say, "No more babies, Mammy. No more."

"Yes, Miss." I don't say, "Master Gerald ain't never gonna have no son,'"count I don't got to.

I wash the little body, which ain't hardly been with us long enough get dirty. I sing old song to them gentle spirits what care for babies and small helpless creatures. I don't want name this baby Three, but that name stick in my head.

That night Master Gerald sit in drawing room with he decanter and nobody dare go inside.

Next day, Miss Ellen get out of bed. She pale 'n' puny, but work don't quit needin' done 'count no baby die.

Big Sam, he dig grave alongside baby brothers, and Elijah makes cedar coffin. Gerald and Ellen didn't bring no priest; I don't reckon they could stand it. Morning fog writhin' off trees when we gathers. Cotton harvest waitin', horses and wagons waitin', sacks waitin', men standin' with they hats in they hands and womens in best kerchiefs. Pork, he tote box to the grave, solemn as can be. Master Gerald have Miss Ellen's arm, and Big Sam standin' close behind, case she faint. Pork kneel in his best pants to set the box into the hole. Carreen, she 'bout ready to scream, but Miss Katie squeezin' she hand like it might bolt. Afterwards Master Gerald see to the ginnin' and Miss Ellen go to office and plantation books, I walks the girls upstairs to the nursery. At the door Miss Katie turn to tell me, "Mammy, I think I'll call my Colt Beelzebub."

I stops dead like, if I still enough, might be her words go away. Miss Katie shakin' like leaf in windstorm. She little shoulders shakin' and she not meet my eyes. Poor child don't know how she want to feel. I puts my arm round her. "Beelzebub a good name, honey. A very good name."

How Young Master
Wilkes Come Home

SO WE DON'T go to Savannah. Ellen's sister Pauline write that Master Pierre divide he competence among he daughters, except he gives Nehemiah L'Ancien Régime and set him free. Don't know how Nehemiah fare 'thout Pierre. It one thing pretend you Master when you gots Master, another be Master youownself.

In December a crate come to express office at Jonesboro depot and Big Sam and Prophet fetches it. It the painting of Mistress Solange from Pink House mantel, which, Miss Pauline's note say, am willed to Miss Ellen.

Miss Ellen have Master O'Hara's Irish painting took upstairs to their bedroom and hang Miss Solange where Ireland been. Master O'Hara, he doubtful. He clasp he hands behind he back and say, "I dunno, Missus O'Hara. Won't I be sittin' here of an evenin' and feel her eyes fixed on me like she is the great lady and I am her stableboy?"

"Mr. O'Hara," Miss Ellen says. "Every grand planter needs a French aristocrat over his mantel."

But Master Gerald mind ain't easy, so she say, "Dear Mr. O'Hara, Solange Robillard died so I could be born."

So that be that. Sometimes, when he think nobody watchin', Master Gerald raise he glass to Mistress Solange. Master Gerald grateful for what he got.

First time she see her grandma hangin' there, Miss Carreen gasp like she seed a ghost. Miss Katie, she study Miss Solange for a spell afore she asks me, "Am I to be like Grandma, Mammy?"

Somethin' flickers behind my eyes. It like I awake but dreamin' same time. Dreamin' I at big junction, more roads than I can count. I can go down ary of them, but I walk down Miss Katie's, and here she am wearin' a green dress which match her eyes and her hair pulled back in comb and she a woman growed. But Miss Katie ain't satisfy. It comes to me she ain't satisfy.

I rubs my eyes and slip out of that dream and clutch that old horsehide sofa. If I clutch hard enough, I doesn't faint. I say, "No, honey. Not yet you ain't." Cold chill come over me and Miss Katie ask what wrong and I says, "Someone steppin' on my grave. It's nothin', honey. You go on."

I don't know how it happen that them what wants to see can't and them what don't want to see, they gots to.

———

Young Mistress Katie O'Hara didn't want be no woman. If she could have been horse, she would have been horse. She always with that Beezlebub and can't talk 'bout nothin' else. Miss Ellen worryin' 'bout her daughter deportment 'count girls s'posed to admire men riders, not *be* one. Miss Katie impatient with pretty dresses Rosa sew for her, and them fine crocheted collars and cuffs her aunts send her for Christmas go in the chifforobe and nevermore see the light of day. Miss Katie wear boys' long pants and boys' corduroy shirts and ridin' boots. Sometimes she forget take off her spurs, and sofa foot, which is carved like a big lion paw, have lost he toe and he claw.

She bein' on that horse from can to can't. I can't get her do nothin' round the house.

Suellen and Carreen growin' up like they s'posed. They *understands* deportment, which Miss Katie plain don't. Gettin' Miss Katie deportment is like kneadin' dough without no yeast. No matter how you grunts and shoves, it gonna be one sad loaf.

Miss Katie think she got all the deportment she need, and Mistress Beatrice, 'stead of checkin' and reinin' Miss Katie in, lets her run wild.

Master Gerald, he ain't discipline Miss Katie neither. All them things what girls ain't s'posed to do, he forgives.

After three Baby Geralds, somethin' in Miss Ellen lost. She still do: she run the household, visit the sick, help them what needs help. Every day she has family prayers, and sometimes she take train into Atlanta for Catholic church. But her heart not with us. Her heart with them Geralds.

In August, Miss Eleanor Wilkes dies. Young Master Ashley be off in Europe when he Momma pass. Miss Eleanor laid out in Twelve Oaks withdrawing room, and womens sit round the coffin whilst men on veranda drinkin' whiskey and talkin' hushed. Miss Eleanor daughter Miss Honey Wilkes, she swoons, so Miss India got be Twelve Oaks Mistress. Wilkes children never had no Mammy, and it shows.

Couple evenin's after his wife buried, Master Wilkes ride over sit with Master Gerald on Tara front porch. They talkin' late and decanter empty afore Master John ride home. Master Gerald come in all gloomy and take hold of Miss Ellen and hugs her like he 'feared she gonna disappear.

Not long after, I come from church, still in my Sunday clothes, when Miss Katie come into kitchen with saddle blanket wrapped round her and she nods like "Mammy, I needs you" afore she start up back stairs. In bedroom she drop saddle blanket and the back of her britches bloody. I gasps, but Miss Katie cool like nothin' at all.

She drop britches to the floor and steps out of chemise. "Don't stand there gawking. Fetch me a washcloth."

"It's the Jack, honey." I dip cloth into washbasin, clean her up.

"I know what it is." She more annoyed than affrighted. "Haven't I helped Beatrice breed Papa's mares?"

I gasps out. "What you done?"

She shake her head like she so tired. "Now, Mammy . . ."

"No young lady doin' that sort of thing! I gots tell you Momma!" Miss Katie wrap she Papa round her little finger. Not she Momma—Katie got respect for Miss Ellen!

"Mammy! It's natural!"

"That don't make it right. Young ladies, they don't got know nothin' 'bout such things." All the time I wipin' on her, thighs and bottom, and I folds a clean towel tucked in there and we both looks at each other and Katie a woman and Ruth a woman and I can't help grin findin' my face.

"Are you laughing at me?"

"No, ma'am, Miss Katie Scarlett O'Hara. Take a brave man to laugh at you."

Which was how Miss Katie becomes a woman. She didn't care for it, not a little bit.

Grass growin' over them three little graves. Flowers open and bloom and die, Miss Ellen havin' ladies' teas again, and one by one she blue cups broke. Fairhill and Twelve Oaks and Tara and Calverts and Munroes havin' barbecues, one, two, three a month. I don't know how nothin' get done. Jincy, Twelve Oaks coachman, play fiddle so good he don't drive no rig from June to September!

Honey Wilkes mournin', but you think that keep her from flirtin'? Not on you life! Honey admirin' them boys' thisnesses and thatnesses, callin' arybody "honey," which is how she get her name. At Calvert barbecue, Honey say, "Oh, Brent, I declare I never saw a finer horseman," which Miss Katie overhear, and ridin' back to Tara afterwards, she say over and over until I thinks Suellen gonna hit her, "Oh, Brent! You ol' horseman you!"

Miss Ellen say, "Katie, it is good manners to praise a gentleman's accomplishments."

"Oh, Momma, they're not accomplishments. The Tarleton twins can sit a horse. But Brent? Beatrice talks about buying him a mule because Brent'd look *better* on a mule. Why does Honey lie about him?"

"Honey isn't *lying*. Not exactly. Flattering, yes. Honey was flattering Brent. The ability to make a man feel good about himself is a lady's special gift."

"Brent Tarleton sits a horse like a sack of flour."

"I'm sure Brent is well aware of his shortcomings, my dear. Aren't we all?"

Since I don't think Miss Katie think she got *ary* shortcomings, I smiles, and she get on me 'stead of her Momma.

"Mammy, doesn't the Bible say we shouldn't lie?"

"I dunno, baby. We ain't supposed to use the Lord's Name in vain, but that special kind of lyin', not everyday lyin'. Plenty times, I expect lyin' better'n next worst thing."

"Oh, Mammy!"

Had her way, Miss Katie wouldn't go to no barbecues, but she don't gets her way. When Miss Ellen say, "The O'Haras will attend," she mean ary O'Hara and house servants too, 'count we O'Haras, even the blackest.

But when Miss Katie havin' her own way, she off ridin' that red devil Beelzebub. Horse never know'd no other rider, ain't nobody ever been on he back 'cept Miss Katie. When she walk to the pasture, break of day, fog still hangin', he come runnin' and nickerin', glad be alive and glad be Miss Katie's horse. Katie closer to that horse than her own flesh and blood. She don't pay hardly any mind to Suellen and Carreen 'less they blockin' her way.

She Papa's Darlin', and there's many an afternoon I seen Master Gerald and Miss Katie ridin' out together like father and son.

'Thout Miss Eleanor and with Master Ashley away, Master John Wilkes don't know what do with heself. Evenings, when Master Gerald ain't at Twelve Oaks, Master John at Tara, where they talkin' 'bout cotton and horse races and "the Compromise," somethin' 'bout havin' slaves in Kansas—do they got slaves or don't they?

Them Four Horsemen of Apocalypse comin', but nobody want remark it. When them Millerites was sayin' world gonna end, everybody jabberin' mornin' to night how Jesus comin' and world gonna end. Which, come the day He don't and it don't and everybody forget 'bout Rev. Miller and he prophecy.

But war comin' so big and quick I 'most 'spect to hear drums beatin'! But nobody talk 'bout no war. It like talkin' gonna bring war on so shut your mouth! Instead, they talks about President Pierce what he doin' and Stephen Douglas and Henry Clay what they doin', and they drink they whiskey till decanter empty.

Master Ashley Wilkes been gone near three year. He been to England and France, all them places. He all the time writin' Master John 'bout them places.

Master Gerald particular glad Master Ashley comin' home. Miss Ellen glad too, 'count she hopin' when Master Ashley home, Master John not bein' so lonesome. All O'Haras 'cept Miss Katie at Twelve Oaks when Master Ashley comes home. Miss Katie has sprain her ankle and she stay home.

Jincy gone for to collect him, and we waits on Twelve Oaks veranda drinkin' sweet tea. Miss Ellen and Wilkes girls fannin' theyselfs. Bees buzzin' through rosebushes Miss Wilkes plant, which ain't lookin' so pert since she pass. Master Wilkes white as a cotton boll but smilin' like he ain't done in ages, and him and Master Gerald be drinkin' juleps Pork make, 'count Pork famous for he juleps. They discussin' how hot it am and how yesternight Master Hugh Calvert get so drunk he falls off he horse and break somethin', and both them sinners laughin' like they never been drunk theyown-selves. Twelve Oaks house niggers hangin' round and won't shoo when Miss Honey shoo 'em.

When Jincy bring buggy up lane we quit talkin'. Young Master been gone such a time we wonderin' if he still that boy born and reared on Twelve Oaks plantation. Am he who he been?

Before buggy quit rollin', Young Master Ashley jump down and take his Papa arms, like he never seed him before. They alike, but John Wilkes tired as old scrip and Ashley Wilkes bright and sharp edge as new copper penny.

Ashley changed. He were a quiet boy with gray eyes seem like he just got here and gone blink of your eye. Master Ashley changed. He done knowed women and ain't no boy no more.

He ain't lost that way of seemin' to see what nobody else do, but he don't stay away so long as before. He smile sweet and easy and sad.

Master John ask 'bout Rome and Greeks, and Master Gerald ask 'bout Ireland. Master Ashley been visitin' them places Masters care 'bout. He ain't visit Haiti nor Africa.

We all crowded around jabberin'. Jincy sets a parcel aside Twelve Oaks's front door.

"I found it in Paris," Master Ashley say.

Master John raise he eyebrows.

"I thought you'd like it. It's sentimental."

Laugh burst out of Master John, and pretty soon we all laughin' even though we ain't got the joke.

It painting of soldiers in a battle who ain't fightin' a war 'count they tendin' a little wounded dog.

"Vernet," Master Ashley tells his father, solemn as a judge.

Master John, solemn too, though he lip quiverin'. "For the hall? The withdrawing room?"

Only Wilkeses grinnin'. Us folks admirin' Master Vernet painting of soldiers tending a hurt dog whilst war goin' on. Why don't they take hold of that dog and run for they life, is what I'm thinking.

Master John have he tongue in he cheek. "Sublime."

"Man's inhumanity to dog," Master Ashley say.

Somethin' in Master John's eyes change then, 'count joke ain't funny no more. "Man is meant to mourn." Ashley Wilkes's papa ain't talkin' 'bout no painting no more.

"Mother didn't suffer?"

Master John about to break down, which he would have hated front of all us. "Death was merciful. Eleanor is in her Savior's arms."

"Oh, Ashley. Dear Ashley!" Honey and India Wilkes break the spell. They hugs him so hard, he catch his balance and sayin', "Please, please! Don't knock the weary traveler off his feet!"

Honey stick out she tongue.

Everything back to where it been. Master Gerald askin' 'bout Ireland, and he ain't satisfied till Ashley tells him day by day how he gets from Dublin to Cork and how it rain every day and the sun didn't really set so much as it slink into the mist.

"Oh, it's wet all right," Master Gerald crows and slaps his thighs like he made it wet heownself.

"And how is our dear nation? Shall we elect Frémont or Buchanan?"

His Papa say Buchanan, and Master Ashley say how Europeans think we goin' to war, and I feel a stab to my heart and I sits down in chair which am Miss Eleanor's favored rocker. I fannin' myself and gaspin' and folks' faces blurry and voice in my ear am Miss Ellen, who press tea glass into my hand.

"I be all right," I say. "I just don't want no war."

"Sensible minds will prevail, Mammy," Master John says.

But Master Ashley raise his sad eyes and says, "Will they? The fool does not delight in understanding. He delights in his own mind."

"Of course they will." Master John put a snap in he voice.

Me? I'm thinkin' with Master Ashley.

Then six-horse wagon rolls up Twelve Oaks lane with a great crate tied down with ropes.

Master Ashley, he tell Mose get a gang to Momma's rose garden. They's to bring skids and block and tackle and pry bars and such.

Well, we troops down to garden where Mistress Eleanor plant so many roses two coloreds busy day in day out carin' for 'em. Them roses get better care'n some childrens. Field hands skid crate off wagon and Mose take pry bar to crate, which has got a metal horse. Green horse rearin' and wavin' it hoofs about. I seen better-lookin' horses.

Master John wipin' tear from he eye.

"Etruscan," Master Ashley announce, like Master Etruscan particular good maker of green metal horses.

"Eleanor . . . she . . . she would have been delighted."

"I bought it for Mother. Her lovely garden begs for a fountain."

"She often spoke . . ."

Well, everybody feels like we is where we ain't s'posed to be, like we somewhere private. Wilkeses, they got a way of makin' folks feel that way.

That big green horse ain't no end of what in that crate. Master Ashley got a silver cup from Ireland for Master Gerald. I don't know why it call "stirrup cup"—child couldn't get a foot in it. Master Gerald fit to be tied. He want know 'zactly where Master Ashley buy it, and when Master Ashley says, Master Gerald grinnin' 'count he know silver shop well, pass by it many a time.

Master Ashley has a fine lace shawl for Miss Ellen and lace collars and cuffs for he sisters. Might be he buy the shawl for his Momma Eleanor, but gives it to Miss Ellen.

When Master Ashley ask for Miss Katie, Miss Ellen tell him, "She was thrown yesterday and slightly injured. I insisted she stay home."

Master Ashley grin like Miss Ellen and him knows somethin' other folks doesn't. "Miss Katie . . . thrown? She's more cocklebur than little girl."

"No longer a 'little girl,' Ashley," Miss Ellen say.

"Ah."

Later that evenin' I keepin' Miss Katie company on Tara porch when Master Ashley ride up. That man always dress right. Even when he was little boy I never seed him mussed. He done change he travelin' clothes and he boots shined blood red and he gray trousers, which are tighter'n needs be, and a white shirt, which don't look like it ever been wore afore, and a gold tie pin and hat 'most as white as he shirt.

He doff hat to Miss Katie and smile. She sit bolt upright like lightning done hit her. He come up the stairs and kiss her hand like a Frenchman and says how she's growed up. She don't say nary one word. Might be she can't.

He say, "I'm sorry about your fall."

Miss Katie start to 'splain, but she choke. "Tree limb" is all what come out.

"Ah well, if you must gallop through the woods." He dip in his pocket for little blue silk pouch.

For a second I thinks he gots a ring in there, but it a wore-out piece of brass.

"Put this on his harness and Beelzebub will shun low branches."

Miss Katie don't know to thank him. She blush. He say, "This horse brass decorated a Roman bridle two thousand years ago."

"I know when the Romans were," Miss Katie say, sharper than she means to.

"I'm sure you do," he say, smilin' that sweet smile, and Miss Katie don't know 'zactly what to do so she bob her head like little girl. When she figures how silly that look, she straighten to say, stern-like, "Thank you, Mr. Wilkes. Beelzebub will treasure it always."

Why Gentlemen Favor Sidesaddles

IT WERE FLAT brass with rubbed-down face I can hardly make out, some king's face, I reckon, but Miss Katie, she think high on it and has Toby wire it to Beelzebub bridle, double-wired so it can't come loose. She tell Beelzebub he a Roman warhorse now, and horse look at her like he do, interested but not knowin' a thing, and she stroll round him so she can come up on that brass like she never seed it and say, "Why, Beelzebub. Where'd you get this? Gift from an admirer?"

She sassy 'bout the whole thing.

When she ain't ridin' with her papa, she ridin' with Miss Beatrice. Her and horse off to Fairhill most every day. While she out gettin' sweaty, young county gentlemens buzzin' round Miss Honey and Miss Suellen like bees. Them girls spring honey—watery but so delicate and sweet!

Them girls and Miss Carreen and Miss India Wilkes too, they got deportment. They passin' through they days with nary a ripple. Miss Katie, she ripple like catfish in the shallows. Even when you don't sees Miss Katie, you knows she there!

Most Mistress no more free do what they want than I is or Pork is or ary colored. They gots to wear they bustles and they gots to keep they pale face out the sun and they gots tell ary gentleman within hearin' how he mostest gentleman ever strut the earth. That ain't Miss Katie O'Hara!

Other womens brings Miss Ellen they troubles. They brings they secrets and troubles to Miss Ellen 'count Miss Ellen patient like them saints she studyin' when she was little. Womens ain't gonna ever come to Miss Katie. Even when Miss Katie growed ain't no woman gonna tell her no troubles. Miss Katie ain't no saint like Miss Ellen. She ain't no part of no saint. When Miss Ellen see hurtin', she do somethin' 'bout it. Miss Katie don't see no hurtin', she don't see no sufferin', what she see is sheownself!

I ask myself why I loves her? Why I want know everything she up to? Why I follow everywhere she go? She ain't one bit like me. She ain't like most folks!

'Count who she am! She more Miss Katie than Miss Carreen Miss Carreen, even Master Ashley ain't so much who he am as Miss Katie am who she am! She like sun goin' down and moon comin' up. Ain't nothin' you can do 'bout it but be glad.

Deportment only thing stand between you and the Devil. Only shield chase Satan away is deportment and big smile. If you actin' happy and got deportment, Ol' Devil pass you up, find some other sinner do mischief to.

Miss Beatrice, she don't got deportment, but Miss Katie throw her up to me. "Beatrice this" and "Beatrice that," like Mistress Beatrice Tarleton and her brood are 'zample. "Beatrice doesn't care if her skin is 'pearly white,' Mammy," Miss Katie say. "Beatrice believes most 'gentlemen' are fools."

Distaste for that woman so strong I gets knots in my throat.

I don't dare tell Miss Katie what Miss Beatrice don't know nothin' 'bout. Here what I want say to her:

Yes, Miss Beatrice, she work hard, yes, she doin' Mistress things, and prayin' 'bout 'em, and she brave and she don't let herself do foolishness and she know more 'bout them horses than most men. But Miss Beatrice husband, Master Jim, own thousand acres and all the money he want. Now 'n' again Master Jim go Georgia legislature to make them laws everybody else gots to obey. Even important white Masters listen to Miss Beatrice and smile like fools no matter what foolishness she sayin'!

But that 'count of who she marry! If Miss Beatrice white trash like Mrs. Slattery or colored girl like Teena, she best hold her tongue and clap a big smile on she face!

All Miss Beatrice got, she got 'count she marry Master Hugh. That's how come Momma and me fret 'bout who you marry, 'count you marry wrong man you ain't gonna be nobody. You might be drunkard wife or gambler wife or pauper wife. And if you don't marries, you be spinster sittin' at the foot of the table not darin' say nothin' to distress you kin. Oh, Miss Katie be mealymouth then! Woman who don't never marry and woman marry a fool, they life be blight!

———————

Eight year ago, Miss Katie climb on her first horse. She always ridin' astride like a boy, but now she growed, so Miss Ellen have Jonesboro saddlemaker make a fine sidesaddle, red just like Beelzebub.

Now Miss Katie, she afeared of Momma, so she don't sass or nothin'. She thank her Momma, but week after, Big Sam ask me what that lady saddle doin' hangin' in the tobacco barn and why do Toby unsaddle and saddle twict every time Miss Katie go ridin'.

So I asks Miss Katie, and she say she "prefer" ride just like she done, just like Papa Gerald do.

So I tells her, "Honey, ain't no lady ever ride a horse like a man."

She answer back. Miss Beatrice has told Miss Katie that "Catherine the Great" rode man saddle and told her "ladies in waiting" ride man saddle too. I tells Miss Katie, if they them "ladies in wait-ing" been waitin' for husband, they waitin' long time.

Miss Katie ain't goin' Fayetteville Female Academy till next fall, but she already know everything. She tell me "ladies in waitin'" is important ladies at court; them ladies ridin' man saddles with Cath-erine the Great be Masters' daughters.

"Catherine the Great weren't no Georgia lady," I says. "Maybe them 'ladies in waitin'" weren't after no husbands. Maybe they caught husbands already."

Katie forehead crinkle up. "Why would any husband care if I ride sidesaddle?" Miss Katie dewy eyed like a child.

I don't say no more. Some things even Mammies ain't 'splainin'.

Come summer, Wilkeses' cousins Charles and Melanie Ham-ilton visit Twelve Oaks and come to all the barbecues. Hamiltons' Papa and Momma dead, so they in Atlanta with they Aunt Pittypat, who would talk a mockingbird to death! 'Count Charles Hamilton livin' in Atlanta, Charles ain't bold like the Tarleton twins. Miss Melanie shy little thing but got good deportment.

Charles and Melanie friends with Wilkes girls and Suellen, but Miss Katie don't pay 'em no mind.

Sometimes Miss Katie ride out with Master Ashley. They ain't gallopin', they talkin'. Master Ashley think Miss Katie still a child 'count she ridin' like a boy. It ain't no secret they ridin' out, but they don't flaunt it neither.

Master Ashley, he safe. He ain't gonna take no advantage. Tar-leton twins and them Calvert boys, they ain't safe, but Miss Katie'd rather show her heels to 'em than set in some shady spot with some boy and get to know him too good.

The Twins' body servant, Jeems, growed up with them, and Jeems know what Twins doin' and what arybody else doin' too! Jeems welcome in Tara kitchen arytime! Cook pour Jeems tea and he yarnin'.

Jeems say it *funniest* thing. "Stuart and Brent Tarleton, they bestest, fastest riders in Clayton County, 'cept for a *girl*."

Jeems slap he thigh. Yesterday mornin' they chase after Miss Katie, Stuart in the lead and Brent fallin' back, through the woods, over the plowed ground, then Brent leadin' and Stuart fallin' back and splashin' through river fords until they horses winded and Miss Katie gettin' smaller and smaller till they can't see her no more. "Spawn of the Devil," Jeems tell us. "That what they call that Beelzebub horse: 'Spawn of the Devil.'"

I don't tell Miss Ellen 'bout lady saddle gatherin' dust in the tobacco barn and Big Sam don't neither, but Miss Ellen finds out she daughter ridin' boy-like 'stead of girl-like, and Miss Ellen tell Miss Katie she has been deceitful and ladies ain't never deceitful, no matter what. She tell Miss Katie man saddle unladylike and no girl ever get husband ridin' unladylike.

Now Miss Katie pretend she repent, but she's backslid before she done repentin'! She set her lip and gonna find some other way of ridin' astride, like a boy.

Me, I don't like what Miss Beatrice up to, tryin' turn Miss Katie into someone like her. Miss Katie ain't got no fine house and ain't got no plantation and ain't got no money and she keep this foolishness up she ain't gonna have no husband give 'em to her!

So I tells Miss Katie her Momma right. If she keep ridin' like a boy, she disappoint her husband somethin' terrible.

Now Miss Katie don't really care whether she catch no husband or not. Exceptin' that dreamy Ashley, she ain't got time of day for ary boy.

But she don't want be told no neither. Bein' told no gravel her.

Miss Katie ask why ridin' like a boy gonna disappoint man she marry, and I gets a wicked notion. I christened Catholic, married AME, and sits in the garret of Jonesboro Baptist Church every Sunday. I know what Satan's mischief look like. Look like my notion!

Master Gerald been 'couragin' Miss Katie in this horse foolishness 'thout puttin' he name to it. Master Gerald ride out with her of an evening and they jumpin' fences when they thinks nobody sees. Master Gerald all the time throwin' up Miss Beatrice: Miss Beatrice this and Miss Beatrice that. Miss Ellen smilin', but her smile peaked. Me, I figure Master Gerald got debts to pay. So I sweet as sweet potato pie when I tell Miss Katie, "You got to ask your papa 'bout that, honey. Got to ask a husband what a husband be lookin' for."

That were Satan mischief. I knows it were. I prays forgiveness.

Miss Katie waits talk to she Papa until family done eatin' dinner and Miss Ellen upstairs with Carreen, who has got the sniffles.

Master Gerald in the chair Miss Ellen brought in when she gives he old chair to Big Sam. After so many years, new chair look as poorly as old chair. Everything get poorly 'thout we noticin'.

This evenin' Master Gerald am satisfy. Prices good, we had good rains, and cotton bolls tight and burstin'. Master Gerald has bit he cigar and poured he drink of whiskey not knowin' a powder keg 'bout to explode. I sets down in a side chair with my sewing basket. I takes out darnin' and holds torn sock up, which he can't help seein' out corner of he eye, and I mutterin' 'bout "certain gentleman don't know enough to roll they sock afore they draw it on," not loud, just loud enough he hear. If I not mutterin', Master Gerald don't know I breathin'.

Miss Katie come in and sit on the floor at his feet and make eyes at him. She jumps up to light his cigar. She ask if maybe he want water for to mix with he whiskey.

They talk horses. She reckons ain't nobody could ride Beelzebub 'cept her 'n' her Papa, not even Miss Beatrice. She tells him how, in Jonesboro t'other day, Storekeeper Kennedy say, "Your father, Gerald, he's short and he's Irish but he's *mighty*!" Master Gerald like that fine and he swell up some, but he no fool and Miss Katie ain't the first try slip somethin' by him. He say, "Flattery, puss. Flattery has brought many a good man down." But he pleased too and wouldn't mind more of what bring them good men down. He say how President Buchanan sidin' with planters 'gainst them Yankees, and Miss Katie, her mouth drop open, like she 'stonished her Papa know what the President do. Master Gerald roll President Buchanan's words round in his mouth. "What is right and what is practicable are two different things."

Miss Katie wants know "What's 'practicable'?"

Master Gerald say " 'Practicable,' puss, is what can be accomplished. I've always favored what's 'practicable' meself."

She amazed, plumb amazed, how wise her Papa be, and her face shinin' and he puffin' on he cigar and I peerin' into basket of unmended socks tryin' not to laugh.

Miss Katie knowin' 'zactly what I thinkin', and she glance and glare fierce as a raccoon in a trap, which naturally sets me quiverin' like shook jelly, and I looks off 'count I dare not look no more.

Miss Katie figures she better get to it 'fore I gets hilarious, so she put this sweet, sweet look on her puzzled little face. "Daddy, can I ask you a question?"

Dead serious he say, "No you can't, Miss Katie. Master Gerald O'Hara is NOT to be approached!" and he chuckle and pat her shoulder. "You know I can't resist a pretty girl."

She make a puss-face at that, which I see, but he don't. In her softest sweetest voice, Miss Katie say, "Papa, some silly people are sayin' I must ride sidesaddle—instead of as you and Miss Beatrice do. When I ask why, they don't answer or they beat around the bush. Somehow, if I do ride astride, when I marry I'll disappoint my husband. I may not marry. I may never marry. But if I do, I'd so hate to disappoint my husband. What can they possibly mean? Exactly *how* might I disappoint him?"

Master Gerald spray whiskey out he mouth like he swallow

soap and he cough and choke and he stub he cigar and he cough so hard Miss Katie jump up pattin' he back and Master Gerald red as ripe apple.

When he settle, he drink he whiskey and swallow and she perchin' on the arm of he chair, sayin', "You know everything there is to know about horses, Father dear. How could riding astride disappoint my husband?"

Master Gerald look to me for help, but right away he knows who put Miss Katie up to this, and I smiles to let him know Mammy ain't bailin' him out. He dab he mouth with handkerchief and cough again—just to pass the time. "Katie, Katie, I believe I would like some water after all."

Soon she gone Master Gerald glower like to melt me down!

When she bring he water, he sip it and smile one of them weak smiles growed men puts on pretendin' be little boys and tell Miss Katie her Momma will explain 'bout the sidesaddle. He say, "Perhaps, she's cautioned you already."

Which notion gets me snortin' into my handkerchief, but I pretends I blowin' my nose.

Miss Katie wail, "But why? How can I hold a horse if I'm perched on his side like a saddlebag?" She march out and clump upstairs, and Master Gerald, he shake he finger at me but he don't say nothin'.

I don't know whether Katie ever ask her Momma how ridin' astride would damage a maiden. Miss Katie never quit doin' it.

How I Is Judas

TARA COTTON BRING twelve cent, which was the only good news that fall. Wheat half what it been and white folks' banks and railroads start failin', and in Kansas, abolitionists and slavers shootin' each other. I thinkin', Not again. Spirits dim and restless, swirlin' all round like they makin' room.

Dilcey visit Tara with her fool daughter, Prissy. We sittin' on the kitchen porch. Everything hush like big storm a-gatherin'.

Dilcey tells me, "General Jackson kill Grandpap at Horseshoe Bend. Grandpap a Red Stick. 'Twas their land. *This* land"—(she look around like Red Sticks behind every Tara bush)—"be Creek land. Right here!"

I say, "Folks always killin' folks. Seems like they can't help theyself."

She say, "Gonna do it again."

Spirits flutterin' round us like moths 'gainst window light. I shiverin'. I say, "Ain't nothin' you nor me can do."

Dilcey say, "Them Redsticks knew how to die. Reckon Masters be any good at it?"

Tara gettin' on like always. After supper, Pork put flowers in O'Hara bedroom. Miss Ellen gallivant round the county seein' to arybody can't do for theyownself. Overseer Wilkerson not so mean he's been. Big Sam tell me Overseer got a woman.

Saturdays, Sam and Master Gerald go into Jonesboro sell cotton and stay for horse and slave sales. Sam say more Masters sellin' they coloreds than buyin' 'em. When Masters afeared, coloreds grieve.

When Master Gerald sell cotton, he stick he money in Frank Kennedy safe. Time to time, him and Big Sam load they pistols and ride train into Atlanta, where they put Tara money in Georgia Railroad Bank.

When they comes home, Master Gerald tell Miss Ellen Georgia Railroad Bank strong like rock. Georgia Railroad Bank ain't gonna fail like them other banks.

Miss Ellen, she look at her husband long time 'thout sayin' nary word. "Mr. O'Hara. My three daughters and I have confidence in your good judgment."

Master Gerald step out on the porch to smoke he cigar. Late, 'thout makin' nothin' of it, he ride to Twelve Oaks askin' have Master John hear ary rumors 'bout Georgia Railroad Bank?

Sundays be quiet and peaceful and wind whisperin' cedars round Jonesboro Baptist Church, where whites and coloreds prays things get better afore they get worst. Preacher criticizin' Jonesboro racetrack. He say "racin' fever" worse than dropsy or yellow fever, but that don't stop the bettin'. Seem like less money Masters got, more they chance it.

Tarletons bettin' 'gainst Calverts, Calverts bettin' 'gainst Wilkeses, Wilkeses bettin' 'gainst Tarletons. Masters smilin' and noddin' like no hard feelin's, but they hands next they pistols.

Twelve Oaks cotton harvest month later than Tara cotton, so

Wilkeses cotton harvest after panic start when cotton buyers vanish like smoke. Dilcey say Master John wins most he bets but sometimes "quiet as the grave" Sunday morning.

————

Most mornings Miss Katie and that red devil Beelzebub already out when I comes into the kitchen, and sometimes they ain't be home till dark. Miss Katie afeared of she Momma. When Momma scold, Miss Katie hang she head and repent, but she out very next morning.

Miss Beatrice call on Master Gerald, and I serve 'em myself.

Miss Beatrice sittin' bolt upright in the hard horsehide chair. She wearin' she ridin' garb, long leather gloves in she lap. Master Gerald pretendin' she come visit him every single day, all the time, that this nothin' unusual.

I sets tea tray on side table and goes stand in the corner, where Pork stand when he servin'.

Miss Beatrice say, "Gerald, when I must speak uncomfortable truths, I prefer something stronger than tea."

It don't take him no time to fetch he decanter. He glass dirty and he gonna send me for a washed glass, but Miss Beatrice say, "Just pour it in my teacup, Gerald."

Which he do. She drinks it and holds her cup out again.

He wait on her till she wag she finger so he can sit down. "It's your daughter, Gerald."

"Which of my daughters, Beatrice?"

She give him a look. "If you believe Katie's been at Fairhill riding with me, she hasn't. Every morning I expect her, but usually, I am disappointed. I do not fear for her as a rider, she's better than most men, certainly she's better and safer on a horse than my sons. I worry about her reputation, Gerald. And, as you must know, I am less concerned with reputation than any woman in the county."

"But . . ."

"Your daughter is wild as a Cherokee. She startles deer in the woods and field hands in the wheat bottoms. While Wilkeses and Calverts and (I regret to say) Tarletons are wagering their respective competences at the Jonesboro track, your daughter associates with the grooms and jockeys, whites *and* coloreds, preparing horses for the races. Katie O'Hara is, Jeems assures me, a great favorite with those people."

So that evenin' when Miss Katie come in, Master Gerald be waitin' to pounce. He don't 'low me into the drawing room whilst he reprovin' her. Miss Katie come out white faced and silent like I never seed her. She never say no more 'bout Miss Beatrice and she never ride Fairhill no more.

But she ain't cured. Not by no long shot. Very next morning she and that horse out afore arybody arose, and when she come home the sun done set.

Master and Mistress distress and don't know what to do. They feelin' like viper in they bosom! Mistress don't want switch the child—won't do no good anyhow. Master Gerald don't want sell she horse. They ain't gettin' nowheres!

Miss Katie don't tell me what she feelin' or thinkin'. She don't tell nobody, 'lessn she tellin' that darn horse. Beelzebub livin' up to he name.

Dilcey don't gets to church often, but she come that Sunday just to catch me after.

Preacher done preach a good sermon, and I feelin' "saved." "Wilkeses still wagerin'?" I asks.

"They is. Mammy . . ."

I don't give a hoot what the Wilkeses do. What Wilkeses do am their affair. I tryin' to put off what comin', whyfor Dilcey come to church this Sunday and whyfor she layin' in wait. Heart know what comin' afore head do.

Dilcey say Mose, Master Ashley Wilkes's body servant, was at the races yesterday and while the Masters at the rail bettin', Mose with jockeys and grooms and he spot Miss Katie. Miss Katie got her beautiful hair tucked up in a man's hat and she wearin' boys' ridin' clothes and she look 'zactly like a black-haired, green-eyed boy. Farmer Able Wynder am talkin' with Miss Katie. Farmer Wynder don't know who she am. He wantin' hire Miss Katie for a jockey. "If you can handle that red brute, young fella, you can handle my filly. I'll pay a dollar up front and half your winnings."

Mose tell Dilcey Miss Katie weren't talkin' like herself neither. She talk deep down and growly like a boy. Miss Katie don't race that day, but she considerin' it!

Well, I ain't gonna let Dilcey get one up on me, so I pretends it don't matter. "Oh, she just foolin'. Master Gerald know all 'bout it."

Dilcey put that "caught you in a lie" smile on she face and say, "Sometimes I wish I was 'saved,' but I repents of it."

Which she think funny and I doesn't.

All next week I watchin' Miss Katie like a hawk. I gets up afore even she do, and I offer make her breakfast since Cook ain't woke. No, she ain't hungry. No she don't want no coffee nor tea. "Early for you, isn't it, Mammy?"

"Somebody got keep an eye on you."

She smile like the pretty little girl she am and pops her riding crop 'gainst pant leg as she goin' out the door.

When she gallop off, sun just a pink line over the Up-country. Cook in her nightshirt, yawnin'.

"Gracious, Mammy!" she say. "Is you right?"

"I glad you finally risin'," I say. "Stove already stoked."

I ask Big Sam and field hands keep they eyes peeled, and afore Miss Katie come home of an evenin', I knows most where she been. I know when she jumpin' fences and when she racin' through stumps been pulled but not yet burned.

Miss Ellen, she desperate. She thinkin' send Miss Katie to Miss Pauline in Savannah. I shudders to think of them two under one roof, and I guess Master Gerald shudder too. Maybe he believe heself when he tells he wife, "Puss'll grow out of it."

Week come to an end. Saturday I up and doin' when Katie come in the kitchen. No, she don't want eat nothin' and it no business of mine where she ridin' today. Miss Katie got stubbornest look on her face. Why she hair tuck under she cap? She ain't sayin'.

After she gone I wakes Pork and Toby. I tells Toby rub sleep out of he eyes, harness trap, and bring it round. Then I goes upstairs along to Master's bedroom. I slips in 'thout knockin'. Master Gerald stretchin' one bare leg out of he tangled covers and Miss Ellen sleepin' so calm like she in she coffin.

I shakes Master Gerald shoulder, and he come out of sleep easy. He sit up and glance at Miss Ellen, but I put finger to my mouth and jerk my head toward the hall. When we outside, I says, "Master Gerald, you oldest daughter need you."

Pain flitter 'cross he face, but he get dressed.

Pork at the front door with Master Gerald best jacket and hat and coffee what got whiskey in it. Master Gerald give him a look, wonderin', "You in this too?" but Pork solemn as church.

Toby drive with Master Gerald beside. I rides in back with my feets danglin' over the backboard.

I expect we drive straight to racetrack, but when we gets Jonesboro, we draws up behind Frank Kennedy store. Inside Master Gerald buy some of that horehound candy I favors.

Plenty farmers and overseers. They done sold they shoat or colt or colored boy and buyin' plug tobacco or whiskey or hoof trimmers or turpentine for to doctor they animals—all manner of store goods.

Master Frank live above he store and start early and stay late. Frank Kennedy plain as mud hen, but we all knows he gonna be rich one day. He been buyin' land which is cheap 'count of the Panic and most folks not havin' no money.

"Top of the mornin', Frank."

"Gerald. Good of you to stop." Master Frank don't ask Master Gerald why he in town 'thout bein' at the sale, 'count Mister Frank never ask Master Gerald nothin' Master Gerald not want him ask. Mister Frank ask 'bout Suellen, how she health and spirits. He sweet on Suellen. Master Gerald say she at Female Academy study French and dancin' and fancywork and such.

Master Gerald recalls Frank's father, who he knowed from when he come to Up-country. "Grand fella," he say. Grand fella, your Dad." Frank Kennedy father were Irish.

Farmer interrupts wantin' number eight fullered horseshoes.

"Take care of this fella, Frank. He's doin' honest work!" Big wink. Master Gerald pull out his watch. After the big noon race, they three, four more races afore the farmers' races, which aryone and ary horse enters.

Master Gerald sit on a nail keg and take out he pipe. I goes outside and gives Toby a couple horehound candies.

People, horses, wagons. I don't see Miss Katie nowhere.

So I sits with Master Gerald knittin' baby socks. I ain't no shakes at knittin', but I never met no baby particular 'bout socks nor no new Momma wasn't glad to get 'em.

Frank Kennedy brings *Macon Telegraph* newspaper, which Master Gerald read pass the time.

Farmers come say howdy and gossip. He nod short at Angus MacIntosh, who nod short at him. Somethin' happen in olden days twixt Master Gerald kin and Master Angus kin, and they carryin' on quarrel 'cross the ocean many years later. Folks remember they hurts and cherish 'em.

Master Gerald friendly with Amos Trippet, who ain't no gentleman but raise best Ossabaw hogs and Dominique chickens. Amos promise four hogs for Tara come killin' time. Master Gerald tap his newspaper and tell Amos, "You ever heard the like of this: 'I am not, nor ever have been, in favor of bringing about in any way the social and political equality of the white and black races, that I am not, nor ever have been, in favor of making voters or jurors of Negroes, nor of qualifying them to hold office, nor to intermarry with white people; and I will say in addition to this that there is a physical difference between the white and black races which I believe will forever forbid the two races living together on terms of social and political equality.' What do you make of Mr. Lincoln, Amos?"

"I think he wants to be elected senator." Old Amos got red hair and skinny neck like one of his Dominique roosters. Amos don't favor me. He thinks I gets above myself. "What do you make of the man, Mammy?"

"Never knowed no Lincolns. No Lincolns in Clayton County I ever heard 'bout."

"Don't trifle with Mammy, Amos. Get crossways with Mammy, your best hogs will get cholera and your mules will come up lame."

Both men laugh to show how they's foolin' and not nervy. Not a bit.

What do I think? I think it don't make no nevermind what some Illinois Master say to get elected.

Well, they talkin' politics until Amos and Master Gerald can't think nothin' more. Amos go 'bout he business and Master Gerald wander store like he might spy somethin' he ain't thought of but might need. Store smell like molasses and sulfur and neat's-foot oil.

We waitin' till Miss Katie get so deep into wickedness, she can't wiggle free.

Master Gerald visit with every customer come in Kennedy store, just like he proprietor, and if Master Frank don't like it he can't object 'count he Frank and Gerald Gerald.

I tear out missed stitches and knit 'em again. When church bell jangle noon Master Gerald roust Toby awake. Me and Toby in back, Master Gerald drivin'. We trot past farmers drivin' or leadin' cows and sheeps and pigs they bought. Pair young colored boys led by halters round they necks.

We encounters Wilkeses, father and son. Master John red faced. He say, "I've never seen the like, Gerald. Our horse had the field by a length!"

Young Master Ashley say, "I can't think Gerald is as interested as we are in our undeserved good fortune." He pulls out his watch. "The Atlanta train? Meeting our cousins?"

Master John must have won big. "Friend Gerald, can you believe Melanie and Charles Hamilton prefer the city to our glorious countryside?" He waves his hands, meaning everywhere round.

"Do bring them to Tara, John." Master Gerald tip he hat and cluck and we off.

Horses lined up for the race. Colored jockeys and white boy jockeys, serious as can be, talkin' to they mounts, tellin' 'em, askin' 'em, beggin' 'em, do best they can. Master Gerald crack he whip, and we canter through the infield so fast me and Toby clingin' on with both hands. Beelzebub ain't hard to see.

Horses prancing and dancing and circlin' they so excite. Short man in a red vest and top hat have he pistol in the air. Mens jumps out of our way. Mens shoutin' at us and boy snatch for our reins, but we through the crowd, onto the track, and straight to the start line.

Miss Katie wearin' boy clothes with big cap over she hair. She waitin' starter gun shoot, but starter ain't shootin' 'count our rig on the track.

People yellin' curses. Riders peerin' and wonderin'.

Miss Katie look mighty like a boy. Miss Katie browner any lady s'posed be and sittin' her horse like she jockey all her days. Her hands too fine for boy, but they brown too.

I knows what she thinkin' too. She thinkin' put spurs to Beelzebub and race down the track, but ain't no racin' 'lessn somebody racin' 'gainst you.

Master Gerald look fierce at Miss Katie and grab Beelzebub bridle.

She say, "Papa! Please! We can win." Beelzebub neck arched and a-quiverin' with wantin' to run. "We can win!"

"Katie, you're a girl," her father say. "You can't even try."

How Miss Katie Come
to Be Miss Scarlett

MAMMIES DOESN'T PREEN theyselfs. They see what they gots see and knows what they gots know and sometimes they says what they knows but mostly they don't. Mostly, they let folks tell 'em what they already knowed yesterday. Mammies nods and smiles. Nods and smiles.

Cook beatin' biscuits. Cook tellin' 'bout Miss Katie and Tarleton boys and I listenin' with one ear, rollin' round in my mind what I seen when Miss Katie rides in last night.

Cook think it big joke. "Anyway, Miss Katie she ride up on that big red horse where Suellen and India Wilkes is havin' they picnic. Cade Calvert and Tarleton twins fetchin' dainties from the hamper though them girls perfectly able get up and help theyselves. 'Can I get you a cup of water, Miss India?' 'Won't you sample a ginger cookie?'" Cook cacklin'. "Them girls high-and-mightiest girls in North Georgia."

"That's what Jeems say?"

"He with the twins, ain't he? Like I was sayin' afore you interrupt: 'long comes Miss Katie, who been ridin' since daybreak. Miss Katie splattered with red clay and her horse plumb filthy. She gallop in, stirrin' so much dust, them girls get to coughing and beatin' dust off theyselves, and my, ain't they cross!"

I tells Cook, "Pass me them biscuits. You gots to whop 'em more'n what you doin'."

Miss Katie been ridin' round devilish since her Papa makes her quit that fool horse race. Every day and all day, she ridin'. Might be she puzzlin' and ridin' round helps her do it.

Master Gerald, he never tell nothin' what happen in Jonesboro race day and Miss Katie don't tell nothin' and I don't neither. Most what you wants hid don't stay hid, but no 'count blabbin'. Mammies don't blab.

Half Clayton County was at the racetrack that Saturday, and them what wasn't hears from those what was, but Master Gerald and Miss Ellen go 'bout their business like always, pretendin' nothin' happen.

Miss Ellen tell Miss Katie if she ever do such a thing again, she sent to Savannah with them Baptists and pray four times every day and all-day sermons Sunday.

But Miss Katie puzzlin'. Somethin' change that day, and she ain't caught up to it.

Cook tellin' me how Miss Katie interrupt them girls' picnic. "Miss Katie, she don't care nothin' 'bout Miss Suellen nor Miss India neither. She want them boys saddle up and race her to the river."

I sighs. "Poor child."

"'Poor child,' my foots! Young Mistress need took down a peg or two. That what I say! Miss India and Miss Suellen, they aggravated. Here they was enjoyin' they outing and young boys dotin' on 'em and now they bonnets dusty with Miss Katie dust. Miss India pour tea out her glass and say, 'Brent, please fetch fresh tea. We seem to have been transported to an Arabian dust storm.'" Cook press the back of she hand 'gainst she forehead like Miss India do when distress.

Now I knows Miss India don't care nothin' for Miss Katie. She don't like Miss Katie ridin' out with Master Ashley, no matter they innocent as babes. Miss India don't think no daughter of no Irishman good enough ride out with she brother.

Cook say, "Miss Katie ignore Miss India and Suellen like they ain't nothin'. She means go ridin' and want boys ride chasin' her, but them young Masters ain't rushin' do her biddin' like they done yesterday and day afore."

"Probably tired of gettin' beat," I say.

Cook say, "Miss Katie horse tramplin' round and them girls makin' mean faces and boys scuffin' dirt with they boot toes and sayin' nary word." Cook cackled.

I say, "Miss Katie love that horse."

"Be that like it be! Be that like it be! Miss Katie, she say, 'Brent. I'll reach the ford before you will.'

"'Don't feel like ridin' today, Katie,' that boy mumblin'.

"Miss Katie, finally she get it. Oh, she get it good! World turn upside down! Them boys—who always favor her over the other girls—don't favor her no more."

I ponderin' what in Miss Katie little head. She didn't race no horse Saturday. Now boys won't chase horse no more. *That* chasin' done.

"Jeems say Miss Katie white as a hant. She don't give up, though. Not our Miss Katie. She say, 'Two bits says I reach the ford first.'

"Young Master Brent, he scratch his head and says, 'Shucks, Miss Katie. It's too hot for ridin'. Tie up your horse and sit a spell.'

"Miss Katie get quiet. Thoughts buzzin' through her head like hornets. Jeems, he behind a tree lest Miss Katie gallop Beelzebub through them girls' picnic. But she don't. Miss Katie say, 'Brent, I never knew you to refuse a challenge.' Then that child ride off by sheownself."

———

It dark when Miss Katie finally gets home. Master and Miss don't know nothin' happened, but coloreds know. Pork so low-down Master Gerald ask am he sick. Pork favors Miss Katie like me.

I sees her in the lantern light at the stable door and goes to help how I can. She brushin' Beelzebub hard, like she want rub brush right through him.

Horse, he wore out. He head hangin' down. Poor beast been rid half to death.

No use pretendin' I don't know what's goin' on. I says, "It's all right, honey. It's all right. One day soon you be doin' what ladies got do. All Georgia ladies do same. Ladies unalike as your Momma and Missus Tarleton got be ladies. It ain't terrible. You get you a home and plenty eat, husband what love you and babies to tend. Been like that since Eve and Adam. Honey, you ain't no boy, and you surely don't want to be. Boys gets to ride in horse races and sits in high offices, but it's boys what gets killed in wars and boys what gets hanged."

Miss Katie didn't say nary word. She didn't want nothin' from me nor nobody else neither. She don't come in for dinner.

———

Morning after that picnic where Katie can't get no boys chase after her, Cook still laughin' 'bout it and I whoppin' biscuits. Beaten biscuit, gots be *beat*. I looks up when Miss Ellen come in the kitchen and say, "Don't start the eggs. Katie isn't down yet."

I say, "Miss Katie never this late. Her and that horse out ridin'."

Miss Ellen smile like one of them saints knowin' what nobody else knows.

Cook set sausages on platter and slides 'em into the warming oven.

What now? I wonderin'.

Hour later, when Miss Ellen comes back, she happy as can be. "Mammy, would you serve?"

Rosa or Cook always serves breakfast. Pork serve supper and dinner and for the gentlemen's drinkin'. Mammies don't serve at table. I surprise.

Miss Ellen clap her hands together. "Mammy, this is the Day of Jubilee!"

Day of Jubilo is when we be freed. That in the Bible. I ain't seen Miss Ellen so happy in months but ain't heard nothin' 'bout nobody gettin' freed.

"Yes, Missus," I say. Cook quick scramble eggs like Master Gerald likes 'em and set sausage and biscuits on plates. "Miss Ellen want me to serve," I say.

"'Tain't proper," Cook say.

"Miss Ellen, she Mistress, 'lessn somethin' ain't what it been." I puttin' plates on tray.

"Don't you drop nothin'," Cook say.

"Wouldn't hurt you sausages if they *is* drop," I say, 'count I don't want think why this Day of Jubilo.

In dining room, Miss Katie settin' in same chair like always. She hands folded in she lap.

Master Gerald ain't lookin' at he daughter. He ain't lookin' at nothin'. He stab finger under he collar and tug at it. He glad to bow his head when Miss Ellen say the blessin', "Heavenly Father . . ."

Me, I want gnash my teeth. I want shout, "I you Mammy! I'd helped you if you just ask!"

Miss Katie weren't nobody to laugh at. I believe she'd have killed aryone laugh at her. I clamp my mouth shut.

She'd let her curling irons get too hot, and her beautiful black hair was scorched and patchy and frazzled. Her green eyes were red and sore, and she had flecks of burnt cork clingin' from her eyelashes. She'd laid on face powder like it were axle grease.

". . . In Christ's name. Amen." Miss Ellen took up she fork.

Miss Katie's bosoms was pushed up by she corset and she waist squished to little or nothin'. She wearin' them green dancin' slippers what was she Momma's.

Miss Katie pickin' at she food.

"Sister Katie." Suellen didn't snicker. Just. "Don't you look lovely."

"Dearest Katie." Miss Ellen nipped that in the bud. "Tomorrow morning, Rosa will help you dress."

"I can help too." Suellen been most happy to help, yes she be. Miss Katie's look could have froze salt water.

Miss Katie dab her napkin to her lips. She look round at all of us. "Henceforth, please call me Scarlett." She turn to her father. "In honor of my dear Papa's Momma."

Master Gerald took aback. "Why, uh . . . puss . . . Scarlett . . . that's grand."

"Dearest Grandma . . ." Scarlett drop she head like she thinkin' on old lady she never knowed.

Master Gerald don't hardly know what say.

I can't look at this and can't look away. My Baby Katie like pretty bird, tossed and feathers plucked out by hurricane. So proud. Fierce proud. I smiles like I got to and take up coffeepot and pours.

Miss Carreen know somethin' happened but can't figure what. "But . . . Scarlett," she say, "Katie . . . ?"

"Dear Sister, Katie is no more. Papa, you're unusually quiet this morning."

"Thinkin' about things, sweetheart. Just thinkin' 'bout . . . things . . ."

Miss Ellen has got what she wanted. Me too, I s'pose. Miss Ka——, Miss Scarlett gettin' deportment, and I wished I felt better 'bout it.

"Where will you ride this mornin', darlin'?"

Scarlett rolls her napkin and shove it into her napkin ring. Napkin come loose, but she stuffs it partway so it sprawl next her plate lookin' foolish. "I shan't be riding this morning," she say.

"Oh?"

"I shall not be riding today."

"Oh."

"Father, perhaps you'll take him out."

"But, I . . ."

"It would be best if the horse was exercised." She laughs a little laugh, but nothin's funny. "He's accustomed to"—she almost break, but she catch herself—"a . . . considerable exercise."

I'm thinkin': And you ain't? But I ain't say nothin'. Ain't my place be sayin'.

"Papa, don't you like the horse?"

"To be sure I do, puss, but . . ."

Things might have gone one way or t'other. Miss Scarlett was on knife edge when she say, just like it were joke betwixt them, "Surely there's no better horseman than Gerald O'Hara."

Master Gerald were pleased, like she knew he'd be. He wearin' that stupid look men wear when a pretty girl tell 'em 'zactly what they wants to hear. And Master Gerald, he growed man! Them neighbor boys: them Tarletons and Calverts and Fontaines—they child's play.

I wasn't lookin' at her no more, 'count of I didn't want to watch Miss Scarlett tryin' not cry.

I thinkin', Poor child.

I thinkin', Poor Beelzebub.

I thinkin', Poor young gentlemen.

How Miss Scarlett Breakin' Hearts

IF THERE WAS ary unbroke boy's heart in Clayton County, he never met Miss Scarlett O'Hara.

That child weren't no fool, and didn't take her long to figure what boys were about. Scarlett wasn't no pretty girl—oh, I mean, she weren't homely like Miss India, but she wasn't no head turner neither. She studied on boys, and in no time 'tall, she made herself into a trinket them boys kill to have. Precious trinket just out of they grasp.

She lays on the gravy. Think Scarlett don't know how boy lights up when pretty girl comparin' him—comparin' him *favorable*—to Andrew Jackson or Joshua or—without comin' right out with it— the best bull in the pasture?

It didn't always come natural. 'Twere struggle for her bein' helpless. But if young ladies got be helpless . . . "Please help me down. My stirrup is so far from the ground!" 'Tweren't easy for her. She were a sight abler than them boys she pretend be helpless with.

Lord have mercy—the child who jumped the highest rail fences for miles around has to have a boy's arm from mounting block into coach and "Please don't drive so fast." Goodness gracious, no. Miss

Scarlett delicate tummy did "flip-flops when you drive so daringly."

No, 'tweren't easy. Early on when some poor boy ditherin' whilst decidin' what do next, Miss Scarlett lose patience and do it herself. But as she learn what boys am, she get weaker and weaker until a puff of air give her the jimjams!

Her bestest trick come natural. Miss Scarlett, she always could bear down on one thing 'thout fussin' 'bout ary other thing. When she was jumpin' them fences, fence jumpin' were ALL she were doin', she weren't thinkin' 'bout maybe her shirt come loose and maybe showin' what it shouldn't whilst she jump fence, nor was she thinkin' had she done her chores nor how'd she pray tonight at family prayers. When Miss Scarlett bear down on what she wants or wants to do or wants think 'bout or wants have, that one thing was what she thinkin' 'bout, not two thing, not even one and a half. When Miss Scarlett turn them green eyes of hers on some boy not long out of short pants, that boy didn't have no more chance than a snowflake in Georgia July! No matter what he thinkin'—if he thinkin' at all—he ain't gonna slip free of them green eyes which is weighin' him up, all he parts, toe to head, like nobody never did afore, 'cept maybe he Momma when he baby. That boy never knowed before how the sun and moon revolve round him and no other boy! He never know'd he was so darn clever! He never know'd he was strong as that bull in the pasture, which no lady ever inspect up close but every lady know they needin' somethin' like that bull onct they marry. Might be tips of boy's ear turn red and maybe he stutter, but ain't no boy, never ever, none of 'em ever turn away from Miss Scarlett's gaze until she shake her head and dismiss 'em like they am nothin' but a frippery. Her gaze natural to Miss Scarlett. It were her bestest weapon.

'Tweren't too long before boys comin' to Tara like bees to spilled honey. They boys on the porch in the morning and boys dwaddlin' about when lamps lit at dusk. Miss Ellen enroll Miss Scarlett at the

Fayetteville Female Academy. Miss Scarlett need more deportment afore it too late!

Miss Scarlett don't want go. She missin' them barbecues and picnics and ball dancin', but she go anyway. Only thing in the world Miss Scarlett 'feared is she Momma.

First time Master Gerald gets on Beelzebub, horse throws him. Second time too. Master Gerald fine rider, but he ain't Beelzebub rider. Saturday after Miss Scarlett off to Fayetteville Academy, Master Gerald take horse to Jonesboro and sells him.

When Miss Beatrice hear what he do, she spittin' mad. She don't approve anybody buy Beelzebub, and if Miss Scarlett ain't gonna ride him, Master Gerald best return horse to Fairhill. Miss Beatrice strong 'bout that. She so strong us Taras don't go to next Fairhill barbecue. Miss Beatrice sons don't pay they Momma wrath no mind. They can waste time in Fayetteville just as easy as Tara, so that what they doin'.

When Miss Scarlett come home, Master Ashley and her ridin' or talkin' or havin' they picnics like they done when Miss Scarlett a harum-scarum. After they picnic in Twelve Oaks gardens, Miss Scarlett comes home tell me, "Bourbon roses have existed since King Bourbon's day."

Scarlett ask Master Ashley was it true roans are faster than duns and is a white-headed horse more likely to go blind? If Master Ashley notice she ridin' sidesaddle now, he never say nothin'.

Master Ashley full of himself and too much the gentleman, but he were good to Miss Scarlett and no mischief happenin' betwixt 'em. Them two never need no chaperone.

Master Gerald fond of Master Ashley and keeps to heownself that might be Master Ashley should pull he head out of he books and pay more attention to cotton plantin' and hoein' and harvestin'.

When Miss Scarlett hear Beelzebub sold, she ask Master Gerald do he sell harness with that old horse brass? He say harness went with the horse. She more distress 'bout that horse brass gone than horse gone. Like I tellin' you, Miss Scarlett workin' only one task at a time.

She don't care for no Female Academy and ask her Momma what use French and rhetorics be for lady what gonna marry and rear babies and manage house servants. Miss Ellen say young womens got more opportunity than they used to and Miss Scarlett should be grateful.

Miss Scarlett wonder if things change so much: isn't men mens and women womens?

Miss Ellen say mens and womens mostly the same but gentlemen and ladies, every generation they different. "We change, dear. You may not think so, but we do."

"A girl at the Academy said no Irishman can be a gentleman."

"Dear, dear Scarlett," her Momma said, chuckling 'count she ain't never heard nothin' foolisher, "*some* people will believe anything."

Me, I wouldn't want be ary girl insult Master Gerald. Miss Scarlett loves her Momma and Poppa and Tara. I reckon she loves me a little too.

Miss Scarlett don't care for schoolroom with other young mistress, but she don't mind Female Academy so much after the boys start callin'. Miss Scarlett and schoolmarm sittin' in parlor drinkin' tea with young boy who don't know what say and Miss Scarlett not helping him. Toby drives me over one afternoon, bring dresses she wants, so I in the room while Brent Tarleton talkin' 'bout politics and cotton prices, which ain't come back, nor the 'conomy, which ain't come back neither. Miss Scarlett so, so interested and so grateful Brent knows these *important* things so girls don't need trouble they heads 'bout 'em!

Beelzebub killed. Man who buys him can't ride him and man he sell horse to can't ride him neither. So he killed. I don't say nothin' to Miss Scarlett, but I reckon she know. Miss Beatrice start sayin' Scarlett is a "two-faced little green-eyed baggage."

War clouds gatherin', and Miss Ellen prayin' fierce. When Tara ain't too busy, she take morning train into Atlanta for Catholic Mass.

Summer done and most Tara cotton picked when news come 'bout Master John Brown. Overseer Wilkerson run to Tara House with pistols, big one and little one, stuffed in he belt. Master and Mistress with Suellen on the porch. Right away Overseer ask where Miss Scarlett and Miss Carreen?

Master Gerald say Miss Carreen in her room and Miss Scarlett is in Fayetteville, if you must know. He peeve 'count Overseer bust in when him and Miss Ellen talkin' together.

But Miss Ellen hearin' *how* he ask. "What's wrong, Wilkerson?"

Pork watering flowers in window box and I takin' my ease and Overseer look at us and say, "Leave us."

Pork frown. He Master Gerald's servant. I don't even bother frown.

Overseer put hand on big pistol and say in a voice mean somebody gonna get hurt, "You have heard my order."

Master Gerald stand up. He mouth narrowin' and he gettin' red, but Miss Ellen catch he arm. "Please, Gerald. Pork. Mammy. Give us a moment alone, please."

So Pork and I grumblin' but we go.

Straight out back into the yard find out what's this ruckus.

Turns out: Big Sam and Overseer been at Kennedy store crack of dawn buyin' plow points when telegram come which rile Masters up. Telegram 'bout Virginia slave uprisin' led by white man, John Brown. Big Sam say: "Wilkerson search me and he takes my jack-knife and hold he pistol on me all way home."

There in that kitchen yard things spinnin' round me and I gaspin' like I gonna faint. Big Sam and Pork sets me down and Rosa bring

343

water and cool cloth. I wants shut my eyes but don't dare 'count spirits dancin' inside of my eyelids, spirits I don't wants never see again.

Jonesboro Masters lockin' they coloreds in sheds and meat houses, anyplace got stout door with lock on it. Big Sam say Georgia Militia is called out and young Masters ridin' with they swords and guns and coloreds what ain't locked up makin' theyselfs scarce.

Nobody know 'zactly what happenin' and nobody know what to do. Masters don't know nor coloreds neither.

Later we hear Overseer Wilkerson all for lockin' Tara up. Overseer tell Master Gerald he too good to niggers and that why niggers rise up. Miss Ellen, she say Master Gerald be Master, and if Overseer don't agree with Master Gerald, might be he could find 'nother plantation more to he liking.

Master Gerald send Big Sam warn Master John Wilkes. Master Ashley, he gallop to Fayetteville to collect Miss Scarlett, who ride home on back of he horse.

Well, we doesn't get locked up that day or night, but Master Gerald and Mistress and girls all sleep in bedroom with Master Gerald's pistols. Pork take shotgun and set chair outside door. Don't want walk upstairs hallway that night till Pork snorin'!

Young Masters out patrollin' the roads, and I wouldn't want be no colored caught without he pass.

Next morning Miss Ellen in kitchen while Cook fixin' breakfast. She watch so close, Cook nervy, drop a platter and break it in three pieces. I says, "Miss Ellen, you was a little wrinkled baby when I first take you in my arms. You babies—Scarlett and Suellen and Carreen—with these hands I cuts they cord."

So Miss Ellen say, "I'm sorry, Mammy. This dreadful Brown business . . ." She go back to dining room, where she belong.

Jonesboro telegraph rattlin' day and night. John Brown risin' stopped and he surrounded. Day after, soldiers march in. Day after, he captured.

Brown have lost he wits! Was that fool thinkin' I should kill Miss Scarlett? Big Sam should hold down Carreen whilst Pork cut her throat? Ary slave speculator got better notion who coloreds is than John Brown do. Brown talkin' to heownself; thinkin' blood solve things. Blood am blood. Blood am blood!

Miss Scarlett's birthday seven days after Master Brown uprisin'. We ain't wantin' no celebration, so Miss Ellen invite the Wilkeses for tea 'stead of throwin' a barbecue. Charles and Melanie Hamilton and Aunt Pitty comes with 'em. Miss Pitty can't talk 'bout nothin' but white folks murdered in they beds. She say, "Just like that Denmark Vesey in Charleston. Hundreds of innocents slain in their beds."

I doesn't correct Miss Pitty. Not good time for coloreds correctin' white folks.

White Masters say they can't stay in no Union where John Brown's doin' uprisin's. Master Gerald and Master John mad at Master Jim Tarleton 'count of favorin' the Union. Miss Ellen say take their politics outside, onto the porch please, and they take whiskey decanter with 'em.

Master Ashley praisin' some book and Miss Scarlett noddin' like she read that book and a good many others besides.

I in kitchen layin' out sandwiches and cakes when Miss Melanie come to help. When I thanks her but don't need no help, she say, "More hands makes lighter work, don't you think?"

"Not if they white hands," I say, and she startle afore she laugh. For little bitty girl she gots big laugh.

"Well, Mammy," she say, "I shall try hard to meet your expectations."

"Ain't got none," I tells her. "Lost them expectations long time ago."

Her little face thoughtful. "You're joking?"

Partly I am but ain't gonna confess it.

"I should be very unhappy, without the very highest expectations. Can't we at least hope for the best?"

She am so earnest I can't help answerin' true. "Most times things don't turn out like we hopes."

"That's so," she say. "But as St. Paul writes, 'For our light affliction, which is but for a moment, worketh for us a far more exceeding and eternal weight of glory; while we look not at the things which are seen, but at the things which are not seen: for the things which are seen are temporal; but the things which are not seen are eternal.'"

"Mmmm," I say. "We 'temporal' for sure."

Miss Melanie smile brighten that kitchen like sun walk in the door. I smiles—can't help myself. Cook grinnin' too.

"With hope for eternity." Miss Melanie take my cookie tray. "When we will again be with those we love."

Miss Melanie done lost her Momma and her Papa. She and her brother, Charles, they orphan child. Orphan child know all they is to know 'bout "temporal."

Miss Melanie serve Miss Ellen first, then Miss Pittypat. Then she serve the younguns. She carry cookies onto the porch for the gentlemens afore she serve her brother, Charles, and take just one cookie for herself.

Miss Melanie Hamilton, she got deportment!

John Brown or no John Brown, we gots harvest the cotton, and Tara hands pickin' soon as dew off the bolls. Master Gerald, he ridin' from field to press and back, assurin' heself things done right. When ain't got enough hands, he climb off he horse and pickin' heself!

There am three new babies in the Quarters, and Miss Ellen and me busy with 'em atop arything else we gots do. Toby drive Miss Carreen and Suellen to Twelve Oaks every morning get tutored with Miss India and Miss Honey. Master Ashley turn library into schoolroom.

Miss Ellen gets letter from Miss Pauline sayin' Nehemiah have passed. Miss Ellen hand shake and she cryin'. *Savannah Gazette* tell how Nehemiah were the best-regarded free-colored businessman in the city.

Nehemiah die without never jump no broomstick with nobody. I don't like think 'bout that so I don't. I wonder if he have ary brothers or sisters. He never say nothin' 'bout none.

Miss Scarlett back at the Female Academy, where all them boys makin' nuisances of theyselfs.

Second of December Master John Brown gets hanged. Miss Scarlett say, "Brown was good enough to ruin my birthday; I'm so grateful he didn't spoil Christmas."

That year Tara have one of those newfangled Christmas trees in the drawing room. I don't understand what cedar tree have to do with Baby Jesus, but white folks favors 'em. First Twelve Oaks have a ball, then Tara have a ball, then Fairhill ball, but some folks don't go to Fairhill 'count Master Jim bein' for the Union. Miss Scarlett don't go 'count of Miss Beatrice still mad at her 'bout Beelzebub.

We Be Seceded

I DONE LOST most them I loved, and most my beloveds die ugly.

Storm of war roarin' down on Tara like a ravin' lion and I get to rememberin'. I couldn't help myself! I hates close my eyes. Night after night I recallin' that wove basket which were too big for the manioc but we didn't have no other. I'd hide inside pretendin' nobody could see me, and I guess that were true, 'count they never see me when they come.

I'd hide in that basket. *"Ki kote pitit-la?*—Oh, where is that child!" Momma'd sing, and I'd cover my mouth to not be gigglin'.

Planters ain't hardly talkin' 'bout the weather no more, nor what cotton fetchin'. They talkin' 'bout who wants be President and what Congress doin' and suchlike. When planters ain't cussin' weather or crop prices, somethin' terrible wrong.

All they lives they been plantin' and hoein' and tendin' and worryin'. Livin' so slow you could hardly see no changin'. No more. Things movin' faster than Atlanta locomotive! That spring Democratic party splits in two and the Constitution Union party gets up and runnin', and some Masters be for one and some for t'other.

Fourth of July, all us go into Jonesboro for Congressman Stephens speechifyin'. Miss Ellen don't want go, but Master Gerald says Master John Wilkes be on the platform with Stephens and white trash might get rowdy and Master John needin' all the friends he got.

Pork tell me Master Gerald got two pistols in he coat, but I'ze not to tell Miss Ellen nor the girls. Pork, he don't come. Pork say coloreds got no place in Masters' quarrel.

Jonesboro am red, white, and blue banners and buntings everywhere you look. Over the tracks under shade trees am a platform with more buntings where Master John Wilkes and Master Jim Tarleton talkin' with somebody so small he like little boy in he Poppa's suit. Little man pale like he been dead since yesterday, but he talkin' hot and clampin' Master Jim's arm so fierce he coat dented. Reckon that man Master Stephens.

White mens holdin' for secession with they friends east of the depot, and them which is for the Union to the west. Older Tarleton boys near their Papa. Boyd carryin' one of them leaded canes, and Tom have he hand in he pocket. Raif and Cade Calvert not four feet away. Calvert boys' Momma, she Yankee.

Miss Ellen talkin' to Mistress Calvert 'count nobody else will.

It July hot. Ladies shadowed under silk parasols. They wavin' palmetto fans.

Tarleton twins, Stuart and Brent, payin' politics no nevermind. They off under a shade tree sparkin' India Wilkes.

It gettin' on to noon and men be grumblin', which stop when whiskey casks arrive. I figure they purposed slow. Whites and whiskey don't go good together.

I on depot platform far from the crowd. Master John's body servant, Mose, the only other colored.

"What you make of this, Mammy?"

"I thinkin' we ain't where we ought be."

Shout at the whiskey keg done for us. We slip inside depot, where we can see through window but ain't easy seen.

Timetable next ticket window. Mose can read a mite and tells me Jonesboro got six trains goin' south and eight trains comin' north every day 'cept Sunday. I say I don't need know how read know that. Mose say two more goin' north than comin' south, so one day the South gonna run out of trains. I don't know nothin' 'bout no trains. "See Miss Scarlett," I say. "See how she strollin' at them Tarleton twins, like she got nothin' on her mind. Nice day take a stroll. 'Why, hello, Stuart! Hello, Brent! Fancy meetin' you here'!"

Mose say, "Miss Beatrice say Miss Scarlett am a—"

"I know what Miss Beatrice say," I say. "Arybody know."

Although Master John Wilkes favor stayin' in the Union, nobody mad at him 'count Master John all the time readin' books and plantin' he cotton late. But folks distress Master Jim Tarleton for the Union 'count he rich and he hunt and he gamble and he gallop 'round and he drink and he cotton fetch top price. Since Master Jim favor the Union, might be they catch favorin' it too like childrens catchin' measles?

This rally for Union, but most everybody come here is for secedin' from the Union, which is why the whiskey slow gettin' here. Master Jim, he hold he hands up and everybody quieten 'cept them what ain't got they cup filled yet.

He introduce the skimpy man who am Congressman Stephens like I thought. Master Jim say Master Stephens a very great Georgia white man 'count what he am and what he done.

I can see from India Wilkes's homely face, Miss Scarlett has made her move on them Tarleton twins. Them boys gapin' like babes what lost they nipple.

Folks give Master Stephens some clapping and some boos. He voice bigger'n he, and far away as we is, I hears ary word.

"O Jerusalem, Jerusalem, how did thou killest the prophets and stonest those that are sent to thee . . ." which shuts up booin' 'count Stephens make it so cussin' him might be cussin' God. He don't stay biblical long but get right to the point everybody fussed 'bout: "Shall the people of Georgia secede from the Union if Mr. Lincoln is elected to the Presidency of the United States? My countrymen, I tell you frankly, candidly, and earnestly, that I do not think that they ought."

God or no God, that draws boos. Men at whiskey wagon particular strong booers.

Master Stephens says planters prospered "in spite of the general government." But he say 'thout that government they not doin' so good as they done. He calculate property in Georgia is worth twict what it been ten years ago 'count of that government. I wonders is me and Mose counted in that property?

Folks hear Master Stephens respectful, but they cheer when he finish he speech sayin' if Georgia do secede, he secede with her. "Their cause is my cause, and their destiny is my destiny; and I trust this will be the ultimate course of all." Everybody clap till they hands hurt, them Tarleton and Calvert boys too. Them boys never seen blood drippin' through a manioc basket.

———

We enjoys a fine slow fall. Them leaves turn blood bright and yellow gold to remind us what we stands to lose. Lincoln elected, and them which was for stayin' in the Union start talkin' secession and them Unionists which hasn't changed, quieter what they been.

After Miss Scarlett finish at Female Academy she come home to Tara. When it mild, Miss Scarlett ride out with Mister Ashley, and when it cold or blowin' they in Twelve Oaks library. Miss Scarlett don't know nothin' 'bout no paintings nor Europe countries and don't care to read no books, so I guess she mostly listen. Might be Master Ashley deportment rubs off.

Up-country Christmas balls ain't Savannah, but this year they grand as can be. All the plantation house gots one of them newfangled trees. Munroe tree catch fire but they puts it out. Hetty Tarleton gown get too near fireplace and lit afire, but she Papa and Master Jim rolls Miss Hetty on floor and puts fire out afore she burnt up. Ashley Wilkes tells Miss Ellen Tara ball grand as any he gets to in Europe. I reckon Europe ain't so grand as Savannah.

Miss Scarlett cuttin' a swath through young gentlemen like they ripe wheat. Cade Calvert, he so shy he stutters when he try talk to her, so he ride over to leave a flower on Miss Scarlett porch chair. Come every morning to leave one flower. Most times when he leave his flower, yesterday flower just where he set it down, so he exchange old flower for new one. When there ain't no flowers flowerin', he leave bunches of winter berries, serviceberry, and bird cherry.

South Carolina done secede from the Union, so Georgia want secede too and they call out the legislature figure how. Master Jim Tarleton go to legislature, and oldest sons, Boyd and Tom, goin' with him. Master Jim say they "witness history."

After legislature vote leave the Union, county planters starts up a militia. They want call they militia somethin' strong, like Clayton Grays or Inland Rifles or Rough and Readies. Missus Calvert sews a flag which has got a cotton boll and "Clayton County Volunteers," but some militia don't grow cotton and Missus Calvert a Yankee, so they thanks her and calls they troop the Troop, which is what they been callin' it all along. Ashley Wilkes, he captain, and Raiford Calvert be lieutenant. They run out of gentlemens afore they got enough troopers, so them nongentlemens what can't afford horses is give horses by them what can. When Miss Beatrice gives her horses, she say she want 'em back sound as they been. Everybody figure to fight one battle, Yankees run away, and Georgia be seceded.

When the Troop drill on the Jonesboro racecourse, a-laughin' and wavin' they swords, mist hang about them so thick I ain't sure they in this world or one foot in the next. Laughin' boys, sad boys, high-spirit boys, sour boys, brave boys, and affrighted, mist cover all same.

Yesterweek, Dilcey comin' home in Master John's coach from Slatterys', where Miss Slattery gonna have baby. Storm thunderin' and lightnin' and rain pour down, and when Dilcey look out coach window she see horse legs alongside. How big is horse with legs high as coach window? Dilcey close her eyes shut. When she ask Jincy, he ain't seed nothin'.

Some nights, them four horsemen am comin' so closeby Tara I hear they hoofbeats.

What it gonna be like lose everything? No Tara, no Twelve Oaks, no Jonesboro, no Atlanta, no railroad, no cotton fields, no milk cows, no chickens, no hogs, nothin'? How it gonna be when all them Up-country boys lyin' beside the three Geralds?

I sit up mendin' past midnight. Miss Ellen says mendin's beneath me, that Rosa could do it. I don't tells her I stayin' awake 'count of manioc basket and my darlin' Martine and poor Jehu, who got hanged for wantin' hold his head high.

———

Everybody enjoyin' them boys wavin' swords in the air and men bowin' to ladies and Tarleton twins racin' up and down the racetrack and old Mr. MacRae, who fought in Mexican War, is tellin' boys who never seed no war how bad it am which sound glorious. Can't be too terrible for them! Master Ashley got a drill book he studying and he sayin' commands and they slip they swords away and gets more or less lined side by side and when Captain Wilkes gives 'em a holler, they draws they swords at once and such a glitterin' and screechin' I never heard and never wants to hear no more.

Ary boy she lets be in love with her in love with Miss Scarlett.

Girls jealous. Honey and India Wilkes, Betty Tarleton, Sally

Munroe—even Miss Scarlett's own sisters jealous. Do Miss Scarlett fret? She do not. She bedazzle ary boy she want to, and before they done preenin' she walkin' off.

Miss Scarlett like thrush, so fixed on singin' she don't care who hear song. Maybe she don't intend be triflin' with them boys, but triflin' what she do.

When Stuart Tarleton get throwed out of college, he tell Miss Scarlett he got throwed so he could be with her. Miss Scarlett pretends she believe him! She tell young Master Stuart he "musn't throw your future away over me."

Stuart say might be he ain't got no future, not meanin' it, the way boys don't mean things, but sayin' it to shine brighter in Miss Scarlett eyes.

Boys ain't got no "hold up" nor "wait a spell." They wants what they wants afore soon. Girl what got deportment can fend 'em off. Girl ain't got deportment half-promise and wink till she get clear and they cools off. I don't want know 'bout them boys' night dreams.

The Troop drill twict a week, and after they done wavin' they swords they gets up to Robertson Tavern 'count patriotism thirsty work.

Jeems with the Tarleton twins, like always. Jeems rapscallion. He got him a woman at Munroes', and Tarletons' Missy carryin' he child. Jeems only colored 'lowed in Robertson's when Troop congratulatin' theyownselfs and bein' fierce and drinkin' and scarin' Yankees if any happens in. Jeems know how fade away. He fade when he needin' to.

Them boys drinkin' and boastin' 'bout what they gonna do to them Yankees until Cade Calvert says, "Yankees ain't all bad. Some Yankees glad to see us secede."

"Ain't no good Yankees," Stuart Tarleton say.

Cade's Yankee stepmother and Stuart Tarleton's Papa votin' 'gainst secession means both boys got plenty to live down.

Cade Calvert been hearin' 'bout his stepmother since he were small. Stuart been kicked out of two colleges and 'bout to be kicked out of third. "Let's hope the Yankees are glad to see us go," Cade Calvert say. "Good riddance."

"What you mean by that?" Stuart Tarleton say.

"What'd you mean 'What do I mean?'" Cade Calvert say. For good measure he say, "You redheaded son of a bitch." He dip in he pocket. Turn out, he ain't got nothin' in that pocket but he pipe, which he gonna smoke, showin' he contempt for Stuart Tarleton, but Stuart believe he reachin' for pistol and pull he own, which shoot afore he got it proper pointed, so ball goes into Cade Calvert's leg and Cade shout, "Damn," and knocks over a table as he fall to the floor.

Young Doc Fontaine take over and cut away Cade pant leg to see what's what, and Cade mad as a wet hen 'count them's he uniform britches.

Bullet gone right through, didn't hit no bone and Cade Calvert didn't bleed to death, so arybody make a joke out of it.

White Masters likes to joke when they scared.

When Miss Scarlett hear 'bout it, she want know smallest detail until she learns they was fightin' 'bout politics not 'bout her.

How I Meets the Hangman's Son

UP-COUNTRY PRETTIEST PLACE Le Bon Dieu ever made. 'Taint Paradise, but it near as us sinners gonna get. Master Gerald got a big heart and Miss Ellen heart distract but she always tryin' do what right. Miss Scarlett, she . . . who she am. Every girl child I ever know had a mite part of Miss Scarlett, but not one had every bit Miss Scarlett 'ceptin' Miss Scarlett!

Morning of the Wilkeses' barbecue all the clouds rolls away and everybody happy as can be! Big Sam, Teena, Rosa, Dilcey, and Cook already gone to Twelve Oaks helpin' out. I gonna stay Tara with Miss Ellen but day too fine! Master Gerald drivin' like he always do. Young folks lively. I never knowed 'em so lively. Oh, they was beautiful and fine. Young girls loves to love. Young girls same as music boxes, music boxes got no more say 'bout what music they play than young girls do.

Spicebush and redbud and crab apple and laurel and wild plum blossomin', and as we goin' down the road we drivin' through spice-bush smell then crab apple, then wild plum like overhearin' smidgens of talk in French then Creole then English then Cherokee.

Master Gerald bought Dilcey and Dilcey fool daughter, Prissy.

I suppose I glad. I reckons Dilcey and me fuss and paw the dirt for a time, but 'ventually we sort it out. Master Gerald finally got shut of Overseer Wilkerson. 'Tweren't none too soon.

I forgets my sorrows and am lively and gay in Le Bon Dieu's grateful sunshine. Whatever I do, what gonna come gonna come.

When we comes to Twelve Oaks, we gets greetin's and greetin's. Wilkeses' stableboys hold our team while O'Haras descend into the fete. Frank Kennedy sparkin' Suellen, so he help her down and ask can he fetch her somethin' afore she can hardly draw breath. Master Gerald greetin' Master John and Honey at she Poppa side actin' lady of Twelve Oaks. O'Hara girls cooin' and babblin' like they do, 'cept Miss Scarlett be holdin' back 'count she Miss Scarlett.

Twelve Oaks grandest house in the county. It got columns. It ain't got front porch like Tara got, Twelve Oaks got "veranda." Twelve Oaks even got curved staircase, though not so fine as Jehu's. Rose smells from the garden mix with cookin' from the barbecue out back.

Man half in shadow on the veranda. He apart. Ain't from here. Black-haired man considerin' Miss Scarlett. Not makin' no move or nothin', just considerin'! I don't need ask is he dangerous. First time you hear canebrake rattler shake he tail you know he dangerous!

It like sun slip behind a cloud and our gaiety nothin' but play-actin'. Somebody steppin' 'cross my grave.

Enough of that! I goes round back where coloreds cookin' barbecue and fixin's. Picnic tables set under shade trees, and Pork and Mose layin' out silver. Big Sam, he sweatin' at the barbecue pit. Big Sam notorious for barbecue.

Ain't just Masters and Mistress got have deportment. Barbecue got have deportment too. Barbecue got be open air, no sittin' in no stuffy dining room. Barbecue smoke get in ladies' hair so they smell of it, and whiskey and wine hid behind boxwood hedge so Baptists can pretend they ain't none. You got have too much barbecue so everybody eat more'n they should, beat biscuits, dandelion and poke greens for white folks, chitlins, hocks, and yams for coloreds. Colored tables far enough from white tables so coloreds ain't over-hearin' but near enough to jump up when they called.

Able Wynder's hams got deportment. Them hogs in the woods grazin' on acorn till fall, when nights cold. When hogs killed they steamed and scraped, blood and liver sausages made that day, and chitlins scrubbed and brined. Hams take they cure for ten days afore they can enter smokehouse. They rotated every day so they don't settle to one side or t'other, and fire never 'lowed get so hot you can't pass your hand twixt fire and ham. Hams *smoked* not *burnt.* Two months they smoked. Then they hang in cool dark meat house to collect theyselves. We eatin' hams smoked last fall, afore Lincoln was elected and South Carolina secede and Young Masters goin' to war. These hams got history in 'em. These hams what am!

They's birthday barbecues and baptism barbecues and funeral barbecues. Today was Ashley Wilkes birthday barbecue and he engagement barbecue. Melanie Hamilton engage to marry Ashley Wilkes. They sits a little apart. He perch on milkin' stool at her feet. They smilin' like they was Adam and Eve, onliest people in the world.

Sometimes I remember how that felt, but mostly I doesn't. Some things is for young folks feel and old folks regret. Sometimes I wonder how I comes to be here. Sometimes I thinks I s'posed be somewheres else.

When white folks has all they wants, coloreds set down. Rosa and Toby has armchair for me at head of colored table. Mose on my right hand, Pork on my left, Big Sam aside him. Jeems sittin' in the grass at our feets. We talkin' 'bout this and that and I ask about black-haired man who is done ate and is smokin' cigar with Master John.

Mose say man comes with Frank Kennedy. Dark-haired man doin' business with Master Frank, buyin' every bale cotton Frank

Kennedy gots to sell. "Master Butler say we goin' to war. Federals gonna blockade us. So what cotton gonna get sold to England best go while the gettin' good."

"Butler?" I whisper.

"Master Rhett Butler," Pork say.

"Where he call home?"

Pork say, "Charleston. He family got plantation on the Ashley River."

Sun go behind a cloud again and this time don't come out. It like I been struck. Pork and Mose don't pay no mind, but Jeems ask do I want some tea, some springwater?

Pork and Mose happy talk about black-haired man 'count he scandalous! He business shine a red lamp in front window and respectable men slip up the back stairs do their buyin' and sellin'. Black-haired man been to Yankeeland so much it like he Yankee heownself. He got bastard son in New Orleans . . .

I lays down my fork. I drinks springwater. Swallowin' hurt. Black-haired man, he stay out all night with a young girl, and when she brother challenge him, he shoot brother dead.

Everything spinnin' round. Jeems ask is I all right.

"Course I is!"

Frank Kennedy know this scandal but do business with the man?

Pork say, "Master Kennedy telegram bank. Butler credit good." Pork pause. "Might be he gentleman, but he ain't no *Savannah* gentleman."

Jeems say barbecue best he ever ate.

Mose say, "Same like always."

Rhett Butler is that boy baby born with the caul in he fist. Smell of roastin' meat so rich and thick it choke me. I gets up sudden and Pork ask whyfor, but I beeline to the necessary and lose all I ate.

When I comes out, Dilcey gives me damp rag, which I wipes my sweaty forehead. Dilcey and me gonna get along. I drinks water and spits and wipes my mouth too.

When I sets again I angles my chair so I can watch Butler, who am watchin' Miss Scarlett, who am queen bee in a bee swarm, all them men and boys buzzin' round her. I watchin' Butler and he watchin' Miss Scarlett and—I gots be mistook! Gots to be!—she can't be watchin' Master Ashley! But she am!

My head spinnin'. All my griefs alive and writhin' in my head and Miss Scarlett peekin' at Master Ashley and I been mistook 'bout that too. Mammy ain't s'posed be mistook! Nobody noticin' what Miss Scarlett up to but me and that Butler and might be Master Ashley, though he give no sign he payin' mind to aryone 'ceptin' Miss Melanie. Oh, he adorin' her! And Miss Scarlett, she signalin' she who he ought be adorin' 'count, look! how many other mens at her feets!

I never knowed. I figured they like brother and sister, I never thought Miss Scarlett want Master Ashley. They unlike. They unlike as Up-country and Paris, France!

Butler, he feel my eye on him and he turn and smile and raise one of he eyebrows, like we in this together, like him and me only ones knows what goin' on. He ain't all high-and-mighty, no; he eyes laughin'. I drops my gaze.

After a time, white folks done eatin' and men smokin' they cigars. Master Wilkes take Miss Melanie plate. Miss Melanie feel my eye and smile at me like we is kin, which we ain't. Coloreds stirrin', pickin' up plates, fetchin' wine or whiskey to gentlemens and second desserts to them what wants 'em.

Somebody say somethin' political, primin' that pump. Womens groan and hurry up leavin' while mens flock together like dogs wantin' to fight. Pork keeps on tellin' more'n I wants know 'bout Rhett Butler. How he daddy important man, how he daddy disown him. Oh, Pork, I know everything I got to know 'bout them Butlers!

Jeems pipes up, "Master Stuart don't care for Master Rhett. Stuart say Master Rhett thinks too high of heself. Stuart thinkin' to try him!"

I wearied to death of mens, all they struttin' and paradin'! Who biggest! Who got more money! Who got big house! Who other men bows afore! I sick to death of mens!

Rhett Butler start talkin', and I thinkin' might be Stuart get he chance try him. Clayton County mens of one mind 'bout this war: they's bound to fight and they's bound to win. Them which had doubts done chewed 'em up and swallowed. Ain't no doubts 'lowed here!

But this Rhett Butler, who ain't got no good name and no friends nor Up-country kin, he sayin' they gonna get whupped by Yankees and they's too root-hog ignorant to know it!

Stuart ain't the only one get his back up. They grumblin' and murmurin' and spittin' they tobacco juice like 'twere into Butler eye.

Just need one more word. They beggin' for that one word so's this be affair of honor. They achin' for it.

Butler stop short, one scant word short. That the cruelest thing he done that day. Master John goes to him, and they talk quiet like there ain't a score of men bristlin' and wantin' kill somebody. Them two walk to the house like best of friends! So that be that. Nobody cross Master John at his son engagement party. Stuart say, loud enough others can hear, "I 'spect we'll meet Mr. Butler again someday." They's nods agreein' to that.

So menfolks leavin' and coloreds cleanin' up and women in the house restin' for the dancin' later in the evenin'.

Though I ought be up and doin', I can't raise out my chair. Coloreds movin' round quiet, and the green day flickerin' like when sunlight tickle Flint River. Under that bright river I sees Miss Scarlett and Rhett Butler; they's standin' front a coffin so small gots be a child. They side by side but ain't together and ain't holdin' hands.

Sun bounce that water, and he and she gallopin' a buggy through city streets with houses and buildings and everything burnin' round 'em. Dilcey sayin', "Mammy . . . ?"

I sayin', "I fine," and squeeze my eyes so tight I squeezin' them spirits right out of 'em. I does not want know! I does not. Le Bon Dieu help me!

Dilcey croonin' and wipin' my forehead like Momma with child, and almost I lets her do it, it been so long . . .

I opens my eyes. "I take a drink of water," I say, and she bring it.

Benches stacked. Chairs atop each other, big pots and platters and long tongs washed and spread on grass to dry. What white folks do 'thout us? How they plant and hoe and pick they crops and have they kitchens and they barbecues 'thout they coloreds?

Folks restin' up. The O'Haras in Honey Wilkes's bedroom, girls' ball gowns hangin' on door of the chifforobe, Carreen and Suellen curled up on the floor and Master Gerald in the sleigh bed. He smile a question when I looks in, but I nod like I got important business needin' done and he sink back into he pillow.

Miss Scarlett ain't in yard nor veranda, and nobody in the kitchen but Wilkeses' cook snorin' in she chair. I rememberin' Miss Katie on that Beelzebub, girl's hair tuck under she cap, wantin' so fierce to race, to beat all them mens, and I fears for her then and I fears for her now. I Miss Scarlett Mammy! I she Mammy!

I comin' down hall when I hear Scarlett cry out mad and hurt. Cry raise hairs on my head.

Master Ashley fly out library like a man escapin' jail. He don't see me or nothin' else. He still am where he just been.

The silence am so loud I hears sunlight tappin' dust motes. Then there a nasty crash come from library like somethin' broken. My heart comin' out my breast. Devil been busy today. I hears two voices talkin' but can't make out what they sayin'.

Next, Scarlett burst out same like Master Ashley and her face white and ragin'. After her like dog after rabbit am a man's mockin' laughter. Scarlett so raged she pass by me without signifyin', though I can touch her if I wants. Everything get still again. Hall clock deliverin' it seconds and minutes and years.

I hears match scratch. Man hummin' to heownself. I smells cigar.

Despite myself I drawn into that room.

All the walls am books. Books over windows and under 'em. Red books and black books and green books and blue. Books on tables aside the couch and chair where Rhett Butler smokin' he cigar. Them what's seen Lucifer say he beautiful. He hair black as moonless night, eyes laughin' when he mouth not. Like a cat, he ripplin' and sly. Like Beelzebub, he kill you afore he let ary man ride him.

I kneels to collect dish what broke. Rhett Butler considerin' what he considerin'. I ain't nothin' to him: fat old colored servant pickin' up the leavin's.

I collect little broke pieces in the corner and behind the chair and along the baseboard. Ain't never gonna be glued. Never be whole no more. All but one Miss Solange's blue teacups broke too.

I brush broke pieces into my apron and gets on my feet and waits until he notice me.

He smile puzzled but 'tain't unkind.

"Master Butler," I says to him, "your Papa hanged my husband."

That snatch him back from whatever he considerin'. He eyes harden and he see me like I ain't often seed.

He hold my eyes fast, but I has told truth, so after a time he let air out in a little puff and say, "My father has fewer compunctions than most."

Whatever a compunction am, Langston Butler surely ain't got none.

I gots so much to say I can't hardly speak. "I seed you."

Master Butler say, "I can't say I'm delighted. As a rule, I'd rather not be seen. As you may know, one thrives on underestimation."

Donald McCaig

Once I puzzle that out, I nods. I sees him and he sees me. Lord, how I wants weep! I ain't can't do nothin' with this man, no more'n with Miss Scarlett.

"I regret your loss," he say like he means it.

He smile at me, like he don't mean none of the harm he and Miss Scarlett gonna do 'count lovin' each other. I don't tell him what I knows am comin'.

I take the broken crockery out of Master John's library to the yard to throw it away. I goin' upstairs then, walkin' slow like the old, fat nigger I has come to be.

Ki Kote Pitit-la?

HURRICANO DO WHAT it got to and goes out to sea. All them boys and girls wants to wed been wed and boys what goin' to war gone.

Dice am throwed!

After Twelve Oaks barbecue, Master Charles Hamilton decide he don't love Miss Honey Wilkes much as he love Miss Scarlett O'Hara, which ain't no kind of news, but Miss Scarlett sayin' yes make everybody jaw drop!

Most folks believin' she marryin' 'count young gentlemens goin' to war so young girls hurry-up marryin' 'em.

I don't 'spose that so. Miss Scarlett don't pretend she care 'bout no war or brave young gentlemen or ary that. She never once done arything 'less somethin' in it for Miss Scarlett!

Same day as barbecue, same day I meets Master Rhett Butler, President Lincoln proclaim to them Southern states which ain't seceded they got to provide troops to attack them states what has. Up-country folks got kin all through the South, and if they was havin' trouble makin' up their mind 'bout fightin', they mind made up now.

War have found us. Roadsides bright with redbuds and locust

365

bloomin', cattle grazin', hogs eatin' they slops, milk cows mooin' when need be milked, old folks complainin', boys and girls fallin' in love, but everything different now. War have found us.

Tara in a tizzy 'bout Miss Scarlett wed. Even Miss Ellen don't know what to do. Confusion makes her forget what she tryin' say, and she droppin' things. Miss Scarlett wed wearin' Miss Ellen wedding dress. When she come downstairs on her Papa arm, I sheds a tear. I ain't Katie Scarlett O'Hara's Mammy no more.

That night I helps her undress and I snuffs candles afore Charles comes in. I go downstairs feelin' like Scarlett be sacrifice to what or who I doesn't know.

Plain to see Master Charles happy and grateful he wedded husband, but Miss Scarlett dazed. Ain't first time bride dazed discoverin' why girls ride sidesaddle, so I don't think much 'bout that.

Master Ashley and Miss Melanie marries too.

Them boys go to war figurin' they be home afore summer's out, and everybody at Jonesboro depot see 'em off. Twelve Oaks and Tara and Fairhill, everybody. So much mist minglin' with smoke over young men train, I scarce can look at 'em.

After they gone, Scarlett mopes round the house for days and days. Miss Ellen thinks she miss Charles too much and all the time brewin' her sassafras tea. I asks Miss Scarlett what she dreamin' 'bout. She dream 'bout fish mean she carryin' Charles's child.

Since Master Gerald dismiss Overseer, he overseein' Tara heownself. Field hands don't got work so hard but gets more done when Master Gerald oversee. Master Gerald gloomy 'count of the war and don't put he work down till dark and never ride over to Twelve Oaks no more. Suellen and Carreen and Honey and India gets together to knit socks for soldiers.

Everybody holdin' they breath. Old world gone, new world ain't got here yet. Look to be a hard birthin'. Hot and damp for early in the summer and hard to catch breath. Birds quit singin' afore dew off the grass, and hummingbirds trudgin' from flower to flower.

I'm takin' my ease on the porch with glass of water when Miss Ellen comes out. "Don't leave, Mammy. Please."

So I sits back down. Miss Ellen ask where the girls, and I say they off to Twelve Oaks. Miss Scarlett goin' with 'em.

"It's good Scarlett is getting out of the house. She seems so unhappy."

"Yes'm."

Miss Ellen sigh. "Poor child. Bride for just one week before his duty takes her husband away."

I don't got to say nothin' 'count Rosa bring out a tray with a white teapot and Miss Ellen blue teacup. Miss Ellen keep blue cup in withdrawing room glass cabinet, and nobody 'cept her drinks from it.

"Scarlett is Mr. O'Hara's favorite," Miss Ellen say.

"Yes'm."

"The last of my mother's cups." She hold it to the light. "I'd so hate to lose it."

"You Momma had them cups in Saint-Domingue. She and Captain Fornier brought 'em from France."

"How old were you?"

"I dunno. Didn't have no birthdays on Saint-Domingue."

"Do you remember anything else?"

"Ki kote pitit-la?"

"French?"

"Creole. My mother played a game with me. I don't speak no Creole no more."

"Your mother . . ."

"Don't remember her. Just that she played a game."

"Surely . . ."

"I were baby child, Missus, when Captain Fornier find me. Cap-

tain Fornier just about my firstest memory." I is more upset than I
showin'. I don't want remember, no.

"Captain Fornier. That affair of honor . . ."

"That were just one of them stupid things white gentlemen gets
up to!"

"Ruth, honor . . ."

"'Must be satisfied.' White folks always sayin' that. You know
whats I think? I think honor be 666, Beast of the Apocalypse, all
eyes and grins and teeth!"

"A gentlemen's honor . . ."

"How comes colored mens get along without it?"

Miss Ellen got answer on she tongue but don't let fly. She pour
her tea. Spoon clink 'gainst she blue cup. "Will Scarlett be happy,
I wonder."

I drinks my water.

"Ruth, you know my daughter best."

"Yes'm. I knowed your mother and I knowed you and I knows
Katie Scarlett, and, if Le Bon Dieu willing, I gets know Miss Scarlett's childrens too."

"Well?"

Mammies don't say what they know. Mammies don't *ever* say
what they know. But I do. Don't know why, but I do. "Scarlett don't
give a hang for Charles Hamilton. She marryin' to spite Ashley
Wilkes."

I hears Miss Ellen's cup rattlin' 'gainst saucer. "Mammy!"

"Yes, Missus. You want I say somethin' else, I will."

"Have I ever sought anything but the truth?"

I takes that in. I takes my sweet time takin' it in. I takin' so long,
Miss Ellen impatient. "Ruth . . ."

"Reckon you same like most Mistress. You knows what you
wants know and lets everything else go by."

"Will my daughter be happy?"

"Charles Hamilton got deportment and plenty money, but he ain't no match for Miss Scarlett. That Beelzebub would have killed Charles quick as a wink. Charles ain't long for this world aryway."

Like I done said, Ellen knows what she want know and lets the rest go by, and what I'm sayin' ain't to her likin'. "Ah, so you *know* this."

Contrariness rise up strong and hot, and I says, "I sees things, Miss Ellen. I don't wants see, but I does."

"Ah," she say. She say, "It is a beautiful spring, isn't it, Mammy. I can't remember a finer."

I plain can't turn loose of it. "Scarlett and Rhett Butler get together one day," I say. "Them one of a kind. Maybe they buck and jibe and fight the bit, but they two am halves a broke plate. Only be whole when you glues 'em together."

She smile like somethin' addle my wits. "Mr. Butler is a scoundrel, Mammy."

I looks her right in the eye. "Master Butler same like Master Philippe. No God Damn different."

Smile drop off Ellen face, and she hits back, "Philippe died in an affair of honor. At least he wasn't hanged."

Which leave me gaspin'. Morning swim round me: blue skies, green earth, porch flooring painted gray. "How you know . . . How you know 'bout . . ."

"Philippe and Jack Ravanel were friends, Ruth. Good friends. You wouldn't want to know that, I suppose. You wouldn't want to know Philippe admired your husband."

I gape like fish out of water.

"Philippe said had their positions been reversed, he'd have been a rebel like Jehu Glen. 'Give me liberty . . .'"

"'Or give me death.' Most times death." I so distress I speak without hardly knowin' what I say.

Ellen distress too and take her sweet time sayin, "Yes." Her hand shakin', and she set cup down careful. "Philippe was half Muscogee. In his grandfather's time, he'd have fought us at Horseshoe Bend."

I nods.

"Before he was ready, no more than a boy, his father died and Philippe was the man in his family." Ellen look off where I weren't. "I am sometimes reminded of him; a shadow's odd shape, a warm spring rain, an unexpected burst of children's laughter. I am invariably surprised and . . . stung when I remember my Philippe."

"Spirits stay near them they loves. They impatient we join 'em."

"Ruth, do you think it possible to love more than one man. Can both halves of a divided heart be true?"

"Only ever loved one man. Jehu, he . . . he had the beautifulest hands."

"Philippe would sing sometimes. Silly rhymes. 'Here's my Ellen. Not much for hellin' . . .'"

"Philippe might have growed up be different. Philippe die afore he was who he am."

"Can we hope for what can't be undone?"

"Some men particular difficult. Yet we loves 'em. Them men don't leave much room for woman to be." It were my turn to pause. "Philippe and Rhett Butler don't got deportment."

She smiles. "Philippe? Deportment? No. But Ruth, truly graceful folks don't need that. Grace is how they move, and, God knows, Philippe was graceful."

"You got money enough and power enough and you white, maybe you don't need deportment. Other folks—it all they got."

Ellen get up then and step off the porch to pull a weed in the flower patch. She shake dirt off it root. She wipe she hands with a handkerchief. "Scarlett . . ."

Oh, I burstin' today. Old nigger woman, can't write she own

name! Just burstin'! "Scarlett rise above. Ain't nothin' put her down. I don't want be the fool stand in her way."

Ellen lookin' past Tara lawn down to the Flint River, which am high and brown 'count it springtime.

After her poor Momma pass, I holds Baby Ellen. Maybe she rememberin' that. I don't expect she wants to. Rememberin' ain't what you wants to do much of. Rememberin' stab you heart.

I say, "I sees things."

She looks at me like we not Mistress and Mammy, we two womens makin' our way in the world. "I know," Ellen say. "I've always known."

I say, "I lost 'em all."

Kindly she say, "Them?"

I say *"Ki kote pitit-la?"* not knowin' why I'm sayin' that. In this moment Ellen let me say arything I wants.

I say, "Jehu Glen, my Martine . . ."

"Yes."

"Captain Augustin, Missus Frances and Penny and Miss Solange and Master Pierre and Nehemiah. And . . . each of them Baby Geralds."

"Yes," Ellen say. "Yes. Each precious one of them."

Almost we falls into each other arms, but that can't ever be took back, so we doesn't.

I say, "War comin' worse than what Babylon done to Jerusalem. I sees fire and blood. War, fire, and blood."

She say, "We've only prayer. Sometimes I believe that's all . . ." She touch me then, gentle as a sparrow lightin'. "I did love Philippe. I do. Do you think that's wrong? We love always with a divided heart. I can't 'see.' I'm grateful for that. I can only heal those wounds under my hands. We can't protect them, Mammy. We must try, but they do as they will. However we try, however we pray, they will do as they will."

Her hand tremble when she touch rim of teacup. No stronger'n eggshell and come all the way from France, then Saint-Domingue, then Savannah, then Tara.

We has said too much already. No more can be said without we go where we can't never come back.

Miss Ellen say, "Mr. Wilkerson's accounts are a shambles."

I gets up. "I be seein' to Teena's newborn."

We never lost no newborn at Tara. None but Miss Ellen's.

Ki kote pitit-la? . . . Oh, where is that child?

Well, Momma, here I am. Here am where I gots to.

Acknowledgments

MY GRATEFUL THANKS to those whose knowledge, kindness, faith, and forbearance helped Mammy come alive:

Mr. Paul Anderson Sr.
Mr. Paul Anderson Jr.
Mr. Peter Borland
Ms. Gillian Brown
Ms. Susan Brown
Ms. Mia Crowley
Ms. Kris Dahl
Dr. Laurent Dubois
Dr. Douglas Egerton
Ms. Julia Gaffield
Dr. Philippe Girard
Dr. Joan Hall
Ms. Anne McCaig
Dr. Jeremy Popkin
Dr. J. Tracy Power

Ms. Laura Starratt
Mr. Kerly Vincent
Mr. John Wiley, Jr.

The Atlanta History Center
Cathedral of St. John the Baptist
The Davenport House
The Georgia Historical Society
The Hermitage
The Owens-Thomas House

And, in special,

Ms. Margaret Munnerlyn Mitchell